2 95

two at a crime

Lust, greed, lies, and family ties—they're all *Deadly Allies* in a feast for mystery lovers presented by the Private Eye Writers of America and Sisters in Crime in this collaborative anthology featuring twenty stories by America's finest mystery writers.

"A treasure trove for crime buffs!"
—*Marlboro Enterprise/Hudson Daily Sun*

SARA PARETSKY's tough-talking detective V. I. Warshawski must prove a tennis star's innocence in a bizarre murder in "Strung Out."

"The best anthology of the season."
—*The Virginian-Pilot* and *The Ledger-Star*

CAROLYN G. HART's sassy newswoman, Henrie O, proves a nose isn't all it takes to get the news . . . and solve a murder in "Nothing Ventured."

"All of the stories are first-rate . . . imaginative, suspenseful, well written, and entertaining. . . . The right gift for any mystery fan and the perfect bedside companion."
—*The Ormond Beach* (Fla.) *Observer*

Kinsey Millhone's favor for some very wealthy clients turns into a good deed on behalf of her favorite bank robber in SUE GRAFTON's "A Little Missionary Work."

"Super . . . a must read for mystery fans."
—*Merrillville Herald*

"*Deadly Allies* will provide many hours of enjoyment in a variety pack of suspense, mystery and entertainment."
—*The Southbridge News*

In JULIE SMITH's "Silk Strands," a poet reflects on the permanent erasure of a lover who was an emotional cipher.

"Outstanding! . . . Along with all the big names, there is some remarkable new talent displayed."
—*Senior Beacon* (Texas)

Three-time Shamus Award winner **LOREN D. ESTLE-MAN** deals his PI Amos Walker into a poker game with the highest possible stakes in "Safe House."

"Fine introductions to some top-rate mystery writers."
—*Beverly Times*

Sunny paradises are the setting for "Sex and Violence" in **NANCY PICKARD**'s plain-titled story, and greed and death in **BENJAMIN SCHUTZ**'s "Mary, Mary, Shut the Door."

"Excellent . . . A superb example of what's good and exciting in current mystery fiction. . . . A 'must' for mystery devotees."
—*The Oak Ridger*

deadly
allies

*PRIVATE EYE WRITERS OF AMERICA/
SISTERS IN CRIME
COLLABORATIVE ANTHOLOGY*

EDITED BY
ROBERT J. RANDISI
AND
MARILYN WALLACE

BANTAM BOOKS
NEW YORK • TORONTO • LONDON • SYDNEY • AUCKLAND

This edition contains the complete text
of the original hardcover edition.
NOT ONE WORD HAS BEEN OMITTED

DEADLY ALLIES

A Bantam Crime Line Book / published by arrangement with Doubleday

PUBLISHING HISTORY
Doubleday edition published April 1992
Bantam edition / July 1993

CRIME LINE and the portrayal of a boxed "cl" are trademarks of Bantam Books,
a division of Bantam Doubleday Dell Publishing Group, Inc.

In the story "Louise" by Max Allan Collins MS. TREE and supporting cast copyright Max
Allan Collins and Terry Beatty. MS. TREE is a trademark of DC Comics, Inc.

ISBN 0-553-29631-0

Published simultaneously in the United States and Canada

Bantam Books are published by Bantam Books, a division of Bantam Doubleday Dell Publishing
Group, Inc. Its trademark, consisting of the words "Bantam Books" and the portrayal of a
rooster, is Registered in U.S. Patent and Trademark Office and in other countries. Marca Regis-
trada. Bantam Books, 1540 Broadway, New York, New York 10036.

PRINTED IN THE UNITED STATES OF AMERICA

RAD   0 9 8 7 6 5 4 3 2 1

contents

contents

foreword

Long hours alone at a desk and the subsequent inability to remember the simple conventions of social exchange . . .

Lack of information about current developments in one's chosen profession . . .

Occasional and overwhelming suspicions that you are alone in your goals, problems, pleasures, frustrations . . .

Such might be the plight of the writer, if not for the existence of writers' organizations. Through newsletters and meetings, information is disseminated, achievements are celebrated, and fellowship is enjoyed.

Prior to 1981 there existed only one organization for mystery writers, the Mystery Writers of America (MWA). Perhaps as a result of the growth of popularity of the mystery and the subsequent increase in the numbers of mystery writers, the 1980s saw a burgeoning of writers' organizations. The first to arrive was the Private Eye Writers of America (PWA), followed by Sisters in Crime (SinC) and the American Crime Writers League (ACWL). The Horror Writers of America (HWA) was born; many of its members also write mysteries.

All of these organizations are well-meaning, but with such a proliferation, it was easy to look at them as being competitive. Perhaps the two deemed by the uninformed as the most competitive were PWA and SinC.

PWA, after all, glorified storytelling that was tough and masculine—although much of the best work being done in that form at present is being done by women, as you will see in this collection.

In its desire to gain respect for women's writing, it might have appeared to some that SinC was against anything "masculine," but it has never been the goal of Sisters in Crime to exclude or to put at a disadvantage the male members of the crime writing and reading family.

A little background about the two groups will help put their parallel aims in focus.

The PWA was formed in 1981 by Robert J. Randisi to foster support and respect for the private-eye form. The first PWA Shamus Award was presented in 1982 at the Bouchercon World Mystery Convention, held that year in San Francisco. An award has been presented every year since for the best in the private-eye genre: Best Novel; Best First Novel; Best Paperback Novel; Best Short Story; and a Life Achievement Award.

The first president of PWA was Bill Pronzini, the first vice-president Bob Randisi. The 1991 president was Jeremiah Healy, and Jerry Kennealy was the vice-president. Bob Randisi continues to serve as permanent executive director.

Among past winners of the Life Achievement Award— The Eye—are Ross Macdonald, Mickey Spillane, William Campbell Gault, and Richard S. Prather.

In the ten years since its inception, PWA has made great strides toward achieving its aims and goals. In support of the PI form it has published an anthology of original PI short stories every other year since 1984. Many of these stories have been nominated for Shamus and Edgar awards. The organization also cosponsors a Best First PI Novel contest with St. Martin's Press. The winner receives ten thousand dollars and is published in the U.S. by St. Martin's and in the U.K. by MacMillan, Ltd. Past winners of the award include Les Roberts, Gar Anthony Haywood, and Karen Kijewski.

It has been an exciting first decade, and PWA intends to make its second decade even more productive.

In order to be a member of Sisters in Crime, you don't have to commit a felony or live in a convent or even be female. The organization is made up of writers, editors, librarians, literary agents, booksellers, and readers who enjoy —and wish to help others enjoy—mystery and suspense fiction written by women. Founded in 1986 by Sara Paretsky at an informal breakfast at the Bouchercon World Mystery Convention in Baltimore, current international membership has grown to about 1,200.

At that first meeting, several themes emerged from the comments of the thirty-five participants. Many wondered whether mysteries by women were reviewed as often as were mysteries by men. Several speakers were concerned that books depicting gratuitous and often prurient violence toward women received disproportionate publicity. Still others felt that more should be done to help promote public awareness of mysteries by women.

Since then, under the direction of presidents Sara Paretsky, Nancy Pickard, Margaret Maron, Susan Dunlap, and Carolyn Hart, Sisters in Crime has been involved in several exciting projects, at the same time providing a strong sense of community for its members.

Major metropolitan newspapers across the country have been monitored by volunteers to determine the proportion of women's mysteries receiving review attention. In 1989, for example, the figures ranged from 19 to 39 percent in a year when, according to best estimates, at least 40 percent of mysteries published were written by women.

A booklet entitled "Shameless Promotion for Brazen Hussies" is now available, offering the accumulated wisdom of members to aid women writers in effectively promoting their books. A listing of members' books in print is distributed semiannually to bookstores and libraries in the United States and Canada. A map of the United States depicting scenes from members' books is being sold in bookstores and other retail outlets.

Now, with *Deadly Allies*, Private Eye Writers of America and Sisters in Crime have combined to bring readers an exciting collection representing the work of each organization's members.

What fun to have stories in the tradition of the American private eye, that brave loner with a commitment to a particular morality, side by side with the evolving mystery fiction of women who have taken the venerable mystery traditions and added their own spin of compassion, humor, and cooperation! If our experiences as readers and as editors told us anything about contemporary mysteries, it was that whether the main character was a man or a woman, whether the setting was in the middle of a mean street, behind the closed doors of small-town America, or in corporate boardrooms, we could expect to see a tough, independent individual who cared about other people and who understood that legal and moral right aren't always the same.

As we suspected all along, the similarities are more striking than the differences. All twenty stories share a concern for justice, a real and deeply felt sense of the dynamic relationship between individuals and the society in which they live, and most especially, a delight in presenting complex characters in fascinating situations—in short, good storytelling.

Deadly Allies proves without a doubt that PWA and SinC are after the same thing, and that we can work together to achieve it. The stories in this book are presented in pairs— one from a PWA member and one from a SinC member— according to theme. Each pair of stories is preceded by a brief discussion of the common thread that binds the two stories; the editors collaborated on these explanations, as they did on this main introduction. Each individual story is also preceded by an introduction. The PWA introductions were written by Bob Randisi, the SinC introductions by Marilyn Wallace.

No doubt the 1990s will see the birth of other writers' organizations. To that end, we'd like to found the first one right here. It's called BASIC—Brothers and Sisters in Crime. There are no dues and the requirement for membership is very simple: you simply want to be a member—and if you want to, you are.

And so for all our sisters and brothers, for every relative of any description who takes pleasure in an intriguing story well told, we offer *Deadly Allies* for your enjoyment.

Robert J. Randisi
Brooklyn, NY

Marilyn Wallace
San Anselmo, CA

deadly allies

The common thread between Lia Matera's story and Jeremiah Healy's may be the most obvious. Both are attorneys, and both use their knowledge of the law to give their stories an extra edge of realism, excitement, and depth.

———————

easy go

LIA MATERA

Lia Matera's fans are delighted that she's writing fiction instead of briefs. A lawyer herself, she has created two memorable lawyer-protagonists. Willa Jansson, featured in 1987 Anthony nominee Where Lawyers Fear to Tread, A Radical Departure *(nominated for an Edgar and an Anthony),* Hidden Agenda, *and* Prior Convictions, *is a clever social observer, bent on fighting the cannibalism of left-wing politics, and concerned with the conflict between personal versus professional ethics. Ambitious, aggressive Laura Di Palma of* The Smart Money *and* The Good Fight, *offers a more cynical perspective on contemporary moral issues—with the mastery of story and language readers have come to expect of a Matera mystery.*

Trouble seems to come so easily into the life of lawyer Frances Valentine that she hopes it's also "Easy Go."

I kept my eyes on the sidewalk, on river patterns of sticky urine congealing in the morning sun, catching pigeon feathers. Around me old men scratched and coughed and slid up walls they'd hugged for shelter in the night. Now and then, a briefcase darted by, a pair of shined shoes hurried toward City Hall, toward the Federal Building, toward the State Court of Appeal. I kept my eyes lowered. I knew too many lawyers in San Francisco, and they knew too much about me.

The offices of the State Bar of California are just a few blocks from the heart of San Francisco's Tenderloin. And the Tenderloin does have a heart: for the thousands of teenage prostitutes of both sexes, for the rummies and runaways and addicts at peep shows, there is at least a soup kitchen, at least a church with gaudily uplifting angels. But try to find the State Bar's heart. It doesn't have one, just a ledger.

I climbed the steps. I should have been glad to climb them; I'd waited three years to do it. Three years plus one day since they'd cut off my buttons and epaulets. Three years of paying an "inactive status" fee (and galling it had been, believe me). Now, for an additional four hundred and thirty dollars and proof I'd retaken the professional responsibility exam, I would once again receive a flimsy paper card with perforated edges. Frances Valentine, it would read, Active Member, State Bar of California.

The State Bar. After my disciplinary proceeding, a tragic-faced girl stopped me in the hall to say that the State Bar was hiring. You don't need anything but a law degree to work there; it didn't matter that my license had been suspended. I'd bitten my lip to refrain from telling her I'd rather empty bedpans; she didn't deserve the splash of acid that had grown to replace pleasantries in my conversational style.

I didn't empty bedpans. I took a bus to a hot griddle of a town with too many Burger Kings. I bought a newspaper and found a job in a title company with a tiled roof. That was the first of six white collar jobs I took in different valley towns, most of them with a Denny's and a Woolworth's and not much else.

I could have done it differently, could have gone to some little gem of a seacoast town, maybe worked as a paralegal, maybe taught in some small college. I could have done myself and my résumé that favor.

But I wanted Bradley Allen Palmer to know he'd ruined me. I wasn't sure he cared, but I wanted him to know.

• • •

My Persian carpet was soiled and stained after three years of rough treatment by the woman to whom I'd sublet my apartment. The afternoon light showed water spots and gouges on the dusty oak desk and table. Fleas hopped on the sofa, searching frantically for the cat I'd evicted.

I opened the bay windows, grateful that my Chinese neighbors still cultivated small flowering trees, still hung vegetables to dry like laundry, still maintained their tiny fish pond. The twin spires of St. Ignatius, blurry with fog, hovered over distant rooftops. Damp wind rustled the want ads spread out on my desk: want ads from both San Francisco papers, from the Oakland paper, from the *Advocate Journal*, from *California Lawyer*.

I'd crossed out a few ads: sole practitioners who couldn't afford to be fussy, couldn't afford to worry about a little moral turpitude in their employees' past—maybe even had a little in their own. Men paying seventeen, eighteen thousand in a town where forty is considered low. But they all knew my story, let me know there were thousands of virgin lawyers out there. One expressed amazement that I hadn't been disbarred. A distinction without a difference, if no one would hire me.

I'd had my résumé redone. Three-quarters of the page listed my honors in painful detail: top five percent; law review; student article published; clerk for the Honorable Steven K. Dresge; another article published; teacher of legal writing at a downtown law school; associate with Winship, McAuliffe, Potter & Tsieh, one of the better criminal-law firms. Then a paragraph headed "Subsequent Employment" condensed the last three years of my life into categories: escrow clerk, loan officer's assistant, registrar's aide, junior budget analyst. At the bottom of the page, because honesty required it, I had written, "License to practice before the California Bar reinstated" and the date.

I felt a wrench of nausea: rent due soon and not much money in the bank. I remembered the hurry-up anxiety of a waiting time clock, deadening days of shuffling of preprinted forms. Maybe the new résumé was an exercise in false hope. All recredentialed and no place to go.

Bradley Palmer had made partner by now, pulling down a salary of $150,000 and a partnership share of that much or more. He'd taken me to Chez Panisse the night Millet, Wray & Weissel hired him, a three-hundred-dollar dinner for two, six years ago.

The last time I'd made love to Brad, it had been a foregone conclusion that we'd marry. We'd been in my apartment. This room had smelled of blossoms from the Chinese couple's trees. Now there was a faint zoo smell in the air, from cat puddles sunbaked into the carpet.

Brad Palmer had prospered while I sweltered in secretarial-beige cubicles, spurning consolation. It wasn't *his* nose I'd cut off to spite my face.

If I closed my eyes, I could see Brad on top of me, his chest damp and hirsute, his arms tensed to support his weight, his wide-set eyes half closed, a vein standing out on his broad forehead, sweat beading on his flat cheeks, his thin lips parted, honey-colored hair damp at the hairline, stiffly combed back by my own fingers.

But then, I could also see him sitting in the State Bar hearing room, straight and handsome in his banker's blue suit, testifying against me.

I rode the elevator to the twenty-first floor of the financial district monolith. I walked into the offices of Millet, Wray & Weissel and handed their aristocratic, carefully painted receptionist my résumé.

The woman took it, thanking me dismissively.

"Will you make sure Bradley Palmer gets it?"

It was halfway to the "in" basket. Sighing, she diverted it to the blotter and scribbled "Attn: BAP" in the top corner. Then she glanced at the typeset name beneath her scrawl. Pencil arrested, she looked at me with startled interest. "Frances Valentine?"

I fought an impulse to deny it. "Yes."

"If you'll be seated a moment." She pressed a buzzer on her space-age telephone, mumbling something to someone.

Two minutes later, Brad stepped into the reception area.

He wore navy pin-striped wool, a white shirt, a maroon tie. His hairline had receded slightly. He sported a coppery new mustache that disguised the thinness of his lips and lent his face an air of reserved goodwill. His eyes were brighter blue than I remembered, his brows thicker, nose straighter, face bigger, shoulders wider. He even seemed taller.

I'd had three years to think about him. I'd experienced every shade of emotion, from crazy fury to tender regret, thinking about him. But I hadn't quite realized until yesterday, crying over want ads, that I didn't love him anymore. There was nothing left to fuel the rage.

There seemed to be several of me, rising simultaneously, to greet him. I shook his hand because the receptionist seemed to expect it of me.

She handed Brad my résumé.

It took me a minute to find my voice. Three years is a long silence to break. "Do you need a law clerk? Or a paralegal?"

His eyes strayed to the bottom of the page to see how I'd handled my disgrace. A bit of color crept into his cheeks.

He murmured, "This way." As he led me down a suede-walled corridor, he kept glancing back, making sure (or maybe fearing) that I followed.

He preceded me into his office.

I walked around the room, looking at the plush wheat carpeting, the natural suede walls, the golden oak desk, the sienna leather chairs, the unglazed pottery, the Georgia O'Keeffe on a pine easel.

Brad watched me, a vein standing out on his forehead, his eyes bright.

"I need some kind of transition on my résumé, Brad. I want to practice law again."

"Why here?"

"No one else will hire me." *And maybe you think you owe me a favor.*

"Frannie, it would be a hard sell. To say the least."

I visualized him in front of the hiring committee. How would he explain what I'd done? Baldly perhaps: You see, colleagues, Ms. Valentine was convinced her client would be killed in prison. So she tried to buy him a forged passport. She contacted the passport forger herself. She then told her fiancé (maybe Brad would let the word hang in the air) what she'd done. Her fiancé was sure she'd get caught if she followed through. Her fiancé thought she'd gone a little crazy; maybe even thought she was a little in love with her handsome client. With characteristic paternalism, her fiancé contacted the State Bar to keep her out of worse trouble. (Or maybe he was jealous and angry. Who could tell, with his lawyer face wiped clean of emotion?)

Her fiancé didn't care if her client was blinded and carved up with sharpened spoons. Didn't care if he lay in a pool of blood for hours while the prison guard ignored him. Didn't care if it took him four slow days to die. Said she was lucky he'd died, in fact. Lucky because the government was too embarrassed to indict her. Lucky because it remained a State Bar matter.

Lucky. Even Brad's facial flaws, the tired lines and receding hairline, were signs of success.

"Plus . . ." Brad remained poker-faced, straight-spined. "I don't want to be a target of recriminations. If I go to bat for you, I'll want some assurance that you don't blame me; that you've accepted the consequences of your actions."

I turned to the wall of windows on my right, stood there feeling like Kirk at the helm of the *Enterprise*. The detail was magnificent: furbelows and banners and awnings, Peter Max colors in plate-glass reflections, churches and Victorians hoisted to eye level by distant hills, buckets of cut flowers polka-dotting corners, bobbing streams of pedestrians, a brick plaza and its windblown fountain, the slow, noisy jerk of traffic. More to see in Brad's window than in entire inland valleys.

"The thing is, Brad, Raul Alegría accepted the consequences of your actions."

"You'd have been prosecuted if you'd gone any further." His voice seemed a dead and distant thing, the sentence three years stale.

"That was my risk to take. Or it should have been."

I heard the sigh of leather cushions, the creak of a swivel chair. "What do you want from me, Fran? I don't hear from you for three years. Like I'm the fucking bad guy. For keeping you out of jail. So? What do you want from me now?"

I considered leaving. But I'd already thrown away three years. Three years of flat horizon, static air, cloudless blue-white sky; like being trapped in a vast stoppered jar. What the hell had I proved? That I could make myself suffer?

I turned to face him. His arms were folded across his chest, his chin tucked down. Guarded.

I didn't love him anymore. Such a relief.

"No one will hire me," I said carefully. "You know how I feel about my work."

"Come on—how good's it going to look, a year or two here as a glorified law clerk?"

"Look where I am now. Look at my résumé."

He scowled at his desktop. He was motionless at first, then he nodded slightly.

"Most places, I can't even get interviews. Even fly-by-night lawyers won't touch me." *And nobody in town owes me a favor; nobody but you.*

"Okay, Frannie." The new mustache hid the pained twitch of muscle at the corner of his mouth. I saw it in the paralyzed misery of his cheeks. I knew the face so well. "I'll square it somehow. Come in Monday."

I told myself it was the smartest thing I'd done in a long time. I told myself I was nothing but a whore. Probably both were true.

It was law clerk's work, writing up the results of my research so someone else could go into court and argue the actual motions. But that was okay.

The job wasn't as exciting as my old job at Winship, McAuliffe. But after three years of invisibility, that's not what I compared it with.

At the end of the second week, John V. Cusinich, a senior partner with Coke-bottle glasses, a thin, pinch-lipped face, and slicked-back hair, came into my office. I was surprised. Cusinich was being considered for a federal court judgeship, adding much to his already considerable consequence. Until that morning, he'd barely deigned to nod to me. "You did this memo?" His magnified eyes examined the small, unadorned room with distaste.

"Yes. Is there some problem with it?"

"No. It's excellent. I didn't think we had any basis for our claim, but this is a very clever argument." He very nearly smiled, I think. "Good use of case law. I understand you have more experience than our other—than our clerks."

"I passed the bar six years ago. Clerked for the Northern District—Judge Dresge—and then spent two years at Winship, McAuliffe, Potter and Tsieh."

"Bradley mentioned that. Criminal law background. Actually,"—he brushed imaginary lint from his sleeve—"I talked to Roland Tsieh about you this morning. We've been asked to take on a criminal matter as a favor to a corporate client. You should look at the file. See what you think."

I already knew what I thought. The firm should take the case and let me handle it.

Watching Cusinich inspect my undecorated burlap walls, I felt light-headed, realized I was holding my breath.

That afternoon, a large abstract oil painting was removed from above the Xerox machine and brought to my office. A man identifying himself as "maintenance" asked me where I wanted it. I didn't particularly like the splashes of ocher, tan, and pink, but I knew a vote of confidence when I saw it. I had the man hang it above my desk, where it was clearly visible from the door.

The next day, Brad brought me a file folder. He glanced at the painting. "John Cusinich suggested I assign you this case."

"Is it the criminal matter he mentioned?"

"Yes."

I flipped the file open. A few notes on a phone conversation: client busted for growing marijuana in the Santa Cruz Mountains. No mention of when or how much. I'd need details, and I'd need them soon. "This office doesn't usually handle criminal cases, does it?"

"This is the only one. The defendant's father owns a brussels sprouts farm down the coast. We handle all his business affairs. That's why the son thought of us. We did tell him a criminal law firm might do a better job. But I guess he really wanted us. Asked John Cusinich if we had anybody here with criminal defense experience. I told John about you."

"I want the arrest report, indictment, all that stuff. Meet the client. Check out the scene."

A hesitant shuffle.

"I'm sure you know"—trying not to take the hesitation personally—"that it's a quick deadline for Motions to Suppress Evidence. Most of these cases are won or lost on that motion. I'm not trying to shirk my other work, but I need to move—"

"I'm just wondering. . . ."

I looked up at him. "I remember how, Brad. Believe me."

"Okay."

With a parting glance at the oil painting, he left me to my first case in over three years.

•   •   •

When the client phoned Cusinich back, Cusinich put him through to me. His file was significantly thicker by then. I had an arrest report from the Santa Cruz County Sheriff's office, an indictment from the DA, and a Motion to Suppress Evidence well under way.

The client gave me directions to the mountain property from which police had seized twenty-six marijuana plants.

I drove down the coast, trying to enjoy the scenery. It was a clear, breezy day, the sky streaked with clouds, the air fresh and salty. Men in straw cowboy hats bent over rows of greenery between the highway and the ocean cliffs. Some of the farm workers were gathered around a pickup truck just off the road; most were Hispanic men, short with broad chests and dusty clothes.

When I'd heard about Raul Alegría, I'd driven to a coastal farm and found Raul's mother in the middle of a field, sobbing and being comforted by men who looked like these men. I'd driven her to Folsom Prison, to the infirmary there. The drive had taken four hours, more or less, and Martina Alegría, a strong-looking woman with rough hands, had spent most of that time telling me what a good baby Raul had been, how he'd wanted to nurse all the time, and been bigger than the other farm workers' children.

I'd seen Martina Alegría again when I'd moved to Fairfield. She'd been picking lettuce and had a raw-looking pesticide rash on both arms. She'd come to the title company to bring me a plate of fried cookies and an icon of the Madonna. She'd cried a little and promised to buy a Mass for me next time she burned a candle for Raul. I hope she remembered.

About three-quarters of the way down to Santa Cruz, I turned left, heading up Ben Lomond Mountain.

Half an hour later, I approached a rustic, plank-sided A-frame.

A man paced the road beside the driveway, running his hand over a lank mane of black hair. He motioned me to pull over, then helped me out of the car, murmuring, "Jerry Riener. Hi."

He might have been six four if he'd stood straight. He had puffy-lidded eyes and a square, stubbled jaw. He looked pale, maybe sick, maybe hung over. In top form, he'd have been male-model handsome, but he was far from top form. He wore a quilted jacket, patched and stained, shiny jeans, muddy boots.

For a second, he gaped at me in my city-slicker clothes. Then he said, "Oh man, I hope you can keep me out of jail. They'll kill me in there."

Something Brad had coached him to say? "Why would 'they' do that—whoever 'they' are?"

He reeled slightly, as if my scorn had physical mass. "Don't you know what I used to do for a living?"

"No." I stuffed my hands into my jacket pockets. It was sunless and gloomy under the canopy of pines and redwoods. The air smelled musty, fungusy, of damp roots and rotting leaves.

Reiner's eyes narrowed. Suspicion? Displeasure? "I thought I—" He sighed. "You mind a short hike? I'll take you where they harvested the pot."

We crossed the road, heading away from the house. The woods ended almost immediately and we walked uphill, onto acres of tumbling meadowland, knee-high in swaying grasses. Miles away, at the foot of the mountain, the sea glimmered, flecked with whitecaps.

Reiner inhaled deeply. "Botanically, it's very rich. Seventy percent of the plants in Thomas's *Flora of California* are in these mountains." He uprooted a pad-shaped bit of greenery. "Miners' lettuce. Edible." He squatted in the tall grass, shading his eyes as he looked up at me. "I've learned what's edible and what isn't in the last few years."

"What did you used to do for a living?"

"Prison guard. Soledad, among other places."

A prison guard. I thought of the guard who'd let Raul lie there half a morning bleeding. Folsom Prison had fired him, but no other action had been taken. He'd vanished before I had a chance to spit in his eye. Scot-free.

I heard myself murmur, "Do you know David Williams?" Reiner shook his head. "Should I?"

"He was a guard at Folsom. . . . Never mind." I felt a needling of irritation. New case, new start. Forget Raul. "Go on with what you were saying."

"Well, it's not a very popular profession." A hint of rueful grin, then: "The way you're looking at me—you know, somebody's got to do it. There's some hard, nasty folks in there and we can't *all* rely on someone else to watch them."

He stood, eyes flashing with defensive anger. Or maybe just fear. Soledad was a big place. No matter what jail Reiner ended up in—if he ended up in one—there would be a former Soledad inmate coming through, eventually.

"If someone did recognize you, what would he tell the other inmates about you?"

He stroked his jaw. "A diplomatic way of asking if I'm a sadistic asshole?"

"Are you?" My tone was sharp. Almost unprofessional.

"Goddamn." A stillborn grin. "Lady, who do you think is in there? Christian martyrs? We're talking serious gangs—people who literally bite each other's fingers off, ears off. Not nice people."

My first case in three years. Had I forgotten how to act professional? "I'm asking how they saw you, not how you saw them."

An exasperated wave of the arm. "I wasn't any rougher than I had to be. Maybe they thought I was an asshole, at times. Sometimes you have to clamp down for their own protection." He looked suddenly weary. "It can be a real horror show, you have no idea. You start taking shit and there's no end to it. On the other hand, get too much in the middle and you get hurt big-time. To some extent, you leave it alone. Other times, you get heavy. It's a very fine line."

A screwed-up system, my old boss used to say. Accept that or find some other kind of law to practice.

"Tell me about your arrest."

Reiner brushed a lock of hair off his forehead. His hand was callused, nails trimmed but rough. His hand was shaking.

"It seems from your arrest report that the state has a very strong case against you, Mr. Reiner. If you are guilty . . ." Playing harbinger, my former boss called it; part of the job. "It might be possible to bargain the charge down to simple possession, if you're willing to plead guilty. It could mean a much shorter sentence. And something else you should consider: There's a statute allowing the government to confiscate your land if you're convicted of cultivating marijuana on it."

Jerry Reiner folded his arms over his chest. His eyes were open wide, unblinking. He looked like a wax statue.

I expected him to rail at the unfairness of the statute, the unfairness of the system. Most clients would. He didn't.

It was a minute, maybe longer, before he spoke. His lips moved without sound, at first. His color flooded back. Fight, not flight. "Look, I mean it: they'll kill me in there. So I'll just have to take my chances, okay?"

My mouth felt dry, my throat tight. Three years of bitter nostalgia for criminal practice, but I'd let myself forget this part of it. Let myself forget how it felt to share a client's fear. Except Raul's.

Raul had said to me, "I won't last a week in there, Frances." And I'd replied, "Tell me what to do, and I'll do it."

To Jerry Reiner I said, "It's your decision, not mine."

His lips pursed and his brows pinched. There was determination in his eyes, raw and reckless. But no hint of supplication. No favors asked.

"So you won't buy me a fake passport?"

The air temperature seemed to drop twenty degrees. I felt myself take a slow step backward.

"I kept track of you after the State Bar gave you that little slap on the wrist!"

"How did you know about—"

"Alegría was scum. A punk. A snitch."

The landscape seemed to tilt. "How did you know Raul?"

He pointed at me, two quick stabs of the index finger. "I think it's bullshit you're at a fancy law firm now! What's the point of getting disbarred if you can go to work for a fancy law firm?"

"Why do you know this?" Why do you care?

"It's not right." Somewhere between a whine and a shout.

"Are you Jerry Reiner?"

"No." He shook his head widely, emphatically. "Never heard of him, except what I read in the paper about his arrest. The article said his father's a big-time farmer. I don't know what made me run down who the father's lawyer is. It was just a feeling I had—that he was your firm's client. It was just"—he kissed his fingertips—"karma."

I scanned the meadow. It ended in a tangle of shrubs. Then more forest.

"Who are you?"

"A three-year suspension—a fucking slap on the wrist! Now you're back at a fancy law firm."

"As a law clerk."

"You know what I've been doing for the last three years? Grunt fucking labor. When I can get it."

"David Williams. You're David Williams." You let Raul die. Let him lie in his own blood for hours.

He nodded. His eyes glinted, maybe with tears.

"It doesn't matter." I was chilled to the marrow in my wool suit. "Doesn't matter what happened to me." God knows I suffered as much as I could make myself suffer. "That's not the point. What about Raul? How could you leave him lying there?"

"I told you! Sometimes you can't get in the middle. You've got to let them put the message out: Here's what happens to guys who try to rat out their friends and make a deal."

"Our system's based on making deals. If you can't protect a prisoner who's testified—"

" 'You.' If 'you' can't." He ran both hands over his hair. "Leave it up to the prison guards, the garbage collectors. Sure, shun them, act like they must be mean stupid sons of bitches to want to do the job, but leave it to them to keep the psychos chilled! 'You'! You have any idea what kind of powder keg it is? How rigid the codes are? Fuck. Sure, I could have jumped in the middle when they went for Alegría, maybe started a fucking riot, lots of gunfire and stabbing and maybe hostages and people dying, because that's the kind of place Folsom is. I could have rushed Alegría to the infirmary, but you know and I know he wouldn't have lasted an hour longer. Or even if he'd made it, they'd have got him next time, no joke."

There were times, living in Fairfield, in Woodland, that I'd stared at the flat line of sky on field and become overpowered by a sense of unreality. I'd attributed it to the sensory deprivation of a barren landscape.

But now, with grasses tickling my ankles and distant sea sparkling in my peripheral vision, I felt the same disconnection. Raul was dead. The man who'd let it happen shouted at me. Defending himself. Like I could ever forgive him.

"And then a bunch of fat bureaucrats sit in judgment— why didn't you stop it, all that bullshit. But if you're not there, you don't know. You can't know."

"I heard you got fired."

"Fucking right." He took two angry steps toward me, his face flushed red. "And what else am I trained for? Odd jobs, farm labor—fuck, I've been living in a Volkswagen squareback for three years, you know that? You know how hard it is to get by, get enough food when you're trying to save for rent? Find any kind of decent job—never mind meet women—when you're living out of a car?"

What was it Brad had said? Accept the consequences of your actions?

"Why?" I wondered. "Why did you go to all this trouble? Why lie about who you are? Why not just call me—"

"Oh, spare me! Look at you in your nice suit, working for a hotsy law firm. You never would have talked to me!"

Why am I talking to you now? Why did you bring me here?

He clenched both fists. "You made out like a fucking bandit!"

"No!" I'd had a wider range of options to narrow, but I'd done it. For three years, I'd done it.

He pressed his fists to his eyes. It took me a moment to realize he was crying.

Then his hands dropped. From his jacket pocket he drew a small bundle wrapped in a red kerchief. He held it to his temple.

He said, "I wanted you to see this."

I had no idea what he was doing. It was unreal and I was incorporeal.

Not even the blast tipped me off. And when David Williams fell, the bundle arcing out of his hand, I thought he'd suffered a sudden failure of adrenaline.

I stood there a long time listening to grasses rustle, tree limbs creak. I stared at the dark spot on Williams's temple, the slavering laxity of his mouth, the wide-open sheen of his eyes.

I moved toward him cautiously, crouching beside him and staring. Staring and still not believing he'd shot himself right there in front of me.

When I finally did believe it, I crawled away, scrambling at first on all fours like an animal. Then I ran, ran like hell down the hill, away from him.

Before I reached the woods, a huge man caught me with a flying tackle, knocking the air out of my lungs.

I spat out a mouthful of grit, struggled against the hands on my arms, tried to see through tears and dust.

I panted, "Man shot himself. Up there."

"What I saw was you crouched over him. I think you better wait right here."

And wait I did, with the real Jerry Reiner frog-marching me back to the house so he could phone 911.

"Do I have to tell you again how it happened?"

Roland Tsieh examined the small room with interest. The Santa Cruz County Jail complex was relatively new; Winship, McAuliffe, Potter & Tsieh had never had a client there before. The tall man with the Asian eyes and the supercilious face seemed pleased with me, for once; more pleased than he'd ever been when I'd worked for him.

He nodded. "From the time he's waiting for you in Reiner's driveway."

Roland listened attentively as I went through it again.

"Roland, the physical evidence supports my story, doesn't it?"

"The physical evidence. We have one small-caliber gun wrapped in a handkerchief about four feet from the body—yes, yes, I know it flew out of his hand when he fell. But basically the gun's right where you were standing. It's unregistered—and you are known to have connections with unsavory people like passport forgers, so presumably you could have obtained such a weapon. Also, which I did not realize, you know how to shoot a gun." He shrugged. "Mainly, though, it's who he was. The evil prison guard who let your pet client get killed. That's really why you're in here."

"But I didn't know who he was until I got there. He told me he was Jerry Reiner!"

"That's what you say. It could have been the other way around. You setting up a meeting with him."

"He phoned John Cusinich and pretended he was Jerry Reiner. We can prove that."

"We can prove *someone* did that. It could have been you as easily as Williams. In fact, darn clever, if you'd set it up: you can't make the shooting look like suicide, you claim self-defense. Big guy lures you to the mountains."

"But John Cusinich—"

"Credible lawyer that he is, says he fixed you up with a 'client' who claimed to be Reiner but wasn't." Roland nodded. "Makes it look like Williams set a trap for you. Except you know what the prosecution will say: it could have been any man on the phone. It could have been your passport forger."

Passport forger—again Roland raked me with the words.

"How can they get a motive out of this, Roland? Just because Williams was on duty when they killed Raul—"

"Just because? Hell, Alegría dies and you're in deep mourning for three years." He looked startled by my tears. "You never said anything to anyone about that, did you? Never complained that the guard was an SOB?"

"Only to Raul's mother."

"Great! I can just see her on the witness stand, adding her own bit of venom as she repeats what you said! Anyone else?"

I shook my head.

Roland stood. "You've got the money, I assume? Your ten percent?"

I could get ninety percent of the bail money from a bailbondsman. The rest would come out of my pocket. "If the bail's under twenty thousand."

"Twenty thou!" he scoffed. "Five times that, if we're lucky."

Bail was set at $350,000. It was set unusually high because I had "so recently" demonstrated my willingness to abet a flight from prosecution.

Brad Palmer put up my ten percent. Even in his salary range, it must have hurt to write a check for thirty-five thousand dollars.

I said, "Thank you. I'd have gone nuts in jail."

He said, "I knew that three years ago."

I held his hand, cold and creamed, but it felt like lizard skin to me. I couldn't imagine ever having loved him. I felt nothing but tolerance and distance. But I was glad he'd put up my bail.

It helped square things between us. Close the accounts. Because Brad would lose his bail money. Like I would lose the money I'd spent getting back my license.

I couldn't stick around. I'd been a criminal lawyer too long. I'd watched guilty men go free and nice men go to prison. I'd watched a client die slowly because a cynical guard wouldn't lift a hand to help him. (Yes, I did blame Williams. More than ever.) I wouldn't risk my freedom, my life.

I still knew where to find the passport forger I'd contacted for Raul. The minute Roland Tsieh mentioned him, I knew I'd go see him.

God knew where I'd go from there. Someplace lusher than Fairfield; I would give myself a break, this time. And I was almost used to drifting along without a career.

Maybe when she heard what happened, Martina Alegría would buy another Mass for me.

summary judgment

A JOHN FRANCIS CUDDY STORY

JEREMIAH HEALY

Many people—authors, critics, and readers—feel that Jerry Healy is at the top of the heap, right now. He is a past Shamus Award winner for Best Novel with his John Francis Cuddy novel The Staked Goat, *and probably made the best outgoing PWA vice-president's speech when he complained about the constant flying back and forth in "PWA-2," passing the PWA president in "PWA-1." He is also the only man who ever showed up at a PWA poker game with a "how-to" book.*

In Summary Judgment *Boston-based John Francis Cuddy proves that no case is too small for a man of principle.*

1

Steven Rothenberg welcomed me back to his law office. Cluttered and shabby, it hadn't changed for the better since the last time I'd been there. Neither had Rothenberg.

His beard was a little more trimmed, but the black was losing its battle with the gray, and what was left of his hair already had surrendered. A suit coat hung on a battered clothes tree. His tie was tugged down from an unbuttoned collar, his sleeves rolled up twice, almost to the elbows.

Rothenberg sat behind his desk. I took the chair in front of it. Sunshine from the May afternoon backlit him, a partial view of the Boston Common visible across Boylston Street.

"I remembered you from the Daniels case, Mr. Cuddy."

"You should."

Rothenberg moved his tongue around inside his mouth. "Can I call you John?"

"Sure."

"John, I've got a capital case here, murder one. I'd like you to help me represent my client on it."

"Private or court-appointed?"

"Appointed, but—"

"Be seeing you."

"Wait, wait a minute."

"Look, Mr. Rothenberg—"

"Steve."

I took a breath. "Steve, you can't feed a canary on what the commonwealth allots for investigation in a court-appointed. You know it, and I know it."

"Yeah. But this one's different."

"How?"

"This guy actually may not have done it."

I closed the file folder. "At least your client had enough sense not to talk to the cops."

"A result of his, ah, prior experiences in that regard."

I slid the folder back to Rothenberg. "So I've read the reports. Let's hear your view of it."

The lawyer came forward in the chair, squaring his shoulders for the first rehearsal of a new play. "My client, Jack Funderberk, is a poor homeless man who saved a dog from drowning in the Charles River."

"Said in there the lagoon next to the Charles."

"The lagoon, whatever. It was still January, and therefore freezing and life threatening to him."

"To Funderberk."

"Right."

"Go on."

"The sole reason my client goes for the swim is because the rich owner of the dog, one Leah Bland, Miss WASP of 1938, offers him a hundred thousand to save Jeeves's life."

"Jeeves was the dog?"

"Yeah."

"That wasn't in there."

"So I'm telling you. The dog's name was Jeeves."

"Like the butler?"

"Like the butler. Anyway, after my client risks—"

"I didn't think he was your client yet."

"He wasn't. I'm getting to that. After Funderberk drags the dog safely to shore, Miss Bland and her nephew Norbert, who was also there but not as intrepid as my client—"

"Lose 'intrepid,' Steve."

"Not as *brave* as my client. Miss Bland reneges on the contract. Funderberk hires this hack named Theodore Moone to represent him."

"The homeless man hires Moone to sue the old woman for breach of contract?"

"Right, right. I don't know how Moone ever got past high school, much less law school. Those papers—the civil case—aren't in there because it's the result that counts. Moone loses the contract action for Funderberk."

Our courts were awfully backlogged. "How'd they get a trial in only four months?"

"They didn't. Miss Bland was represented by Drysdale, Coppinger and Sewell. Know them?"

"Not socially."

"Very funny. Their head guy, Drysdale, and some female associate blow Moone out of the water on summary judgment because Moone files just an 'information and belief' counteraffidavit."

My one year of law school was too long ago. "Slow down, Steve."

Rothenberg spread his hands. "All right, it's like this. Drysdale moves for summary judgment just after the complaint is filed, saying basically Moone hasn't got a case because the affidavits of Miss Bland and the nephew show no contract was ever formed. Moone should have filed his client's affidavit, Funderberk swearing based on personal knowledge that Miss Bland said what she said that day at the river."

"Lagoon."

"Lagoon. Moone instead files his own counteraffidavit, saying in it that he—Moone—has the following facts on 'information and belief.' "

"And that's not good enough."

"Right, right. Summary judgment is like a substitute for trial, so you have to have the people in the affidavits giving the kind of information that would be admissible as testimony at trial."

"The contract case gets bounced out of court on that?"

"Yeah. It would have been a tough one to win anyway, but at least Funderberk should have had his chance before the jury."

"I take it Funderberk finds out that he's lost his hundred thousand."

"Right. So he gets himself a baseball bat and goes calling on Miss Bland."

"Allegedly."

"No. No, he admits he did that. Went to her town house over on Marlborough there and banged around the front door a little."

"Then what?"

"Then he claims he went away, came back again, and went to the alley door."

"Behind the house."

"Right, right. He bangs some more with the bat, Miss Bland comes out and gives him what for, and he slams the bat down and stalks off."

"He says."

"Right."

"Then what happens?"

"Maybe an hour later, nephew Norbert finds his aunt bludgeoned to death—"

"Lose 'bludgeoned,' too, Steve."

"No. No, that's the word the cops said the nephew used. 'Bludgeoned.' "

Maybe a Norbert would. "Sorry, go on."

"That's about it. The ME and lab reports all mesh.

Funderberk's prints on front and back doors. Death by repeated blows to the head. Bat found at the scene with more of his prints all over it, even a couple of hers."

"How do you figure hers?"

"Defending herself, she tries to grab it away. Who knows? In any case, there were clumps of her hair and bits of—"

I held up my hand. "I read that part, too, Steve. What do you expect me to do?"

Rothenberg clasped his fingers behind his head and leaned back. "Nobody saw him do it, John. All they've got is motive, means, and opportunity."

"You don't think that'll be enough?"

"I want you to find some reasonable doubt here, something I can take to the mat. Or at least something to bump down the charge, make the prosecutor think he won't be able to persuade twelve citizens good and true that my client whacked Ms. Bland and Jeeves."

"The dog, too?"

Rothenberg moved his tongue around again. "Afraid so."

"The jury isn't going to like the dog, Steve."

"I know."

2

Detective Sergeant Bonnie Cross sat at a desk in front of Lieutenant Robert Murphy's enclosure in Homicide. Reading a case file, she was wearing a blue blazer over a gray skirt. Brown hair framed a sincere, open face and fell to shoulders just shy of horsy. Before she talked, you'd get the impression that in college all her classmates went to her for advice.

"What," she said, not as a question.

"Lieutenant in?"

"No."

"Coming back?"

"On the Twelfth of Never."

"Vacation."

Cross turned a page in the folder. "Right."

"It's only May. How can he be off already?"

"Lieutenant's still working on last year's vacation."

I sank into the perp chair next to her desk.

Cross turned another page. "What."

"The Bland killing. I'm in for the defense."

"Bring your magic wand."

"That bad?"

Cross closed the file. "You're working for the lawyer, you've read the reports we gave him. Unit responding finds devoted nephew cradling battered head of beloved aunt in his lap. Blubbers out a story about homeless guy that stands up like Gibraltar. Prints, blood, and tissue match on weapon, motive A-one, eyewitness to means and opportunity. *You* could prosecute this one, Cuddy."

"I got the impression from the lab report that they made the prints before you picked up Funderberk."

"They did. The Mets booked him two weeks prior."

The Metropolitan District Commission Police patrolled the highways and waterways around Boston. "Charge?"

"Your boy beat up another derelict on the river there."

"Funderberk have much of a sheet?"

"You'd need two hands to lift it."

"History of violence?"

"More like a philosophy of violence. If it moved or talked, he hit or kicked it."

"But he saved the old woman's dog from drowning."

"You figure him out, I got an old professor could do an article on it."

"Name of the guy Funderberk supposedly beat up?"

"Shattles, Benny NMI. Mets sent us a copy of the file. Here."

I skimmed it, pausing over the station photos. Both white males, fortyish with brown hair, stringy like they wore hats a lot and didn't wash much. Given the names on the back, Funderberk wore his hair a little longer than Shattles, but you had to compare them side by side. Funderberk's right cheek and lower lip cut, Shattles's left eye closed and nose broken. Glance at them without the bruises, and you might not be able to tell them apart.

"Anybody talked to this Shattles?"

"Cuddy." Cross waved a tired hand over her desk. You couldn't see the top of it for documents and message slips. "We had four killings in the last thirty-six hours. The drug posses and street gangs in Roxbury and Dorchester are renting *Colors* on videotape, just to make sure they do the drive-bys right. I think we got this Bland case under control, you know?"

"Appreciate your time."

"Don't hurry back."

3

The next morning I drove from the condo I was renting downriver to the MDC station near the Museum of Science. I lucked out with a patrol officer who knew Benny Shattles by sight and had seen him half an hour before on the Cambridge side near the Massachusetts Avenue Bridge.

Cruising Memorial Drive in the slow lane, I spotted Shattles along the embankment, picking up soda cans and tossing them into a green leaf bag he dragged behind him. He wore a ski hat and gloves and too many layers of sweater for the sunshine. Even the leaf bag didn't look like it was on its maiden voyage. I found a parking place and walked back to him.

"Shattles?"

His head snapped up, like a man who was in a foreign country and was surprised to hear someone recognize him. "No."

I moved up close to him, and he backed off a step.

"Nobody's going to roust you, Shattles."

He said, "You're already rousting me." A southwest twang still laced through his voice.

"I want to talk with you about Jack Funderberk."

"That jerk? I ain't got no time to talk about jerks."

I took out a five-dollar bill, creasing it longways like a pup tent. "I'll buy a hundred cans' worth, all right?"

Shattles smiled. Only a front tooth and an incisor on top, the bottom teeth stumpy with gaps between the enamel and gum. The eye was okay, the nose pretty crooked.

Shattles set down the bag, angling a hand wearing an old army wool-liner toward the bill. I let him take it.

Stuffing the five into his belt, he said, "This won't go that far, you know."

"Far enough. Want to sit down?"

There was a grassy area under a failing tree held up with

rubber hoses and wires. I wasn't sorry when Shattles sat downwind.

He tugged on the cuffs of his sweaters. "So talk."

"I understand you and Funderberk had a little disagreement."

"Berk the Jerk? I whipped his butt for him."

"Why?"

"He damned near gets hisself killed swimming after some broad's hound, then thinks a lawyer's gonna get him his money. That's sure a jerk in my book."

"You fought about his lawsuit?"

"Naw, naw. That's just how it got started. I was stretched out here on the river, over by the BU bridge. Nice night, river curves so you can see all the lights downtown in the skyscrapers with the working stiffs still in them. I had a bottle, not a big one, just enough for the night. Then Berk comes along, he's down in the dumps. I asks him, how come? He says, his lawyer's gone and booted the money the old lady owes him. I says, how's that? He says, the lawyer screwed up the paperwork somehow, he's not getting a dime. I says, when'd you ever know a lawyer got something right? Then I offers him some of my bottle, buck him up some. He gets nasty, like he always does, won't give it back. That's when I whipped his butt."

"When was this?"

"When? I don't know."

"The police hauled you in?"

"Yeah, yeah. Woulda been okay, except somebody heard me whipping him, they called the cops from one of them emergency stands. They hadn't pulled me off him, I woulda killed the guy."

"You figure Berk could have killed the old woman?"

"Berk the Jerk? No way, man. He's just a loser. He went to see a lawyer, for chrissakes."

"Do you remember where you were when you heard about it?"

"Heard about what?"

"The killing."

"Sure, sure. I was here, right here. Policing the area. Some reporter comes up, wants to know if I know Berk. I told her to get lost."

Policing the area. "You ever in the service, Shattles?"

He lost the cockiness. "Yeah. Two tours in-country, first one Khe Sanh. You?"

"Saigon, mostly."

"How about a little extra then?"

"Extra?"

He pointed to his belt. "A little more veteran's benefit, from a rear-echelon type to a grunt in the boonies."

I laid another five on the grass and left him.

4

Boston's Charles Street Jail has about ten years on the Civil War. The cells are arranged in tiers around a central, open shaft. A giant cage for birds without wings. A federal court order restricted the number of inmates it could hold, and a new jail for pretrial detainees is supposed to open over by the Registry of Motor Vehicles on Nashua Street. One way or the other, I didn't think Jack Funderberk would ever see it.

A Suffolk County sheriff's officer brought Funderberk into the glass-walled room. The officer stepped outside, and Funderberk yanked a chair from the scarred wooden table to sit across from me. The facial bruises were healed, and he'd been shaving regularly. His hair was a little cleaner, too, parted in the center and pulled back behind the ears. His arms and face and neck looked bleached, the skin already taking on the ghost pallor of being inside all day.

I explained to Funderberk why I was there.

He sneered. "Just punching the clock on another loser, huh?"

"Probably."

We waited each other out. Funderberk looked down between his knees. He slapped his hand on the flat of the table. The officer on the far side of the glass took a step forward. I motioned him back.

Funderberk looked up at me. "I didn't kill that old broad, man. I should of, but I didn't."

"Tell me about it."

"Won't make no sense unless I start with the stuff from January."

"That's fine."

"All right. I'm at the river, see? I'm just walking. It's a

sunny day, only since it's not lunchtime yet, there ain't a lot of people walking around."

"How did you know it wasn't lunchtime?"

"There's like this tower. Across the river, Cambridge side. You can see the clock in it. Wasn't noon yet."

"Go on."

"All right. Like I said, there wasn't much happening. Just this old broad and this kind of short, wimpy-looking guy with her."

"And the dog."

"Right, and the dog. Jesus, man, you'd think somebody like her'd have enough sense not to let the thing run wild, but no, she's got this leash folded up in her hand, dog's off running."

"What kind of dog?"

"Wirehaired terrier. The kind they had in those old *Thin Man* movies. 'Asta.'"

"How do you know?"

"How do you think? I seen the movies."

"I mean how did you know it was a wirehaired terrier?"

"Oh, I . . . when I was a kid, I worked for a vet after school."

"Okay."

"Okay. So the dog's running around, and it sees these ducks out on the lagoon. Now, you got to remember, man, it's like the January thaw, the ice on the lagoon is all yellow and you can see open water here and there. Well, the stupid dog goes nuts after the ducks. So what happens?"

"The dog falls through the ice."

"Exactly. Exactly what happens. Only it don't go under. Under the ice, I mean. It's like in the water, trying to get back up on the ice, but it can't and it's really, like—what's the word?"

"Floundering?"

"Yeah, yeah. Floundering. And the old broad, she's pitching a fit on the snow there, and the wimpy guy with her, one look at him and you can tell he's gonna be no good. So I run up to them and I says, 'Hey, pinheads, your dog's drowning out there."

"Then what?"

"The old broad starts talking real fast. Not crazy, just real upset. She says, 'Please, please save my dog.' Actually she says, 'Please save my Jeeves,' and I says, 'Who?' and she says,

'Jeeves, Jeeves, my dog.' I look out at the dog, who's maybe going down for the first time, and I says, 'Are you kidding me, lady? I could drown out there.' Then she says, 'You save my dog, I'll give you a hundred thousand dollars.' Just like that. A hundred thousand. The wimp starts screaming at her. 'Auntie Leah, what are you, nuts or something?' like that. So I cuff him one, just to shut him up, and meanwhile this dog's going down for the second time. I says to her, 'Lady, you serious or what?' She says, 'I'm serious, I'm serious. You go save my dog, and the hundred thousand's yours.' I says to her, 'You promise?' and she says, 'Yeah, yeah. I promise, I promise.'"

Funderberk worked his rear deeper into the chair and set his feet harder on the floor. "So I take off my coat there, man, and I pull off some clothes and I jump in. The bottom's all mucky, and I'm losing my balance even before I get twenty feet, and I says to myself, 'Jesus, the hell am I doing this for?' My feet are already numb through the shoes and socks, so I decide to turn back. Then the dog sees me, and the thing starts barking and yowling and trying to get to me. And it's taking a lot of water. So I slog out a little more and I get near it, and I can hear its front claws, scratching on the ice, trying to get up out of the hole of water."

Funderberk swiped the back of his hand across his eyes. "Its paws are bleeding, see? Its paws are bleeding 'cause it's trying so hard to get up on that ice. Well, I finally get to it, and I grab it and kind of half swim back to shore."

Funderberk's face darkened. "I'm so beat I can't hardly stand up, man, but I set that dog on the ground, gentle as a nurse with a baby. Now, what does the old broad say? 'Oh, thank you so much'? 'Oh, where can we send the money'? No way, José. She grabs the dog and starts running all stiff-legged, 'cause she was old, see? And the wimp starts after her, but he can't even run as fast as the old broad. And I'm starting to really freeze up, so I yell, 'Hey, hey! I'm going into shock or something here. I need a doctor and a warm bed somewheres.' And they just keep running up that ramp there across Storrow Drive toward the houses. And I'm yelling 'Where's my hundred, lady? Where's my hundred thousand?' And they just keep going, her with the dog and him after her."

I said, "Anybody else see this?"

"No. Nobody, like I said before. Nobody else around. But that's what happened, goddammit! Just like I said."

"What did you do then?"

"I near died, man."

"After that."

"I watched out for them, see? For a week, maybe more. They didn't come back to the river. So I start walking up and down the streets. I spot the wimp guy, carrying some groceries and going into this la-di-da doorway on Marlborough. I get the name and address, and I check out the phone book over to the drugstore and bingo! I got Miss Leah Bland, man. I got her."

"Then what?"

"I go to this lawyer. I'm just walking down the street, trying to figure this thing, and I see his sign in the window there, so I go in. I figure, this is an easy case, right? I mean, everybody and his brother can see the old broad owes me the hundred grand. So I sit down with this guy Moone, and he listens to my story and he takes down the information. He didn't have no secretary or nothing, that should have tipped me right there. But I always had PD's before, and they come right to the courtroom or the holding pen, you don't ever see their office, like. Anyway this Moone, he tells me he's gonna bring a lawsuit against them. He says he's gonna bring them to their knees."

"But he doesn't."

"Oh, man. He screws it up. Royally. He gets us tossed out of court because of some kind of paperwork he files or don't file that doesn't have my name on it, I don't know. I get nuts about it, I take it out on this other guy by the river there."

"Benny Shattles."

Funderberk looked surprised. "You know Benny?"

"I read the file. Go on."

"Anyway, I take it out on Benny, then I stew about it some, then I get good and loaded one night and I really feel like crap the next morning. So I go to her house and—"

"With a bat."

"Right, yeah. With this bat. I go—"

"Where did you get the bat?"

"Where?"

"Where."

"Jesus, man, I don't—wait a minute. Down by the river

there. Yeah, by the ball field over near the tugs, you know? I go down there, watch the softball. Most of the guys use the metal bats now, but they was using one of the wood ones, I guess, and it cracked, so they just left it, and I picked it up."

"And went visiting."

"Right. I wasn't drunk or nothing. But when I go to the front door, the wimp sees me through the curtains and starts yelling for me to go away. The dog, Jeeves, he's at the window, too, front paws up on the glass, barking and wagging what tail he's got, like he's glad to see me. I start banging on the door with the bat, and this other old bag in the next building starts yelling down at me from her window. Saying she was gonna call the cops, I didn't quit. So I go around the block to think about it, then up the alley and start banging on the back door. This time the old broad, Bland herself now, opens up the back door. Jeeves comes out, jumping and licking my hand, like he remembers me and all. The old broad, though, she starts yelling at me and I start yelling at her, and pretty soon the other old bag is leaning out another window, yelling at both of us and saying that's it, she's calling the cops. Well, I slam down the bat and get out of there. I'm mad as hell, but I leave and I don't hurt her, man, I swear it."

"Why'd you bring the bat?"

"Huh?"

"You weren't going to hurt her, why'd you bring the bat?"

"I don't know, man."

"You don't know."

"You don't think of that kind of stuff. You're hung over and feeling screwed and you just have the bat 'cause you picked it up before you thought about going to see her."

"That'll never fly."

"Hey, I don't know what flies and what don't, see? That's why I don't got no job and no house and no money."

"Don't forget no future."

"Real funny. Whose side you on, anyway?"

"I'm going to talk to the nephew and the neighbor who saw you that day. Anybody else you can think of?"

"No. Yeah, talk to Moone, willya? Tell that shyster how he screwed me up."

I stood.

Funderberk used the table to get to his feet. In a different tone, he said, "Hey, man, when you see the wimp nephew, make sure he's feeding Jeeves, all right?"

I looked at Jack Funderberk. "Whoever killed Miss Bland did the dog, too."

Funderberk blinked, dropping his head without closing his eyes. "Aw, no, man. No, no."

I started to feel what Steve Rothenberg had said.

5

Theodore Moone's office made Rothenberg's look like the Taj Mahal.

I climbed the third flight over the dry cleaners. I'd seen the sign in Moone's window from a block away. Up close, it was hand-painted. Probably with the stick Moone had used to stir the paint.

Moone himself told me to step right in. He oozed into a sports jacket that looked like spun Cream of Wheat. His shirt was wrinkled from waist to shoulders, the tabs sproinging away from each other. His tie was twice as wide as the one I was wearing. The red toupee was so obvious that the too-high part actually made it look more natural. Flushed face, small eyes, big Irish jowls. I shook a sweaty palm and got the kind of grin that made me want to button the pocket holding my wallet.

"Take a load off and tell me your problems, sir."

I eased into a folding chair with "Wilkie's Funeral Home" stenciled on the back of it. When Moone plopped into a tufted desk chair, some stuffing poofed out like dandelion seeds.

Moone made a ritual of clicking a ballpoint over a yellow legal pad. "If I could just have your name?"

"John Cuddy." I took out my ID and showed it to him.

Putting the pen back into his shirt pocket, Moone exhaled forcefully. "Now what?"

"You represented a man named Jack Funderberk on a case that went sour."

"Sour? I tried to help that bum out, and he commits murder. You got any idea how long it'll be before I live down the bad publicity?"

"Let's talk about the civil case for a minute."

"The Board of Bar Overseers wouldn't like that."

"Why not?"

"Client confidentiality."

"You think the board would like me telling them you just called your client a murderer?"

Moone puckered his mouth. "What do you want to know?"

"How come the case went sour?"

"Look, I get all kinds in here, all right? All kinds. This Funderberk, he comes in, I wanna open a window. But I hear him out, and what he says makes a little sense. So I call this Miss Bland on the telephone, and she's frosty, she says to call her lawyers. Not her lawyer, her lawyers, plural. Gives me Drysdale, Coppinger—"

"And Sewell."

"Right. That gets me thinking, she's already talked this over with some high-powered people. Maybe Funderberk really has something. So I file a complaint, on this Funderberk's say-so, now, and I get back the telephone book."

"A motion for summary judgment."

"With attached affidavits and exhibits and memorandum in support of this and that. A tidal wave of paper."

"Which amounted to what?"

"Funderberk says she offered him a hundred thousand *before* he went in the water. She and her nephew say she offered Funderberk a hundred bucks *after* he brought the dog back alive."

"Sounds like something a jury should decide."

"Yeah, well, it didn't sound that way to the judge. I did the best I could for this Funderberk, but I was buried. This Drysdale and some little superstar in a slit skirt ate my lunch for me. I'm lucky I didn't end up having to pay some of Drysdale's fees."

"Why didn't you file Funderberk's own affidavit?"

Something moved behind Moone's eyes. "You go to law school or what?"

"A year's worth, nights."

"Yeah, well, they don't teach you in law school how you're supposed to reach your client when you need him and he don't have a permanent address or job. I needed him, but he never called me or came to see me. I did what I could."

"What kind of contingency were you on?"

"None of your business."

"I can ask Funderberk about your fee."

"Go ahead. At least now I know where you can find him."

6

Picture Humpty-Dumpty just before the fall and you'd have a pretty good image of Norbert Bland. He met me at the door to the Marlborough Street town house wearing a brown cardigan sweater over a frayed white shirt and brown pants. Fifty or so, his fingers were short and blunt. Though thinning, the hair and eyebrows were both that glossy black that God gives to wing of crow and Clairol puts in bottle of dye.

As he looked at my ID a pointy nose appeared to be his most expressive feature. "If we must talk, come in, come in."

The interior door opened onto a hallway, the staircase marching straight to the second floor. Bland led me into a small parlor decorated in Edwardian furnishings. I took one of two straight chairs with oval backs upholstered in faded maroon. Bland took the other.

"I want to be a good citizen, Mr. Cuddy, but I'm not sure how much I should help the man who killed my auntie."

The last seemed an odd word coming from a man his age. "I appreciate your talking to me at all, Mr. Bland, but I'm really just interested in what you saw that day."

The eyes narrowed. "Which day?"

"Let's start with the incident on the river."

"Oh, really. That's already been resolved by our attorneys."

"Just what you saw and heard, please."

A sigh of resignation. "Auntie and I took Jeeves for a walk. Auntie named him Jeeves because he'd rush to the door like a butler whenever someone rang. Jeeves liked his outings, and Auntie let him off his leash. I'd warned her about that—endlessly, in fact—but to no avail. As luck would have it, Jeeves went bounding after some waterfowl and plunged through the ice, flailing about madly. Well, I don't swim, and Auntie was beside herself, when this homeless fellow approached us and said"—Bland scrunched up his face and dropped his tone an octave—"'Don't worry there, lady, I'll get him for you.'"

"Funderberk."

"As we later discovered."

"He just volunteered?"

"Precisely. I don't doubt his bravery, but after the rescue, naturally Auntie wished to rush Jeeves back here before he caught his death. However, she did pause to offer your Funderberk a hundred dollars for his trouble. A noble gesture, really. Well, the fellow grew nasty, bellowing that he wanted a hundred *thousand* dollars. Can you imagine? So naturally Auntie scooped up Jeeves and began to run while I lingered back a bit, to protect her in case your Funderberk decided to become even nastier. We arrived home safely, and Jeeves made a complete recovery."

"When did you next hear from Funderberk?"

"*I* didn't. Auntie called DeWitt Drysdale. She was always a stickler for advising our attorneys of any potential difficulties, and DeWitt said he would take care of it. Well, thereafter, Auntie got some sort of threatening call from a dreadful man named Moone who presented himself over the telephone as a lawyer, though you would scarcely have guessed it hearing him talk."

"You met him?"

The eyes narrowed again. "Just over the telephone."

"Then what happened?"

"Well, one day this Funderberk fellow came storming up our front steps, brandishing a baseball bat. He was shrieking obscenities and demanding to be admitted to discuss 'what he had coming to him,' I believe was his phrase. Naturally, I refused to open the door. By shouting through the windows, Mrs. Van Nuys—in the next building—and I repelled him."

Repelled. I bet myself that Norbert was going to use "bludgeoned," too. "Did you call the police?"

"No. No, but Auntie may have called DeWitt, because I did hear her use the telephone. I went upstairs to bathe."

"You took a bath?"

"This Funderberk, your client, upset me. I find it relaxing to bathe after I'm upset."

"Go on."

"Well, I was in the tub with the water running and the door closed when . . . when . . ." Bland's voice seemed to catch, and he wet his lips. "When Funderberk returned, to the back door this time. Auntie was always a . . . feisty person, Mr. Cuddy. And I imagine it didn't take much to trigger

your client's rage. When I finished my bath, I came out in
my robe and started to my room, but I could feel a draft."

"A draft?"

"Yes. As though a door or window were open. Auntie
usually kept all the windows closed during the day, you see.
Too much soot about for the curtains and draperies. Well, I
sensed something was amiss, so I called her name. No reply.
I called Jeeves. The same. I went downstairs and Auntie
was . . ."

Bland put one of the blunt little hands to his face and
spoke through the splayed fingers. "Auntie and Jeeves both
were in the back hall, the outside door open. I went to
Auntie and tried to pull her up, to get her to a chair, you see.
I don't believe I realized she . . . until I saw the blood and
the . . . her head had been bludgeoned, and Jeeves had
been smashed almost to pulp. I picked him up—I had to
move him to close the door—and that's when I saw the bat,
just lying on our patio, drenched in . . . in everything."

"You picked the dog up?"

Bland nodded through the hand.

"Instead of just dragging him away from the door?"

The hand came down. "He was our . . . pet, sir."

"I'm sorry. Anything more?"

"Precious little, I'm afraid. I dialed the police, then tried
to . . . I believe that when they arrived, I was sitting on the
floor, cradling Auntie's head. I don't . . . I don't really remember much after that."

"Did you happen to see anyone else around?"

"Anyone else?"

"Another derelict, maybe."

"Derelict? I assure you, sir, one caller like your Mr.
Funderberk was quite sufficient contact for this family."

"But you never actually saw Funderberk after he left the
first time, out by the front door."

"That is correct. But Mrs. Van Nuys did. Shall I arrange
an introduction?"

7

"Sit down, young man. Sit, the chair will hold you."

I took a doilied easy chair across from Mrs. Van Nuys, the four-posted walker between us, her gnarled fingers caressing the rubber handgrips like a six-year-old kid with his first two-wheeler. Bluish hair worn in a ponytail and half glasses on her nose, it had been a while since her first two-wheeler.

"Leah Bland and I debuted together, Mr. Cuddy. My family was from the Hudson Valley originally, not Yankees like the Blands. But we got along famously, just famously."

"So you've known the Blands most of your life?"

"That's right. Leah's father and brother were giants, sir, giants of their times. But I don't expect you've come to hear about them."

"That's right. I believe Norbert Bland explained on the telephone?"

"You must do your duty, sir. And I mine as a citizen. I'm prepared to testify, and I'm certainly not afraid to tell my story more than once."

"I'm listening."

"Well, it was a fine day, the dogwoods and magnolias blooming, the scent of spring in just everything. I'd opened all the windows on this floor—unlike Leah, you see, I enjoy the fresh air. Furniture be hanged, if you can't live with the soot, get out of the city."

"With the windows open you could hear what happened next door?"

"I could. I condominiumized, if that's the word for it, several years ago at the advice of DeWitt Drysdale, and I must say I haven't regretted it one instant. Fine unit owners around me now, much less upkeep—did you know that all Norbert ever does all day long is clean and maintain that house? Oh, Leah would buy everything for him, the mops and gloves and cleaning fluids and all, but he spends every day keeping that house spotless. I decided to retain the third floor here as my apartment. It has just the nicest bay window in the house and the best sun as well."

"So you heard something that day?"

"I did. I was reading here, thank God for my eyes, still sharp as an eagle's, when I heard this commotion on Leah's front stoop. I made my way to the window, and I could see this disreputable character with a baseball bat, pounding on the door and swearing like a sailor. Well, he seemed quite mad to me, so I advised him that I would summon the police if he didn't go on his way. That seemed to discourage him, and he left."

"Can you describe who you saw?"

"I can. A tramp, approximately forty, I would say. Hair like one of those hippie creatures, brown to black from being filthy. The word 'disheveled' would be generous regarding his clothes, far too many layers for the weather."

"Go on."

"Well, I thought we were quit of him, and never called the police, more's the pity. Then, a short while later, I heard something from the back as well."

"How long after?"

"Oh, minutes."

"Two minutes, ten minutes?"

"Perhaps fifteen or twenty."

"What did you hear then?"

"More shouting. His voice, I was sure. The same man, I mean. I made my way to the rear—I'm surprisingly adept with this contraption." Mrs. Van Nuys almost managed to flex her fingers around the rubber grips. "I thought I would hate having to use it, but quite frankly it's a godsend. I don't have a nephew like Norbert to look after me."

"When you got to the back, what did you see?"

"The same tramp, ranting at Leah and she giving no ground. That woman was an oak, Mr. Cuddy. Unbending, unyielding. I was just so proud of her, but also concerned for her. I advised the man that I was calling the police, and that seemed to spook him again. He threw the bat down on the ground and strode off, swearing still. I asked Leah if she wanted me to summon the police, and she said no, not to bother. She seemed so . . ."

I waited.

"I'm sorry. She suddenly seemed so distracted . . . uncertain. And that was quite unlike Leah, as I've said. However, I thought that she was probably just reacting from the confrontation, so I left the window. . . ." Mrs. Van Nuys bit her lower lip. "If I had called the police that instant, I can't help but think that Leah would be alive today."

"I wouldn't hold yourself responsible for that."

The eyes came over the half glasses. "I would."

"Mrs. Van Nuys, did you ever see that man come back?"

"Come back?"

"After you saw him drop the bat—"

"*Throw* the bat."

"After you saw him throw the bat down, did you ever see him again?"

"No. As I said, I left the window."

"You never saw him strike Miss Bland?"

"No."

"Did you ever see any other men like this one around the Bland house?"

"Any others? Heavens, no! Do you mean there are more like him?"

8

DeWitt Drysdale's office was the Taj Mahal.

Drysdale, Coppinger & Sewell occupied the entire top floor of a fifty-story tower, the kind that's becoming a little hard to rent after the demise of the Massachusetts Miracle. Drysdale himself had a corner office with a sweeping view of Boston Harbor. The mahogany desk matched the mahogany credenza, bookshelves, and chairs. The rugs would have cost the Kubla Khan half his empire, and the paintings were by artists so famous their signatures were illegible.

"Mr. Cuddy, please take a seat. The attorney who sat second chair on the motion for summary judgment, Ms. Talitieri, will join us shortly."

DeWitt Drysdale accentuated the "Ms.," as though he were still getting used to pronouncing the word. In fact, everything about Drysdale was accentuated. Widow's peak of gray hair, brushed stylishly back over his ears. Chiseled chin, complete with cleft. Glasses, the metal frames probably platinum, the faintest tint to the lenses. When we shook hands, I noticed he wore French cuffs under the sleeves of his suit jacket.

I heard the door swish open behind me.

"Ah, Nina, thank you. Nina Talitieri, John Cuddy."

Talitieri was short, even in high heels. Brown eyes, a hint of makeup, curly black hair abruptly chopped off at the neckline. White stockings over the heels, blue two-piece suit, ruffled white blouse. Formidable until she smiled, when you got the feeling she might be a nice person after all.

"Mr. Cuddy."

When we all were settled, Drysdale said, "Just so the ground rules are clear, Mr. Cuddy; I'm not deeply versed in criminal law, but I do know the discovery opportunities for the accused are rather limited. Accordingly, I'm happy to permit you this interview, although all attorney-client communications are obviously out-of-bounds."

"Fair enough."

"Where would you like to begin?"

"Did you ever meet Jack Funderberk?"

"No. Nina?"

"Never."

"Is it typical for you never to even meet the opposing side to a lawsuit?"

Drysdale smiled condescendingly. "I'm not sure there is a 'typical' in our practice, Mr. Cuddy. As you can see, we've done quite well over the years, yet still have time for the unusual case."

"Like *Funderberk* v. *Bland.*"

"Correct."

"You never even tried to depose the guy?"

"Mr. Cuddy, you must understand. There are various devices for disposing of nonsense cases like Mr. Funderberk's. Summary judgment is one of them. As soon as we received the complaint, I was certain it required no formal discovery, such as deposition. Based on the accounts of Leah and Norbert Bland as reflected in their affidavits, there was no need to run up the tab, so to speak. After Nina performed some confirmatory research of law, we were prepared to dispatch Mr. Funderberk, and his attorney, rather swiftly."

"Tell me, Mr. Drysdale, if the case had gone to trial and Funderberk won, I take it Miss Bland was good for the hundred thousand?"

A veil slid down over Drysdale's face. "I'm afraid I can't discuss my client's financial position, Mr. Cuddy."

"Leah Bland is dead."

"That makes no difference."

"My guess is you're probating her will up at the courthouse. I can just go read it."

"That you can, Mr. Cuddy. But you can't expect me to be talking to you about it, now can you?"

"Could the Blands have lied to protect their nest egg?"

I tried to watch Talitieri as Drysdale heartily reminded me why the word "guffaw" was coined. The young associate's face gave the impression she was playing poker, and I wondered why she wasn't at least smiling, too.

Drysdale composed himself. "Mr. Cuddy, if that's your best argument, I'm afraid you should be advising your client to bring his toothbrush to court."

I addressed Drysdale but I was pitching to Talitieri. "My client isn't in a position to pop into a drugstore, counselor. My client is keeping a six-by-nine warm at Charles Street Jail."

Drysdale stiffened. "And with good reason, sir. He brutally murdered a defenseless, elderly woman. And Leah Bland never told a lie in her life, much less one under oath in a formal document like an affidavit."

"Did Leah Bland ever indicate to you any uncertainty about her version of what happened down by the river?"

"Clearly immaterial, sir. And, in any case, within the privilege."

"Did she ever contact you about Funderberk after the summary judgment motion?"

"Same."

"Mr. Drysdale, if my client is innocent, and there's anything you can tell me to establish that, how're you going to feel if you sit on the lid and claim privilege?"

I hoped I wasn't gilding the lily. I felt, rather than saw, Talitieri shift in her chair.

Drysdale tented his fingers over the slate blotter on the polished desk. "An attorney has no choice but to invoke the privilege, Mr. Cuddy. The privilege survives even the grave."

"I wish I was a privilege."

9

There was a coffee shop at street level across from Drysdale's skyscraper. I had a hot chocolate and then told the inquiring waitress I'd be happy to pay for five more so long as she didn't have to make them and I didn't have to drink them. That made her happy.

I figured that a law firm like Drysdale's probably expected an associate like Nina Talitieri to work well into the evening. That's why I was pleased to see her coming out of the building's revolving door with a herd of secretarial and other staff people just after five. I'd gotten to her.

Talitieri wore a trench coat and carried a leather briefcase. She walked down to the harbor, lost in thought and bumping into at least three people I noticed. At the water's edge, the young lawyer stood for a while, elbows on the railing, staring past the sloops and yawls dropping their mainsails and furling their jibs and motoring into their slips for the night. I anticipated her direction and took a seat on a stone bench a minute before she started moving again.

As Talitieri drew even with me I said, "Let's talk about it."

She jumped, but not much. After watching me for a moment, she sat at the far end of the bench, close enough to talk easily, enough apart to give the impression to a passerby that we weren't together.

Talitieri kept her eyes on the sailboats, as though she were trying to learn how to rig one. "You did a good job back there. Drysdale never noticed."

"Thanks. How'd he get to be where he is? Being dense as a post, I mean."

Almost a smile. "When he was starting out, the road was already paved, you know?"

"By pater and his pater before him?"

A smile and a glance. "Roughly." The smile drifted away. "Whatever I tell you can't be used unless you can figure it out from some other source, right?"

"Sounds fair."

"That's what you said to Drysdale back there."

"All right. I promise."

The head swung around, like she was following one of the boats in particular, but her voice sounded surprised. "You mean that. I mean, you really do mean that, don't you?"

"Yes."

Talitieri leaned back, folding her hands on the buckle of her trench coat. Only the tips of her toes touched the granite blocks set into the ground. "In law school, I had this professor for professional responsibility. That's the ethics course? He used to say, 'Whenever you're representing a client, you have to remember, there are other people around, too.'"

"People like Jack Funderberk."

"His lawyer . . ."

"I've met Moone."

"People in law firms like ours call people like Moone 'hacks.' "

"So would I."

"But this was different. I've only been a lawyer for two years, but Moone . . . Moone gave up too easily, even for a hack."

"What do you mean?"

"All he has to do is file a 'personal knowledge' affidavit in a timely manner and he's all set. He had weeks to find his client and get him to come in."

"Weeks."

"He told the judge, 'I can't find the plaintiff, Your Honor. This counteraffidavit is the best I can do.' God, the rule itself says that's not good enough."

"So?"

"So Moone could have fought a little. He could have jumped up and down, filed his own affidavit stating why he couldn't file a personal knowledge one. That would have gotten him a continuance and bought the time to find his client."

"But he didn't think of it, huh?"

"Aw, the judge even suggested it to him. 'I don't think it'll do any good, Your Honor. This guy's a bum.' He actually said that. In open court, the other lawyers waiting their turn, having a good laugh over it."

"Moone gave the case away."

Another quick side glance. "That's how I saw it, anyway."

"What did the Blands tell you about the incident on the river?"

Talitieri shook her head. "No. No, here's what I'm going to tell you about that, and no more. Miss Bland called Drysdale just after it happened, but Norbert is the one who came in to see me. I don't know why. All I know is that Norbert told me the volunteer version that appears in his and Miss Bland's affidavits. I drafted them up that way, sent them out to the Blands for signature, and they came back signed. 'Under the pains and penalties of perjury.' "

"So, not notarized?"

"No. Not necessary. Just the signatures, under oath."

I thought about it. "Were the Blands good for the money if Funderberk won?"

"Sort of."

"What does that mean?"

"Look, you'll have to work that out. Start with the will itself. The probate and family court at Pemberton Square."

I turned it over some more. "Was Miss Bland at the hearing?"

"On summary judgment?"

"Yes."

"No, of course not. Just Drysdale and me."

"Did you ever speak to Miss Bland after the hearing?"

"No. But she did try to call."

"You?"

"No, Drysdale. I overheard his secretary telling him he had a phone message from Miss Bland. The day of the murder. It's the kind of thing you remember."

Talitieri checked her watch. "Look, Mr. Cuddy, I have to go."

"Right. I'll wait here till you're a ways off."

Talitieri stood up, then fussed with her buckle and briefcase enough to say one more thing, out of the corner of her mouth. "Be sure to read that will, now."

10

I followed Nina Talitieri's advice. After spending most of the next morning plowing through papers at both the probate and superior courts, I took the subway over to the offices of Theodore Moone, Esquire. I pointed out to him the reasons why he probably wasn't going to be an esquire too much longer. After about half an hour, he told me what he knew. It wasn't much, but I thought it would be enough.

The door opened a crack. "Mr. Cuddy, isn't it?"

"That's right."

When I made no effort to move through the door, he said, "Well, what is it?"

"I think we need to talk."

I still hadn't moved, and he seemed to be nervous about it.

"Talk about what?"

"Oh, you know."

He backed away from the door. I caught it with the heel of my hand and followed Norbert Bland into the parlor.

"You really shouldn't have lied about hearing Moone's voice only over the telephone, Norbert."

Bland squirmed in his chair. If he resented my using his first name, it got lost in the wash.

I said, "You were happy as a clam when poor Jeeves went through the ice, weren't you?"

"I don't know what you're talking about."

"I'm talking about the burden that would have lifted from your shoulders."

"If DeWitt Drysdale shared that sort of information with you, I'll—"

"Drysdale didn't say a word, Norbert. I read the will, on file in the probate court."

Bland stared at me.

"You were to get the house, and the liquid stuff, so long as you properly attended to old Jeeves. Aggravating, wasn't it, Norbert?"

He fumed.

"You didn't dare poison Jeeves. But what the hell, Auntie Leah was old, and sooner or later you could manage something. Just one problem, though. The incident at the river really did happen just the way Jack Funderberk said it did. And you were blind scared that if it went to court, to trial, that is, your aunt might even back up his version of it."

"She didn't back it up! She signed her affidavit, just as I did mine."

"No, Norbert. You signed her affidavit just like you did yours. Nobody had to appear before a notary, so you just signed both and sent them back to Drysdale's office. I compared the signature on her affidavit to the signature on her will, Norbert. With no one questioning the signatures in the contract case, you were pretty safe. But if I could spot a problem comparing them, imagine what an expert could do."

"You're bluffing."

"I'm guessing that your aunt really was torn when she

thought about what had happened down at the river. I'm guessing you spoke to Drysdale just after the lawsuit was filed. You assured your aunt that you'd take care of it for her. Then, just after the summary judgment hearing, you told your aunt that Funderberk's case had been thrown out on a technicality. When Funderberk came a-calling, you managed to shoo him away out front. But then he reappeared at the back door, maybe yelling something about her lying in the paperwork. Mrs. Van Nuys says your aunt looked upset after that, and Mr. Drysdale did tell me that Leah Bland never lied. Ever."

Bland's Adam's apple bobbed twice before he spoke. "That's . . . that's . . ."

"You took a bath all right, and overheard your aunt hanging up after she tried to reach Drysdale. It was smart of you to admit that, because the secretary at the law firm would remember that your aunt tried to reach her attorney just after talking with Funderberk at the back door. It was also smart to say you hadn't seen Funderberk hit her. Don't want to make things too neat for the cops. But tell me, Norbert, what did you say to her? 'Auntie, why were you trying to call DeWitt?' "

Bland shuddered, his face like a dam breaking. "Auntie Leah left word for DeWitt to call her back. Something that . . . that hobo said set her off. She confronted me, demanded to know what had happened. I tried to explain it to her, deflect her. But no, she knew what an affidavit was. A statement under oath. She knew she'd never signed one. She called me a liar, that wretched little dog of hers jumping and yapping and snapping at me."

Bland seemed to lose focus. "All it ever did was track dirt into this house, on the rugs, the furniture, everywhere. It was . . ." Norbert came back to me. "I tried to reason with her. I was only trying to protect us from that hobo's insane lawsuit."

"To protect your inheritance, which was why you offered Moone five thousand dollars to take a dive."

"That fool! He responded to DeWitt's motion in order to lose the case but ensure a handsome fee for himself. He wanted more, but he took five and was glad for it. Probably more than he makes in a . . . a . . ." Bland seemed to struggle for an appropriate wage period, but he'd been out of the stream too long to be sure.

"So your aunt said she was—"

"Auntie Leah was going to turn me in! For perjury, a crime. She said I'd go to prison for that."

"Where was the bat?"

"Inside the back door. Auntie had picked it up from the patio. She was walking back to the telephone, to call DeWitt again. I didn't know what to do. I grabbed it and I hit her. And her damned dog, too. I crushed him, and then I picked him up and flung him against the door. I didn't know what I was doing."

"You knew enough to wear gloves to avoid leaving your prints on the bat."

"I was already wearing the gloves upstairs, when I heard her on the telephone. Rubber gloves."

"Tidying up a bit?"

"No, no. For my . . . my hair. When I dye it, I wear the gloves. I was just about to when I heard her speaking to DeWitt's office."

"Come on, Norbert. You also knew enough to be sure to move your aunt's body. Getting her blood and brains on you to cover the stains from cracking her skull."

He shook his blunt little index finger at me. "She was going to send me to prison! Her own family. Do you know what happens in jail to men who . . . who can't protect themselves? I couldn't convince her. I had to deal with her immediately, quickly. Don't you understand?"

"Summary judgment."

"What?"

"Never mind."

Sue Grafton and Sue Dunlap illustrate how much trouble you can get into when you do something, or take on a job, without giving it enough thought. Some might call it acting on a whim, or just plain bad decision-making. But perhaps it's more like climbing the mountain because it was there.

a little
missionary work

SUE GRAFTON

*What can we say about Sue Grafton that wouldn't
sound like we were gushing? Okay, so we'll gush.*

*Sue Grafton has taken her PI, Kinsey Millhone,
right to the best-seller lists—or is that the other way
around? Starting with "A" Is for Alibi, she has so far
worked her way to "I" Is for Innocent, virtually
without a misstep. She has done for the female PI
what Robert B. Parker did for the male PI: she's
given her a very high visibility factor, and made it
possible for others to follow in her footsteps.*

*"A Little Missionary Work" gives us a look at
some different sides of Kinsey Millhone, but there's
one side of Kinsey that is always apparent—the top
side. She does what she has to do to come out on
top, as you will see here.*

Sometimes you have to take on a job that constitutes pure missionary work. You accept an assignment not for pay, or for any hope of tangible reward, but simply to help another human being in distress. My name is Kinsey Millhone. I'm a licensed private eye . . . in business for myself . . . so I can't really afford professional charity, but now and then somebody gets into trouble and I just can't turn my back.

I was standing in line one Friday at the bank, waiting to make a deposit. It was almost lunchtime and there were eleven people in front of me, so I had some time to kill. As usual, in the teller's line, I was thinking about Harry Hovey, my bank-robber friend, who'd once been arrested for holding up this very branch. I'd met him when I was investigating a bad-check case. He was introduced to me by another crook as an unofficial "expert" and ended up giving me a crash course in the methods and practices of passing bad paper. Poor Harry. I couldn't remember how many times he'd been in the can. He was skilled enough for a life of crime, but given to self-sabotage. Harry was always trying to go straight, always trying to clean up his act, but honest employment never seemed to have much appeal. He'd get out of prison, find a job, and be doing pretty well for himself. Then something would come along and he'd succumb to temptation— forge a check, rob a bank, God only knows what. Harry was hooked on crime the way some people are addicted to cocaine, alcohol, chocolate, and unrequited love. He was currently doing time in the federal correctional institution in Lompoc, California, with all the other racketeers, bank robbers, counterfeiters, and former White House staff bad boys. . . .

I had reached the teller's window and was finishing my transaction when Lucy Alisal, the assistant bank manager, approached. "Miss Millhone? I wonder if you could step this way. Mr. Chamberlain would like a word with you."

"Who?"

"The branch vice-president," she said. "It shouldn't take long."

"Oh. Sure."

I followed the woman toward Mr. Chamberlain's glass-walled enclosure, wondering the whole time what I'd done to deserve this. Well, okay. Let's be honest. I'd been thinking about switching my account to First Interstate for the free checking privileges, but I didn't see how he could have found out about *that.* As for my balances, I'd only been over-drawn by the teensiest amount and what's a line of credit for?

I was introduced to Jack Chamberlain, who turned out to be someone I recognized from the gym, a tall, lanky fellow in his early forties, whose workouts overlapped mine three mornings a week. We'd exchange occasional small talk if we happened to be doing reps on adjacent machines. It was odd to see him here in a conservative business suit after months of sweat-darkened shorts and T-shirts. His hair was cropped close, the color a wiry mixture of copper and silver. He wore steel-rimmed glasses and his teeth were endearingly crooked in front. Somehow, he looked more like a high-school basket-ball coach than a banking exec. A trophy sitting on his desk attested to his athletic achievements, but the engraving was small and I couldn't quite make out the print from where I stood. He caught my look and a smile creased his face. "Var-sity basketball. We were state champs," he said as he shook my hand formally and invited me to take a seat.

He sat down himself and picked up a fountain pen, which he capped and recapped as he talked. "I appreciate your time. I know you do your banking on Fridays and I took the liberty," he said. "Someone told me at the gym that you're a private investigator."

"That's right. Are you in the market for one?"

"This is for an old friend of mine. My former high-school sweetheart, if you want the truth. I probably could have called you at your office, but the circumstances are unusual and this seemed more discreet. Are you free tonight by any chance?"

"Tonight? That depends," I said. "What's going on?"

"I'd rather have her explain it. This is probably going to seem paranoid, but she insists on secrecy, which is why she didn't want to make contact herself. She has reason to be-lieve her phone is tapped. I hope you can bear with us. Believe me, I don't ordinarily do business this way."

"Glad to hear that," I said. "Can you be a bit more spe-cific? So far, I haven't really heard what I'm being asked to do."

Jack set the pen aside. "She'll explain the situation as soon as it seems wise. She and her husband are having a big party tonight and she asked me to bring you. They don't want you appearing in any professional capacity. Time is of the essence, or we might go about this some other way. You'll understand when you meet her."

I studied him briefly, trying to figure out what was going on. If this was a dating ploy, it was the weirdest one I'd ever heard. "Are you married?"

He smiled slightly. "Divorced. I understand you are, too. I assure you, this is not a hustle."

"What kind of party?"

"Oh yes. Glad you reminded me." He removed an envelope from his top drawer and pushed it across the desk. "Cocktails. Five to seven. Black tie, I'm afraid. This check should cover your expenses in the way of formal dress. If you try the rental shop around the corner, Roberta Linderman will see that you're outfitted properly. She knows these people well."

"What people? You haven't even told me their names."

"Karen Waterston and Kevin McCall. They have a little weekend retreat up here."

"Ah," I said, nodding. This was beginning to make more sense. Karen Waterson and Kevin McCall were actors who'd just experienced a resurgence in their careers, starring in a new television series called *Shamus, PI*, an hour-long spoof of every detective series that's ever aired. I don't watch much TV, but I'd heard about the show, and after seeing it once, I'd found myself hooked. The stories were fresh, the writing was superb, and the format was perfect for their considerable acting talents. Possibly because they were married in "real" life, the two brought a wicked chemistry to the screen. As with many new shows, the ratings hadn't yet caught up with the rave reviews, but things looked promising. Whatever their problem, I could understand the desire to keep their difficulties hidden from public scrutiny.

Jack was saying, "You're in no way obligated, but I hope you'll say yes. She really needs your help."

"Well. I guess I've had stranger requests in my day. I better give you my address."

He held up the signature card I'd completed when I opened my account. "I have that."

I soon learned what "cocktails five to seven" means to the very rich. Everybody showed up at seven and stayed until they were dead drunk. Jack Chamberlain, in a tux, picked me up at my apartment at 6:45. I was decked out in a slinky beaded black dress with long sleeves, a high collar, and no back; not my usual apparel of choice. When Jack helped me into the front seat of his Mercedes, I shrieked at the shock of cold leather against my bare skin.

Once at the party, I regained my composure and managed to conduct myself (for the most part) without embarrassment or disgrace. The "little weekend retreat" turned out to be a sprawling six-bedroom estate, decorated with a confident blend of the avant-garde and the minimalist; unadorned white walls, wide, bare, gleaming expanses of polished hardwood floor. The few pieces of furniture were draped with white canvas, like those in a palatial summer residence being closed up for the season. Aside from a dazzling crystal chandelier, all the dining room contained was a plant, a mirror, and a bentwood chair covered with an antique paisley shawl. Très chic. They'd probably paid thousands for some interior designer to come in and haul all the knickknacks away.

As the party picked up momentum the noise level rose, people spilling out onto all the terraces. Six young men, in black pants and pleated white shirts, circulated with silver platters of tasty hot and cold morsels. The champagne was exquisite, the supply apparently endless, so that I was fairly giddy by the time Jack took me by the arm and eased me out of the living room. "Karen wants to see you upstairs," he murmured.

"Great," I said. I'd hardly laid eyes on her except as a glittering wraith along the party's perimeters. I hadn't seen Kevin at all, but I'd overheard someone say he was off scouting locations for the show coming up. Jack and I drifted up the spiral stairs together, me hoping that in my half-inebriated state, I wouldn't pitch over the railing and land with a splat. As I reached the landing I looked down and was startled to see my friend Vera in the foyer below. She caught sight of me and did a double take, apparently surprised to see me in such elegant surroundings, especially dressed to the teeth. We exchanged a quick wave.

The nearly darkened master suite was carpeted to a hush, but again, it was nearly empty. The room was probably fifty feet by thirty, furnished dead center with a king-size bed, a wicker hamper, two ficus trees, and a silver lamp with a twenty-five-watt bulb on a long, curving neck.

As Jack ushered me into the master bathroom where the meeting was to take place, he flicked me an apologetic look. "I hope this doesn't seem too odd."

"Not at all," I said, politely . . . like a lot of my business meetings take place in the WC.

Candles flickered from every surface. Sound was dampened by thick white carpeting and a profusion of plants. Karen Waterston sat on the middle riser of three wide, beige, marble steps leading up to the Jacuzzi. Beside her, chocolate-brown bath towels were rolled and stacked like a cord of firewood. She was wearing a halter-style dress of white chiffon, which emphasized the dark even tan of her slender shoulders and arms. Her hair was silver blond, coiled around her head in a twist of satin ropes. She was probably forty-two, but her face had been cosmetically backdated to the age of twenty-five, a process that would require ever more surgical ingenuity as the years went by. Jack introduced us and we shook hands. Hers were ice cold, and I could have sworn she wasn't happy to have me there.

Jack pulled out a wicker stool and sat down with his back to Karen's makeup table, his eyes never leaving her face. My guess was that being an ex–high-school sweetheart of hers was as much a part of his identity as being a former basketball champ. I leaned a hip against the marble counter. There was a silver-framed photograph of Kevin McCall propped up beside me, the mirror reflecting endless reproductions of his perfect profile. To all appearances, he'd been allowed to retain the face he was born with, but the uniform darkness of his hair, with its picturesque dusting of silver at the temples, suggested that nature was being tampered with, at least superficially. Still, it was hard to imagine that either he or Karen had a problem more pressing than an occasional loose dental cap.

"I appreciate your coming, Miss Millhone. It means a lot to us under the circumstances." Her voice was throaty and low, with the merest hint of tremolo. Even by candlelight, I could see the tension in her face. "I wasn't in favor of bringing anyone else into this, but Jack insisted. Has he explained the situation?"

She glanced from me to Jack, who said, "I told her you preferred to do that yourself."

She seemed to hug herself for warmth and her mouth suddenly looked pinched. Tears welled in her eyes and she placed two fingers on the bridge of her nose as if to quell their flow. "You'll have to forgive me. . . ."

I didn't think she'd be able to continue, but she managed to collect herself.

"Kevin's been kidnapped. . . ." Her voice cracked with emotion and she lifted her dark eyes to mine. I'd never seen such a depth of pain and suffering.

At first, I didn't even know what to say to her. "When was this?"

"Last night. We're very private people. We've never let anyone get remotely close to us—" She broke off again.

"Take your time," I said.

Jack moved over to the stair and sat down beside her, putting an arm protectively around her shoulders. The smile she offered him was wan and she couldn't sustain it.

He handed her his handkerchief and I waited while she blew her nose and dabbed at her eyes. "Sorry. I'm just so frightened. This is horrible."

"I hope you've called the police," I said.

"She doesn't want to take the risk," Jack said.

Karen shook her head. "They said they'd kill him if I called in the police."

"Who said?"

"The bastards who snatched him. I was given this note. Here. You can see for yourself. It's too much like the Bender case to take any chances." She extracted a piece of paper from the folds of her long dress and held it out to me.

I took the note by one corner so I wouldn't smudge any prints, probably a useless precaution. If this was truly like the Bender case, there wouldn't be any prints to smudge. The paper was plain, the printing in ballpoint pen and done with a ruler.

Five hundred thou in small bills buys your husband back. Go to the cops or the feds and he's dead meat for sure. We'll call soon with instructions. Keep your mouth shut or you'll regret it. That's a promise, baby cakes.

She was right. Both the format and the use of language bore an uncanny similarity to the note delivered to a woman named Corey Bender, whose husband had been kidnapped about a year ago. Dan Bender was the CEO of a local manufacturing company, a man who'd made millions with a line of auto parts called Fender-Benders. In that situation, the kidnappers had asked for five hundred thousand dollars in tens and twenties. Mrs. Bender had contacted both the police and the FBI, who had stage-managed the whole transaction, arranging for a suitcase full of blank paper to be dropped according to the kidnappers' elaborate telephone instructions. The drop site had been staked out, everyone assuring Mrs. Bender that nothing could possibly go wrong. The drop went as planned except the suitcase was never picked up and Dan Bender was never seen alive again. His body . . . or what was left of it . . . washed up on the Santa Teresa beach two months later.

"Tell me what happened," I said.

She got up and began to pace, describing in halting detail the circumstances of Kevin McCall's abduction. The couple had been working on a four-day shooting schedule at the studio down in Hollywood. They'd been picked up from the set by limousine at 7:00 P.M. on Thursday and had been driven straight to Santa Teresa, arriving for the long weekend at nine that night. The housekeeper usually fixed supper for them and left it in the oven, departing shortly before they were due home. At the end of a week of shooting, the couple preferred all the solitude they could get.

Nothing seemed amiss when they arrived at the house. Both interior and exterior lights were on as usual. Karen emerged from the limo with Kevin right behind her. She chatted briefly with the driver and then waved good-bye while Kevin unlocked the front door and disarmed the alarm system. The limo driver had already turned out of the gate when two men in ski masks stepped out of the shadows armed with automatics. Neither Karen nor Kevin had much opportunity to react. A second limousine pulled into the driveway and Kevin was hustled into the backseat at gunpoint. Not a word was said. The note was thrust into Karen's hand as the gunmen left. She raced after the limo as it sped away, but no license plates were visible. She had no real hope of catching up and no clear idea what she meant to do anyway. In a panic, she returned to the house and locked herself in. Once the shock wore off, she called Jack Chamberlain, their local banker, a former high-school classmate— the only person in Santa Teresa she felt she could trust. Her first thought was to cancel tonight's party altogether, but Jack suggested she proceed.

"I thought it would look more natural," he filled in. "Especially if she's being watched."

"They did call with instructions?" I asked.

Again she nodded, her face pale. "They want the money by midnight tomorrow or that's the last I'll see of him."

"Can you *raise* five hundred thousand on such short notice?"

"Not without help," she said, and turned a pleading look to Jack.

He was already shaking his head and I gathered this was a subject they'd already discussed at length. "The bank doesn't keep large reservoirs of cash on hand," he said to me. "There's no way I'd have access to a sum like that, particularly on a weekend. The best I can do is bleed the cash from all the branch ATMs."

"Surely you can do better than that," she said. "You're a bank vice-president."

He turned to her, with a faintly defensive air, trying to persuade her the failing wasn't his. "I might be able to put together the full amount by Monday, but even then, you'd have to fill out an application and go through the loan committee."

She said, "Oh, for God's sake, Jack. Don't give me that bureaucratic bullshit when Kevin's life is at stake! There has to be a way."

"Karen, be reasonable. . . ."

"Forget it. This is hopeless. I'm sorry I ever brought you into this."

I watched them bicker for a moment and then broke in. "All right, wait a minute. Hold on. Let's back off the money question, for the time being."

"Back *off*?" she said.

"Look. Let's assume there's a way to get the ransom money. Now what?"

Her brow was furrowed and she seemed to have trouble concentrating on the question at hand. "I'm sorry. What?"

"Fill me in on the rest of it. I need to know what happened last night after you got in touch with Jack."

"Oh. I see, yes. He came over to the house and we sat here for hours, waiting for the phone to ring. The kidnappers . . . one of them . . . finally called at two A.M."

"You didn't recognize the voice?"

"Not at all."

"Did the guy seem to know Jack was with you?"

"He didn't mention it, but he swore they were watching the house and he said the phone was tapped."

"I wouldn't bet on it, but it's probably smart to proceed as though it's true. It's possible they didn't have the house staked out last night, but they may have put a man on it since. Hard to know. Did they tell you how to deliver the cash once you got it?"

"That part was simple. I'm to pack the money in a big canvas duffel. At eleven-thirty tomorrow night, they want me to leave the house on my bicycle with the duffel in the basket."

"On a bike? That's a new one."

"Kev and I often bike together on weekends, which they seemed aware of. As a matter of fact, they seemed to know quite a lot. It was very creepy."

Jack spoke up. "They must have cased the place to begin with. They knew the whole routine from what she's told me."

"Stands to reason," I remarked. And then to her, "Go on."

"They told me to wear my yellow jumpsuit—I guess so they can identify me—and that's all there was."

"They didn't tell you which way to ride?"

"I asked about that and they told me I could head in any direction I wanted. They said they'd follow at a distance and intercept when it suited them. Obviously, they want to make sure I'm unaccompanied."

"Then what?"

"When they blink the car lights, I'm to toss the canvas duffel to the side of the road and ride on. They'll release Kevin as soon as the money's been picked up and counted."

"Shoot. It rules out any fudging if they count the money first. Did they let you talk to Kevin?"

"Briefly. He sounded fine. Worried about me . . ."

"And you're sure it was him."

"Positive. I'm so scared. . . ."

The whole time we'd been talking, my mind was racing ahead. She had to call the cops. There was no doubt in my mind she was a fool to tackle this without the experts, but she was dead set against it. I said, "Karen, you can't handle something like this without the cops. You'd be crazy to try to manage on your own."

She was adamant.

Jack and I took turns arguing the point and I could see his frustration surface. "For God's sake, you've got to listen to us. You're way out of your element. If these guys are the same ones who kidnapped Dan Bender, you're putting Kevin's life at risk. They're absolutely ruthless."

"Jack, I'm not the one putting Kevin's life at risk. *You* are. That's exactly what you're doing when you propose calling the police."

"How are you going to get the money?" he said, exasperated.

"Goddammit, how do I know? You're the banker. You tell me."

"Karen, I'm telling you. There's no way to do this. You're making a big mistake."

"Corey Bender was the one who made a mistake," she snapped.

We were getting nowhere. Time was short and the pressures were mounting every minute. If Jack and I didn't come up with *some* plan, Kevin McCall was going to end up dead. If the cash could be assembled, the obvious move was to have me take Karen's place during the actual delivery, which would at least eliminate the possibility of her being picked up as well. Oddly enough, I thought I had an inkling how to get the bucks, though it might well take me the better part of the next day.

"All right," I said, breaking in for the umpteenth time. "We can argue this all night and it's not going to get us anyplace. Suppose I find a way to get the money, will you at least consent to my taking your place for the drop?"

She studied me for a moment. "That's awfully risky, isn't it? What if they realize the substitution?"

"How could they? They'll be following in a car. In the dark and at a distance, I can easily pass for you. A wig and a jumpsuit and who'd know the difference?"

She hesitated. "I do have a wig, but why not just do what they say? I don't like the idea of disobeying their instructions."

"Because these guys are way too dangerous for you to deal with yourself. Suppose you deliver the money as specified. What's to prevent their picking you up and making Kevin pay additional ransom for *your* return?"

I could see her debate the point. Her uneasiness was obvious, but she finally agreed. "I don't understand what you intend to do about the ransom. If Jack can't manage to get the money, how can you?"

"I know a guy who has access to a large sum of cash. I can't promise anything, but I can always ask."

Karen's gaze came to rest on my face with puzzlement.

"Look," I said in response to her unspoken question. "I'll explain if I get it. And if not, you have to promise me you'll call the police."

Jack prodded. "It's your only chance."

She was silent for a moment and then spoke slowly. "All right. Maybe so. We'll do it your way. What other choice do I have?"

Before we left, we made arrangements for her to leave a wig, the yellow jumpsuit, and the bicycle on the service porch the next night. I'd return to the house on foot sometime after dark, leaving my car parked a few discreet blocks away. At 11:30, as instructed, I'd peddle down the drive with the canvas duffel and ride around until the kidnappers caught up with me. While I was gone Jack could swing by and pick Karen up in his car. I wanted her off the premises in the event anything went wrong. If I were snatched and the kidnappers realized they had the wrong person, at least they couldn't storm back to the house and get her. We went over the details until we were all in accord. In the end, she seemed satisfied with the plan and so did Jack. I was the only one with any lingering doubts. I thought she was a fool, but I kept that to myself.

I hit the road the next morning early and headed north on 101. Visiting hours at the federal correctional institution at Lompoc run from eight to four on Saturdays. The drive took about an hour with a brief stop at a supermarket in Buellton, where I picked up an assortment of picnic supplies. By ten, I was seated at one of the four sheltered picnic tables with my friend, Harry Hovey. If Harry was surprised to see me, he didn't complain. "It's not like my social calendar's all that full," he said. "To what do I owe the pleasure?"

"Let's eat first," I said. "Then I got something I need to talk to you about."

I'd brought cold chicken and potato salad, assorted cheeses, fruit, and cookies—anything I could grab that didn't look like institutional fare. Personally, I wasn't hungry, but it was gratifying to watch Harry chow down with such enthusiasm. He was not looking well. He was a man in his fifties, maybe five five, heavyset, with thinning gray hair and glasses cloudy with fingerprints. He didn't take good care of himself under the best of circumstances, and the stress of prison living had aged him ten years. His color was bad. He was smoking way too much. He'd lost weight in a manner that looked neither healthful nor flattering.

"How're you doing?" I asked. "You look tired."

"I'm okay, I guess. I been better in my day, but what the hell," he said. He'd paused in the middle of his meal for a cigarette. He seemed distracted, his attention flicking from the other tables to the playground equipment, where a noisy batch of kids were twirling round and round on the swings. It was November and the sun was shining, but the air was chilly and the grass was dead.

"How much time you have to serve yet?"

"Sixteen months," he said. "You ever been in the can?"

I shook my head.

He pointed at me with his cigarette. "Word of advice. Never admit nothin'. Always claim you're innocent. I learned that from the politicians. You ever watch those guys? They get caught takin' bribes and they assume this injured air. Like it's all a mistake, but the truth will out. They're confident they'll be vindicated and bullshit like that. They welcome the investigation so their names can be cleared. They always say that, you know? Whole time I'm in prison, I been saying that myself. I was framed. It's all a setup. I don't know nothing about the money. I was just doing a favor for an old friend, a bigwig. A Very Big Wig. Like I'm implying the governor or the chief of police."

"Has it done you any good?"

"Well, not yet, but who knows? My lawyer's still trying to find a basis for appeal. If I get outta this one, I'm going into therapy, get my head straight, I swear to God. Speaking of which, I may get 'born again,' you know? It looks good. Lends a little credibility, which is something all the money in the world can't buy."

I took a deep breath. "Actually, it's the money I need to talk to you about." I took a few minutes to fill him in on the kidnapping without mentioning any names. Some of Karen Waterston's paranoia had filtered into my psyche and I thought the less I said about the "victim," the better off he'd be. "I know you've got a big cache of money somewhere. I'm hoping you'll contribute some of it to pay the ransom demands."

His look was blank with disbelief. "Ransom?"

"Harry, don't put me through this. You know what ransom is."

"Yeah, it's money you give to guys you never see again. Why not throw it out the window? Why not blow it at the track?"

"Are you finished yet?"

He smiled and a dimple formed. "How much you talking about?"

"Five hundred thousand."

His eyebrows went up. "What makes you think I got money like that?"

"Harry," I said patiently, "an informant told the cops you had over a million bucks. That's how you got caught."

Harry slapped the table. "Bobby Urquhart. That fuck. I should have known it was him. I run into the guy in a bar settin' at this table full of bums. He buys a round of tequila shooters. Next thing I know, everybody else is gone. I'm drunk as a skunk and flappin' my mouth." He dropped his cigarette butt on the concrete and crushed it underfoot. "Word of warning. Never confide in a guy wearing Brut. I must have been nuts to give that little faggot the time of day. The money's gone. I blew it. I got nothin' left."

"I don't believe you. That's bullshit. You didn't have time to blow that much. When you were busted, all you had were a few lousy bucks. Where's the rest of it?"

"Uh-uh. No way."

"Come on, Harry. It isn't going to do you any good in here. Why not help these people out? They got tons of money. They can pay you back."

"They got money, how come they don't pay the shit themselves?"

"Because it's Saturday and the banks are closed. The branch VP couldn't even come up with the cash that fast. A man's life is at stake."

"Hey, so's mine and so what? You ever try life in the pen? I worked hard for that money, so why should I do for some guy I never seen before?"

"Once in a while you just gotta help people out."

"Maybe you do. I don't."

"Harry, please. Be a prince. . . ."

I could see him begin to waver. Who can resist a good deed now and then?

He put his hand on his chest. "This is giving me angina pains." He wagged his head back and forth. "Jesus. What if the cops get wind of it? How's it gonna look?"

"The cops are never going to know. Believe me, this woman's never going to breathe a word of it. If she trusted the cops, she'd have called them in the first place."

"Who are these people? At least tell me that. I'm not giving up half a million bucks without some ID."

I thought about it swiftly. I was reluctant to trade on their celebrity status. On the other hand, she was desperate and there wasn't time to spare. "Swear you won't tell."

"Who'm I gonna tell? I'm a con. Nobody believes me anyway," he said.

"Kevin McCall and Karen Waterston."

He seemed startled at first. "You're kidding me. No shit? You're talking, *Shamus, PI*? Them two?"

"That's right."

"Whyn't you say so? That's my favorite show. All the guys watch that. What a gas. Karen Waterston is a fox."

"Then you'll help?"

"For that chick, of course," he said. He gave me a stern look. "Get me her autograph or the deal's off."

"Trust me. You'll have it. You're a doll. I owe you one."

We took a walk around the yard while he told me where the money was. Harry had nearly two million in cash hidden in a canvas duffel of his own, concealed in the false back of a big upholstered sofa, which was locked up, with a lot of other furniture, in a commercial self-storage facility.

I headed back to Santa Teresa with the key in my hand. Unearthing the money took the balance of the afternoon. The couch was at the bottom of an eight-by-eight-foot storage locker crammed with goods. Tables, chairs, cardboard boxes, a desk, a hundred or more items, which I removed one by one, stacking them behind me in the narrow aisle between bins. The facility was hot and airless and I could hardly ask for help. By the time I laid my hands on the canvas tote hidden in the couch, there was hardly room in the passage-way to turn around. By six o'clock, feeling harried, I had set aside a half million and Harry's tote to take with me. The rest of the stash I stuffed back into the couch, piling furniture and boxes helter-skelter on top of it. I'd have to return at some point . . . when the whole ordeal was over . . . and pack the bin properly.

The drop played out according to the numbers, without the slightest hitch. At ten that night, I eased through a gap in the hedge on the north side of the Waterston-McCall property and made my way to the house with Harry's canvas bag in tow. I slipped into the darkened service entry where Karen was waiting. Once the door shut behind me, I shoved Harry's canvas tote into the larger duffel she provided. We chatted nervously while I changed into the wig and yellow jumpsuit. It was just then 10:30 and the remaining wait was long and tense. By 11:30, both of us were strung out on pure adrenaline and I was glad to be on the move.

Before I took off on the bicycle, Karen gave me a quick hug. "You're wonderful. I can't believe you did this."

"I'm not as wonderful as all that," I said uncomfortably. "We need to talk the minute Kevin's home safe. Be sure to call me."

"Of course. Absolutely. We'll call you first thing."

I pedaled down the drive and took a right on West Glen. The cash-heavy duffel threw the bike out of balance, but I corrected and rode on. It was chilly at that hour and traffic was almost nonexistent. For two miles, almost randomly, I bicycled through the dark, cursing my own foolishness for thinking I could pull this off. Eventually, I became aware that a sedan had fallen in behind me. In the glare of the headlights, I couldn't tell the make or the model; only that the vehicle was dark blue and the front license plate was missing. The sedan followed me for what felt like an hour, while I pedaled on, feeling anxious, winded, and frightened beyond belief. Finally, the headlights blinked twice. Front wheel wobbling, I hauled the duffel from the basket and tossed it out onto the shoulder of the road. It landed with a thump near a cluster of bushes and I pedaled away. I glanced back only once as the vehicle behind me slowed to a stop.

I returned to the big house, left the bicycle on the service porch, and made my way back across the blackness of the rear lawn to my car. My heart was still thudding as I pulled away. Home again, in my apartment, I changed into a nightie and robe and huddled on the couch with a cup of brandy-laced hot tea. I knew I should try to sleep, but I was too wired to bother. I glanced at my watch. It was nearly 2:00 A.M. I figured I probably wouldn't get word from Karen for another hour best. It takes time to count half a million dollars in small bills. I flipped on the TV and watched a mind-numbing rerun of an old black-and-white film.

I waited through the night, but the phone didn't ring. Around five, I must have dozed, because the next thing I knew, it was 8:35. What was going on? The kidnappers had had ample time to effect Kevin's release. If he's getting out alive, I thought. I stared at the phone, afraid to call Karen in case the line was still tapped. I pulled out the phone book, looked up Jack Chamberlain, and tried his home number. The phone rang five times and his machine picked up. I left a cryptic message and then tried Karen at the house. No answer there. I was stumped. Mixed with my uneasiness was a touch of irritation. Even if they'd heard nothing, they could have let me know.

Without much hope of success, I called the bank and asked for Jack. Surprisingly, Lucy Alisal put me through.

"Jack Chamberlain," he said.

"Jack? This is Kinsey. Have you heard from Karen Waterston?"

"Of course. Haven't you?"

"Not a word," I said. "Is Kevin okay?"

"He's fine. Everything's terrific."

"Would you kindly tell me what's going on?"

"Well, sure. I can tell you as much as I know. I drove her back over to the house about two this morning and we waited it out. Kevin got home at six. He's shaken up, as you might imagine, but otherwise he's in good shape. I talked to both of them again a little while ago. She said she was going to call you as soon as we hung up. She didn't get in touch?"

"Jack, that's what I just said. I've been sitting here for hours without a word from anyone. I tried the house and got no answer."

"Hey, relax. Don't worry. I can see where you'd be ticked, but everything's fine. I know they were going back to Los Angeles. She might have just forgotten."

I could hear a little warning. Something was off here. "What about the kidnappers? Does Kevin have any way to identify them?"

"That's what I asked. He says, not a chance. He was tied

up and blindfolded while they had him in the car. He says they drove into a garage and kept him there until the ransom money was picked up and brought back. Next thing he knew, someone got in the car, backed out of the garage, drove him around for a while, and finally set him out in his own driveway. He's going to see a doctor once they get to Los Angeles, but they never really laid a hand on him."

"I can't believe they didn't call to let me know he was safe. I need to talk to her." I knew I was being repetitive, but I was really bugged. I'd promised Harry her autograph, among other things, and while he'd pretended to make a joke of it, I knew he was serious.

"Maybe they thought I'd be doing that. I know they were both very grateful for your help. Maybe she's planning to drop you a note."

"Well. I guess I'll just wait until I hear from them," I said, and hung up.

I showered and got dressed, sucked down some coffee, and drove over to my office in downtown Santa Teresa. My irritation was beginning to wear off and exhaustion was trickling into my body in its wake. I went through my mail, paid a bill, tidied up my desk. I found myself laying my little head down, catching a quick nap while I drooled on my Month-at-a-Glance. There was a knock on the door and I woke with a start.

Vera Lipton, the claims manager for the insurance company next door, was standing on my threshold. "You must have had a better time than I did Friday night. You hung over or still drunk?" she said.

"Neither. I got a lousy night's sleep."

She lifted her right brow. "Sounds like fun. You and that guy from the bank?"

"Not exactly."

"So what'd you think of the glitzy twosome . . . Karen and Kev."

"I don't even want to talk about them," I said. I then proceeded to pour out the whole harrowing tale, including a big dose of outrage at the way I'd been treated.

Vera started smirking about halfway through. By the end of my recital, she was shaking her head.

"What's the matter?" I asked.

"Well, that's the biggest bunch of horsepuckey I ever heard. You've been taken, Kinsey. Most royally had."

"*I* have?"

"They're flat broke. They don't have a dime."

"They do, too!"

She shook her head emphatically. "Dead broke. They're busted."

"They couldn't be," I said.

"Yes, they are," she said. "I bet you dollars to donuts they put the whole scam together to pick up some cash."

"How could they be broke with a house like that? They have a hot new series on the air!"

"The show was canceled. It hasn't hit the papers yet, but the network decided to yank 'em after six episodes. They sank everything they had into the house up here when they first heard they'd been picked up."

I squinted at her. "How do you know all this stuff?"

"Neil and I have been looking for a house for months. Our real-estate agent's the one who sold 'em that place."

"They don't have *any* money?" I asked.

"Not a dime," she said. "Why do you think the house is so empty? They had to sell the furniture to make the mortgage payment this month."

"But what about the party? That must have cost a mint!"

"I'm sure it did. Their attorney advised them to max out their credit cards and then file for bankruptcy."

"Are you sure?"

"Sure I'm sure."

I looked at Vera blankly, doing an instant replay of events. I knew she was right because it suddenly made perfect sense. Karen Waterston and Kevin McCall had run a scam, that's all it was. No wonder the drop had gone without a hitch. I wasn't being followed by kidnappers . . . it was him. Those two had just successfully pocketed half a million bucks. And what was I going to do? At this point, even if I called the cops, all they had to do was maintain the kidnapping fiction and swear the bad guys were for real. They'd be very convincing. That's what acting is all about. The "kidnappers," meanwhile, would have disappeared without a trace, and they'd make out like bandits, quite literally.

Vera watched me process the revelation. "You don't seem all that upset. I thought you'd be apoplectic, jumping up and down. Don't you feel like an ass?"

"I don't know yet. Maybe not."

She moved toward the door. "I gotta get back to work.

Let me know when it hits. It's always entertaining to watch you blow your stack."

I sat down at my desk and thought about the situation and then put a call through to Harry Hovey at the prison.

"This is rare," Harry said when he'd heard me out. "I think we got a winner with this one. Holy shit."

"I thought you'd see the possibilities," I said.

"Holy shit!" he said again.

The rest of what I now refer to as my missionary work, I can only guess at until I see Harry again. According to the newspapers, Kevin McCall and Karen Waterston were arrested two days after they returned to Los Angeles. Allegedly (as they say), the two entered a bank and tried to open an account with nine thousand dollars in counterfeit tens and twenties. Amazingly, Harry Hovey saw God and had a crisis of conscience shortly before this in his prison cell up in Lompoc. Recanting his claims of innocence, he felt compelled to confess . . . he'd been working for the two celebrities for years, he said. In return for immunity, he told the feds where to find the counterfeit plates, hidden in the bottom of a canvas tote, which turned up in their possession just as he said it would.

a good judge
of character

SUSAN DUNLAP

Susan Dunlap has a singular talent for finding the murderous pulse of a community. Perhaps the only woman to write three series featuring each of the major types of detective—a police officer, an amateur detective, and a private investigator—she was the 1990–91 president of Sisters in Crime. Berkeley Homicide Detective Jill Smith solves crimes in seven novels, most recently Diamond in the Buff *and* Death and Taxes. *Utility-company meter reader Vejay Haskell is featured in three books, including* The Last Annual Slugfest. *And Kiernan O'Shaughnessy, a former forensic pathologist whose San Diego beach house is tended to by an ex–offensive lineman, investigates murder in* Pious Deception *and* Rogue Wave.

What does it take to get away from it all for a while? What talents help you succeed in fulfilling your dreams? Surely being "A Good Judge of Character" is very important. . . .

━━━━━━━━━━━━━━

Have you ever had the urge to do something suicidal? Walking past an eighth-story window, you stop and look out, your gaze drawn down to the street far below. Suddenly the pull is almost irresistible and you have to brace your hands against the ledge to keep yourself from jumping.

Or you're stopped in your car at a railway crossing at night. The train whistle cuts the dark, it vibrates your flesh. You can feel it in the hollow of your stomach. The white light on the train races at you, taunting: *Can you beat me?* Your foot hits the gas pedal; the car surges forward, smashes through the wooden barrier, jolts over the tracks just in front of the train. The engine roars behind you, a gust of air batters the back of your neck as you crash through the far barricade.

And when the engine actually does race by, horn blasting against your ears, you can hardly believe you haven't moved at all. You sit there, shaking all over, wondering how close you really came to killing yourself.

That type of thing happened to me not long ago. And yet now it seems ages ago. It was in the third week of what was to be a six-week stay in a sleepy beach town near San Luis Obispo. After a hectic year as director of the convention bureau in San Francisco, forced to be pleasant to the head of every professional association, brotherhood, sisterhood, political party, or union that might possibly be wooed to convene in the City, I'd needed to be someplace where no one knew me. Director was one of those jobs whose reward is a lot of show and responsibility rather than much pay. The thrill of being in the public eye had faded. The stress had mounted and I'd made snap decisions, taken chances, acquired things I never would have considered at a more normal time. And my lover, Jeff—one of those new and questionable acquisitions—and his demands had only made the pressure worse. Even he—especially he—had agreed I had to get away.

There in the beach town nothing much happened. My biggest decisions each day were whether to wear a one- or two-piece bathing suit, and when to turn over on my towel and sun my other side.

I was walking along the sand as I did at the tail end of most afternoons. The beach was crowded during the days, with radios clashing, volleyball nets strung up, and teams shrieking and groaning, halfhearted body surfers riding too small waves. But as soon as the first shadow of fog climbed over the horizon the beach emptied. That was my favorite time, when I could pretend the beach was all mine. With five hundred thousand dollars, I'd say to myself, I could buy a retreat with a secluded beach that no one would walk on but me.

The beach was wide there; the palm trees grew close to the walkway. I liked to amble between the trees and the water and pretend the wooden walkway and the road beyond didn't exist. The day had been hot, but now fingers of fog inched their way in from the Pacific, tentatively caressing the sky like a hand in the dark, like a new lover. I'd put a yellow flowered shirt and cutoffs over my bathing suit. My skin prickled against the rough fabric, and I felt, as you do at those times, icy but with shots of fire cutting through. My feet were bare, my hands empty. A couple of dollar bills in my pocket rubbed the point of my hipbone.

It was almost dusk, the light too dim for a family to be taking pictures.

I don't know why I even looked over and noticed that family. What momentarily caught my eye was one of those clear plastic name tags with the red and gold ribbons we use at the convention bureau. The smallest child was wearing it in the middle of his T-shirt; it covered half of his chest. I was only a few feet away from the low cement wall that separates the beach from the walkway. The camera sat on top of the wall. The father, a short, ripply-fleshed man in blue-and-white bathing trunks and a white short-sleeved shirt hanging open, a man in his mid-forties, had set the camera timer and was walking stiffly back to the others. I remember this part very clearly. The two small boys, maybe three and six, were yelling at him to hurry. "Ten seconds, ten seconds! Come on, Daddy!" The older one was wearing a San Francisco 49ers cap. A teenage girl stood, weight on one leg, arms crossed in exaggerated boredom. Divorced father, weekend family, I remember thinking.

The father threw himself on the ground in front of the

boys and grinned at the camera. The smile stopped at his upper lip, and his eyes had a tight, wary look that was out of place in this quiet beach town. The effect was jarring. I can still see that stiff grin painted on for the camera.

And that's when life shifted, like the train whistle daring me. My scalp quivered. Suddenly everything was crisper; the dusk sun shone noon-strong off the sand. I started to run, pushing back the sand with the balls of my feet. My steps were light, my gait fluid. I picked up speed, veered right toward the family. The camera sparkled. I scooped it up and didn't even break pace. I pushed off the cement base of the wall with my right foot and ran faster, striding like a wild horse, full out down the beach beyond the line of palms.

The family's shouts burst up behind me. *They* were the train, the thousands of tons of steel bearing down on me. My bare feet dug hard into the sand. The roar of their voices shifted, the kids' mixing like the clack of wheels on the track, the father's—loud, grating—cutting through the evening breeze, like the train horn shrieking in my ears.

"Hey," he yelled, "you drop that Spectra!"

I didn't look back. My head throbbed. I pressed my feet harder against the sand as I ran past the empty lifeguard chair. I looked up, knowing it was after hours now, but still half expecting to see the guard's blond hair creeping out from under his billed cap.

And that's when life shifted back again. The throbbing of my head evened out; my eyes seemed to refocus. My steps were leaden, my breath short. I glanced down at the camera. No sun hit it now. It was a Polaroid. My fingers were pressed white against its surface. The picture was pushing out between them, scratching my skin. *What was I doing with this thing?* I asked myself in horror. *What had possessed me to steal it?*

I should have just stopped and handed it back to the man, fallen all over myself apologizing, told him that my mother was dying, or my husband leaving me, or made up some tale. I knew that then. But I couldn't. Suppose he recognized me.

He was no more than twenty feet behind me, panting between his shouts of "Thief. I'm going to get you. Thief! I know cops all over the state. That's an expensive camera. You're dead, unless you drop it."

I ran on. My shins ached, the insides of my knees burned, and each new breath seared my lungs.

"I'll get you for this! I don't forget."

What I did then was the worst of all possible moves. I lobbed the camera over my head, high in the air. The picture came free in my hand. I looked back, just long enough to see the camera fall, neck strap sailing behind it. It came down, right through his hands and smashed into the hard sand. His face flushed; he looked humiliated. He glanced up in time to see that I had seen.

He skidded to a stop. I kept running. I was panting so hard I could barely hear his shout. "I know what you look like. In an hour every cop in the state'll have your description." His voice was gravelly but the rage was clear. It didn't fit with the image of the wary man I'd first seen.

I was gasping, my throat and lungs yanking in the air. I wasn't a runner, and my legs felt like cement, the sand like quicksand.

He could still see me, I was sure, when I came to the street that led to my motel. I ran on, but I knew he wasn't following anymore and the adrenaline from that danger was just about used up. I was moving barely faster than a walk.

At the next corner I looked back. I couldn't see him. But I could still feel the ache of fear in my ribs. I hadn't been thinking at all when I grabbed the camera. Now I was running eight tracks of thought at once: reconstructing that moment, asking myself what had possessed me, figuring the way to the motel, picturing him at the motel, picturing the town cops there, and interspersing it all with remembrances of that cold rage on his face, and single-frame shots of my dire future. I was a good judge of character—that skill had saved me more than once. At lightning speed I'd judged this man, and I'd been eons off on him. That frightened me. If you can't judge people, you're dead. I would never had suspected he'd have so violent a reaction.

It wasn't till I got to the motel that I noticed the picture crumpled in my hand. A new wave of panic chilled me. The last thing I needed was to be found with the evidence of my crime right in my hand. I could see the headlines—CONVENTION BUREAU DIRECTOR IS THIEF! That would be it for me! I started to toss the photo in the nearest trash can, but couldn't resist stretching it out for a look. There were nothing but lines and shadows with clumps of dark where the family would have been. You wouldn't even have realized they were people.

Still shaking, I dropped it in the trash. But I wasn't going to escape so easily. It would be simple for him to find me in this small beach town. There were only a few motels here. Exhorting myself to move faster, I trudged to my room. When I opened the door, the phone was ringing. Automatically, I picked it up. "Hello?" I could hear someone at the other end, then the phone clicked dead. Shaking harder, I stood staring at it. Slowly, I put it down. How could he have traced me so soon?

The phone rang again, but I didn't touch it. I threw my clothes into the back of my car, paid for the room, and headed out of town, slowly, careful not to do anything that would draw the police. Maybe he didn't know police all over the state, but just maybe he did. Maybe he hadn't been the hang-up call either.

I stopped for gas near San Jose. I hadn't eaten since lunch and it was nearly 10:00 P.M. now, but the idea of eating seemed as alien as shoving Styrofoam into my throat. I drank a Coke for the sugar and caffeine and drove on, still shaking with fear. You were overreacting about the phone call, I told myself. There's no proof it was him. He's not coming after you. But I couldn't make myself believe that.

When I had left San Francisco, Jeff and I agreed we'd have no contact at all for six weeks—a sort of trial separation, he'd said laughingly. He'd make do with a photo of me he'd cut out of the paper. The plan was the sensible thing to do, we'd agreed on that. Then at the end of that time we'd go to Mazatlán. It galled me to be the one to break our covenant. It had taken us ages to work everything out, and now as I headed toward the city, I wasn't at all sure Jeff would be glad to see me.

Thick streams of fog blew down the streets in the city. A hundred feet ahead everything was whited out. I had the windshield wipers on. I passed Jeff's apartment, the lower floor of a Victorian. His light was on. I let out a long breath, and felt myself safe, even though I knew coming to his place was another panicky run from danger, as illogical a reaction to stress as grabbing the camera.

"What are you doing here?" was his curt greeting. It didn't encourage me to tell him about stealing the camera, and that a man with police connections was after me.

"I needed a change. It's just for a day or two."

"We agreed you wouldn't come here." He stepped back and let me in. "Where are you parked?"

"Next block." His was an iffy neighborhood, with lots of auto heists and cops making rounds. "I didn't leave anything in plain sight in the car."

He shrugged, clearly uncomforted. "You can stay tonight, but you have to leave tomorrow."

"Jeff—"

"No. We made this agreement for a reason. Don't blow it all on a whim."

I started to protest, but I'd been as much a party to the covenant as he. I sank down on the bed, still wired from the day and the drive. Patting a spot next to me, I grinned and said, "I could sleep on the couch."

Jeff plopped down and ran a hand down my thigh. "Since you are here, we might as well make the best use of the time." His kiss was gentler than his words. It reminded me why I kept him around.

"You know," I said at some point during the night, "I may just be encouraging you because you're so good in bed. You're really not my type."

"What is your type?" he asked, clearly not put off.

"Well, not auditors." I grinned. "Auditing isn't very exciting."

It was too dark to see his expression, but I knew from the shift of his head and the tiny snort that he was smiling, too. "My sentiments exactly. If you saw me in my dark auditor's suit, heading into Creston's Hardware or Minton's Jewelry, you'd be even more convinced. But don't you worry, I won't even pack it for Mazatlán."

But in the morning there was no cheery talk of Mexico. As Jeff pointed out it was better that I left before rush hour. And in the light of morning, my escapade with the camera seemed more ridiculous than alarming. Chances were that by now I was nothing more than a bizarre story for the camera owner to tell at dinner.

He was vacationing with his kids; he probably only got them a couple weeks a year, he wasn't likely to ruin that time chasing after me.

Jeff was in the shower when I left—not a very positive indicator for our relationship. I took his blue carry-on bag and headed out to my clothes-strewn car trunk. Auditors understand the importance of keeping your things orderly and where you can find them. It was just 7:03 when I got to my car. There was a ticket on the window! Panic shot through me. Meter maids don't work at night. This ticket had been written by a patrol officer! Impeding a driveway, it said. Shaking, I looked at the front bumper. It was a couple inches past the edge of the driveway—normal for San Francisco. Patrol officers don't spend their nights flashing lights on the edges of driveways, not unless they're called specially, or they are looking for something, or someone. *I know cops all over the state!*

So much for being no more than a dinner story. The man was after me, and he knew where to find me! No longer could I wrap myself in illusions of safety. It was the last thing I wanted to do, but there was no avoiding it: I had to go back and make amends. If I offered a sincere apology, told him I felt like a fool—which I certainly did—and said I'd pay for repairs or replacement, surely he'd forgive me, and call off his cop friends.

Shaking harder, I started my car. Rush hour had already begun. I avoided the freeway entrances, afraid to sit stopped in traffic on display to the world. Instead I wound through South San Francisco and caught 101 nearer to the airport. Why had he only had my car ticketed? Why hadn't he just sent the police to Jeff's apartment and had them drag me out? It wasn't till I was on the freeway that I thought maybe he didn't know about Jeff; he might have gotten my license number from the beach motel and had his police buddies look out for it. In which case the highway patrol would still be watching for me.

I pulled off the freeway at the next exit and drove south through the peninsula towns. He couldn't have friends in every police department in every suburban town.

The drive took forever. I must have stopped at fifty red lights before I got to San Jose. My head throbbed; my teeth hurt from biting back the urge to yell at the fools who didn't signal, the double-parkers, the mothers moseying along at twenty miles per hour. By the time I hit the open farmland around Monterey, the air seemed to become thicker. It pressed in on my lungs, weighed down my arms, made every move an effort, like I'd never stopped running on the beach.

Somewhere this side of San Luis I did think that maybe the hang-up call at the motel was no more than a wrong number, and maybe some San Francisco neurotic had had it with people blocking his driveway and called the police. The thoughts were momentarily comforting, but I didn't believe in coincidence. And I certainly wasn't about to go back to my beach motel for another night and let him take me unawares. I had to have my wits about me when I saw him. I stopped in a Motel 6, transposed two of my license-plate letters on the registration form, and made myself walk to the restaurant across the street and order a hamburger I couldn't eat.

I didn't bother to set the alarm. No need. By eight the next morning I was up, showered, and checked out. At nine I was on the beach watching for the camera man and his kids. I paced along the sand, all the way south to where the pampas grass grew, back north past the spot where I'd seen him, and on to the waterbreak, and then back again, all the time practicing my apology. God, I hated being in this position, cringing, ready to grovel. Beaten.

By six in the evening I was sunburned and exhausted. He hadn't shown up. Had he taken the kids to the mountains for a day or two? Would he be on the beach tomorrow? Maybe. But I knew I couldn't go on as haphazardly as I was. Stealing the camera had been stupid, and this method of hunting the owner showed not much more sense.

I was tempted to give up, get in my car, drive south to Mazatlán. My reservations about Jeff didn't seem so important compared with this threat. Get away from the camera man, part of me insisted. Keep out of his sight. But I felt too uneasy about him. He'd reacted so violently that I couldn't be sure he'd ever let go. And if, as I was coming to believe, he really did know cops all over, he could hound me till he found something; we all have secrets. I wouldn't be hard to find. In a job like director of the convention bureau everyone in the city knew me. Maybe the camera man had recognized me. If I didn't deal with this guy now, I'd be looking over my shoulder forever. Cringing, beaten. And, I had to admit, there was the issue of having misjudged him. I'd always been a good judge of character. It frightened me to think I was losing it.

What to do? I could check at all the motels. There were only five or six. But my description of him and his kids could have fit any number of families. He could be at any motel, eat at any restaurant, be on the beach, or out sailing, or playing miniature golf.

But there was only one photography shop in town, a family operation with cameras, processing, picture frames, and postcards. I'd stopped there for postcards last week. Or that was my excuse. There were two or three points in my stay that I'd gotten lonely enough to pay fifty cents for an excuse to talk to someone.

The Polaroid camera I'd grabbed was expensive, or so the man had said. Surely he would have taken it in to see how costly was the damage. If he'd left it, I'd have an address.

Feeling in control for the first time in a week, I checked into a different motel, walked to a Mexican café—my favorite here—and had a man-sized meal.

The next morning it took me twenty minutes of small talk with the camera-store owner to discover that my harasser had refused to leave his camera, but not before the store owner had written up the repair slip. The name on it was Lawrence Leavenworth, the address: 36 Seaview Street, Eden Valley.

It hadn't occurred to me that Lawrence Leavenworth wouldn't be at a motel here in town. I didn't even know where Eden Valley was. Thirty miles inland, the store owner told me, with a scornful smile. He hadn't liked Lawrence Leavenworth—acted like a pushy tourist, he said. The impression I got from him was that staying in Eden Valley was an appropriate punishment for ungracious behavior to shopkeepers.

I sat in my car a few minutes, trying to figure which of the facts I had about Leavenworth was worth anything. Could Leavenworth be a San Francisco cop? But if he were a cop he'd be here on vacation and he'd be staying at the beach. If you get your kids a couple weeks a year, you want those to be special, and Eden Valley sounded anything but. That made me even more uneasy. Maybe I'd be better off looking over my shoulder forever rather than walking into a place I had no clue about.

The thirty-mile drive was along a winding two-lane road, with few turnoffs and lots of spots where it would be easy to run someone off into the underbrush below.

Eden Valley was an anachronism for this part of California, a tiny town that seemed to have no purpose, on the road to nowhere, with no beach, no mountains, no rivers or movie sets. It would have been at home in the San Joaquin Valley, or in the middle of Kansas. Five streets ran east-west. Inaptly named Seaview Street was the last of them.

Number 36 was a single-story Victorian with dust-scraped white paint. I pulled up across the street. The hot sun prickled my arms. On sunny days like this I had sat out on a plastic-stringed deck chair on the cement walkway in front of my motel door each morning, drinking a cup of the pale coffee from the Mr. Coffee in the motel office. It had pleased me then to not read a newspaper, not plan the day's activities, not have any commitments at all, just to think of Jeff making his rounds to one small business after another till he did the books at Minton's once more. He'd done Minton's the day before I'd left. After he finished there the next time, he'd be in a deck chair south of Mazatlán.

Leavenworth's little boys' cycles—one tricycle, one small bike with training wheels—lay in the burned grass of the front yard, clearly where they'd dropped them last night. I found myself surprised. The Lawrence Leavenworth I'd seen was Mr. Uptight. *His* sons would put their bicycles in the garage and wait for him to lock the door.

The door to the house opened. A small boy in a fresh red and tan SF 49ers cap scooted out, grabbed the bicycle, and pulled it toward the sidewalk.

"Take care of your cap, Larry. You want it to still be nice when Daddy comes back."

"Ahh, Mom!" little Larry grumbled. He was nearly in front of me when he climbed awkwardly onto the bike. He was a sturdy, fleshy child, the image of his father. He didn't have that conventioneer's wary look that had "graced" his father's face. Not yet, anyway, but he looked like a child who could throw a tantrum. He lurched once then pressed hard on the pedal and moved more quickly, though still cautiously down the sidewalk.

His mother brushed her long blond hair off her forehead. In the sunlight her smooth skin glistened. She had wide-spaced blue eyes, pouty mouth, and leaned one hip against the doorjamb. She was the "teenager" I'd taken to be Leavenworth's daughter. I'd misjudged her, too! I really was losing it. Sweat coated my face; my hands were clammy against the steering wheel. I hadn't been like this in San Francisco. I hadn't! I'd walked confidently on dark, deserted Market Street at 2:00 A.M., seen men lurking by the door, and knew I could handle them. I'd been a good judge of character when it counted.

But I hadn't had a decent look at this woman on the beach. If I'd had a chance to study her then, I wouldn't have made a mistake. It had been her bored-teenager stance more than anything that I had noticed. I was still okay! Now in the morning light, of course, I could see that she was older. But early twenties at the outside, hardly old enough to have a cycling son. She was wearing pale jeans with the knees ripped. Her feet were bare. And on her toenails was bright violet polish. All in all she looked like the type of California beach girl whose husband was more likely to be selling speed than nabbing speeders. No wonder I'd thought she was a teenager.

She stepped back inside the house. I didn't even try to follow her. I was too sweaty and nervous and confused. Nothing was right here. I'd been so far off base on Leavenworth I couldn't hang on to anything as "fact."

I drove slowly around the block till I spotted little Larry in his 49ers cap. Hopping out in time to intercept him, I said, "Larry, where do you live?"

"Thirty-six Seaview Street," he rattled off, blond hair bouncing above his eyes. Then suddenly he realized how close he was to me. He stood on the brakes. The metal screeched. The bike was a couple sizes too big for him, the bar too high. He lurched to the right. I caught him and held on while he yanked his leg over the bar.

"Did your daddy give you the bike?"

"He mailed it for my birthday. He goes away."

In a fit of inspiration I asked him, "What school do you go to?"

"Eden Valley. I don't know you. I'm not supposed to talk to strangers about Daddy."

I wanted to ask more, but I didn't dare chance headlines screaming: CONVENTION BUREAU DIRECTOR ATTEMPTS KIDNAP! THIEVING DIRECTOR STEALS CHILD!!! I got back in the car before the child had remounted the too-big bike.

As I drove the winding road back to the beach I tried to view Leavenworth afresh. He didn't live in San Francisco, he lived here—with a wife young enough to be his daughter, with a six-year-old whose birthday he wasn't home for. The bicycle looked pretty new; that birthday couldn't have been more than a month or so ago. He'd come home sometime after that and brought the boy a billed cap that said "SF 49ers" and given the younger one his convention tag.

It pleased me to conclude that Leavenworth wasn't what he seemed—not just an outraged father. But perhaps a man who's hiding something. I smiled. A man with a secret isn't so likely to be contacting the cops.

Freed from the panic that had driven me for days, I treated myself to dinner at the Ocean Side Hotel, where I could watch the sun set over the Pacific. The clouds were green and pink and golden yellow at dusk. I ordered one of those rum drinks with the paper umbrella, and sat watching the sun drop and pondering the rest of my stay here, lying safely on the beach, practicing my Spanish.

I was supposed to be relaxing, but my stomach was still queasy. And as I had my second drink I recognized the nagging doubt that was still clutching me. How could I, a good judge of character, not have suspected him? Was I losing it? That scared me more than he had. The man had threatened me. He'd bluffed and almost beaten me. Almost.

I ordered grilled swordfish steak and pondered Leavenworth and whatever he might be hiding. Everything had shifted again; I wasn't cringing anymore. Now the possibility of his secret began to have the same irresistible pull as the oncoming train.

Leavenworth and Eden Valley didn't fit. The family lived there. But he *sent* his son a bicycle. He wouldn't have done that if he had been away from home for a short time. No, that was the action of a man gone a lot. A father gone so much he can't recall what size bicycle his child needs.

Wherever Leavenworth was the rest of the time was just where I wanted to confront him. I smiled. An apology wouldn't be necessary to a man with a guilty secret. For the first time I felt like my old self, back at the convention bureau, the director.

I gobbled down a few bites of fish, called for the bill, and was out of town in half an hour. It was after midnight when I got back to San Francisco. Pages of newsprint blew down Market Street, the occasional trolley moved along the tracks, its light emphasizing its empty seats. The only life to be seen was a cop in a patrol car and a street person sleeping in the doorway of the building I'd come out of just a month ago. It had seemed much warmer then, but that was 2:00 A.M. instead of midnight and I was weighed down.

As I had a month ago, I parked my car a block off Market. But this time I passed Minton's and headed straight for the convention bureau. I'd kept a key, just in case. The watchman must have been on rounds. Once inside I made my way up the stairs and into the office unseen.

The convention bureau wouldn't have a list of individuals in every profession or trade, but if there was a state, national, or international fraternity that could be wooed to assemble in San Francisco hotels, the address would be here. If they had assembled here, there would be a booking list and a group photo. And I was betting that Leavenworth had picked up the convention badge he'd given his younger son while he was out of town missing the other's birthday. A convention badge isn't something you hang on to. You only bring it home if you're coming right from the convention.

I opened the bureau door, went to the files. I'd been gone for three and a half weeks. To be safe I decided to cover the last two months. I picked up the schedule for May and groaned silently. May was one of our most popular months. The city is warm then, the skies a clear California blue, and the problem was not luring groups but finding enough hotel space. I checked the rosters for Pharmacists, Philatists, Freight Forwarders, Fruit Growers, Root Growers, and eighty-seven other groups. It took me two hours, kneeling behind the desk, beaming a flashlight on the lists, terrified all along that even with those precautions the night watchman would spot something amiss, or that the batteries would give out. All that and I found not one Leavenworth among the attendees of any of the ninety-two conventions. Could the photo-store man have misread his name?

Each of the convention groups sent us an official group photo. I could look for him. I snorted at the monumental ludicrousness of that scheme. Ninety-two group photos, the head of each conventioneer an eighth of an inch tall!

Defeated, I turned off the flashlight and slumped back against the desk drawers. In the dark the cable car bell outside clanged menacingly; police sirens rose and fell but never stopped. When I had worked here, I never noticed the sirens, but they must have been shrieking then, too. I just hadn't thought about them then. No reason why I would have.

But when I stole his camera, Lawrence Leavenworth (or whatever his real name was) came up with his police threat right away. It wasn't the generic threat: I'll call the cops. It was *I'm going to get you. I know cops all over the state*, the threat of a man who really did have some connection with the cops.

Two-thirty-seven A.M. My eyes were barely focusing. I turned on the flashlight and checked through the list of organizations again, this time for ones that had some law enforcement connection. I was in luck! There were only three: The California Court Reporters, the National Bailiffs' Association, and the National Association of Juvenile Court Justices. I scanned the rosters and was almost relieved to find no Lawrence Leavenworth. Not just relieved, but excited. I could feel the train barreling down the track, challenging me. Lawrence Leavenworth's secret was real!

I walked to the pile of group photos on the back table. It was in the Juvenile Court Justices' Association picture that I found him.

It took a magnifying glass to make out Leavenworth's face. But he was there all right, smiling that fake smile. A shiver ran down my back. How awful would it be to see that face across the bench at you when you were in the dock?

Still, a judge—that pleased me a lot—a man in a very visible position. I knew what that felt like from my time as director. I knew the pitfalls. I could almost hear the train whistle, feel its pull. A judge with an alias. A judge who is away from home so much he can't remember how big his son is.

But without Leavenworth's real name I was not a whit closer to finding him. In fact I was worse off. I didn't know any more about him except that the guy was a judge, so he really did have friends in the police and on the bench, and he'd have no trouble convincing the cops to put out an all-points bulletin for me.

Sticking the roster of juvenile judges under my shirt, I made my way down the steps and back outside. Had I known how easy this building was to break into, I would have been a lot more nervous when I'd worked late alone.

Going through the roster, particularly when I didn't know what I was looking for, was going to be a long and tedious task. I couldn't sit in a lighted car without drawing the police. Even twenty-four-hour coffee shops made me wary. But years in the convention bureau had taught me the one place you can sit at any hour: the airport.

A little over an hour later I paid for a burger and coffee and settled in the United area with the roster.

Joseph Acker, Professional Building, 55 Bellingham Drive, Cincinnati, OH.

Mary E. Allen, 907 West Loma Linda, Ste. 107, San Diego, CA.

It wasn't till I got to Richard Prescetti, 8 East Seventh Street, Leavenworth, KS, that I felt a tickle of reward.

Leavenworth, *Kansas. Lawrence Leavenworth.* Business address in Leavenworth. Where would his home be? I called information in *Lawrence* Kansas and found that yes, a Richard Prescetti did have a phone there.

The next flight to Kansas City left at 7:00 A.M. I tossed my clothes in the front and slept a couple hours in the back of my car, then changed clothes. It would be hot in Kansas this time of year, but I didn't want beach clothes, not for this. I pushed Jeff's carry-on aside and pulled out one suitcase from the trunk, but it had winter clothes. The next had jackets and accessories. But the third had a black striped business suit that would do just fine. Tucked in among the socks was a small gray cloth bag with a big "M" on it. I stuck it in my purse.

The plane touched down in Kansas City at 11:03. I checked the luggage at the airport. By ten after I was looking up Prescetti in the phone book. His office address—his chambers?—were in Leavenworth and his residence in Lawrence.

I called his office. A woman, doubtless his secretary, announced he wouldn't be back till Monday. He'd been at the convention out in California.

Was he still out there? I couldn't stand it. I started to dial his home and caught myself just before the phone rang. No. If he was there, I didn't plan to take the chance of tipping him off.

I wanted to see his face when I arrived at his door.

Even with a map it took me a while to find it. The house was a brick ranch type that could have been in any upper-middle-class suburb. The grass had been mowed short, but it was still green. The shrubs had been trimmed. A Cadillac stood in the driveway. This was certainly nothing like his wife's place at the beach.

I walked up and rang the bell.

But it wasn't he who opened the door. It was a woman in

her late thirties, in shorts and a striped blouse. She had flour on her hands. "Sorry," she said, "I'm just in the middle of—"

"Mrs. Prescetti?"

"Yes?"

I smiled. "Is Richard at home?"

"Yes?"

"He's expecting me. My name's Valley, Ellen Valley." I smiled and hoped that smile didn't look too satisfied at my little play on names.

She shrugged, as if he'd forgotten to tell her things before. "He's still asleep. He got in real late from his convention last night."

"I don't want to disturb him," I said with a straight face.

"He's not a late sleeper anytime. I think I hear him stirring already. I'll just go let him know you're here. Why don't you come in and wait?"

"Thanks." She was a nice woman. She deserved better than a bigamist for a husband. I followed her in and settled on the sofa. In her absence I took the gray cloth bag I'd had wadded up in my purse and stuffed it under the sofa. The big "M" stenciled on it particularly pleased me. A fishbowl of quarters sat on the end table by the door. I amused myself trying to guess how many. Scooping out a handful I counted sixteen, so there had to be . . .

Footsteps on the stairs startled me. I stood up, jammed the quarters in my pocket, and walked to the bottom of the stairs. "You remember me from the beach, Mr. Leavenworth."

Clearly, he did. His ripply face paled and it was a moment before he croaked out, "My name isn't Leavenworth."

"And mine isn't Ellen Valley. Or Eden Valley, either."

"I don't know what—"

"And you don't own a Polaroid Spectra. Come on, Larry," I said with delicious sarcasm.

He glanced nervously up toward the kitchen, checking whether his wife, *this* wife, was in hearing distance. He lowered his voice, "Okay, let's cut the crap. How much do you want for the picture?"

It took me a moment to recall the Polaroid shoving out that overexposed picture I'd crumpled and tossed out. I smiled. So that was what Leavenworth was worried about, the picture of him and his other family! I should have realized the significance of the photograph sooner: Leavenworth and his other family.

I'd learned the hard way that it's dangerous to be photographed unawares, particularly if you're emptying Minton's safe. If you put your mind to it when you're going over a business's financial records, you can collect a lot of miscellaneous information. You get some from the records themselves, some from conversations, and the rest by just keeping your eyes open, or so Jeff said. Jeff had given me the door keys, alarm code, the safe's combination, but he must have forgotten about the surveillance camera. While he was in Los Angeles creating an alibi I had been making photographic history slinking out of the jeweler's, cash bag in hand.

"How much?" Leavenworth demanded. The man was condescending. A judge dealing with a thief! I glared up at that ripply face, the lips pressed so hard they bunched the skin at the corners.

Bargaining from a position of power was fun. Whatever the judge came up with would be gravy. I didn't *need* his money.

Leavenworth-Prescetti began to tap his finger. *Tap tap tap,* the judge calling for order.

It would have been the decent thing to tell his wives about each other. But I am a good judge of character, and I realized then that "doing the decent thing" was no longer part of my character.

Prescetti's finger tapped more insistently.

How often is an excess of money a problem, I asked myself? Prescetti already supported two women, why not add a third? It wouldn't take long to detour by his bank for a down payment. I'd get just enough to make him uncomfortable.

I had judged Prescetti correctly, all right. That pleased me. Like the men waiting outside Minton's jewelry store the night I took the money Jeff had known would be in the safe. I knew they were just street people, not undercover cops. I had been a good judge of character—of everyone but Jeff. An auditor is a meticulous type—not a person who sets up a robbery and "forgets" there's a camera above the safe. And when the story broke in the papers, the blurry picture that accompanied it was of me. Nothing connected Jeff to me; he'd seen to that.

And nothing did now. Jeff's blue carry-on bag, the one he kept the money in, is a common make.

Nothing connects me to Minton's anymore either. After all, I was supposedly in the beach town when the robbery occurred. On the other hand, Richard Prescetti has doubtless made a lot of unexplained trips to California, and his convention was in the city around that time.

I made one call before boarding my plane. The police in Kansas should have found the gray cotton bag from Minton's safe in Prescetti's living room by now. I wonder which he'll have harder time explaining, his connection to the theft or the bigamy.

I won't be going back to the beach town, or to Mazatlán. I think Barcelona is more my style. But I'll have to be careful. These thefts have to be the last potentially suicidal things I do, because I can't always count on racing across the tracks before the train hits me.

They loved not wisely but too well. . . .

They were drawn like moths to the flame of love. . . .

Apt descriptions of behavior likely to lead to trouble—and when that trouble is compounded by high stakes and the swift current of strong passions, as it is in Nancy Pickard's "Sex and Violence" and Ben Schutz's "Mary, Mary, Shut the Door," the results may reverberate for a long time, through many lives—and a few deaths.

sex and violence

NANCY PICKARD

Nancy Pickard, the 1987–88 president of Sisters in Crime, is the creator of Jennifer Cain, mistress of the clever aside. A cheerfully cynical sleuth, Jenny is educated, compassionate, and gracious without being a one-dimensional "good girl" or a loner stalking the mean streets. The Jenny books include Say No to Murder, *an Anthony winner;* No Body, *an Anthony nominee;* Marriage Is Murder, *an Anthony nominee and Macavity Award winner;* Dead Crazy, *an Anthony and Agatha nominee;* Bum Steer, *an Agatha winner; and* I.O.U. *Nancy's short stories explore a darker side of the human condition; "Afraid All the Time" was nominated for an Edgar and an Agatha and won a Macavity, an American Mystery Award, and an Anthony.*

In "Sex and Violence," a woman finds that in

*love as in other areas of life, it's sometimes not over
even after it's over.*

———————————

The call came at 10:30 on a Saturday morning in January.

When her phone rang, Amy Giddens was still in her white chenille bathrobe, seated in her rocking chair in front of her gas fireplace, her slippered feet up on a hassock. She was drinking coffee and reading *The Kansas City Star;* the crumbs of a croissant lay on a plate on the floor beside her. A fragrance of bayberry rose from a fat green candle on the hearth; a scent of cinnamon drifted into the living room from a pot of apple cider that simmered on the stove.

She picked up the phone and said hello.

"Oh, Amy, something awful has happened."

It was her friend, Kathy Weltner.

Amy sat straight up, sweeping the newspaper off her lap.

"Of all people," Kathy said. "I mean, I thought he'd live forever. Oh, Amy, Ross Powell is dead." Her voice broke. "I knew you'd want to know. It's just so . . . unbelievable."

Inside her, Amy's voice cried, *No.*

As she listened to Kathy, she stared out her own picture window, noticing in some part of her consciousness that this was just the kind of grey, bitterly cold day that would have inspired Ross Powell to take off for some place like Portugal, where the sun was always shining. She felt a big, lonely emptiness begin to inflate her body, and into the emptiness there poured the huge, silent *No.*

She managed to inquire: how, where, what happened?

"He drove over a cliff." Kathy laughed a little wildly, but the sound got snagged on her tears. "In France. Above Monte Carlo. I mean, of course. Like Princess Grace. Oh God. It's not funny. But if he had to go, I'll bet this is how he'd want to do it, except maybe if he could have had a heart attack while he was fucking, that would have been even better. Maybe that's how he drove off the cliff." Again, she half laughed, half cried, "It would have been just like him, wouldn't it?"

At the word "France," Amy was jolted by a wave of nos-

talgia so strong that it shocked her. It was three years since
she'd seen him, but at that moment she remembered Ross as
clearly, as vibrantly, as if he were that moment leaning over
her, just as he had towered over the Europeans in the train
stations. He was so much taller than most of them that she'd
always been able to spot him easily in crowds. She saw his
shoulders, such all-American male shoulders, that strained
the leather of the jacket he bought in Spain; and his arms,
which were longer than normal, giving him a simian, disproportionate appearance that you couldn't detect face-on, but
which you caught sometimes when you glanced at him out of
the corner of your eye; and the curly brown hair that hadn't
looked so rebellious in Europe where so many other men
also wore ponytails; and his mustache that drooped to the
corner of his mouth when he frowned; and his lips and nose
that were too large for the rest of his face, giving him a lazy,
sensuous look; and his hazel eyes that held a woman's for a
promising, tantalizing moment before sliding away, as if he
knew a sexy secret or had told her a lie. In that startling,
vivid instant, Amy could even smell him, and the greatest
shock was remembering that his after-shave had smelled like
bayberry, just like her favorite kind of candles.

"Amy? Are you there . . . are you all right?"

The memory disappeared. Amy wanted to cry out: *No!
Wait!*

"When did it happen?" she managed to say.

"Last week. I heard it from somebody who heard it from
Ross's mother. They say it was at night, and they think he
was alone—"

"Think?"

"Well, the car just sailed off a cliff into the Mediterra-
nean. They say he probably died on impact, instead of
drowning, although they won't know for sure until they find,
oh God, his body. So it was probably instantaneous. I hope. I
can't bear to think how he felt on the way down, can you?"

"So there's no funeral?" Amy felt as if she had to pull her
voice up from deep inside a great, hollow well.

"His mother will hold a memorial service of some kind, I
guess, but we're having everybody over here tonight for a
sort of party in his honor. I know you didn't care about him
anymore. And I know he was such a jerk to you. But he was
Ross, you know? And everybody from the old days will be

here. And they'll all want to see you. So you'll come, won't you, Amy?"

She promised to.

After she put the receiver down, Amy stared into her real fire burning between her phony logs. And it was at that moment that her memories began, as if by some sort of romantic, nostalgic alchemy, to transform themselves from bitter into sweet. *He was in a good mood that last morning in Albufiera. And earlier, he had looked so sexy, so tempting, lying asleep in their room. What if she had slid back into bed with him? What if she had smiled back at him at the café, forgiven him, kept traveling with him? Would he still be alive?*

Five years ago . . .

Outside the drawn curtains of their hotel room in Albufiera, the morning sun had struck the rough surfaces of the whitewashed buildings like a match, shooting fierce sparks into the cool air. A thin beam of light had filtered through the muslin and it lay like a warm dime on Amy's cheek. Her mind came reluctantly awake before her eyes opened; it took a few foggy moments for her to comprehend the nature of the unexpected heat on her face.

Sun? she thought, unbelieving.

She was afraid to open her eyes and look for fear this blessing might fade back to darkness in her dreams. She squeezed her eyelids tighter and prayed to whatever gods had been harassing her, Let that be the sun shining. Then she opened her eyes cautiously, only to snap them shut when the glare hurt them. Blessed pain.

"Thank you," she murmured into her pillow.

Amy lay still in the expanding pool of warmth, and listened for sounds from the other side of the bed. Ross was breathing deeply, but he wasn't snoring. He never snored. It was one of those qualities of his for which she had continued to try to feel grateful. He was funny, when he wasn't depressed, that was another one. He was tall. Charming to strangers. Kind to dogs. "Arf," she said softly, and stifled a giggle. God knew she'd wagged her tail for him. "Arf, arf."

And he was incredibly patient when she made major blunders—like the time she left her passport on a table in a cafeteria in Paris—even if almost everything else she did annoyed him. One memorable night, he'd been angry because she left food on her plate. Food on her plate, for God's sake, as if she were five years old!

"I'll order the child's plate next time," she'd snapped back.

"Well, that would be appropriate in more ways than one," he'd said coolly, so that she'd had to bite back the tears that would have seemed to him to prove his point.

In point of fact, she was twenty-six and he was thirty-one. His life was devoted to finding jobs that paid enough for nine months to allow him to escape to the south of Europe every winter; her life, for the past two years, had been devoted to saving enough money to join him this time. It had been, mostly, a disastrous idea, she had finally admitted to herself: she couldn't get close enough to him; he couldn't get far enough away from her.

But this is this morning, Amy thought, lying in bed, and the sun is shining. It was not a trivial thought, she knew; in long, cold, grey winters, the sun was never trivial, and its promises were not to be taken lightly.

Amy still had not opened her eyes again, but at least she knew where she was. No small accomplishment that, considering the rate they'd been traveling. "I am on the Algarve," she recited reassuringly to herself, "in the south of Portugal, on the Iberian Peninsula, on the continent of Europe, northern and western hemispheres, third planet from the sun." She smiled. "No wonder it took so long to get here."

Then she discovered another miracle.

She put a doubting hand to her abdomen just to be sure; she pushed in, then out. No cramps, no nausea. Her stomach had unclenched itself in the night.

She'd been the sickest two nights before, in Lisbon.

"Maybe I'll die," she'd told Ross, and had imagined a flicker of hope in his eyes. "For heaven's sake, go to dinner without me."

"I'll bring you back something," he'd offered, looking resentful. Then without waiting for a reply, he had rendered the offer meaningless. "I'll probably stop for a drink, so don't wait up for me."

"I'm not likely to do that," she'd said, dryly.

It seemed to her that everything she said lately was dry, as if to compensate for the eternal rain. Or, possibly, because she herself had condensed. When she met strangers on the road, she wondered if they could tell she had turned into a block of dry ice, expelling lifeless steam instead of air.

Ross had returned to their room after midnight when she

was aching with fever and wretched from hours of diarrhea and vomiting.

He had not inquired about her health.

"I found a wonderful bar," he'd exclaimed, full of the energy of his evening. Rapidly, he'd stripped down to naked, talking all the while. "In the old part of town, down this wonderful windy street, all cobblestones. And there was a Fado singer you would have been crazy about, all melancholy and kind of haunting. I met this old guy there—"

He'd jabbered on while she'd huddled in a fetal position, resenting the hell out of him, yet glad that he was talking to her again, and smiling. She was worn down by the mercurial changes in his temperament, depressed one week, manic the next. And he accused her of being emotional! Was he crazy? she wondered as she lay aching, or just selfish? If he was crazy, as in truly mentally ill, did she have to feel sorry for him and keep loving him? If he was just selfish, *could* she stop loving him?

And then he'd crawled into the bed and pressed himself against her burning back. He'd wanted sex. She was too sick and weak to fight about it, and so she'd let him do it. And hated him.

Finally, she'd hated him.

Months later, she confided to a friend about that night in Lisbon, and was surprised and embarrassed when the friend called it "shocking," and said he had "raped" her. "Oh no," Amy protested, "I could have said no, and he wouldn't have done it, it isn't the same thing at all, I'm sorry I ever said anything about it, and please don't tell anybody else, okay?" After that, she didn't confide to anybody certain things about her relationship with Ross. Like the time they were screaming at each other in their room, after too much beer, in a hotel in Germany, and the manager intervened because she said that Ross was so much bigger than Amy that the manager was afraid "the little American girl" might get hurt. He never would have done that, Amy, thoroughly mortified, told the woman; he would never lay a hand on her in violence. And he certainly never had, except for that time in Florence when he slapped her when she cried hysterically because he hadn't spoken to her in five days. But that didn't count, and besides, it worked. She stopped weeping and he started talking. They'd been cooped up together too much, that was all. And that German manager, she was just overreacting out of some sort of guilt left over from World War II, Amy figured out, that was all, like maybe she hadn't protested when the Nazis took her Jewish neighbors away, or something like that. Anyway, that was her problem, not Amy's or Ross's.

Maybe it's the weather that makes us crazy, she thought as she lay in bed, in Albufiera, as the sun radiated into her vital organs.

They'd been weeks in search of the sun, or was it years? They'd chased its winter shadow from London down to the Atlantic. But even on the road from Lisbon, it had rained and they'd despaired of ever feeling warm again. Amy had wrapped herself in a blanket that Ross had stolen from their hotel and she had huddled in the passenger seat of the rented car and shivered with the flu. All the way along the two-lane blacktop, through green fields of black olive trees, she'd shivered. Past square, one-room houses painted brilliant pastel colors that shone fluorescent in the rain, she had shivered and sweated into the scratchy wool. Halfway, they got stuck behind a funeral cortege. The coffin, a simple wooden affair loaded onto the flatbed of a clean truck, was trailed by somber men on motorcycles and squat, walking women in black. Amy had gotten the feeling she was the corpse and the world was mourning. Knowing better, but playing for sympathy, she'd confided her hallucination to Ross. He'd suggested it was time for her to take another Tylenol. . . .

She slipped out from under her covers and stood beside him, staring down at him in bed. One or two people had told her he reminded them of the actor James Coburn. In the sunlight, Amy examined the long, lean body that gave him that look, and the high cheekbones and the wide mouth, and the creases around his eyes that hinted at intelligence and cruel wit.

"I've known you to be gentle," she whispered. "I've even known you to be kind."

But not lately.

He slept snorelessly on.

She padded barefoot across the rug to her suitcase to scoop up underwear, slacks, and a shirt. Then she went quietly into the bathroom to shower and dress, anxious to avoid the heat of his glance on her nakedness. She didn't want him to want her this morning. Most of all, she didn't want to want him.

A few minutes later, before she left their room, she looked back at it. It appeared so elegant to Amy, and it was cheap, to boot. God, she loved Europe. She had yearned to come here almost as much as she had desired to be with Ross this winter. And now here she was, existing on two different planes—still thrilled by the journey, but miserable with loneliness and resentment. She knew she would never have taken this trip without him; basically, she was a sedentary person, not an adventurer like Ross. Loving him had freed her to do this extraordinary thing—to quit her job and to travel for three months in Europe. Without him, she wouldn't have had the nerve. If she left him, she wouldn't have the courage to continue traveling by herself, she'd probably fly straight home, and even the thought of managing *that* by herself made her feel sick with nervousness. They were both free, and yet he felt imprisoned by her presence and she felt imprisoned by her own fear. Weird. In the bed, Ross moved an arm. Amy quickly, quietly, closed the door.

Ross found her two hours later on the veranda of the big luxury hotel on the beach. The sun was just coming over the building, and there was a slight breeze, so the morning wasn't really all that warm yet; Amy was glad that she'd slipped a sweater on over her shirt and jeans. The Atlantic Ocean, looking gray and restless, was only a strip of beach away from her table. She had known that Ross would have to wander in this direction to find breakfast.

"Hi," he said, and smiled down at her.

"Hi."

He leaned down to kiss her, lingering a moment on her lips, so she knew this day he would honor her with the privilege of one of his good moods.

He dragged a chair up to her table in a rectangle of sun, put an exuberant arm around her shoulders and hugged her with every evidence of fondness.

"Café au lait," he said to the waiter. "I mean, *con leche.*" He laughed, as if the waiter and Amy would enjoy his predicament, and threw up his hands. "Christ, what country is this? Which language this morning?"

The waiter didn't appear to get the joke.

"Can you believe this glorious day?" Ross squinted into the sunshine, looking as pleased as if the day had been especially arranged for him.

She put a finger in her mystery novel, and closed it.

"Yes, it's wonderful."

"How're you feeling?"

"Okay. Good."

"Thought you were going to die on me."

"I felt like it, I guess."

He gazed at her appraisingly, but in a friendly way, over his steaming coffee cup. "You look better," he said finally, and then he grinned. "Good enough to eat."

"Try a croissant, instead," she said, and felt the steam come off the dry ice again.

He leaned back in his chair, and laughed.

"Listen," he said suddenly, eagerly, like a small boy with a big plan. He grabbed her free hand and squeezed it. "How about if we take the car and drive on down the coast for the day? Maybe have lunch on the beach somewhere, get some wine and cheese, what do you say?"

"Ross," she said, then bit her lip.

"All right!" He released her hand, then leaned back again, appearing satisfied with the state of things. "All right."

No! Amy's voice cried inside her head: *It isn't all right!*

"Ross?"

"What?" Was there a hint of awareness, a suspicion at the back of his eyes? Then he smiled again, and whatever she thought she read in his glance was gone. "What, honey?"

"I can't stand—" *to ride your roller coaster again! Stop it! Or let me off!* But for a moment, she lost her nerve.

"What can't you stand? You don't want to go to the beach? It'll be gorgeous. What?"

"Nothing."

"Oh, that!" he teased. "Well, that's nothing."

"Ross?"

"What?" He laughed. "What, *what*?"

"Nothing." Suddenly she was furious, at him, at herself. *I'm getting off, damn you!* "I'm leaving, I'm getting off!"

He looked utterly surprised, and the beginning of angry. How could she ruin their day? he'd demand to know. How could she throw a stupid, goddamned tantrum on a gorgeous day like this? What in the hell was the matter with her?

"Nothing!" she said, and other customers turned to look. *"Nothing!"* As Ross stared at her, Amy pushed back from the table, threw down her napkin, and ran from the veranda.

She slowed to a walk near their hotel.

There would be buses returning to Lisbon that very day.

And from Lisbon there would be planes to carry her home. She hadn't meant to do it this way, but it was better than . . . nothing. Yes, she was frightened, but a smile was growing on her face. *It is,* she thought, *so good to leave on a sunny day when the world is bright and clear and sharp.* The winter sun was strong and hot on her back, like a warm, moist hand, pushing her. . . .

It was the last time she saw Ross.

She thought she had left him forever. She thought she had left herself with only a healthy residue of bitter memories of a selfish man. She had married somebody else, and divorced that man. Dated other men, broken a couple of hearts, and suffered her own being broken again.

But five years later, upon hearing that Ross Powell was dead, Amy was awash in a passionate, sentimental longing for him. He'd been so much fun, she'd loved him so much, and she felt sure that he'd cared about her too, in his own strange way, that maybe he'd even loved her more than he'd ever loved any other woman, and that he'd missed her terribly when she was gone, and that he was sorry for all the times . . .

Oh, God, if only she could love him one more time.

He couldn't be dead. No!

Although she hated the idea of what the "memorial service" represented—that he was really dead—she couldn't stay away.

Kathy Welty and Sam DeLucca had married in the old days when the whole gang, including Ross and Amy, worked as copywriters or artists in the advertising department of Macy's, back when there was a Macy's in Kansas City. There'd been many pairings back then, but Sam and Kathy were the only two who were still a couple.

"It's your three kids that keep you together," proclaimed Steve Allison, as he set down his contribution to the evening: a case of Budweiser, which was Ross Arlen's favorite back in the good old days. "You can't either of you bear the thought of being left alone with the kids."

"Not a problem Ross ever had," Sam DeLucca observed, his dry wit still intact after all those years. "God love him."

"At least not that we ever knew," his wife, Kathy Welty, added in her own tartly distinctive style, which had also distinguished her writing. "It's difficult for me to believe, however, that there aren't a few little Jays—or Jayettes—scattered about the globe, you know?"

"God, what a terrifying thought," said Lara Eisenstein, who was still an advertising illustrator in town. "I loved him, too, but . . . clones of Ross? Mothers, hide your daughters."

"My theory," Steve said, as he popped the tops on Budweisers for each of them, "is that he didn't accidentally go over that cliff at all. He was too good a driver. So I figure a woman killed him. It's only logical—"

"Inevitable, you mean," Sam said, and they all laughed.

"Not to mention justifiable," Kathy interjected.

"Okay," Steve said, "so maybe it was that one who went after him with a knife that time, remember her? What was her name? Or the other one—the accountant—who rammed her car into the back of his. And then into the front. On purpose. And there was that lady, God, poor thing, who tried to kill herself when Ross left her." He took a swig of Bud, wiped his mouth, and smiled. "I think one of them pushed him over the cliff, and who could blame them?"

"Maybe they all got together and did it," somebody called in from the living room. "All the women he ever dumped. You know, like that Agatha Christie mystery, what was it called? *Murder on the Orient Express?* Where they all took a stab, pardon the pun, at the victim?"

"They never called *me*," Amy said.

Sam DeLucca laughed loud enough for his amusement to carry in to the gang in the living room. "Ross, as victim? You expect us to buy that? No way! Ross was a penetrator . . . excuse me . . . perpetrator if there ever was one!"

"Very funny," his wife said. "You're all wrong, anyway. It was a jealous husband or boyfriend."

"Couldn't be," Lara Eisenstein objected. "Ross never dated married women. Remember? It was a principle of his—"

"Principle!" Sam and Kathy hooted at the same time, and Kathy added, "The man hadn't seen a principal since he left high school."

Lara laughed, and made a face at them. "No, really, I mean it was a prin-ci-ple of his never to date married women because . . ." She looked around at each of them, smiling, and shaking her head. "Why should he mess with that kind of trouble, when there were so many other women who were so utterly available to him?"

Kathy suddenly turned toward Amy. "Oops. Listen, guys, maybe this is not tactful. I mean, obviously, it's tasteless, which is only fitting considering the subject, but maybe it's also tactless? You want we should shut up about Ross and his other women, Amy?"

"Don't be silly," Amy said, "it's history."

"I don't get it," Steve said. "How could a man who wouldn't hurt a flea inspire so much violence in so many women? I always thought he was kind of a gentle guy, you know? I mean, he was a good friend, loyal, do anything for you, give you the shirt off his back—"

"Big deal," Sam laughed. "K mart special, all polyester."

Steve laughed, too, but he said, insistently, "All right, but you know what I mean. He was a hell of a lot of fun to be around. I thought he was a nice guy." He took another drink of Bud. "So there, asshole."

"He was nice if you were his friend," Kathy said, in a reflective tone of voice. "That's true. Although he could drive you crazy, the way he used to just drop by any time of day or night, like just when we would be trying to get the kids to sleep. But for his girlfriends"—she glanced at Amy with a smile full of sympathy—"I think there was a lot of wear and tear."

Lara Eisenstein laughed. "You make him sound like a Laundromat."

"I'll tell you what I could never understand." Sam affected a woebegone expression that made him look like his own golden retriever. "What was it about him that attracted women like flies? Begging your pardon, ladies. But I mean it was like they were the flies and he was the screen door. Or they were the flies and he was the garbage . . . no, no, I didn't mean that, that can't be right. Do you understand it, Stevie? Hell, he wasn't even good-looking. What did he have that we don't have?"

The women in both rooms smirked, with the exception of Amy, and one of the men in the living room called out, "You had to ask, dummy!"

"He had glamour," Kathy said. "And style. All of those trips to Europe. Those sports cars he drove, because he didn't have to pay for a mortgage or for preschool like the rest of us. What was attractive about Ross was the life he led, which consisted of periods of compulsive responsibility interspersed with total abandon and adventure. Like a Yuppie Indiana Jones." Her smile was self-deprecating. "I guess it's obvious that I've been thinking about it a lot since he died." Suddenly there were tears in her eyes and in the eyes of several other people there, as well. "Ross was bigger than life. Shouldn't that mean that he wasn't supposed to die?"

Sam slapped his beer can angrily down on his kitchen counter. "What the hell was he doing there, anyway? Wasn't he getting a little old for that stuff?"

"He'd been working for one of those Texas savings and loan companies," Steve said. "One of the ones that went belly up. I think he took his last paycheck and said, adios, guys, have a good time in court, I'm off to Europe."

There was a moment of silence in both the kitchen and the living room. Finally, somebody said, "Let's pretend he's not dead, he's just late to the party."

"Okay then, here," said Steve, holding high a Budweiser, "this is to the late Ross Powell, who's going to walk in that door any minute now and tell us it was all a joke on us. Ha." He drained his beer and then set the can quietly on the counter. "Ha." In a choked voice, he said, "Well, he hated winter, and now he'll never have to see it again. It'll always be summer on the Riviera for Ross."

"We agreed that he wasn't really dead," Sam snapped at him. "He's merely late to the party, probably out picking up a woman somewhere. So cut the sentimental crap. Shut up and drink."

Later, when they had a moment alone in the bathroom, Kathy said to Amy, "You're so quiet. Are you feeling just too sad? Are you okay?"

"I'm not sad," Amy said, and it was true, she wasn't. What she was, was excited. She didn't have to pretend, as the rest of them did. In her heart, she was beginning to feel it was true: Ross couldn't be dead, because he *wasn't* dead. It really *was* unbelievable that he could be dead . . . because it literally . . . wasn't . . . true. They might play around with the idea of what had "really" happened to him, but she had known him better, more intimately, than any of them ever had, and she knew that only she was able to put the facts together to fit the only possible conclusion. *Fact one: they'd found a car, but no body. Fact two: he'd walked off with money from the failed savings and loan company in Texas, probably more than they knew, possibly even a lot of it, and he may have even stolen it. Fact three: if that were so, it would have been just like him to stage his ultimate escape.*

It was all she could do to restrain herself from grabbing Kathy and hugging her and exclaiming, "I think he's alive! And I can find him!"

Once she had the notion, she couldn't shake it.

Driving to work, eating lunch with her friends, talking on the phone to her mother, going to the bathroom, taking a shower, putting on makeup—at all times, a part of her mind was doubting. That he was dead. Hoping. That he was alive. Figuring out. How it could be possible. Dreaming. What she might do about it.

Amy didn't say a word about what she was thinking to anybody, not even to Kathy. She knew that anybody she might confide in would think she was nuts; worse, they'd say she was still in love with him, and they'd feel sorry for her.

Well, maybe she was still in love with him.

But they didn't need to pity her.

They should envy me, Amy thought when she had it all figured out, *because I'm the only one of them—of his friends, of his family, of all of the people who ever knew him—who may get one more chance to see him again.*

Deep down, she wondered—she fantasized—about how he might, by now, be desperately hungry to connect with somebody who really knew him, about how glad he'd be to see her again, about how he might invite her to slip inside his new life, to start all over again with him now that they were older and wiser, about how he might beg her to share his last, best escape.

But most of the time she told herself she only wanted to see him. One more time. One last time. It would be a sort of triumph, a sort of victory, a trick on the trickster, but one that would surely make him laugh the hardest of all. It amused Amy so much to think: I escaped from you, lover, but you can't escape from me.

• • •

At work, they only knew that Amy Giddens took her regular two-week vacation and flew off for a glamorous fortnight to Europe. Cyprus. Torremolinos. The Canary Islands. The Algarve. They looked at her travel folders and envied her exotic, sun-stroked itinerary, marveling at the stamina it would take to visit so many wonderful places in so short a time, and at the adventurous spirit that propelled her to make this trip by herself. A few bluenoses at the office sniffed at her spendthrift manner of throwing money away on an outrageously expensive vacation. Amy stared at those same travel folders and saw: Ross Powell's favorite destinations in his search for never-ending summer.

On the airplane, she kept thinking: there are so many places he could be, places she remembered that he had liked, places where the sun always shone, like almost anyplace along the Riviera, Morocco, Tunisia, Majorca. But the most likely place was Albufiera, because nobody Ross ever knew was ever likely to go there, and because Portugal was still cheap compared with the rest of Europe. Amy remembered Albufiera as a town where the only noticeable foreigners were German and British; Americans preferred the resorts north of Lisbon instead of the Algarve to the south.

And, she had to admit to herself, she *wanted* it to be Albufiera. Because it was beautiful, and because its beauty and her melancholy had made her heart ache, and because she had left him sitting there, and it would be so natural to walk back into the café, at the hotel on the ocean, and to find him sitting there again, to go up to his table, to smile as he had smiled at her and to say, "Hi. Can you believe this gorgeous day? Let's take the car and drive on down the beach. We can stop for a bottle of wine, some bread and cheese, what do you say?"

When she thought of how Albufiera looked, she remembered a particular arch that separated the street from the luxury hotel. In her memory, the street was cobblestones; the hotel had no remembered shape at all. But the arch was vivid in its particularity in her memory: lovely in its simplicity, thick as a man's arm from wrist to shoulder, rounded like the innermost curve of a woman's neck; the sun cast half of it in shadow, the other half in light so bright the whiteness of the arch made her eyes hurt when she remembered it; and what she remembered most of all—whether or not it had actually been true—was that when you stepped through the arch you moved out of cool, sad shadow into the light.

Amy's plane landed in Lisbon on a Monday morning. She drove, in a rented car, all the way to Albufiera that afternoon, arriving at dusk.

Leaving her bags in the car, she walked first to the beach where she and Ross had hung out to watch the sun set over the Atlantic ocean. Just as she had remembered, the Portuguese fishermen were pulling in their nets from their brilliantly painted little boats. Women sold glittering silver fish out of buckets set up on wooden tables in the sand. There were tourists there with lighter skin and hair, and men who were taller and thinner than the Portuguese, but none of them was Ross Powell.

As the sunset grew ever more violently pink and orange, Amy abandoned the beach and walked toward a little dinner restaurant that still lived in her memory. It had been frequented by foreigners, and the tables had been so close together that you couldn't help but get to know your neighbors. But when she thought she found the right location, she saw only a gift store selling knickknacks.

It was dark by the time she found the hotel where they'd stayed, and she wasn't surprised when the clerk told her that no Mr. Powell was registered there. Of course, Ross wouldn't use his real name, she realized. She was expecting that problem. But the clerk also volunteered that there were no Americans at the hotel at all. "Australians?" she asked. No, none of those. "English, Scottish . . ." She began to feel foolish, inquiring of various nationalities under which Ross might be hiding. The clerk grew impatient, and resorted to claiming that she didn't speak English, which of course she had been, if haltingly, until that very moment.

"Oh God," Amy said to herself as she left the hotel. "If I'm wrong . . ."

It would be an expensive mistake, not only in terms of her limited funds but also in the amount of time she had in which to look for him. There were so many places he could be, all of them hot and sunny, except . . .

She remembered a bar—long and cool and dim, even in the daytime—manned by a British expatriate who called out your name the second time you came in, and who paid you the compliment of talking to you in a humorous, cynical way about tourists, as if you weren't one. It was a bar where at any time you could find Germans, Scandinavians, British, and Americans, and always somebody who spoke English. Foreigners stuck together in Portugal, she believed, because they felt like time travelers in an earlier century. The natives either didn't or wouldn't speak English, and the English didn't speak Portuguese, which was so different, so separate from Spanish; everybody stuck to their own kind, staring at the others, and wondering, but rarely pushing through the door from one culture into the other. It was such a good place to hide, she knew it was, and she knew that Ross would think so, too. Here, everybody seemed to be hiding something, some secret—the Portuguese, most of all, hiding their glances, their language, and their souls from the foreign tourists, and most of all, hiding their curiosity. They asked no questions, they gave nothing away in their dark faces: perfect people to hide among, because they appeared to take no interest at all in their visitors.

She was willing to bet the English bar owner would still be mixing drinks behind the counter and welcoming strangers as if they were regulars. So what if Ross wasn't at the beach, and so what if that restaurant was gone now? There were cafés where Ross might be eating dinner this very evening.

But first she would try to find that old bar.

Amy stepped into the cool, dim interior of the bar and scanned the length of the room. She didn't see the Englishman. That depressed her so that she was ready to give up and go find a room for the night. Then her heart lurched and she nearly cried out when she noticed the man seated on the last stool at the end. He was tall, too thin, with a full beard and a mustache; he'd brushed his hair back off his forehead and it fell, curly and unbound to his shoulders—which looked too wide in proportion to the rest of his body. His profile, as he raised a glass of beer to his mouth, displayed a wide nose and full lips. He was wearing a battered brown leather jacket over a black turtleneck sweater and well-worn blue jeans.

Amy ducked, so that she could observe the man at the end of the bar without being seen. Was it Ross? It couldn't really be! Suddenly, for the first time, Amy was struck by the absurdity, the absolute unlikelihood of her quest. Ross Powell was dead. He was supposed to be dead, he wasn't supposed to be sitting here, in the same bar where they'd sat together five years before. And even if he was still alive, it wasn't possible that she had really found him. Out of an entire world of places to hide, she couldn't have picked the one. It wasn't possible, this wasn't the man, she was out of her mind, and she ought to face that truth, have a quick drink, go back and pack her bags and go home, clear-eyed and sane once more.

He turned his face in her direction.

It was undeniably Ross Powell.

And he saw her, looking at him.

After the first instant of surprise, he smiled.

His lips moved as if he were saying something to her, and he pushed his weight forward on the palm of his left hand, as if he were going to shove himself off of the bar stool and come toward her.

"Wine!" A woman pushed her way to the bar directly in front of Ross, and she was followed by two other women. "We'd like a carafe of red wine, please."

Amy couldn't see Ross behind the women.

And then the women were joined by three men, and all of them bunched up jovially at the bar, arguing loudly and good-naturedly over whether to order wine or beer.

Rooted to the floor by the shock of actually seeing him, Amy waited for him to get off his bar stool and walk around the crowd and come over to her. When he didn't appear, she took a couple of tentative steps in his direction.

But then the party of six separated enough for her to see that the bar stool behind them was empty. One of the women noticed, and sat down on it.

"Ross?"

A man at the bar turned to stare at her.

Amy hurried forward.

He was gone. Nowhere in the bar. There were some Portuguese coins thrown down on the counter beside his half-finished drink.

Amy started to hurry out the door, to chase him into the night, to find him and grab him.

But was it really Ross she had seen?

Leaving the bar, she wasn't sure any longer.

Such a quick glimpse, after so many years . . .

But that *smile* . . .

Amy stumbled out of the cool, dim bar into the even colder, even darker Portuguese night. And suddenly, she was also aware of how alone she was: a woman alone outside of a bar in a strange country. She suddenly wanted to get back safely to her car, and to find a hotel room quickly.

That smile. *It* was *him. She knew it.*

She'd look for Ross again tomorrow.

Amy slowed down. Or maybe she wouldn't. If he'd stolen money from the savings and loan, if he'd faked his own death, he wouldn't want to be found, not even by her. How could she have been so foolish as to think he would?

She walked into the dark, narrow street that led in the direction of her car. She felt desolate, stupid. And suddenly, frighteningly, she felt as if she were being followed. Amy picked up her pace until she was nearly running.

She heard footsteps running behind her, drawing nearer.

If she screamed, in this foreign country, where everybody ignored her, would anybody help her?

Amy felt a hand land roughly on her back. It pushed her off balance, shoved her into an alley beside the bar. She cried out as it grasped her shoulder and whirled her around.

"Ross!"

She was staring into his face as he grabbed her hair and pulled her head back. Her eyes were still open as he leaned down and kissed her, forcing her mouth open, pushing his tongue between her teeth, shoving her body against the brick wall.

Her eyes closed as she felt his hands meet in a circle around her neck.

mary, mary, shut the door

BENJAMIN M. SCHUTZ

But for Bob Randisi and some others, Ben Schutz might have jumped off a boat in the middle of Baltimore Harbor. That's where he was when he overheard some people talking about his first publisher going "belly-up." Since that time, Mr. Schutz has gone on to win the Shamus Award for Best Novel with his Leo Haggerty novel A Tax in Blood. With "Mary, Mary . . ." he proves himself as adept at writing short stories as he is at novels.

I wonder if he can swim? Oh well, I guess we had our chance to find out. . . .

———————

Enzo Scolari motored into my office and motioned me to sit. What the hell, I sat. He pulled around to the side of my desk, laced his fingers in his lap, and sized me up.

"I want to hire you, Mr. Haggerty," he announced.

"To do what, Mr. Scolari?"

"I want you to stop my niece's wedding."

"I see. And why is that?"

"She is making a terrible mistake, and I will not sit by and let her do it."

"Exactly what kind of mistake is she making?"

"She knows nothing about him. They just met. She is infatuated, nothing more. She knows nothing about men. Nothing. The first one to pay any attention to her and she wants to get married."

"You said they just met. How long ago, exactly?" Just a little reality check.

"Two weeks. Can you believe it? Two weeks. And I just found out about it yesterday. She brought him to the house last night. There was a party and she introduced him to everyone and told us she was going to marry him. How can you marry someone you've known for two weeks? That's ridiculous. It's a guarantee of failure and it'll break her heart. I can't let that happen."

"Mr. Scolari, I'm not sure we can help you with this. Your niece may be doing something foolish, but she has a right to do it. I understand your concern for her well-being, but I don't think you need a detective, maybe a priest or a therapist. We don't do premarital background checks. Our investigations are primarily criminal."

"The crime just hasn't happened yet, Mr. Haggerty. My niece may be a foolish girl, but he isn't. He knows exactly what he's doing."

"And what is that?"

"He's taking advantage of her naïveté, her innocence, her fears, her loneliness, so he can get her money. That's a crime, Mr. Haggerty."

And a damn hard one to prove. "What are you afraid of, Mr. Scolari? That he'll kill her for her money? That's quite a leap from an impulsive decision to marry. Do you have any reason to think that this guy is a killer?"

He straightened up and gave that one some thought. Enzo Scolari was wide and thick with shoulders so square and a head so flat he could have been a candelabra. His snow-white eyebrows and mustache hung like awnings for his eyes and lips.

"No. Not for that. But I can tell he doesn't love Gina.

Last night I watched him. Every time Gina left his side his eyes went somewhere else. A man in love, his eyes follow his woman everywhere. No, he's following the maid or Gina's best friend. Gina comes back and he smiles like she's the sunrise. And she believes it.

"He spent more time touching the tapestries than he did holding her hand. He went through the house like a creditor, not a guest. No, he doesn't want Gina, he wants her money. You're right, murder is quite a step from that, but there are easier ways to steal. Gina is a shy, quiet woman who has never had to make any decisions for herself. I don't blame her for that. My sister, God rest her soul, was terrified that something awful would happen to Gina and she tried to protect her from everything. It didn't work. My sister was the one who died and it devastated the girl. Now Gina has to live in the world and she doesn't know how. If this guy can talk her into marrying him so quickly, he'll have no trouble talking her into letting him handle her money."

"How much money are we talking about here?"

"Ten million dollars, Mr. Haggerty." Scolari smiled, having made his point. People have murdered or married for lots less.

"How did she get all this money?"

"It's in a trust for her. A trust set up by my father. My sister and I each inherited half of Scolari Enterprises. When she died, her share went to Gina as her only child."

"This trust, who manages it?"

"I do, of course."

Of course. Motive number two just came up for air. "So, where's the problem? If you control the money, this guy can't do anything."

"I control the money as trustee for my sister. I began that when Gina was still a little girl. Now she is of age and can control the money herself if she wants to."

"So you stand to lose the use of ten million dollars. Have I got that right?"

Scolari didn't even bother to debate that one with me. I liked that. I'll take naked self-interest over the delusions of altruism any day.

"If they've just met, how do you know that this guy even knows that your niece has all this money?"

Scolari stared at me, then spat out his bitter reply. "Why else would he have pursued her? She is a mousy little woman, dull and plain. She's afraid of men. She spent her life in those fancy girls' schools where they taught her how to set the table. She huddled with her mother in that house, afraid of everything. Well, now she is alone and I think she's latched onto the first person who will rescue her from that."

"Does she know how you feel?"

He nodded. "Yes, she does. I made it very clear to her last night."

"How did she take it?"

"She told me to mind my own business." Scolari snorted. "She doesn't even know that that's what I'm doing. She said she loved him and she was going to marry him, no matter what."

"Doesn't sound so mousy to me. She ever stand up to you before?"

"No, never. On anything else, I'd applaud it. But getting married shouldn't be the first decision you ever make."

"Anyone else that might talk to her that she'd listen to?"

"No. She's an only child. Her father died when she was two in the same explosion that killed my father and took my legs. Her mother died in an automobile accident a little over a year ago. I am a widower myself and Gina was never close to my sons. They frightened her as a little girl. They were loud and rough. They teased her and made her cry." Scolari shrugged as if boys would be boys. "I did not like that and would stop it whenever I caught them, but she was such a timid child, their cruelty sprouted whenever she was around. There is no other family."

I picked up the pipe from my desk, stuck it in my mouth, and chewed on it. A glorified pacifier. Kept me from chewing up the inside of my mouth, though. Wouldn't be much of a stretch to take this one on. What the hell, work is work.

"Okay, Mr. Scolari, we'll take the case. I want you to understand that we can't and we won't stop her wedding. There are guys who will do that, and I know who they are, but I wouldn't give you their names. We'll do a background check on this guy and see if we can find something that'll change her mind or your mind. Maybe they really love each other. That happens, you know. This may be a crazy start, but I'm not sure that's a handicap. What's the best way to run a race when you don't know where the finish is?" I sure didn't have an answer and Scolari offered none.

"Mr. Haggerty, I am not averse to taking a risk, but not a

blind one. If there's information out there that will help me calculate the odds, then I want it. That's what I want you to get for me. I appreciate your open mind, Mr. Haggerty. Perhaps you will change my mind, but I doubt it."

"Okay, Mr. Scolari. I need a description of this guy, his name and anything else you know about him. First thing Monday morning, I'll assign an investigator and we'll get on this."

"That won't do, Mr. Haggerty. You need to start on this immediately, this minute."

"Why is that?"

"Because they flew to St. Mary's this morning to get married."

"Aren't we a little late, then?"

"No. You can't apply for a marriage license on St. Mary's until you've been on the island for two days."

"How long to get the application approved?"

"I called the embassy. They say it takes three days to process the application. I'm looking into delaying that, if possible. Once it's issued they say most people get married that day or the next."

"So we've got what, five or six days? Mr. Scolari, we can't run a complete background check in that period of time. Hell, no one can. There just isn't enough time."

"What if you put everyone you've got on this, round the clock?"

"That gets you a maybe and just barely that. He'd have to have a pimple on his backside the size of Mount Rushmore for us to find it that fast. If this guy's the sneaky, cunning, opportunist that you think he is, then he's hidden that, maybe not perfectly, but deep enough that six days won't turn it up. Besides, I can't put everyone on this, we've got lots of other cases that need attention."

"So hire more staff, give them the other cases, and put everyone else on this. Money is no object, Mr. Haggerty. I want you to use all your resources on this."

My jaw hurt from clamping on the dead pipe. Scolari was old enough to make a foolish mistake. I told him it was a long shot at best. What more could I tell him? When did I become clairvoyant, and know how things would turn out? Suppose we did find something, like three dead ex-wives? Right! Let's not kid ourselves—all the staff for six days—round the clock—that's serious money. What was it Rocky said? When you run a business, money's always necessary but it's never sufficient. Don't confuse the two and what you do at the office won't keep you up at night.

I sorted everything into piles and then decided. "All right, Mr. Scolari, we'll do it. I can't even tell you what it'll cost. We'll bill you at our hourly rates plus all the expenses. I think a reasonable retainer would be thirty thousand dollars."

He didn't even blink. It probably wasn't a week's interest on ten million dollars.

"There's no guarantee that we'll find anything, Mr. Scolari, not under these circumstances. You'll know that you did everything you could, but that's all you'll know for sure."

"That's all you ever know for sure, Mr. Haggerty."

I pulled out a pad to make some notes. "Do you know where they went on St. Mary's?"

"Yes. A resort called the Banana Bay Beach Hotel. I have taken the liberty of registering you there."

"Excuse me." I felt like something under his front wheel.

"The resort is quite remote and perched on the side of a cliff. I have been assured that I would not be able to make my way around. I need you to be my legs, my eyes. If your agents learn anything back here, someone has to be able to get that information to my niece. Someone has to be there. I want that someone to be you, Mr. Haggerty. That's what I'm paying for. Your brains, your eyes, your legs, to be there because I can't."

I stared at Scolari's withered legs and the motorized wheelchair he got around in. More than that he had money, lots of money. And money's the ultimate prosthetic.

"Let's start at the top. What's his name?"

The island of St. Mary's is one of lush green mountains that drop straight into the sea. What little flat land there is, is on the west coast, and that's where almost all the people live. The central highlands and peaks are still wild and pristine.

My plane banked around the southern tip of the island and headed toward one of those flat spots, the international airport. I flipped through the file accumulated in those few hours between Enzo Scolari's visit and my plane's departure. While Kelly, my secretary, made travel arrangements I called everyone into the conference room and handed out jobs.

Clancy Hopper was to rearrange caseloads and hire temporary staff to keep the other cases moving. Del Winslow was to start investigating our man Derek Marshall. We had a name, real or otherwise, an address, and phone number. Del would do the house-to-house with the drawing we made from Scolari's description. Larry Burdette would be smilin' and dialin'. Calling every computerized data base we could access to get more information. Every time Marshall's name appeared he'd take the information and hand it to another investigator to verify every fact and then backtrack each one by phone or in person until we could re-create the life of Derek Marshall. Our best chance was with the St. Mary's Department of Licenses. To apply for a marriage license Marshall had to file a copy of his passport, birth certificate, decrees of divorce if previously married, death certificate if widowed, and proof of legal name change, if any. If the records were open to the public, we'd get faxed copies or I'd go to the offices myself and look at them personally. I took one last look at the picture of Gina Dalesandro and then the sketch of Derek Marshall, closed the file, and slipped it into my bag as the runway appeared outside my window.

I climbed out of the plane and into the heat. A dry wind moved the heat around me as I walked into the airport. I showed my passport and had nothing to declare. They were delighted to have me on their island. I stepped out of the airport and the cabmaster introduced me to my driver. I followed him to a battered Toyota, climbed into the front seat, and stowed my bag between my feet. He slammed the door and asked where to.

"Banana Bay Beach Hotel," I said as he turned the engine on and pulled out.

"No problem."

"How much?" We bounced over a sleeping policeman.

"Eighty ecee."

Thirty-five dollars American. "How far is it?"

"Miles or time?"

"Both."

"Fifteen miles. An hour and a half."

I should have gotten out then. If the road to hell is paved at all, then it doesn't pass through St. Mary's. The coast road was a lattice of potholes winding around the sides of the mountains. There were no lanes, no lights, no signs, and no guardrails. The sea was a thousand feet below and we were never more than a few inches from visiting it.

Up and down the hills, there were blue bags on the trees. "What are those bags?" I asked.

"Bananas. The bags keep the insects away while they ripen."

I scanned the slopes and tried to imagine going out there to put those bags on. Whoever did it, they couldn't possibly be paying him enough. Ninety minutes of bobbing and weaving on those roads like a fighter on the ropes and I was exhausted from defying gravity. I half expected to hear a bell to end the trip as we pulled up to the resort.

I checked in, put my valuables in a safe-deposit box, took my key and information packet, and headed up the hill to my room. Dinner was served in about an hour. Enough time to get oriented, unpack, and shower.

My room overlooked the upstairs bar and dining area and below that the beach, the bay, and the surrounding cliffs. I had a thatched-roof verandah with a hammock and clusters of flamboyant and chenille red-hot cattails close enough to pluck. The bathroom was clean and functional. The bedroom large and sparely furnished. Clearly, this was a place where the attractions were outdoors and rooms were for sleeping in. The mosquito netting over the bed and the coils on the dresser were not good signs. It was the rainy season and Caribbean mosquitoes can get pretty cheeky. In Antigua one caught me in the bathroom and pulled back the shower curtain like he was Norman Bates.

I unpacked quickly and read my information packet. It had a map of the resort, a list of services, operating hours, and tips on how to avoid common problems in the Caribbean such as sunburn, being swept out to sea, and a variety of bites, stings, and inedible fruits. I familiarized myself with the layout and took out the pictures of Gina and Derek. Job one was to find them and then tag along unobtrusively until the home office gave me something to work with.

I showered, changed, and lay down on the bed to wait for dinner. The best time to make an appearance was midway through the meal. Catch the early birds leaving and the stragglers on their way in.

Around 8:30, I sprayed myself with insect repellent,

slipped my keys into my pocket, and headed down to dinner. The schedule said that it would be a barbecue on the beach.

At the reception area I stopped and looked over the low wall to the beach below. Scolari was right, he wouldn't be able to get around here. The rooms jutted out from the bluff and were connected by a steep roadway. However, from this point on, the hillside was a precipice. A staircase wound its way down to the beach. One hundred and twenty-six steps, the maid said.

I started down, stopping periodically to check the railing. There were no lights on the trail. Late at night, a little drunk on champagne, a new bride could have a terrible accident. I peered over the side at the concrete roadway below. She wouldn't bounce and she wouldn't survive.

I finished the zigzagging descent and noted that the return trip would be worse.

Kerosene lamps led the way to the beach restaurant and bar. I sat on a stool, ordered a Yellowbird, and turned to look at the dining area. Almost everyone was in couples, the rest were families. All white, mostly Americans, Canadians, British, and German. At least that's what the brochure said.

I sipped my drink and scanned the room. No sign of them. No problem, the night was young even if I wasn't. I had downed a second drink when they came in out of the darkness. Our drawing of Marshall was pretty good. He was slight, pale, with brown hair parted down the middle, round-rimmed tortoiseshell glasses, and a deep dimpled smile he aimed at the woman he gripped by the elbow. He steered her between the tables as if she had a tiller.

They took a table and I looked about to position myself. I wanted to be able to watch Marshall's face and be close enough to overhear them without looking like it. One row over and two up a table was coming free. I took my drink from the bar and ambled over. The busboy cleared the table and I took a long sip from my drink and set it down.

Gina Dalesandro wore a long flower-print dress. Strapless, she had tan lines where her bathing suit had been. She ran a finger over her ear and flipped back her hair. In profile she was thin-lipped, hook-nosed, and high-browed. Her hand held Marshall's, and then, eyes on his, she pulled one to her and kissed it. She moved from one knuckle to the next, and when she was done she took a finger and slowly slid it into her mouth.

"Gina, please, people will look," he whispered.

"Let them," she said, smiling around his finger.

Marshall pulled back and flicked his eyes around. My waitress had arrived and I was ordering when he passed over me. I had the fish chowder, the grilled dolphin with stuffed christophene, and another drink.

Gina picked up Marshall's hand and held it to her cheek and said something soothing because he smiled and blew her a kiss. They ordered and talked in hushed tones punctuated with laughter and smiles. I sat nearby, watching, waiting, her uncle's gargoyle in residence.

When dessert arrived, Gina excused herself and went toward the ladies' room. Marshall watched her go. I read nothing in his face or eyes. When she disappeared into the bathroom, his eyes wandered around the room, but settled on no one. He locked in on her when she reappeared and led her back to the table with his eyes. All in all it proved nothing.

We all enjoyed the banana cake and coffee and after a discreet pause I followed them back toward the rooms. We trudged silently up the stairs, past the bar and the reception desk, and back into darkness. I kept them in view as I went toward my room and saw that they were in Room 7, two levels up and one over from me. When their door clicked closed, I turned around and went back to the activities board outside the bar. I scanned the list of trips for tomorrow to see if they had signed up for any of them. They were down for the morning trip to the local volcano. I signed aboard and went to arrange a wake-up call for the morning.

After a quick shower, I lit the mosquito coils, dialed the lights way down, and crawled under the netting. I pulled the phone and my book inside, propped up the pillows, and called the office. For his money, Scolari should get an answer. He did.

"Franklin Investigations."

"Evening, Del. What do we have on Derek Marshall?"

"Precious little, boss, that's what."

"Well, give it to me."

"Okay, I canvassed his neighborhood. He's the invisible man. Rented apartment. Manager says he's always on time with the rent. Nothing else. I missed the mailman, but I'll catch him tomorrow. See if he can tell me anything. Neighbors know him by sight. That's about it. No wild parties.

Haven't seen him with lots of girls. One thought he was seeing this one particular woman but hasn't seen her around in quite a while."

"How long has he been in the apartment?"

"Three years."

"Manager let you look at the rent application?"

"Leo, you know that's confidential. I couldn't even ask for that information."

"We prosper on the carelessness of others, Del. Did you ask?"

"Yes, and he was offended and indignant."

"Tough shit."

"Monday morning we'll go through court records and permits and licenses for the last three years, see if anything shakes out."

"Neighbors tell you anything else?"

"No, like I said, they knew him by sight, period."

"You find his car?"

"Yeah. Now that was a gold mine. Thing had stickers all over it."

"Such as?"

"Bush-Quayle. We'll check him out with Young Republican organizations. Also, Georgetown Law School."

"You run him through our directories?"

"Yeah, nothing. He's either a drone or modest."

"Call Walter O'Neil, tonight. Give him the name, see if he can get a law firm for the guy, maybe even someone who'll talk about him."

"Okay. I'm also going over to the school tomorrow, use the library, look up yearbooks, et cetera. See if we can locate a classmate. Alumni affairs will have to wait until Monday."

"How about NCIC?"

"Clean. No warrants or arrests. He's good or he's tidy."

"Anything else on the car?"

"Yeah, a sticker for something called Ultimate Frisbee. Nobody here knows anything about it. We're trying to track down an association for it, find out where it's played, then we'll interview people."

"Okay. We've still got three, maybe four days. How's the office doing? Are the other cases being covered?"

"Yeah, we spread them around. Clancy hired a couple of freelancers to start next week. Right now, me, Clancy, and Larry are pulling double shifts on this. Monday when the offices are open and the data bases are up, we'll probably put the two new guys on it."

"Good. Any word from the St. Mary's registrar's office?"

"No. Same problem there. Closed for the weekend. Won't know anything until Monday."

"All right. Good work, Del." I gave him my number. "Call here day or night with anything. If you can't get me directly, have me paged. I'll be out tomorrow morning on a field trip with Marshall and Gina, but I should be around the rest of the day."

"All right. Talk to you tomorrow."

I slipped the phone under the netting. Plumped the pillows and opened my book. Living alone had made me a voracious reader, as if all my other appetites had mutated into a hunger for the words that would make me someone else, put me somewhere else, or at least help me to sleep. The more I read, the harder it was to keep my interest. Boredom crept over me like the slow death it was. I was an old jaded john needing ever kinkier tricks just to get it up, or over with. Pretty soon nothing would move me at all. Until then, I was grateful for Michael Malone and the jolts and length of *Time's Witness*.

I woke up to the telephone's insistent ring, crawled out of bed, and thanked the front desk for the call. A chameleon darted out from under the bed and headed out the door. "Nice seeing you," I called out, and hoped he'd had a bountiful evening keeping my room an insect-free zone. I dressed and hurried down to breakfast.

After a glass of soursop, I ordered saltfish and onions with bakes and lots of coffee. Derek and Gina were not in the dining room. Maybe they'd ordered room service, maybe they were sleeping in and wouldn't make it. I ate quickly and kept checking my watch while I had my second cup of coffee. Our driver had arrived and was looking at the activities board. Another couple came up to him and introduced themselves. I wiped my mouth and left to join the group. Derek and Gina came down the hill as I checked in.

Our driver told us that his name was Wellington Bramble and that he was also a registered tour guide with the Department of the Interior. The other couple climbed into the back of the van, then Derek and Gina in the middle row. I hopped in up front, next to Wellington, turned, and introduced myself.

"Hi, my name is Leo Haggerty."

"Hello, I'm Derek Marshall and this is my fiancée, Gina Dalesandro."

"Pleasure to meet you."

Derek and Gina turned and we were all introduced to Tom and Dorothy Needham of Chicago, Illinois.

Wellington stuck his head out the window and spoke to one of the maids. They spoke rapidly in the local patois until the woman slapped him across the forearm and waved a scolding finger at him.

He engaged the gears, pulled away from the reception area, and told us that we would be visiting the tropical rain forests that surround the island's active volcano. All this in perfect English, the language of strangers and for strangers.

Dorothy Needham asked the question on all of our minds. "How long will we be on this road to the volcano?"

Wellington laughed. "Twenty minutes, ma'am, then we go inland to the volcano."

We left the coast road and passed through a gate marked ST. MARY'S ISLAND CONSERVANCY—DEVIL'S CAULDRON VOLCANO AND TROPICAL RAIN FOREST. I was first out and helped the women step down into the muddy path. Wellington lined us up and began to lead us through the jungle, calling out the names of plants and flowers and answering questions.

There were soursop trees, lime trees, nutmeg, guava, bananas, coconuts, cocoa trees, ginger lilies, lobster-claw plants, flamboyant and hibiscus, impression fern, and chenille red-hot cattails. We stopped on the path at a large fern. Wellington turned and pointed to it.

"Here, you touch the plant, right here," he said, pointing at Derek, who eyed him suspiciously. "It won't hurt you."

Derek reached out a finger and touched the fern. Instantly the leaves retracted and curled in on themselves.

"That's Mary, Mary, Shut the Door. As you can see, a delicate and shy plant indeed."

He waved us on and we followed. Gina slipped an arm through Derek's and put her head on his shoulder. She squeezed him once.

"Derek, you know I used to be like that plant. Before you came along. All closed up and frightened if anybody got too close. But not anymore. I am so happy," she said, and squeezed him again.

Other than a mild self-loathing, I was having a good time, too. We came out of the forest and were on the volcano. Wellington turned to face us.

"Ladies and gentlemen, please listen very carefully. We are on top of an active volcano. There is no danger of an eruption, because there is no crust, so there is no pressure buildup. The last eruption was over two hundred years ago. That does not mean that there is no danger here. You must stay on the marked path at all times and be very careful on the sections that have no guardrail. The water in the volcano is well over three hundred degrees Farenheit; should you stumble and fall in, you would be burned alive. I do not wish to alarm you unreasonably, but a couple of years ago we did lose a visitor, so please be very careful. Now follow me."

We moved along, single file and well spaced through a setting unlike any other I'd ever encountered. The circular top of the volcano looked like a wound on the earth. The ground steamed and smoked and nothing grew anywhere. Here and there black water leaked out of crusty patches like blood seeping from under a scab. The smell of sulfur was everywhere.

I followed Derek and Gina and watched him stop a couple of times and test the railings before he let her proceed. Caution, Derek? Or a trial run?

We circled the volcano and retraced our path back to the van. As promised, we were back at the hotel twenty minutes later. Gina was flushed with excitement and asked Derek if they could go back again. He thought that was possible, but there weren't any other guided tours this week, so they'd have to rent a car and go themselves. I closed my eyes and imagined her by the side of the road, taking a picture perhaps, and him ushering her through the foliage and on her way to eternity.

We all went in for lunch and ate separately. I followed them back to their room and then down to the beach. They moved to the far end of the beach and sat facing away from everyone else. I went into the bar and worked my way through a pair of long necks.

A couple in the dining room was having a spat, or maybe it was a tiff. Whatever, she called him a *schwein* and really tagged him with an open forehand to the chops. His face lit up redder than a baboon's ass.

She pushed back her chair, swung her long blond hair in an about-face, and stormed off. I watched her go, taking each step like she was grinding out a cigarette under her foot. Made her hips and butt do terrible things.

I pulled my eyes away when I realized I had company. He was leering at me enthusiastically.

I swung around slowly. "Yes?"

It was one of the local hustlers who patrolled the beach, as ubiquitous and resourceful as the coconuts that littered the sand.

"I seen you around, man. Y'all alone. That's not a good thin', man. I was thinkin' maybe you could use some company. Someone to share paradise wit'. Watcha say, man?"

I shook my head. "I don't think so."

He frowned. "I know you ain't that way, man. I seen you watch that blonde with the big ones. What'sa matter? What you afraid of?" He stopped and tried to answer that one for me. "She be clean, man. No problem."

When I didn't say anything, he got pissed. "What is it then? You don't fuck strange, man?"

"Watch my lips, bucko. I'm not interested. Don't make more of it than there is."

He sized me up and decided I wasn't worth the aggravation. Spinning off his stool, he called me something in patois. I was sure it wasn't "sir."

I found a free lounge under a bohio and kept an eye on Derek and Gina. No sooner had I settled in than Gina got up and headed across the cocoa-colored volcanic sands to the beach bar. She was a little pink around the edges. Probably wouldn't be out too long today. Derek had his back to me, so I swiveled my head to keep her in sight. She sat down and one of the female staff came over and began to run a comb through her hair. Cornrowing. She'd be there for at least an hour. I ordered a drink from a wandering waiter, closed my eyes, and relaxed.

Gina strolled back, her hair in tight little braids, each one tipped with a series of colored beads. She was smiling and kicking up little sprays of water. I watched her take Derek by the hands and pull him up out of his chair. She twirled around and shook her head back and forth, just to watch the braids fly by. They picked up their snorkels and fins and headed for the water. I watched to see which way they'd go. The left side of the bay had numerous warning signs about the strong current including one on the point that said TURN BACK—NEXT STOP PANAMA.

They went right and so did I. Maybe it was a little fear, maybe it was love, but she held on to his hand while they hovered over the reef. I went farther out and then turned back so I could keep them in sight. The reef was one of the richest I'd ever been on and worthy of its reputation as one of the best in the Caribbean.

I kept my position near the couple, moving when they did, just like the school of squid I was above. They were in formation, tentacles tucked in, holding their position by undulating the fins on each lateral axis. When the school moved, they all went at once and kept the same distance from each other. I drifted off the coral to a bed of sea grass. Two creatures were walking through the grass. Gray green, with knobs and lumps everywhere, they had legs and wings! They weren't toxic-waste mutants, just the flying gurnards. I dived down on them and they spread their violet wings and took off.

When I surfaced, Derek and Gina were heading in. I swam downstream from them and came ashore as they did. Gina was holding her side and peeking behind her palm. Derek steadied her and helped get her flippers off.

"I don't know what it was, Derek. It just brushed me and then it felt like a bee sting. It really burns," Gina said.

I wandered by and said, "Looks like a jellyfish sting. When did it happen?"

"Just a second ago." They answered in unison.

"Best thing for that is papaya skins. Has an enzyme that neutralizes the toxin. The beach restaurant has plenty of them. They keep it just for things like this. You better get right over, though. It only works if you apply it right away."

"Thanks. Thanks a lot," Derek said, then turned to help Gina down the beach. "Yes, thank you," she said over his shoulder.

"You're welcome," I said to myself, and went to dry off.

• • •

I sat at the bar, waiting for dinner and playing backgammon with myself. Derek and Gina came in and went to the bar to order. Her dress was a swirl of purple, black, and white and matched the color of the beads in her hair. Derek wore lime-green shorts and a white short-sleeved shirt. Drinks in hand, they walked over to me. I stood up, shook hands, and invited them to join me.

"That tip of yours was a lifesaver. We went over to the bar and got some papaya on it right away. I think the pain was gone in maybe five minutes. How did you know about it?" Gina asked.

"I've been stung myself before. Somebody told me about it. Now I tell you. Word of mouth."

"Well, we're very grateful. We're getting married here on the island and I didn't want anything to mess this time up for us," Derek said.

I raised my glass in a toast. "Congratulations to you. This is a lovely place to get married. When is the ceremony?" I asked, sipping my drink.

"Tomorrow," Gina said, running her arm through Derek's. "I'm so excited."

I nearly drowned her in rerouted rum punch but managed to turn away and choke myself instead. I pounded my chest and waved off any assistance.

"Are you okay?" Derek asked.

"Yes, yes, I'm fine," I said as I got myself under control. Tomorrow? How the hell could it be tomorrow? "Sorry. I was trying to talk when I was drinking. Just doesn't work that way."

Derek asked if he could buy me another drink and I let him take my glass to the bar.

"I read the tourist brochure about getting married on the island. How long does it take for them to approve an application? They only said that you have to be on the island for two days before you can submit an application."

Gina leaned forward and touched my knee. "It usually takes two or three days, but Derek found a way to hurry things up. He sent the papers down early to the manager here and he agreed to file them for us as if we were on the island. It'll be ready tomorrow morning and we'll get married right after noon."

"That's wonderful. Where will the ceremony be?" My head was spinning.

"Here at the hotel. Down on the beach. They provide a cake, champagne, photographs, flowers. Would you join us afterward to celebrate?"

"Thank you, that's very kind. I'm not sure that I'll still be here, though. My plane leaves in the afternoon, and you know with that ride back to the airport, I might be gone. If I'm still here, I'd be delighted."

Derek returned with drinks and sat close to Gina and looped an arm around her.

"Honey, I hope you don't mind, but I invited Mr. Haggerty to join us after the ceremony." She smiled anxiously.

"No, that sounds great, love to have you. By the way, it sounded like you've been to the islands before. This is our first time. Have you ever gone scuba diving?" Derek was all graciousness.

"Yeah, are you thinking of trying it?"

"Maybe, they have a course for beginners tomorrow. We were talking about taking the course and seeing if we liked it," he said.

"I'm a little scared. Is it really dangerous?" Gina asked.

Absolutely lethal. Russian roulette with one empty chamber. Don't do it. Wouldn't recommend it to my worst enemy.

"No, not really. There are dangers if you're careless, and they're pretty serious ones. The sea is not very forgiving of our mistakes. But if you're well trained and maintain some respect for what you're doing, it's not all that dangerous."

"I don't know. Maybe I'll just watch you do it, Derek."

"Come on, honey. You really liked snorkeling. Can you imagine how much fun it would be if you didn't have to worry about coming up for air all the time?" Derek gave Gina a squeeze. "And besides, I love the way you look in that new suit."

I saw others heading to the dining room and began to clean up the tiles from the board.

"Mr. Haggerty, would you—" Gina began.

"I'm sure we'll see Mr. Haggerty again, Gina. Thanks for your help this afternoon," Derek said, and led her to the dining room.

I finished my drink and took myself to dinner. After that, I sat and watched them dance to the shak-shak band. She put her head on his shoulder and molded her body to his. They swayed together in the perfect harmony only lovers and mothers and babies have.

They left that way, her head on his shoulder, a peaceful smile on her lips. I could not drink enough to cut the ache I felt and went to bed when I gave up trying.

Del was in when I called and gave me the brief bad news.

"The mailman was a dead end. I went over to the school library and talked to teachers and students. So far, nobody's had anything useful to tell us. I've got a class list and we're working our way through it. Walt did get a lead on him, though. He's a junior partner in a small law firm, a 'boutique' he called it."

"What kind of law?" Come on, say tax and estate.

"Immigration and naturalization."

"Shit. Anything else?"

"Yeah, he's new there. Still don't know where he came from. We'll try to get some information from the partners first thing in the morning."

"It better be first thing. Our timetable just went out the window. They're getting married tomorrow at noon."

"Jesus Christ, that puts the screws to us. We'll only have a couple of hours to work with."

"Don't remind me. Is that it?"

"For right now. Clancy is hitting bars looking for people that play this 'Ultimate Frisbee' thing. He's got a sketch with him. Hasn't called in yet."

"Well, if he finds anything, call me no matter what time it is. I'll be around all morning tomorrow. If you don't get me direct, have me paged, as an emergency. Right now we don't have shit."

"Hey, boss, we just ran out of time. I'm sure in a couple of days we'd have turned something up."

"Maybe so, Del, but tomorrow around noon somebody's gonna look out over their heads and ask if anybody has anything to say or forever hold your peace. I don't see myself raising my hand and asking for a couple of more days, 'cause we're bound to turn something up."

"We did our best. We just weren't holding very good cards is all."

"Del, we were holding shit." I should have folded when Scolari dealt them.

I hung up and readied my bedroom to repel all boarders. Under the netting, I sat and mulled over my options. I had no reason to stick my nose into Gina's life. No reason at all to think that Derek was anything but the man she'd waited her whole life for. Her happiness was real, though. She was blossoming under his touch. I had seen it. And happiness is a fragile thing. Who was I to cast a shadow on hers? And without any reason. Tomorrow was a special day for her. How would she remember it? How would I?

I woke early from a restless night and called the office. Nothing new. I tried Scolari's number and spoke briefly to him. I told him we were out of time and had nothing of substance. I asked him a couple of questions and he gave me some good news and some bad. There was nothing else to do, so I went down to see the betrothed.

They were in the dining room holding hands and finishing their coffee. I approached and asked if I could join them.

"Good morning, Mr. Haggerty. Lovely day, isn't it?" Gina said, her face aglow.

I settled into the chair and decided to smack them in the face with it. "Before you proceed with your wedding, I have some news for you."

They sat upright and took their hands, still joined, off the table.

"Gina's uncle, Enzo Scolari, wishes me to inform you that he has had his attorneys activate the trustee's discretionary powers over Miss Dalesandro's portion of the estate so that she cannot take possession of the money or use it in any fashion without his consent. He regrets having to take this action, but your insistence on this marriage leaves him no choice."

"You son of a bitch. You've been spying on us for that bastard," Derek shouted, and threw his glass of water at me. I sat there dripping while I counted to ten. Gina had gone pale and was on the verge of tears. Marshall stood up. "Come on, Gina, let's go. I don't want this man anywhere near me." He leaned forward and stabbed a finger at me. "I intend to call your employer, Mr. Scolari, and let him know what a despicable piece of shit I think he is, and that goes double for you." He turned away. "Gina, are you coming?"

"Just a second, honey," she whispered. "I'll be along in just a second." Marshall crashed out of the room, assaulting chairs and tables that got in his way.

"Why did you do this to me? I've waited my whole life

for this day. To find someone who loves me and wants to live with me and to celebrate that. We came here to get away from my uncle and his obsessions. You know what hurts the most? You reminded me that my uncle doesn't believe that anyone could love me for myself. It has to be my money. What's so wrong with *me*? Can you tell me that?" She was starting to cry and wiped at her tears with her palms. "Hell of a question to be asking on your wedding day, huh? You do good work, Mr. Haggerty. I hope you're proud of yourself."

I'd rather Marshall had thrown acid in my face than the words she hurled at me. "Think about one thing, Miss Dalesandro. This way you can't lose. If he doesn't marry you now, you've avoided a lot of heartache and maybe worse. If he does, knowing this, then you can relax knowing it's you and not your money. The way I see it, either way you can't lose. But I'm sorry. If there had been any other way, I'd have done it."

"Yes, well, I have to go, Mr. Haggerty." She rose, dropped her napkin on the table, and walked slowly through the room, using every bit of dignity she could muster.

I spent the rest of the morning in the bar waiting for the last act to unfold.

At noon, Gina appeared in a long white dress. She had a bouquet of flowers in her hands and was trying hard to smile. I sipped some anesthetic and looked away. No need to make it any harder now. I wasn't sure whether I wanted Marshall to show up or not.

Derek appeared at her side in khaki slacks and an embroidered white shirt. What will be, will be. They moved slowly down the stairs. I went to my room, packed, and checked out. By three o'clock I was off the island and on my way home.

It was almost a year later when Kelly buzzed me on the intercom to say that a Mr. Derek Marshall was here to see me.

"Show him in."

He hadn't changed a bit. Neither one of us moved to shake hands. When I didn't invite him to sit down, he did anyway.

"What do you want, Marshall?"

"You know, I'll never forget that moment when you told

me that Scolari had altered the trust. Right there in public. I was so angry that you'd try to make me look bad like that in front of Gina and everyone else. It really has stayed with me. And here I am, leaving the area. I thought I'd come by and return the favor before I left."

"How's Gina?" I asked with a veneer of nonchalance over trepidation.

"Funny you should ask. I'm a widower, you know. She had a terrible accident about six months ago. We were scuba diving. It was her first time. I'd already had some courses. I guess she misunderstood what I'd told her and she held her breath coming up. Ruptured a lung. She was dead before I could get her to shore."

I almost bit through my pipe stem. "You're a real piece of work, aren't you? Pretty slick, death by misinformation. Got away with it, didn't you?"

"The official verdict was accidental death. Scolari was beside himself, as you can imagine. There I was, sole inheritor of Gina's estate, and according to the terms of the trust her half of the grandfather's money was mine. It was all in Scolari stock, so I made a deal with the old man. He got rid of me and I got paid fifty percent more than the shares were worth."

"You should be careful, Derek, that old man hasn't got long to live. He might decide to take you with him."

"That thought has crossed my mind. So I'm going to take my money and put some space between him and me."

Marshall stood up to leave. "By the way, your bluff wasn't half-bad. It actually threw me there for a second. That's why I tossed the water on you. I had to get away and do some thinking, make sure I hadn't overlooked anything. But I hadn't."

"How did you know it was a bluff?" You cocky little shit.

Marshall pondered that a moment. "It doesn't matter. You'll never be able to prove this. It's not on paper anywhere. While I was in law school I worked one year as an unpaid intern at the law firm handling the estate of old man Scolari, the grandfather. This was when Gina's mother died. I did a turn in lots of different departments. I read the documents when I was Xeroxing them. That's how I knew the setup. Her mother's share went to Gina. Anything happens to her and the estate is transferred according to the terms of Gina's will. An orphan, with no siblings. That made me sole

inheritor, even if she died intestate. Scolari couldn't change
the trust or its terms. Your little stunt actually convinced
Gina of my sincerity. I wasn't in any hurry to get her to write
a will and she absolutely refused to do it when Scolari
pushed her on it.

"Like I said, for a bluff it wasn't half-bad. Gina believed
you, but I think she was the only one who didn't know anything about her money. Well, I've got to be going, got a plane
to catch." He smiled at me like he was a dog and I was his
favorite tree.

It was hard to resist the impulse to threaten him, but a
threat is also a warning and I had no intention of playing fair.
I consoled myself with the fact that last time I only had two
days to work with. Now I had a lifetime. When I heard the
outer door close, I buzzed Kelly on the intercom.

"Yes, Mr. Haggerty?"

"Reopen the file on Derek Marshall."

acknowledgments

I'd like to thank the following people for their contributions
to this story: Joyce Huxley of Scuba St. Lucia for her
information on hyperbaric accidents; Michael and Alison
Weber of Charlottesville for the title and good company, and
John Cort and Rebecca Barbetti for including us in their
wedding celebration and tales of "the spork" among other
things.

The drama played out between sleuth and criminal is most engrossing when the adversaries are well matched; the wilier the opponent, the more satisfying the victory. Hide-and-seek, parry and riposte, the balance shifts first one way and then the other as one side tries to obscure the truth while the other strives mightily to uncover it. Michael Collins, in "Role Model," and Sarah Andrews, in "Invitation," play out intriguing variations on the theme in two provocative stories.

role model

MICHAEL COLLINS

As "Michael Collins," Dennis Lynds is the creator of one-armed PI Dan Fortune. The first Fortune novel, Act of Fear, published in 1967, won Mr. Collins/ Lynds an MWA Edgar Award for Best First Novel. His most recent Fortune novel, Cassandra in Red, proves that twenty-five years later both Fortune and Michael Collins are going strong. Dennis Lynds has also written successful mystery series as "Mark Sadler" and "William Arden." He is a past president of PWA, a winner of the PWA Life Achievement Award, and a member of Sisters in Crime. He is also living proof that winning a life achievement award does not mean that your achievements are complete.

Role Model is vintage Collins, taking Dan Fortune back to his former haunt, New York City, where many of us miss him since his move to the West Coast.

His voice shook so much it sounded far more than three thousand miles away.

"Brett Darcy, Fortune. They killed Jake. The cops just told me. Get here as fast as you can. All expenses."

It was 6:10 A.M. in Santa Barbara. In bed beside me, Kay rolled over with her head under the pillow.

"Jake who?"

"Good God, Fortune, is there more than one Jake I'd call about at this hour? Jake Butler. Number 99. The Bonecrusher. They shot Jake Butler in some stinking alley."

Brett Darcy owned a football team that had played in more than one city, kept his main office in New York no matter where the team played. He was a lawyer, had a lot of other irons in the fire, New York was the place to be. But the team was the apple of his eye, and Jake Butler had once been the rock the team was built on. I'd worked for Darcy before, but New York has a lot of detectives.

"Why me, Darcy?"

"Because you know that Captain Pearce. I'll cry for Jake, Fortune, he was the best lineman I ever had. But I'd heard he was on the skids, and I don't want it to rub off on the team. I want our own man on the case so we have time to cover any slime."

It was honest. I gave my terms, including a week up front when dealing with billionaire businessmen in case things don't turn out right. He took my terms without a murmur. He's a sharp man, rich and educated. The new breed of sports owner. I promised to be in New York by five or six o'clock, hung up, and got dressed.

"I suppose you have to go back once in a while," Kay said. "Just to keep me from taking you for granted."

"Don't pout, you're too dignified even naked. Get up, I'll cook breakfast."

Captain Pearce's office gets more like old Captain Gazzo's every time I see it, especially now I live out in California and don't see it that often. Messy and neglected, as if he doesn't give a flying damn for such small things anymore. In perpetual midnight, shades drawn all hours. Maybe, in the end, it goes with the job.

"How do you like it in Tinsel Land, Fortune? La-La Town?"

"That's La-La Land and Tinseltown, Captain, and we don't live in Los Angeles."

"Whatever. Where do you live?"

"Santa Barbara. Ninety miles north. Warm days and cool nights. Mountains, sun, and sea. Not too many people yet."

Pearce looked at the drawn shades of his dim and cluttered office. He's a college man, seemed to be wondering how he had ended up where he was. He sighed, opened a folder on his desk.

"Vice found Butler's body early yesterday morning in an alley behind a NoHo club. Shot once in the head, half the head blown away. Five bags of crack in his pocket. Wallet still in his jacket. No cash or credit cards, but everything else including his California driver's license. No jewelry, not even a watch, except his two Super Bowl rings. The—"

"They took his cash, credit cards, and his watch, but left his rings?"

"Left the crack, too. Five good bags."

I looked at Pearce's covered windows that were like blind eyes. "It doesn't make much sense."

"That's not all that doesn't make sense," Pearce said. "The gun was in the alley next to his body. It traces out to a dead end. One of those 'specials' you buy in the right places."

"A gun to do a job like a robbery. The most valuable loot left behind, the gun left behind. Sounds like a plain robbery and the killer panicked, Captain."

Pearce studied his own blind windows. "Shot Butler in the mouth, wiped off his prints, put Butler's prints on the gun, and left it. Does that sound like panic in a dark alley, Dan? *Only* Butler's prints on the gun. The barrel would have to have been put into his mouth to blow the back of his head off. Then the gun was wiped and placed neatly on the ground."

The silent office filled with the noises beyond his closed door. The voices and protests of the accused: outraged and angry, pleading and whining. The cool drone of the police.

I said, "Suicide? He didn't *have* any money, credit cards, or a watch? Hooked on crack, broke, failed his fans? The tarnished role model?"

"The ME says he'd go for suicide ninety percent."

"Not you?"

"We have problems." He rocked in his chair. It creaked.

"Who buys crack and then shoots themselves without smoking the crack first? Few suicides do it alone in a back alley without telling anyone or leaving a note." He continued to rock. "Then there's the blood and bone and brain tissue."

"Blood? Tissue?"

"Not enough, and he didn't walk far with half a head. Not even Jake Butler. Medical examiner can't explain it except by saying we'd had a heavy rain that maybe washed most of it away."

"But you think he was shot somewhere else." Sometimes experience tells you as much as evidence. "What else don't you like, Captain?"

"No word where he made the buy. No word on him at all. And we've pulled in a lot of markers. Not a word to place him in the area doing anything."

"They could be too scared because he was so famous."

"They could be."

Darcy Enterprises, as befits a sports empire, was in a building not far from the new Madison Square Garden. Newly painted and carpeted in the team colors, blue and silver, the offices took an entire floor. The reception room and corridors were lined with action portraits of everyone who had played on the team. Famous, infamous, or also-ran. Larger and more often for the famous, and Jake Butler looked down at me life-size at least a dozen times on my route to the executive suite.

"Sit down, Fortune."

The suite had an outer office, a kitchen, an antechamber with wet bar, and the inner corner office from where Brett Darcy ruled his empire. New Jersey, Brooklyn, the upper bay, and the distant sea all visible in a wide arc through the windows.

"You know my wife?"

"Mrs. Darcy." I nodded to the tall redhead stretched on a dark green velvet couch that faced the windows and Darcy.

"Ms. La Luna. La Luna Cosmetics, you know? My real and business name. In public the business name. How did you lose the arm? The war?"

It was a long couch, but she filled it end to end. A whisper under six feet, her long hair was a rich dark red between auburn and strawberry blond. Her blue slacks were skintight without looking tight. A trick that had cost thousands of dollars she hadn't acquired by being shy. I didn't hit her with one of the snarling stories I have for the curious. She did that to you. You called it refreshing honesty and simplicity, and smiled.

"Something like that."

She was Darcy's third wife, and if she'd set her sights on him she'd gotten a lot more than money. Darcy was a trim six-foot-four, as handsome and athletic as Ted Turner. At forty-one, he wasn't more than two years older than Ms. La Luna. A Rhodes scholar and Harvard Law graduate. Maybe it was love. But love wasn't what Brett Darcy had on his mind.

"What did you get from Pearce?"

I told him the facts I'd gotten from Pearce. "The real kicker is that none of their pigeons or contacts know anything about Butler doing a buy or anything else down there."

"Suicide? Jake Butler?" He swiveled, scowled out his rows of high windows at the Brooklyn half of his view. "That's crazy. Christ, Fortune, he could lift a Honda and break an I-beam in his bare hands. An animal. Animals don't commit suicide. Right, Helen?"

Helen (La Luna) Darcy said, "He was too gentle, Dan."

"You knew Butler well, Ms. La Luna?"

"I know all of Brett's employees." She sat up, shook her head sadly. "Jake was the softest man I ever met. Even shy. I don't think he would be capable of any violence off the football field, especially not against himself. He was almost afraid of his strength. An overgrown boy, really."

She seemed to have as much interest in Jake Butler as her husband, but I had my doubts that boys of any kind would be high on her list of men. Except for that next-to-the-last line: Jake Butler afraid of his own strength, of what he might have done with that strength. Strength would attract Helen Darcy. It wasn't money that drew a woman like her to men like Darcy, it was power. In our society money is power, but not the only kind.

"There's got to be something else, Fortune." Darcy swiveled back to face me. "Five bags of crack. As I said on the phone, I've been hearing about Jake being in trouble. The scum down there could be too afraid of who Jake was to talk to the police."

"The police don't think he was shot in that alley."

Helen Darcy said, "On what do they base that, Dan?"

I told them Pearce's problems. Brett Darcy seemed to think about them.

Helen Darcy frowned. "It could have happened in a room ten feet away. In a car parked in the alley. In any of the buildings that back onto that alley."

"Helen's probably right." Darcy nodded. "But I don't like it. Could be a frame-up that might involve very bad characters. That could rub off on the team." Darcy gave me the exit line. "Cissie outside has your check. Find out what poor old Jake had gotten himself into. Remember, your first job is to keep Darcy Enterprises out of it as much as possible."

I sent the check to my bank express mail. Then I called Captain Pearce. They had thought of everything Helen Darcy had, were checking it all out, but it didn't look promising so far. Except maybe the car theory. A car had parked in that alley that night, left tracks in the mud after the rain.

He talks to few people, his name doesn't matter. It's not real anyway. Not the name he has up here. In Colombia he has a name and a place. A powerful place. Up here he barely exists.

"It will fade away, your drug war. When your administration has a more visible demon. When the more notorious leaders of the cartels have been killed or incarcerated. When the epidemic of crack in your slums has diminished enough to be again useful."

He is an educated man. An American university, our military training school in Panama. Prominent in old-family Colombian politics on the side that happened to be out now, the business associate of both the Medellín and Cali cartels, and of other cartels we don't know about yet up here. He doesn't sell any cocaine or heroin, he supervises. If it wasn't drugs, it would be emeralds or another product. A businessman.

"But the trade will go on?" I said.

"As long as there is a demand, of course."

I had done him favors years ago through my old connections to Andy Pappas and the Mafia. In Colombia, where Side A and Side B of the same oligarchy have been warring and dividing up the wealth for two hundred years, favors are paid.

"Tell me about Jake Butler."

"There is nothing to tell. He appears to have been a most visible man, your Mr. Jake Butler. My people at all levels know of him, if I do not. But here, in the business, he is completely invisible, as I am sure the police have told you."

"They've been checking, too?"

He smiled. "Of course they have been checking, which you know as well as I do. We all have our sources in the enemy camp, yes? It is an ancient game. One wins today, another tomorrow."

"But the people lose every day."

"It is their destiny."

The afternoon sun rested on the city outside. In the empty restaurant only thin shafts of sun through the closed shutters caught the dust motes. It wasn't open, we weren't there.

"No word on Butler buying the crack?"

"He did not buy it in that area, or anywhere in this city. That I guarantee. If he bought the drug, he brought it with him."

"If he bought it? You think it was a setup?"

"The consensus on the street is against it. There seems to be no angle to a setup, no bottom line. No advantage, no profit."

Without an angle, a bottom line, who would set Jake Butler up as a junkie?

Most slum families are large. There isn't much money, there isn't much work, and there isn't much fun. On what money they have they get drunk. Men and women. It's the cheapest escape from pain.

Jake Butler had six brothers and four sisters. Eight had survived to adulthood thanks to a mother who worked long and hard to raise them after her husband died in a street brawl. Only Jake's sister, Maddy, lived in the east.

"Jake, he come to see me maybe three times."

You get out of the slums how you can. For Jake it had been football. For one of his brothers it had been armed robbery. For Maddy it had been marriage to a man with a decent blue-collar job. The house was a semidetached in Queens on a street that had seen better days. But Maddy Johnson, née Butler, had curtains at her windows, a color TV and comfortable furniture in her living room, food in the big freezer-refrigerator in her shiny kitchen.

"What did he talk about, Maddy?"

She shrugged, looked out through her neat curtains. "Jake don't talk much. Now I guess he don't never talk no more."

She started to cry. A solid woman with the soft face of a child and an expression that never changed even as she cried.

"You know what he's been doing since he left football?"

"Jake never done left football, Mr. Fortune. My mom said Jake was playin' semipro out on the coast, helpin' out coachin' at his old high school, workin' nights down to the mall."

"The mall?"

She shrugged again. The gesture of the twentieth century. The shrug of resignation, of what's the use? The dream of the weak and poor to rise as one is gone. The dream now is to get yours. A dream of the aristocrat and the barbarian.

"What happened to all the money he made?"

"He don't make that much. Those was the days before the big bucks. I mean Jake done okay, give a lot to Mom and the family. The lawyers for Todd an' all. Mom say he lost money in a couple o' businesses don't pan out. Some pizza joints. A bar."

"What was he doing at the mall?"

"Security, I guess. He was tryin' to be a fighter, too. I heard some guys wanted him to do that wrestlin'. Jake he said it was all phony, but fightin', it was okay."

"You mean boxing? Professional?"

She nodded. That is the other gesture of the twentieth century. The shrug and the nod. As if there is nothing to say and even less desire to say it.

"He talked about taking up boxing when he visited you?"

"Some. He mostly come to borrow money. For his rent."

"He couldn't pay his rent?"

"He only come in from the coast a month ago, an' he just start workin' with his fighter friend. Walt Green, or Rashid Green. A gym over in Jersey. New Brunswick or maybe Trenton. Mario's Gym."

"Did you give him money, Maddy?"

"What you think? 'Course I give him some money. Ain't got much to give, but me'n Horace done what we could.

Horace offer to try to get him a job drivin' trucks like Horace. Jake said he'd sure think about it, but he wanted to try fightin' an' maybe a couple other ideas first." The tears started again, dropping down her expressionless face. "Last time I seen Jake."

"Was he on drugs, Maddy?"

She was silent. "I been thinkin' about that. Jake done some grass back in California, before and after he was in football, but I never saw him use nothin' heavy. It wasn't drugs Jake got high on, Mr. Fortune, it was football. Sports. Just bein' in that there world, you know? The guys, the crowd, winnin'." She shook her head, shook away a tear. "Ever since he was a kid that there was all the high Jake he ever need."

Brett Darcy had paid for the hotel without protest. The Cavendish is small, tucked away on the East Side, and expensive. Darcy wanted to keep me happy. I didn't think he wanted me so happy he'd sent the lady who waited in the lobby.

"We need to talk," Helen (La Luna) Darcy said. "The bar."

Like everything else at the Cavendish, the lounge was small, quiet, elegant, and expensive, but even it looked drab as Helen Darcy swept into it with me trailing behind. She wore a blue body suit and floppy top that was *très chic* and took panache to wear. She had panache to burn. That's what gets the Brett Darcys. Then, a lot of men have money, it's the panache of a Darcy that gets the Helen La Lunas. Fair is fair.

"I like good white wine."

I ordered the most expensive white wine on the list. It was a Montrachet la Guiche. Even her eyebrows went up.

"Can you afford that?"

"No, but your husband can."

She waved the waiter back, canceled the Montrachet for a good Chardonnay. "I don't want this to draw attention on your report or expense account. The Chalone will make Brett mad enough, but he'll accept it."

They don't serve that kind of wine by the glass. She watched the waiter bring bottle, ice bucket, and glasses, pour my taste, get my nod, pour full, and leave. Her foot swung the whole time.

"Jake Butler was fixing fights out in California."

I drank. It's a great white. "How do you know, and why didn't Brett tell me?"

"Brett doesn't know." She drank. "It would kill him, Dan. He loved that man like a son. Jake was all of Brett's greatest moments. If he knew Jake had a reason to kill himself, and probably did, it would destroy him."

I had trouble picturing anything except the loss of a few billion destroying Brett Darcy. On the other hand, Jake Butler *had* been Darcy's greatest player at his greatest sports moments. Owners can come to think they're athletes and heroes, too.

"How do you know?"

"A team scout out in California heard about it and told me. He knew what it would do to Brett. We kept it quiet, but you should know. It does give poor Jake a motive to kill himself."

"Or to be killed," I said.

"I suppose that, too. Jake was basically such an honest man."

And knew too much. "You know any details?"

She stood. "The fights were all in L.A., the fixer's name is Reuben Huerta. I have to go. Remember, not a word of this to Brett. Maybe it's nothing, but—"

She let it hang as she swirled out of the elegant lounge, leaving a vivid impression of flying red hair and a body made entirely of blue skin. She also left over half a bottle of the Chardonnay. It was good I was going nowhere until morning.

Mario's Gym was in Trenton. The Metroliner got me there before noon, with only a light hangover after a decent breakfast. It took me another hour to find the gym in a run-down section of the grimy New Jersey state capital. As I walked in, a fight was finishing in the center ring.

A training fight—headguards, safety belts, and pillow gloves. An older man was brawling a much younger kid. The older fighter was anywhere from thirty-five to sixty-five, his face battered but his body still taut despite an alligator skin that glistened with sweat. The kid's face was red from some hard shots even the pillows had failed to soften, and as I watched he took a solid left that drew blood from his lip.

"Son of a bitch!"

The kid picked off the old man's right, fired a real right of his own that missed by six inches as the older man moved neatly. Someone rang the bell.

"You see what the old bastard—" the kid yelled at a stocky man in a sweatshirt at ringside.

"I want a rematch," the old fighter said.

"Rematch?" the kid said to the sweatshirt.

"Get your shower," sweatshirt said to the kid. "You can't keep your face out of *his* glove, how you gonna fight someone real?" He turned to the older fighter. "Shower up, Johnny, an' come to the office for your dough."

"Sure, Mario."

Mario patted the older fighter on the shoulder, walked to me. He noticed my absent arm. "I can make a fighter out of almost anyone, but you're too old." He had a nice touch with human relations. "What can I do for you?"

I nodded to the older fighter who still leaned against the ring ropes. "What did he mean, a rematch?"

"What he said." He didn't look back at the older fighter, only at me. "Johnny's got some head damage, thinks every fight is for the money. Thinks he's still fighting for real. It makes him a hell of a spoiler, keeps these kids on their toes."

"Useful," I said.

"What else he gonna do to make a buck?"

What else was Johnny going to do? Shine shoes? Welfare? My guess was Mario paid him pretty well for making the macho kids work harder than they expected, and Johnny got to think he was still a fighter and a human being. Not a bad arrangement.

"I'm looking for Walt Green? Maybe Rashid Green?"

"Or Bucky Taylor or Ali ben Ali or Jack Dempsey the Fourth," Mario said. "Walt—the Salt—Green."

He was telling me that Green was an "opponent." One of that legion of fighters at the bottom of fight posters who fatten the wins of rising young hopefuls. They make it possible for twenty-year-olds to go on ESPN with 19–0 records, compile 19–60 records themselves under ten names in fifteen states and five countries.

"When does he come in?"

Mario looked at the wall clock. "Should be here now. All depends if he can get his car to run."

There have always been "opponents." If a hopeful can't

beat them, he isn't going far. You don't want kids with futures
going around battering each other before either is ready, so
where else are the fledgling Tysons to get their practical experience? Where else are promoters going to get cheap
replacements for no-shows?

"You want to talk to me?"

In ring trunks and headgear he looked like any other
fighter. No more battered, no less. A solid middleweight.
Taller, with a thick neck and bullet head, but longer, thinner
legs. That was good for an "opponent," helped him fight at
any weight from welter to light heavy without looking too
obvious a fraud.

"Tell me about Jake Butler."

He sat heavily on a weight bench. "Shit, that was real
bad, man, real bad. They know who done it?"

"They don't even know why."

"Shit."

"How long had you been teaching him to fight?"

He shook his head and looked at the floor. "They sus-
pends my license a couple years ago, I goes to L.A. Jake he a
fight fan, you know? He come aroun', we gets to talkin'. He
say maybe he be a fighter. I tells him anytime he want to
fight I manage him. He money in the bank. People they
come to see the Bonecrusher fight. A couple, maybe three
weeks ago he calls me."

"You were working with him here? Teaching him?"

"I work with him. Two weeks. Then I quit, I tell him to
quit."

"That bad?"

"Worse, man. I mean, I could beat him in a round. Any
round. An' I'm a middleweight. He was musclebound, got a
glass jaw an' no moves. He too old an' slow. Like, man, we
tried. Maybe, a couple years ago he get good enough he lose
without they throw garbage. Smart manager make a bundle
on him. Not now, an' he Jake Butler, you know? No way I let
Jake Butler be no freak."

"You told him to quit fighting?"

"He never start fightin', man. I tell him quit *tryin'* to
fight. I got to knock the big guy down two, three times 'fore I
makes him unnerstan'."

Playing semipro football on the coast, doing what
sounded like unpaid high-school coaching, and working
nights as a security guard at some mall. Money gone for his

mother and lawyers for his brother. Money lost in some pizza parlors and a bar. Then he had to stop thinking about maybe being a fighter.

"How did he take it?"

"He don't kiss me. But he Jake Butler, he take it okay."

"He say what he planned to do?"

Green shook his head. He was itching to be moving, punching. That was what kept them in the ring, no matter how many fights they lost. The money, yes, what other way to make money did most of them have, but in the end it was the action. Even when they lost two fights in a single night, under two different names at two different weights. Whatever the promoter needed. They knew about the downside, the lies, the fix.

"You know a man named Reuben Huerta? Out on the coast?"

"Shit, yeah. Who don't know that motherfucker? Slimy as a snake an' ten times's crooked."

"There's word that Jake was involved with Huerta, fixing fights on the coast."

"Jake never do nothin' like that. Jake he keep his name clean, you hear? That why he got no eyes for that wrestlin', why he walk away from fightin' when I tell him all he be was a clown worse'n me."

He was punching the heavy bag hard when I left. If Jake tried to fight or wrestle, he'd be a clown. Had it made him look for another choice?

Moving with the sun, the afternoon flight from Kennedy gets into LAX in the early evening. It gave me time to visit with Jake's mother in Oxnard, spend a night at home up in Santa Barbara.

A tall, spare woman with a thin mouth and steel eyes, Alice Mae Butler's gaunt face was suspicious and unfriendly. Raising ten kids alone in an L.A. ghetto slum, watching two die, does not make you especially loving or trusting of your fellow humans. The big house Jake had bought was dirty and ragged among the manicured lawns of an upper-middle-class neighborhood. Ghetto life doesn't foster middle-class standards.

"Jake's dead. What you care who done it?"

"Brett Darcy hired me to find out, Mrs. Butler."

"Ms. Butler. I earn the name, got no part o' that dead fool. What's that Darcy care 'bout Jake? He make a lot o' money, what more he want from Jake?" She might not care about middle-class values, but her ghetto suspicions were finely honed. "He figure Jake he got killed dealin' shit, don't want the good name o' the team dirtied up, right?"

"What do you figure Jake got killed doing?"

"How I know what Jake got killed doin', mister? He as big a fool as that old fool Butler hisself." Anger in her eyes at her son for dying and leaving her without another son as well as no husband. Leaving her without her meal ticket, the only man who'd ever made life sweeter.

In her anger and rage her voice had grown loud. A neighbor across the street glared from behind a lawn mower on his immaculate grounds. A young man and woman came out of the front door behind Mrs. Butler. They both had angry faces and surly eyes, the same slouching manner and ultramod designer clothes. The young woman smoked, her cigarette dangling arrogantly.

"What the fuck's all the noise, Ma?" the young man demanded.

"That honky botherin' you, Alice Mae?" the girl drawled, fixed her vacant gaze on my empty sleeve.

Alice Mae Butler turned on them, snarling. "You call me Ma, girl, an' you mind your mouth, Josh Butler! Get that filthy thing out o' your mouth, Sarah Dee! Look at you, all dressed up. What you gonna do now your brother's dead? Where I gonna get the money so's you can lie aroun' all day?"

The daughter flounced back inside as much as a woman in tight pants and a sequined tank top can flounce. The son stood macho. Jake Butler's younger brother had been made to look like the kid he was in front of a stranger, a one-armed white honky at that, had to save what face he could.

"I don' need no Jake, an' I don't need you, old woman. I'm movin' out o' this dump, gettin' me a big job in L.A."

It's hard for a six-foot male in his twenties to flounce, but he did the male equivalent and followed his sister into the haven of the house that Jake had built and Mama kept. Slums don't necessarily build character. Alice Mae Butler watched the open doorway where they had disappeared.

"They my last two. I don' do 'em no favor lettin' 'em

stay." She sat down on the front steps. "Jake he got killed tryin' to have some kind o' life. Like the rest of us."

"Why was it so hard, Ms. Butler?"

"Why what so hard?"

"Some kind of decent life."

She glared up at me, then looked away again toward the neighbor grooming his lawn. "Jake he got nothin' 'cept bad luck."

I said, "Was he selling drugs, Ms. Butler?"

The anger on her gaunt face had a mean look. She struggled to get up from the steps. Arthritis. I helped her. On her feet she pushed my hand away with bitter violence. "Jake he never sold no drugs, never done no drugs. 'Cept some grass in high school and that there college. Anyone says he done is a liar."

"Trouble with the law?"

"He got no trouble with no one!"

A man who is shot had some kind of trouble, and there is no way a boy in the ghetto, especially an oversized one, doesn't have some run-in with the police sooner or later.

"Was he gambling, Ms. Butler? Fixing fights? Maybe trying to fix football games?"

"You get out! Jake, he dead. What it matter how'r why? Let it rest, mister. You let poor Jake rest."

I got up late next morning, Kay was already gone. She'd had one of our special wine dinners waiting when I drove up from Oxnard.

"You that hungry?" I said.

"You had something else in mind?"

"It could probably be arranged."

"Arrange it then."

Dinner was late, and I overslept. I had to talk to Jake's old high-school coach down in Watts, but decided to brace Manny Baum while I was in Santa Barbara. I got a bran muffin and coffee at Jeannine's, walked to Gold's Gym. Manny's there until noon to watch the kids spar in the hope of finding one worth coming out of retirement to manage.

"The hungry kids, the tigers, don't live in this town," Manny said. "Yeah, I know Rue Huerta. I wish I didn't."

"He's that bad?"

"Rue the Screw. They don't mean a former prison occupation or his sexual ability. Rue would cheat himself and probably has."

"Would he fix fights?"

"Would I eat lox for breakfast?"

"You know the name Jake Butler, Manny?"

"What weight does he fight?"

Next to Thoroughbred racing, professional boxing is probably the narrowest profession.

"Where do I find this Huerta?"

Manny watched a junior bantamweight move with fluid grace. His eyes told me he wondered if the boy could take a punch. "Try Sammy Glick's gym in Venice. Don't mention my name."

Since anyone in their right mind who knows L.A. would do anything to avoid the 405 freeway, I took Highway 1 and the Santa Monica to Jake's high school. The Watts riots are twenty-five years ago. A lot has changed, a lot more hasn't. Failed shops are still boarded up, the morning bars full of men who have nothing else to do.

"Yeah, I heard about Jake." Coach Baines didn't notice my arm, looked past me at his own pain for Jake Butler.

"Was he selling drugs?"

"No."

"Then how did crack get into his pocket?"

"Somebody put it there."

"Why?"

"I'm not a policeman, and I'm not in New York."

"You are a coach, Jake's coach. He was helping you for free. Why not hire him?"

"I wanted to."

"Why didn't you? Gambling? Trouble with the law?"

"No."

We were in his office, and he wished I would go away.

"I've been told Jake was involved in fixing fights here in L.A. If he fixed fights, he fixed other events, too. He——"

"Jake never gambled, didn't fix fights or anything else."

"Reuben Huerta. That's the name that says Jake was a fixer. You know that name?"

"I know that name. Jake wouldn't spit on that slime."

"Then tell me why you didn't hire him, coach. All I've learned tells me Jake needed money. Why not hire him here?"

He seemed to grow smaller where he sat, looked at his

windows as if he wanted to look out at his playing field, his territory. But all the windows were too high in the basement office.

"He wasn't qualified."

"Jake Butler? Not qualified to coach a school team he—"

"Not qualified to teach. To coach high school in California you need a teaching credential."

"Why not help him get qualified?"

"I tried, Fortune. I told him to go back to college, get his teaching credential."

"Why didn't he?"

"Too much work, I guess." He said it, but he looked away.

I said, "Jake wasn't afraid of work."

He had to have that window. He stood, walked to the high horizontal windows, looked out at the grass and the fence and the garbage-littered avenue beyond. He spoke without turning, "Bottom drawer. The manila envelope."

It was a clipping from the *San Vicente Times*, dated a year ago:

Jake Butler, former professional football great in town to apply for a coaching position with the San Vicente Broncos semipro football team, barricaded himself in a room at the Ramada Inn Friday in a tense standoff with local police.

Chief Mark Belden said that Butler, 38, told police he had a gun and held officers at bay for three hours while he shouted obscenities and tossed furniture from his third-floor window. He finally surrendered peacefully to Harold Baines, his former high-school football coach.

Butler was charged with two felony counts of criminal damage to property and a misdemeanor charge of criminal trespass. Chief Belden said no weapons were found in the room. Butler refused treatment at Sisters of Mercy Hospital. Baines, the Reverend Mr. George Ashe, and other community leaders from Los Angeles posted bail and Butler was released.

It was later revealed that Butler had been arrested on Wednesday when he had been unable to pay his lunch bill at a local restaurant. Police stated that at that time it had taken twelve officers to subdue Butler.

A local story in a local newspaper. A story with a gaping omission in it.

"Jake Butler should have made AP, UPI, the works."

At the window his back was still to me. "The team kept it off the wires. The city cooperated."

"You mean Brett Darcy," I said. "It looks like Darcy kept a lid on something else, too. What's missing, Mr. Baines? Why did it happen? Why did Jake go berserk like that?"

Baines turned from the window on his field and his city. "Jake couldn't read or write. He couldn't do basic arithmetic. He couldn't pass a test to get out of grade school. That day up in San Vicente to try for an assistant on a semipro team he hit rock bottom. They turned him down because even a semipro team couldn't hire a coach who didn't know how to read or write."

He walked his bare basement office. "He had gone to this high school and a major college. He'd been ten years in the pros, but had been educated nowhere. He had learning problems that were covered up so he could play. No one cared except that he play football. We all rationalized that it was his only chance to be someone. He graduated from here without learning anything. Four years in college he had a D average in bonehead courses like 'theory of football' and didn't graduate. It was a massive and cynical fraud on everyone, but mostly on Jake Butler."

He walked from wall to wall, anger and guilt on his face. "I don't know what happened in New York, but it wasn't about drugs, or criminal violence, or gambling."

Venice is a raffish oceanfront community. A larger version of Summerland, mixed with some Coney Island and a lot all its own.

It was late afternoon when I got there, the roller skaters out in force, the concrete walk alive with the first of the evening revelers and gawkers. Sammy Glick's Gym was on a street barely inside Venice. A cavernous building that had once been a warehouse. It was even more packed than the ocean walk.

There was no Sammy Glick. Only a manager whose glance swept his domain corner to corner like a prison guard watching the yard.

"Huerta comes around."

"When?"

"Who knows?"

"You have a home address? Phone number?"

"He just comes around."

"I guess I have to hang around."

"I guess." He yawned, looked away. "What you want him for?"

Casual, offhand. It told me he not only knew Reuben Huerta well, he knew exactly where Huerta could be found.

I said, "Tell you what, if he comes around tonight, you say Dan Fortune from New York wants to talk about Jake Butler. I'll be at the Marina Pacific Hotel."

If my hunch was right, Reu the Screw would be at the Marina Pacific to fill my ear with Jake's transgressions before the sun was down. The call came on the house phone after I'd unpacked and showered, but before I went down for the first beer of the night.

"Huerta."

"Room 220."

I slipped my old revolver between the arm and the first cushion of the couch, arranged the other chairs so they would face each other and I could see them all.

"You Fortune? From New York?"

There were three of them. The spokesman, who wore shades and a black silk suit, a monogrammed gray silk tie, pale yellow shirt, and jacket two inches too long, would be Huerta. The other two were smaller and trimmer, nervous in plain slacks, sport shirts, and sport coats. Huerta looked at my empty sleeve without saying anything. He knew I had one arm before he saw me. Maybe the gym manager told him. I sat on the couch. Huerta took the armchair in the center, the other two sat on the edges of the straight chairs. They would be my aces.

I smiled. "So okay. Tell me about Jake Butler and the fights he fixed with you or for you."

He went through the act. "Who tell you Butler fix no fights? I don' know what the fuck you talk. You better—"

I said, "The guy who paid you to tell the story told me, for Christ sake. Who the hell else would know about something that never happened?"

"What the fuck you talk!" He began to sputter. "You want I show you the fights, the dates, the money I pay, the—"

One of the troubles with setting up a frame with small-time punks is that the people you have to use aren't too bright. He'd been paid to tell a yarn, but I wasn't playing right.

"Hell, no," I said. "I know you've got it all. Even those two to say they took the dives Jake 'fixed,' right? The clinchers to make me go home happy."

Huerta was on his feet. Confused, a little uneasy, he turned loud and nasty. "You callin' me a liar, man? What the fuck you come out here an' call me—"

"Did you tell the boys there Jake Butler got murdered?"

If an earthquake had buried us all, it couldn't have been more quiet in the room.

"Do they know they might have to tell their lies in a New York court? You ready for a murder trial, Rue baby?"

One of the trim ones said, "Hey, man, you don'—"

"Shut the fuck up!"

I said, "They found Jake Butler shot in a New York alley five days ago. The guy who paid you to lie about Jake tell you that?"

"Five day?"

"Before you even made the deal, right? That'll look sweet in court. Come on, no one's going to believe Jake Butler fixed any fights. Jake didn't know enough to fix a fight. You couldn't and wouldn't trust him. My guess is you never knew Butler that well."

The second trim one said, "I ain' goin' to no New York, Reu."

"Hey, you don' say no shootin' shit, man."

Huerta might have toughed it out, but the boys wouldn't. I gave him the coup de grace.

"You even knew I had one arm before you showed here. The man told you who'd come asking."

Huerta folded. "Shit, the guy don' pay me for no murder stuff. Okay, he come 'roun the gym, pay me I say Jake Butler help me fix fights. I got to tell on'y one guy. I know the guy 'cause he got one arm. Dates an' names an' bring a couple o' boys to say they took the dives."

"What man came around the gym?"

"I don' know. He Latino guy like me. He pay cash, what the hell, hey? I do job, get same again."

"How were you to get the same again?"

"Phone call."

"Make it."

The number, of course, was out of service. He should have expected that, and so should I. It was his only contact. The unknown Latino would be from somewhere far away, and long gone.

"Shit man, what the hell, hey? I got paid good."

He grinned, herded his boys out. I went down for that first beer. I'd find a nice restaurant in Venice, get a night's sleep, be on the early plane out of LAX for New York and finish it.

It took me a day to find what I knew had to be there, then I went to Captain Pearce. Next morning I made a phone call.

Helen Darcy wore a green tailored suit, green blouse, green shoes, when the maid ushered me into the living room of the penthouse condo the Darcys called home when they were in New York. You could have put most of our Summerland house into the room, and the view over the city and Central Park was so vast I had the feeling that on a clear day you could see Pennsylvania.

"You're finished?"

She reached to take a cigarette from a bright green stone box on an antique coffee table, offered me one. I shook my head. She lit hers with a green table lighter. I wondered if she changed all the accessories in the apartment to match her outfits.

"All finished."

"Then why come to me? Brett hired you."

"Why did he kill Jake Butler, Helen?"

"I beg your pardon?" She didn't even blink. Smoked in the massive living room with its endless view.

"He sent you to me with that yarn about Reuben Huerta and fixing fights. Another smoke screen to go along with the crack and the back alley. Muddy the water, misdirect attention. Anything to keep the police and the publicity away from Darcy Enterprises."

"I don't know what you're talking about. If you have any accusations to make, I suggest you talk to Brett."

I didn't really have to hear the sound behind me to turn and see Brett Darcy in the room. He wasn't alone. The bodyguard had no visible weapon. As big as Jake Butler, he probably wouldn't need one to handle me. They were a team,

Darcy and his wife. I had expected Brett would be around to see why I wanted to talk to her. It gave Captain Pearce more time down at Darcy's office.

"You think I killed Jake, Fortune?"

"Metaphorically," I said. "Jake shot himself in your office. In front of you. He took out that gun, stuck it in his mouth, and blew his brains all over your expensive walls."

"You're insane, Fortune," Helen Darcy said.

"You can't prove such an accusation," Brett Darcy said. "Why would I hire you to—"

"I already have proved it," I said. "I remembered the first day I got here. New paint and carpeting. The whole office. Must have cost you a fortune to get it done overnight, but how else are you going to hide the blood on the carpet, the bone and brains and blood on the walls? And what's a few bucks to Brett Darcy when it involves very bad publicity? You had to do the whole place, one suite would have stood out, looked different."

Darcy sat down on one of his antique Chippendale chairs, said nothing. Helen Darcy wasn't quite as smart as Brett, didn't know yet it was all over. "How do you expect to prove—"

"There aren't a lot of people who could do the job on such short notice. I found them, Pearce has their statements, is checking the tires on all of Brett's and the company's cars right now. When he finds the tires that match the tracks in the alley, he'll find blood inside the car. The crack you planted never did make sense. In that alley it should have been long gone. And the rings. You wanted to be sure the police knew who Jake was."

Brett Darcy said, "You told the police?"

"I told them."

"I hired you to work for Darcy Enterprises."

"They'd have figured it out themselves, sooner or later."

"No," Darcy said, "I don't think so. I made a mistake."

The bodyguard and Helen Darcy watched us, aware that something was going on, aware of Darcy's cold anger. And of mine.

"Why did he shoot himself?" I said. "Why in your office?"

"Because he was dumb and stupid and mentally ill."

"You covered up that time he went berserk out in San Vicente, kept it off the wires, out of anywhere but that backwater daily. That must have cost, too. All those stringers and wire people to pay off, sweet-talk, lean on."

Darcy said, "He snapped then, and he snapped again. Out of his mind."

"Jake Butler, sports hero, couldn't read or write. Four years of high school and four years of college and ten years in the pros, and when the money ran out, he couldn't get a job better than a security guard. Couldn't even coach at the high school that graduated him. He blamed you for it, didn't he, Brett?"

"He was crazy! What did I have to do with him being dumb? I don't run high schools, I don't run colleges. I run a business."

"Not dumb, Brett, uneducated. Jake wasn't dumb. Jake knew that behind it all was the money. All the money to be made on him by you and those like you, *because* of you and those like you. On his ability to play a game. That's all that mattered."

"I hired you to protect me and the company. You didn't do the job. Don't expect a check."

"Why do you think I get paid up front when I work for cheap tycoons?"

Now the bodyguard growled. He would do nothing without a command, and Darcy knew that Pearce knew where I was.

"When did Jake come to you for a job? The day before? A week before?"

"Two days."

The day after Walt Green told him he wasn't good enough to be a professional boxer.

"Why didn't you give him a job?"

"I didn't have a job he could handle."

The doorbell rang. Helen Darcy went to answer it.

"He wouldn't take muscle work. What else could he do?"

Captain Pearce came in with three of his men. He looked at me. I nodded.

"I offered him some bucks, airfare back to the coast."

Two detectives walked to Brett Darcy.

"Why the fuck did he have to shoot himself? In my god-damn office!"

I said, "He was a role model. An example to the nation."

They took Darcy out. Helen Darcy was already on the phone to the lawyers. It was clearly suicide, as the medical examiner had said. Brett wouldn't be held long. But obstructing the police would haul him into court, and the newspapers would get it all. Not that most people would give a damn.

invitation

SARAH ANDREWS

Sarah Andrews, a geologist who has worked the oil fields in Wyoming, Colorado, California, and Texas, and now advises clients about groundwater contamination, appears in print for the first time here. Following the dictate to write what you know, she is completing A Fall in Denver, *an upcoming Doubleday novel featuring Em Hansen, herself a geologist who doesn't believe that the deaths of several coworkers are the suicides they seem to be. A writer equally at home dealing with the wild natural beauty and the elemental emotions of the oil fields or the edgy mental state of a desperate young woman, Sarah's debut here heralds the emergence of a bright new voice.*

In "Invitation," a woman seeking relief from a suitor's harassment discovers that she really gets results when she takes her lawyer's advice.

I didn't think there would be so much blood, Angela thought numbly, watching the stain around the body on the carpet slowly darken. Her arm felt heavy when she lifted it to read her watch; so heavy, she was barely able to turn her wrist. Why hadn't the police arrived yet?

The straight-backed chair pressed against her spine. Her eyes moved randomly about the room, taking in the shattered lamp, the knife, the clutch of flowers lying askew on the floor.

Should I put the flowers in water? The question formed in her mind, hovering just beyond her understanding like a buzzing unseen fly. Drawn by a sudden compulsion to tidy the room, Angela rose from the chair and stepped toward the flowers. And stopped, her breath catching against her stomach like a fist.

Oh God, I almost stepped right over him. Oh my God, please keep me together just a moment longer, just until the police get here, just— She looked at the heavy pile of ruined flesh and leaking blood that occupied the center of her floor: a slab of meat that once spoke and raged and called itself Hank. A tiny bubble of anger broke loose, anger at the police, at God, at a world that tried to kid her that there was a God. Her lips retracted from her teeth as she whispered to the corpse: "If God existed, he wouldn't permit this, would he?" She had tried so hard to prepare herself for anything and everything that might come, but nothing could have prepared her for the imprint of such massive death on the once serene refuge of her home.

Angela's mind sank back into dullness. She sagged into her chair and squeezed her slender body tighter against the slats, girding herself against the hours to come.

Angela slid into a remote field of numbness, a place where only an icy ringing lived. At first she didn't recognize her lawyer, Mr. Ballard, when he arrived at the police station, but his voice brought her to, as he laced into the guard: "Look at her; the girl's in shock. What are you thinking of, putting her next to these animals in the holding cell, with what she's been through? This woman's been hounded near to death. You guys should be ashamed. Bring her to your damned interrogation room." Fixing the guard with a look of pure disgust, Ballard turned his back and started down the hall.

The guard muttered a retort to the lawyer as he approached her, speaking as carelessly as if she were deaf or perhaps some animal who knew no language: "Calm down, big shot, there's nobody in here gonna bother your little sweetheart. Nobody tells me nothing, how's I supposed to know? Besides, all's we got this evening is drunks. Drunks just holler a lot. Calm your mouth, already. Fuckin' lawyers." Taking her by one arm, the guard escorted Angela down the hallway to the interrogation room.

Once the guard had left them, Ballard grasped Angela's arms. "Are you all right?" he asked, peering sharply into her eyes. "You've waited for me, haven't you? You've kept your silence?"

Angela nodded.

"Good. Now they're going to take your statement. Let me lead. You just stay with me, don't say anything more than you have to to get your point across, right? You're going to be fine. I'll have you out of here within the hour, so just keep it together for that long, okay? Then you can let go."

"I'm fine," she lied. The ringing in her ears was growing louder and louder and her scalp felt cool. It's okay, she thought. They'll let me sit down again soon, and I can put my head down if I need to. . . .

The detective came into the room and waved them toward the table with his notebook. Angela followed the man with her eyes. He seemed smaller to her now than when he arrived at her house. In the cool glare of the fluorescent lights, his suit coat was smart but cheap, and she could see his scalp through his thinning gray hair. He looked at her calmly after he took his seat, considering her at his leisure, utterly relaxed.

Ballard settled Angela into a chair and installed himself next to her, making a great show of opening his attaché case and spreading out papers. After asking solicitously if she was warm enough, he swiveled brusquely toward the detective, ran a hand over his already tidy hair, and nodded for the detective to begin.

"I am Lieutenant Taplitz, Mr. Ballard. We could have taken care of this at the lady's home, but she wasn't feeling conversational." He shrugged his shoulders.

Ballard glared at him. "Perhaps you should have done

your homework, Lieutenant. My client has been grievously harassed over the past year. She's had to call on your department no fewer than eight times for assistance, and has received precious little. Surely you can understand her hesitancy to speak to you without an advocate present."

The detective turned toward Angela and sighed. He pointed toward a mirror. "One-way glass. You understand that everything you say is being recorded, that you are on camera, that everything you say can be used against you in a court of law?"

"I do."

"State your full name."

"Angela Post Hingston." Her voice sounded far away, a sound entirely external to her, the names floating into the past on a memory of familial intimacy and obligation. How would Father feel about his little girl now? Could he ever come to understand? A fantasy of his shock, disgust, and final rejection played on center stage in Angela's mind, overriding the detective's voice as he ground methodically through the rest of the preliminaries.

"Are you acquainted with the deceased, Miss Hingston?" he asked, his tone more ominous.

"Don't harass my client, Lieutenant," came Ballard's slightly nasal voice.

"The question stands, Miss Hingston," the detective said.

Angela moved her lips to form speech, but found her throat too tight to comply. Her eyelids sagged shut.

"Is that a yes?"

She nodded.

"State his name, Miss Hingston."

"Hank Stevens. Henry. W. I don't know what the 'W' was for. I—I didn't know him that well."

"Then, in what way did you know the deceased?" the detective asked.

"Socially," said the lawyer. "Let's leave it at that for the moment, Lieutenant; my client's clearly in shock. I must take her to the hospital."

Angela found her voice. "I met him at work. He asked me out a few times. Nothing more." Ballard shot her a look. "No, Mr. Ballard, it's okay." Bitter tears swam in her vision, but she stared steadily into the detective's eyes. "I dated him. Twice. That was before he—um, his behavior—I didn't know—"

Ballard cut in: "The bastard terrorized her. Just look back through your damned blotter, detective. It's all there."

"We need the story from her, not you, Mr. Ballard." Taplitz's gaze stayed steadily on Angela as he replied to the lawyer.

Angela could no longer meet his eyes. As the questioning ground on, her memory spilled helplessly through the months of manipulation and threats, the frightening letters, the attempted break-ins, the grinding court appearances in which she had dutifully walked every last avenue that "the system" paved before her, begging for the fragile armor of restraining orders, her spirit slowly suffocating under the weight of futility, her body weakening with lack of sleep and chronic tension. The mental litany lurched on through lost friendships, shattered dreams, her waning capacities at work, the condescending suggestions from supposed friends that perhaps she was overreacting, had she thought of consulting a psychologist? No one seemed to understand how difficult it was for her to manage even simple tasks while she had to watch so vigilantly for a man who came out of every shadow, who lengthened every night, who finally stalked her even in her dreams.

"So you killed him?" the detective was saying. He planted his meaty hands on the table and leaned toward her, his face as florid as freshly butchered meat.

Something in Angela's mind shifted, and she watched the detective now as if from a distance, his humanity as flat and intangible as an image on a television screen. "I feared for my life," she recited dully. "I fired my gun in his direction to try to stop him."

The detective sighed, leaning back. "You sure did that. You sure did stop him."

"You were great, you did just great," Ballard said as he turned the car onto the highway. "That was truly inspired, when you were telling the detective about dating the bastard. Fantastic. Just the right amount of shame. The limpid look of entreaty. You were excellent. Listen, Angela, you'll be fine, you held up really well in there."

"What's going to happen now?"

"I'm taking you to your friend Karen's house. You'll get some rest—try, Angela. You with me?"

"Yes." Angela pressed herself deep into the soft leather seat of Ballard's Cadillac, wanting to be with no one.

The early morning light gave form to curls of steam rising from black coffee. Angela caught a glimpse of herself in the mirror across the living room and at first did not recognize this face, with its stark lines of fatigue. She closed her eyes, hoping Karen would think for a moment that she was at last asleep, locked upright like a statue in the small overstuffed chair.

A car squealed its brakes a block or more away, and Angela's eyes snapped open.

"Did you get any sleep at all?" Karen asked.

"I don't know."

"I know I must be wishing awfully hard, but I was hoping you could find some peace, now that the bastard's gone. I suppose I'm speaking from the luxurious position of ignorance, not knowing what you went through last night."

Angela was silent.

"You can stay here as long as you like. I guess it would be pretty awful to try to sleep or anything over at your house, so soon after—"

Angela brought her gaze to Karen's face, but didn't meet her eyes. "Thanks for letting me stay here," she said, barely above a whisper.

"Well, you're welcome. Um, but you won't tell anyone where you're staying, will you? I mean, I'm glad to help in any way I can, but I have to think of the baby's safety." Karen squirmed on the green corduroy couch.

"It's okay, Karen," Angela said. "You're a real friend. Nobody knows I'm here except Mr. Ballard, and it's a habit now to make sure I'm not being followed anywhere." She laughed humorlessly. "Although who's going to follow me now?"

"I don't know, maybe the media."

Angela looked up in horror. "You don't really think—"

Karen shrugged. "Listen, the cops and the courts are the least of it. Shit, I may just sell ads for the paper, but I've watched those city-desk reporters. If they smell a story, all hell's going to break loose. Once they're onto it, the goons from TV won't be far behind. Didn't Ballard warn you about that?"

"Yes, but—"

"Yes, but hell. Listen, now may not be the time to tell you this, but you really need to watch yourself around that guy."

"Ballard? But he's my lawyer."

"Lawyers are worse jackals than reporters. Imagine the ego trip he's getting out of this. Lawyers aren't without motives themselves. Sorry, bad choice of words."

"What are you talking about?"

"Oh, come on, I didn't mean to upset you. Here, have some brandy in that coffee; maybe you'll sleep."

"But why would Mr. Ballard be interested in me?" Angela asked bitterly, her eyes suddenly flaring. "I'm a killer, remember?"

"You really don't get it, do you? In some ways that damned lawyer isn't much different from good old Hank, God rest his twisted soul. They see a woman of strength, of power, and they can't resist."

"I have no power."

"You had the guts to pull that trigger rather than let that man rape you. Wake up! Most women would have frozen to the spot in your situation, or dreamed themselves into some fairy tale that they somehow deserved it or that it wasn't really happening to them. Shit, you mustered the resolve to buy a gun and learn how to protect yourself. That's what I mean by power. The power to take action, to stand up for yourself."

"You misunderstand," said Angela, her voice dry and tight.

"God, Angela, for someone who's got so much together, you know damned little about men. Some men see your strength, your self-sufficiency, and they have to conjure up this big illusion that they can control you. What stronger woman is there than one who's pulled the trigger on a man? Shit, it's almost erotic with them. Kind of the flip side of the wounded woman. Remember when I had my leg in that cast in college? Every pervert on campus wanted to know what it was like to have sex with a cripple. And here Ballard's got both items in one package."

Angela shifted uneasily in her chair. "Well, I need to get dressed. I'm late for work."

"Are you nuts? You're not going to work today."

Angela rose to her feet, wobbling slightly. "But I have to go to work. They can't get by without me."

"Honey, I've already called in for you. I've called my

office, too, so I can be here with you. You're really in no
shape—"

"I have to do something!"

Karen sighed. "Sure. No sweat. Fix you right up at eleven
o'clock, with another little trip to the police station."

"What?"

"Ballard phoned while you were in the shower. This
Lieutenant Taplitz has a few more questions for you, now
that you've had some rest. Get it? Now that you've had
some—"

Angela's hands moved erratically through the air, as if she
were trying to swat invisible moths. "But I told him everything already!"

Karen took a deep breath. "Ballard wanted to pick you
up, but I told him I'd bring you down myself. Try to relax for
a while; surely by now you're ready for a good cry."

Angela surveyed the police station with new eyes: Now I
am a woman of strength, she thought ruefully. Now I am a
killer. For the first time in months, she stood almost straight,
squaring her shoulders in the ill-fitting finery of Karen's best
suit. She boldly made eye contact with the policemen, their
leather holsters sticking down like phalluses beside their fat
bellies. Did she note a new glint of respect in their eyes?

Ballard's rasping voice brought her back to reality: "This
way, Angela." The tone of his voice cut deep into her self-
confidence. She looked around the lobby in desperate search
of an ally. Karen was there behind her, giving her a reserved
thumbs-up. What would you think of me if you'd been there?
Angela wondered, returning Karen's glance with a pathetic
attempt at a smile. She longed to know if Karen would truly
stand by her, even if she came to know the darkness that was
in her heart.

Ballard hustled Angela down the hallway, waving his
hand at two reporters who were smoking cigarettes by the
desk. "No statements, boys," Ballard said. The reporters exchanged startled looks that said, Did we ask him for a statement? and straightened up, interest sparking in their
postures. One pulled out a listing of the day's arrests and
dragged a thumb down the column of names. Karen gave
them a goofy smile, as if to say, It's bad taste, boys, but he
makes these little jokes sometimes.

Lieutenant Taplitz looked exactly as he had the night before, no more tired, no better rested. He opened his suit jacket for the first time, revealing a Phi Beta Kappa key and chain hanging from his vest. Angela's muscles contracted even more tightly.

"I just wanted to check with you about this knife the deceased reached for, Miss Hingston. Which hand did he reach with?"

"Which hand? Um, his right, I think." She looked down at her own hands, and pantomimed the confrontation as she concentrated. "Yes, his right."

"Now, I see you're left-handed, and he reached with his right, so he was facing you?"

"Yes. I still had my bag hanging on my shoulder, and my pistol was in it." Angela's voice slipped into an odd rhythm, as if she were reciting a poem from a dream: "I feared for my life, so I reached into my purse and released the safety. He grabbed my hair. I told him to let go, but he wouldn't. He was reaching for a kitchen knife with his free hand. I feared for my life. He had the knife. I fired my gun in his direction to stop him. I fired without aiming, right through the bag."

"Good, good. Now, which way did the body fall?"

But Angela didn't really hear him. She was in a special place all her own, occupied completely in the mental effort of choosing a replacement for the ruined shoulder bag.

The reporters straightened up as Angela stepped out of the room. Ballard hurried her along, down the steps of the police station and across the street to the building that housed his offices, pointedly closing the door before Karen could catch up with them. He said, "Any questions from reporters, your answer is, 'No comment,' okay? You just let me handle them."

"But Mr. Ballard, you said that in a city this big, this is hardly news."

"We can't be too careful, Angela. Drunks and bums shoot each other all the time. Young ladies from good eastern prep schools are another item altogether."

"But I thought you said—"

"Don't you worry about a thing."

Inside Ballard's offices, Angela tried to settle herself in one of the green leather chairs, but found that no position supported her weight comfortably. She looked around the room, recalling the angle of light the sun had cast through the venetian blinds as they'd had their last conversation in that room. Had it only been a week ago? It seemed so much longer.

Ballard barked, "Hold my calls," to his secretary, and firmly closed the door. Arranging himself at his desk, he switched off the intercom and finally brought his gaze around to Angela. Her heart contracted under his scrutiny. Ballard smiled. "We're right on track. I believe this will not even go to a hearing. With the weight of evidence we have in your favor, the most they'd ever charge you with is disturbing the peace." His smile broadened. "Or did you have the presence of mind to use a silencer?"

Angela winced.

"Excuse me, that was a poor attempt at levity. So tell me, was it exactly as you said in your statement?"

Angela's voice rose. "Mr. Ballard—" she began, in that tone halfway between defiance and a whine that said, Daddy, how can you accuse me?

Ballard held up a hand. "You're right. I officially believe your every word. With what you've been through, nothing else matters." He smiled at her, his eyes lingering. He continued, in friendly tones: "But make sure you tell me all your movements leading up to the shooting, so that there won't be any surprises with this lieutenant."

"It's exactly as I told him," Angela said doggedly. "I'd forgotten to lock the door after unloading my groceries. When I turned around, he had come in the door with those flowers, like he had this big fantasy that this was a date. I've told you how he always told people we were engaged, and—anyway, I told him to leave."

Ballard rose, walked slowly around to her chair and grasped her shoulder, and something in the quality of his grip imposed an intimacy that she had struggled for months to ignore.

The headaches had started slowly, but now were almost crushing, and it was getting harder and harder for Angela to draw her breath. She sat crumpled up on the corduroy couch, holding a cold beer to her forehead. Each minute was a labor, and making it through a day had become unbearable.

Maybe if she spoke a few words finally, on some other subject, Karen would quit repeating that phrase, and maybe she'd take that food away before Angela vomited.

"Really, I just want to talk to you," Karen said, for what sounded like the hundredth time.

I just want to talk to you. It seemed everyone was saying that to Angela these days, from the reporters who had tracked her down at work to kids hustling quarters on the street. Was it tattooed on her forehead or something? Or had the universe split open, giving free rein to anyone who wanted to inflict this terrible pressure on her skull?

"Angela, this is important. Just raise a hand to let me know you're listening. Are you okay?"

Angela raised a hand.

"Shit, I'm worried about you, Angela. Will you eat your dinner? Open your eyes, honey, it's your favorite. Jesus, I thought you were on the edge before the shooting, but now this is really getting out of hand. No, dammit, you listen to me, I'm your friend, remember? I'm not just another one of those phonies who hung around you until things got rough, and then rationalized their way out of your life, like you were dreaming up what Hank was doing to you. I know what he did. Remember? Hey, talk to me! What is going on in there? I'm about ready to call a doctor, and it's because I'm worried about you, goddammit, not because I'm trying to get rid of you!"

Angela brought her knees up to her chest, cringing further into herself.

"Angela, listen: what Hank felt for you wasn't love. I don't care what the reporters are saying to you. Harassment is too small a word to describe what he did to you. He tried to rape you. You know that. He was going to carry out his threat. That's what he was there at your house for, to rape you, and rape is an act of hatred, not love. He probably would have killed you when he was done. You did the right thing in protecting yourself. What were you supposed to do, let him at you? If you think you're a basket case now, how would it be if he had actually raped you? And if he killed you then—hey, stop it!"

Angela had picked up the fork and was pressing it into the palm of her hand. In the roaring privacy of her head, she said, All I wanted was to talk to him, that's all, I only wanted to talk to him.

• • •

"Karen tells me you've been through a terrible experience," the woman said, her voice firm but soothing. "I'm here at her request, because of her concern for you. Would it be all right with you if we talked about it?"

Angela sat on Karen's green corduroy couch, her hands clasped over her knees to keep the hem of her skirt in place. She smiled politely at the social worker. Even Karen, she thought. Even Karen thinks I'm crazy. Even Karen doesn't understand that I only did what I had to do. Even Karen thinks he was sane and I was crazy.

"Perhaps it would help you if I explained a little more who I am and what I do," said the woman. "I am a psychiatric social worker. That means I work with the emotional aspects of the difficulties people find themselves in. Not crazy people, just people who have been through very terrible experiences. I help these people process through the feelings that have come up. It can be anything: anger, sorrow, confusion, guilt—"

Angela twitched uncontrollably, then muttered, "I'm sorry Karen wasted your time. I'm quite sure I can't talk with you about this. My, ah, lawyer has told me not to discuss the case with anyone. Sorry."

"I understand. It's good that you protect yourself. Let me explain. You understand that anything you tell your lawyer becomes a matter of professional confidence. That he can't tell anyone what you tell him. Well, that's just the same with me. If you talk to me, anything you tell me becomes a matter of professional confidence, too. It's our agreement that I won't tell anyone anything you tell me. You see, you need a safe place in order to heal from this, and it's my job to help you create that place."

Angela leaned forward. "You wouldn't tell anyone anything?"

"Correct."

"Even in a court of law, if they put you on the stand?"

"That's correct. Only if you wanted me to tell."

"No exceptions?"

"The only exceptions would be things you might tell me that gave me a strong concern that you'd hurt yourself or someone else. Then by law and ethics I would have to take measures so you wouldn't."

Angela stood up and moved about the room, looking out the windows and doorways to make certain they were not overheard. "What do you charge, Miss Chavez?"

"Call me Terry. Normally, sixty dollars an hour. But your friend paid for this visit."

"No. You're not working for Karen, you're working for me." Angela moved to the coat closet and pulled out a tweed jacket. From the right front pocket, she withdrew a checkbook and pen, and wrote a check. "There," she said, thrusting the check at the social worker. "Now you work for me. You are under oath, right?"

"Right."

Angela sat down again and grasped her knees. Her eyes darted around the room, and her lips worked fiercely, silently trying out words. At length she said, "Karen wants me out of here."

"Oh?"

"Yes, she thinks I'm crazy, and she's tired of having me around. I don't sleep much, so I guess I've been making noise, waking her up at night."

"She said you've been screaming in your sleep."

Angela shot the woman an insolent look. "Yeah. That's why I don't sleep. Anyway, I need to go back to my own house, you see. I just need a little help so I can get that far, okay?"

"Fine. That's a good goal. I think I can help you. Maybe we need to examine what happened at the house so that it will be okay to go back there."

"No, that's not the problem. Somebody died there, and that's pretty gross, but that's not the problem."

"Okay, what is the problem?"

"My lawyer."

It was him again. Why did he keep calling? Now the LED flashed insistently over the incoming line on Angela's desk phone. The receptionist's voice had been nagging, even insinuating when she announced the call, and Angela's knuckles were white as she grasped the receiver. That bastard detective, always one more question. She clenched her teeth and punched the button under the flashing light. "This is Angela Hingston."

"Hello, Miss Hingston, this is Lieutenant Taplitz. I just

had one more question about—" The detective's voice droned from the earpiece, rambling along.

Angela cut him short, and was immediately nervous that she had offended him, tempting him to lean on her even harder. "I'm sorry, but you know I can't answer any questions without Mr. Ballard present."

"Oh, okay, Miss Hingston. I was just wondering why someone as frightened as you say you were could carry your groceries all the way into the kitchen, leaving the front door open. Why didn't you kick it shut?"

"I repeat, Lieutenant, I can't answer—"

"Sure, I understand. Perhaps we can all meet for a bite after work, and get all this detail straightened out."

Dear God, not a social occasion! Why can't he close the file? This was supposed to have been over by now. Ballard had said so, promised it would all be over long ago, case closed, simple self-defense. What was taking so long?

Detective Taplitz settled for another meeting in Ballard's office.

When the appointed time came, Angela found herself moving from her car to the office building, but couldn't remember leaving work, or any detail of the drive. Reflexively, she clutched for the reassuring leather of her purse, but found only a small, canvas summer bag at her side. She had to backtrack mentally in order to recall that her leather purse was gone, locked up as evidence on some metal shelf somewhere in the police station. Was there something about that purse that kept the detective after her? Was it that unusual that she'd had a special holster built into its soft leather folds? Angela had never known another woman who carried a gun in her purse, but surely a detective must run into them every day.

This time was even worse than the others. The detective watched her without blinking, staring into her eyes as if a message for him was written on the inside of her skull. I have his letters to you, his voice says, and I have some questions. He waves the letters without breaking his gaze. Ballard croaks like a huge frog higher in the lake, rumbling at the detective about harassing his client, close the goddamn file, why don't you, you sadist? Ballard sneaks a sly glance her way, drooping his eyelids in his little way that suggests intimacy, even possession.

Angela speaks words that sound about right, she thinks they're right, but she can't quite hear.

Angela presses the bullets into the clip, the unjacketed lead bullets leaving a dark streak on her thumb. *Thump, thump,* go the guns on either side of her, in the other lanes of the firing range. She works feverishly, her teeth grinding with the effort of keeping her jaws closed until she can get the pistol ready to fire. *Just a few more seconds, and I can let go. Hold back these words just a little longer, then the bullets will speak for me.*

Angela grasps the pistol firmly in her right hand, taking courage in the familiar feeling of the rubber grip. She jams the clip into the bottom of the grip with the palm of her left hand, then pulls the slide back, her heart rising with the pleasure of the ritual. She sets the safety and lays the gun down gently, as tender as a kitten. She adjusts her hearing muffs, her glasses, turns her shoulder to the firing range, just as she'd been taught. *On the next .45 fired, I go for it,* she muses, *not a .22. Pop. Pop. Those are .22s; little cap pistols.* The smell of gunpowder curls through her nostrils.

Thump! Angela spins toward the range, plants her feet, grasps the pistol, flips off the safety, and pumps off two rounds, and two more. Thirty feet down the range, bits of paper fly from the tatters of her target, the silhouette of the man now almost unrecognizable.

She takes a deep breath now and counts her heartbeats, taking careful aim for the final rounds. *His throat this time,* she muses, *this time he breathes his last.* She squeezes off two final rounds, stitching the target deftly across the larynx, sets the safety, and releases the clip. After slamming another clip into its place, she sets the gun down gently on its side and presses the button to call the target forward along its jouncing wire.

"Hey, lady," she hears, through the muffs. "Nice shootin'." She spins around to find a cop behind her. He's not in uniform, but she'd know him anywhere: he's the first one who arrived on the scene, the one who came into her living room and relieved her of the other pistol, the Beretta she had come to like so much.

Angela observes the cop serenely, enjoying a moment of power among equals. Then a second man steps around the divider from the next booth. Lieutenant Taplitz, wearing his goddamn suit, nodding acknowledgment of her prowess. He stoops to retrieve the brass shells her pistol had ejected onto the floor and proffers them to her like candies. "You were shooting hollow points the night of the killing, weren't you?" he says, gazing into her eyes without blinking.

"Last time we met, you were thinking about telling me what your lawyer had said to you a week before the shooting," Miss Chavez said, in her soothing voice.

"Yes."

"Do you think you're ready to tell me yet? I think it would be good for you to let it out."

"Yes."

"You had told him about how hard it was to go to work every day, having to dress up nicely, and pretend nothing was happening, so no one would think you were crazy, or incompetent."

"Yes. No one understood. Except Ballard."

"What exactly did he say?"

"He said he understood. He said I was overstressed, not bad crazy, like he was."

"Like who was?"

"Like H—" Angela couldn't complete the name.

"Like Hank."

"Yes."

"And Hank was crazy, wasn't he?"

"Yes. He heard voices that weren't there, and he twisted everything I said. But somehow no one else saw how crazy he was, except Mr. Ballard. Mr. Ballard said he'd seen it before, and there was no way out, no deterrence."

"Did you agree with that?"

"Yes. It was true. He was getting worse and worse. Everything I did to try to pull away, he just hung on tighter and tighter. He was getting wilder, trying to get into my house, doing things to my car, smashing it up, moving around in the dark. I was so scared."

"I would be, too."

"You would?"

The social worker stared openly. "Angela, I'm stunned. How can you have gone through what you have and still doubt yourself, still doubt that you were in danger? Really, how can you still trouble yourself with anyone else's pitiful, misguided opinions?" Miss Chavez's eyes swam with tears.

Angela hung her head, sorry for a moment to have troubled this woman. Three sessions now they had sat together, and it was clear that Miss Chavez didn't understand. Angela's remorse quickly stiffened into irritation. No matter if this was one more supposed helper who failed to help, she had made her promise and Angela would hold her to it. She supposed Miss Chavez's plan was to make Angela break down and cry, start to let it out. "It's just the way it is," Angela said.

"Angela, it's time now. What did Mr. Ballard say to you that was so terribly upsetting?"

Angela sighed and looked away, examining the play of light across the window. At length she said, "He told me to kill him."

"Mr. Ballard told you to kill Hank?"

Finally begun, Angela's words came in a rush: "Yes, I was in his office. I'd gotten the restraining order, you see, and been to court to testify and everything, but they let him plea-bargain, misdemeanor disturbance of the peace. And he kept on coming. No one ever saw him, no eyewitnesses, he just kept coming, leaving little clues so I'd know he'd been there. He'd be there, you see, standing in the shadows below my window in the night. The dogs would go crazy, barking at him."

"Tell me what Ballard said to do."

"He said to go ahead and kill him, to make it look like self-defense. He said the law didn't have a provision for rabid animals like Hank, so I must never quote him, but that the thing to do was just kill him. There'd be no problem, because I'd made such a great paper trail, documenting how hard I'd tried to stop him in every other way, and that things were only escalating. He said just to invite Hank over, like I'd had a change of heart and wanted to talk it out, and then when I got him inside, I was supposed to kill him, then call the police. He gave me all the details of what to tell them. But he said I must never, never tell, that it must be our secret. But I had to tell someone, you see? I'm just getting so scared, with all these reporters hounding me, and that detective, and Ballard getting so wild. That's why I had to hire you, because you wouldn't tell."

Miss Chavez smiled kindly. "But really, Mr. Ballard is an officer of the court, and he wouldn't tell you to—"

Angela's pulse raced. "No, you see, that's the problem. He thinks I did it. He thinks I did it just like he told me to."

The last rays of sunset shone through the venetian blinds. The crisp white of his shirt glowed eerily in the fading light. Angela peered into the places where Ballard's eyes must be in the shadows of his face. She could still smell the smoke from the cigarette the detective had smoked an hour earlier during their—what?—seventh visit since the shooting. He had posed just one more question, an insignificant detail, he'd explained, just one little item he had to clear up before he could report his findings. She had thought he'd never leave, but now, alone with Ballard, she wished he had stayed.

Ballard's voice gnawed through the shadows. "You're worried, aren't you?"

"Yes."

"I've told you not to worry. I can handle him."

"But he keeps asking questions." Angela wanted to reach over and turn on the lamp, but she felt frozen to the spot, mired in hatred for the man across the desk.

Ballard moved from his chair. He came slowly around the desk toward her, taking his time, his walk swaggering, seductive. "You're such an amazing woman," he said, almost whispering, casually floating a hand past her head, barely touching her hair. "Few women could have done what you did. I've come to admire you so." He took another swipe, this time grabbing a firm handful of her hair, raising it to his lips to kiss.

The heavy coldness of pure contempt filled Angela's chest. She stood abruptly and moved toward the door. "I'm sorry. I have to leave now."

Ballard moved toward her. "So soon? I was thinking we'd have dinner again."

"No, really, I have to get home. Now that I'm living at home again, there's so much to do, you see? I have to get settled in again." Her voice sounded small and pleading to her. In her fear and rage she began to tremble.

"Why not let me help you?" he said, his voice taking a hard edge. Angela thought she could see his teeth. He said, "You know, we'll always need each other, you and me."

Angela counted five heartbeats before she could think. "Just not tonight, okay? I'll give you a call if I change my mind, okay?"

"Yes," he hissed. "You do that."

The phone was ringing again. The answering machine clicked in, and Lieutenant Taplitz's voice cheerfully reported that he had just one more question, but that he'd catch her at work tomorrow, no need to call back tonight. No matter, thought Angela, he'll have his answers soon enough. No hurry.

She carefully reassembled the gun. It was her evening ritual now, breaking it down and oiling it, piecing it back together.

That crazy Taplitz. Didn't he understand? It really had nothing to do with her. So strange in a homicide detective, that he worked with motives all day long and never understood the big one that stared him in the eye: everyone has a dragon, and they're just looking for someone to slay it for them. That's all she'd been, just a dragon slayer. She'd had no choice. If it hadn't been Ballard pushing her to do it, it would have been someone else, and in fact everyone else had. Everyone from the police to the paperboy had oozed with the expectation that she could somehow stop the monster, proving that fairy tales can come true, that the bad crazy dragon really could be slain. But then that was the sick part of the joke: once the dragon slayer does her job, everyone blames her and treats her like a freak, assigning her to the same hell that the dragon came from.

Such a fine gun. She'd miss it. She inserted the barrel and the spring, then the little pin that held the safety. The bluing on the muzzle was so pretty. Not much longer now, just the piece with the screw that held it all in place.

The phone rang again, switched onto the outgoing message. No one can answer your call just now, so please leave a message at the beep. Karen's voice came on, full of her foolish worry. Why didn't that woman kiss off?

She stroked each bullet as she pressed it into the clip, admiring the soft luster of the silver tips, smiling at the smooth copper of jacketed hardball. She jacked the first hollow point into the chamber, removed the clip, and topped it off with a full metal jacket: the first round for maximum stopping, a second that wouldn't jam in the chamber. Alternate them in the clip, just like he had taught her.

Karen's galling message finally ended, and the machine clicked into silence. Sliding the pistol down between the cushion and the back of the couch, Angela checked the motion one more time: pull and fire. Then she flipped off the safety, replaced the gun, and reached serenely for the phone. She knew the number by heart now, and no hurry, she knew he'd be working late, just as he always did. He answered the call on the second ring. Hello?

"Yes, hello, Mr. Ballard. This is Angela. I've changed my mind. Do you think you could come over? I'd just like to talk to you."

In the early days of detective fiction, the recipe for solving crimes was simple: a bit of perseverence and at least one eagle eye were stirred with a measure of logic and seasoned with a dash of good luck. Modern sleuths use the same ingredients— but they now have the advantage of a brave new world of high-tech equipment to help them sift through evidence and whip up answers. Whether the detective is a private investigator, like Jan Grape's Jenny Gordon or her partner Cinnamon Gunn, or a journalism teacher with never-say-die curiosity, like Carolyn G. Hart's Henrietta Collins, being able to use a computer ensures that she won't come up with any half-baked solutions.

nothing
ventured

CAROLYN G. HART

*Carolyn G. Hart, the 1991–92 president of Sisters in
Crime, is a former journalist who provides double
delight for fans of the traditional mystery. Carolyn's
South Carolina–based mysteries featuring Annie
Laurance, owner of a mystery bookstore, and her
debonair, good-humored husband, Max Darling, are
not only well plotted and full of delicious surprises
but also contain a wealth of information about the
history of the mystery.* Death on Demand *introduced the charming couple, who continued their ad-
ventures in* Design for Murder, Something Wicked
(an Agatha and Anthony award winner), Honeymoon with Murder *(an Anthony winner),* A Little
Class on Murder *(a Macavity winner),* Deadly Valentine, *and* The Christie Caper.

*"Nothing Ventured" is one of the first appear-
ances for Henrietta O'Dwyer Collins, a retired
newspaperwoman subbing as a journalist and pro-*

*fessor, who proves that a nose isn't all it takes to get
the news—sometimes, a computer and a quick wit
are needed.*

━━━━━━━━━━━━

I make it a rule never to involve myself in the personal lives
of my students.

The Meriwether affair was, of course, an exception.
When I pointed this out to Don—Lieutenant Don Brown,
Homicide—I must say he was downright rude about it.
Young people do so hate to admit not seeing the forest for the
trees. Rather an occupational hazard for the young, I'm
afraid. Admittedly, I had an advantage over the police—both
Darrell Meriwether and Barbara Hamish were my students,
and I'd watched the progress of their love affair. Lieutenant
Brown went so far as to suggest that my judgment might be
deficient in gauging passion. I merely raised one sardonic
eyebrow until he looked away. As his face reddened and he
tugged at his collar, he muttered something about the heat in
the room. I forbore to point out that the steam heat is extinguished by the university in April and sharp nights tinge the
rooms with an almost subterranean chill despite the daytime
warmth.

Odd to think Darrell Meriwether's life was forever affected by last Thursday's weather. His life and that, of
course, of his roommate, Paul Feder.

Thursday, April 18, was the kind of spring day celebrated
by poets, billowing flagships of clouds, a robin's-egg-blue
sky, a spurt in temperature sufficient, despite April's chilly
undertone, to draw gardeners forth from winter's hiberna-
tion.

Paul Feder decided to wash his car.

That much was established beyond doubt.

He had time to wash almost half of the jaunty red 1957
four-door Plymouth. A mound of still-damp rags nestled beside a half-full bucket of cold soapy water.

That was the scene in the driveway after Darrell's hoarse
and frantic shouts to the 911 operator brought two squad

cars, Lieutenant Brown's unmarked Ford, and a siren-wailing ambulance to the quiet residential neighborhood.

I didn't know any of this until late that afternoon. I was in my office at the journalism school, where I'd just finished talking to a reporter on our university newspaper, the *Clarion*, which also serves as the newspaper for our town of Derry Hills. The reporter was worried about libel, a specter that haunts all journalists, and I had assured her it wasn't libelous for the *Clarion* to report that the police were seeking a missing bank employee to inquire about the disappearance of a small fortune in bearer bonds that the employee, one Hazel Dublin, had checked out of the vault that morning. The story sounded intriguing, but the reporter knew little more than those facts. The bank president declined to comment. I suggested a number of inquiries to make, felt the old adrenaline surging through my veins, and had just settled back to my grading of the last of a three-part investigative series required of students in Journalism 3705, when Barbara Hamish stumbled in, her narrow, sensitive face white and stricken, her eyes wide with horror and shock. Barbara is the kind of student that teachers, especially old professionals converted to teaching like myself, dream about—articulate, eager, ambitious, with a scholar's love of language and an adventurer's love of life, enough idealism to believe in truth to keep men free yet savvy enough to see the meretricious so inextricably woven into even the most heroic institutions.

In short, nobody's fool. She was presently an outstanding staff member of the *Clarion* and someday she would be a first-class reporter.

But right now she was confronting emotions she'd never even dreamed about.

"Mrs. Collins." Her usually vibrant voice was reedy. "Mrs. Collins—Darrell's roommate's been murdered—and they've arrested Darrell. Please, the police won't listen to me. Please, you've got to help us."

The police in this small college town are well trained, especially my young friend Lieutenant Don Brown, who has a degree in criminology and is going to night law school. He does not arrest capriciously.

But I knew Barbara and I knew Darrell.

This is not to say I consider my students to be exempt from suspicion of wrongdoing merely because they are my students. In fact, I expect any day now to hear of the arrest of my least favorite graduate student for drug dealing. And there is little I would put past the sophomore who is always late for Editing 1003. She is dishonest, unethical, and probably into the kind of sex that Don—Lieutenant Brown—considers an unfit topic for conversation with me.

Therefore, Barbara's impassioned plea that Darrell couldn't be guilty didn't impress me.

What did impress me was the basis for the arrest. The DA, a dark intense young man much given to quoting Freud —I do think someone should inform him that Freud is now hopelessly out-of-date—decided Darrell and Paul were not merely roommates but homosexual lovers and Darrell beat Paul to death in a raging lovers' quarrel.

"That's crazy—so crazy. Oh my God, Mrs. Collins, Darrell wouldn't—Paul wouldn't—they didn't—" Tears streamed down Barbara's face. "It's so awful for the police to say something like that when they didn't even know Darrell and Paul. Just because two guys room together doesn't mean—oh my God, Mrs. Collins, what am I going to do?"

She came to me because at one time in my varied reportorial career I covered the police beat for a large metropolitan daily. And lots of murders. I knew, of course, that Barbara could be wrong. Darrell could be in love with her— and with Paul. In fact, that could provide a pretty motive all its own, a dual involvement. It happened. Lots of things happen. The DA could be right. But he could also be wrong— and if he was wrong, two nice young people's lives would be destroyed.

I only hesitated for an instant. I'd seen the attraction between Darrell and Barbara, watched it grow from hesitant wondering glances to the exchange of lovers' lingering looks, and there was never a false note. And now desperate blue eyes beseeched me. I've never imagined myself as a rescuer of dreams—but life throws us some odd tasks and we are the poorer when we turn our backs on challenge.

"I'll see what I can do. May not be much." I delivered it in my usual crisp fashion.

"Oh, Mrs. Collins. Thank you. Thank God."

That put a heavy burden—and so did the wet warmth of her cheek against mine.

$\bullet$ $\quad$ $\bullet$ $\quad$ $\bullet$ $\quad$ $\bullet$

Don Brown slumped in the hard-backed chair that fronts my desk. It was amazing how quickly he'd arrived on the campus after I'd called to say I'd be dropping by his office to discuss Darrell Meriwether's arrest. Not, of course, because Don was pining for my sage input. Rather, he would do almost anything to keep me away from the crisply modern Derry Hills Police Department. The chief seems to have an almost pathological dislike of elderly women—or perhaps it is one particular elderly woman, Henrietta O'Dwyer Collins.

I was tempted to don (not a pun, I wouldn't do that) my Gray Power T-shirt and sally forth without a prefatory call, but it is never wise to ruffle the feathers of the bird one intends to devour. So I called, and as I expected, Don quickly arrived.

I made no comment about his execrable posture. My own, if not Prussian, is certainly erect, in keeping with my general appearance, a lean and angular body usually attired in sweats, a Roman-coin profile, and dark hair silvered at the temples. I've no intention of going gently into that dark night, and I have no patience with those who confuse age with decrepitude. I know a ninety-two-year-old marathoner. But this was not an appropriate time to encourage Don to mature gracefully. Instead I poured him a cup of my best Kona coffee and assumed a most benign expression, one I'd used successfully any number of times, notably when I shared a cell with an accused murderess and suckered a word-for-word description of a murder-for-hire scheme. She was most indignant when I testified against her. Really, it was one of the high points of my career, a ten-part series entitled "Cellmate with Murder."

"Come off it, Henrie O."

Was it fair for Don to use my late husband's nickname for me? Richard always said it with laughter, claiming I packed more twists and surprises into a single day than O. Henry ever thought about investing in a short story.

I narrowed my eyes, letting the smile lapse.

"That's better," Don drawled. "More than a hint of a barracuda at large." He rubbed the back of his neck. Even sprawled in an uncomfortable chair, Don Brown was, on second glance, an impressive young man. At first glance, one was tempted to see only his carefully blank and unresponsive face, his nondescript sandy hair, his somewhat slight build. It took a second glance or a perceptive viewer to notice his firm chin, his supple, sensitive hands, the litheness of a long-distance runner, the glitter of intelligence in his weary blue eyes.

"So what's your angle on the Feder kill?" He massaged the back of his neck again.

A sure sign of tension.

Why?

With an arrest that quick, it should be open and shut. No problem. No sweat.

I felt a quiver of the old magic, the second sense that a story was out there, just beyond my grasp. Don wasn't certain.

But this wasn't the time for a frontal assault.

I didn't, however, try my benign look again. If it wasn't working, it wasn't working. Indeed, I leaned forward, propped a chin on my hand, and, exuding quiet interest, said merely, "Darrell Meriwether's a student of mine."

Don didn't ante.

"He didn't do it."

"Oh, for Christ's sake." A swallow. "Pardon me, Mrs. Collins."

I raised an eyebrow.

"Oh hell, Henrie O, what do you expect? Don't you think we know our job?"

"You don't know Darrell," I said authoritatively.

It was his turn to look sardonic. "Knowing Darrell doesn't make a difference." He held up his hand to forestall me. "Listen, I know more about Darrell Meriwether now than his mother does, and I'll grant that there's nothing—I mean zero—to indicate he was likely to go off the rails and kill somebody. But it sure as hell looks that way." He sat up straight to snap facts faster than linotype keys used to clatter. "Darrell Meriwether and Paul Feder shared a one-bedroom —two twin beds—garage apartment on Calhoun Street in the old part of town. Victorian houses. Two-story frames, mostly. In good repair. One of those revitalized neighborhoods. An especially desirable street because it dead-ends into a ravine, so not much traffic. The ravine curves around, runs behind the houses on the south side of the block, which includes the Murray property with the garage apartment Meriwether and Feder rented. Thursday morning, April eighteenth, the city sewer department was busy digging up half the street just past the Murray house—four guys, including a foreman. Not a single car went past their excavations between nine and ten A.M. Paul Feder was alive at nine A.M. He called in to the math department to say he would be in later that morning, he had a toothache."

Don gulped his coffee. "That's the kind of fact that drives a detective crazy. Because, you know what Feder did then? Did he go to a dentist? Or to the drugstore to buy some of that red junk that numbs your gum? Nope. He proceeded to wash his car. According to friends, he was nutty about that car. He loved stuff about the fifties. So, was this just one of those little lies people do? Or did he have something special planned? Was he maybe expecting someone to come over? All we *know* is that he started to wash the damn car. Okay, about this time Meriwether decides to cut his morning class and go for a jog. Why? Such a great day. That's what he says, anyway. So neither guy is keeping to his regular schedule. Usually, at nine o'clock on Thursdays Feder would be at the math building and Meriwether in class at the journalism school. So anyway, according to Meriwether, he trots off. There's a bridge that crosses the ravine right behind that property. It connects with a nature path that goes into Primrose Park. Meriwether comes back an hour later. Feder's car is about half washed. The bucket's next to the right rear wheel. Meriwether lopes up the steps to the garage apartment. The door's open—according to him. He opens the screen door and, again according to him, he finds Feder's body sprawled in the middle of the living-room floor, facedown, his head battered to a pulp. Meriwether says he went into shock and he tried to pick up his roommate, carry him to a bed. He says maybe it was crazy, he never thought about it, he was just trying to help, then he realized Feder was dead—very dead—and there's blood everywhere and then Meriwether picks up this golf club—funny thing is, it turns out to be *his* golf club—because he stumbled over it on the way to the phone and he sees it's got blood and hair all over the head, so he starts to throw up—then he calls us and we come. The call logged in at ten-oh-three."

"Why not?" I asked equably.

Don downed the rest of the coffee. "Meriwether was there. We can prove it. His fingerprints are on the golf club. We can prove it. Meriwether's covered with blood. We've got pictures. And there's absolutely no suggestion that anyone else—anyone at all—had any reason for killing Feder. Talk

about a well-liked guy—he was voted the most popular in-
structor in the math department last fall. He was social chairman for the young bachelors' club in town. When he was an
undergrad, he was social chairman of his fraternity. One of
those 'he-never-knew-a-stranger guys.' Bonhomie to the max.
Loud, full of jokes."

"So why did Darrell bash his head in?"

"So who knows? Maybe Feder cracked one joke too
many, and it drove Meriwether nuts."

"I understand the DA says Darrell and Paul were lovers."

Don shrugged. "That's the way the DA reads it. He saw
the shambles of that living room and said it had to be a crime
of passion and that's all he could figure. But nobody may
ever know what triggered Meriwether. Maybe Feder made
some kind of crack about Meriwether's girlfriend. Who
knows? And it doesn't really matter. Cops don't have to
prove motive." He sounded belligerent, but it didn't quite
hide the defensive note. "We have to place the accused at the
scene of the crime and prove opportunity. We can do that.
And besides that, it doesn't look like anybody else *could* have
done it."

Don pulled his notepad out of his pocket, flipped it open,
and handed it to me. As I studied the sketch, he explained.

"Look at it this way, there're two houses on the south
side of the street with a driveway between them, the drive to
the Murray house. At the foot of the drive stands the garage
apartment. Out in the street, maybe twenty yards past the
Murray house—not close enough to see Feder's car in the
driveway but damn sure there—is the sewer crew. Nobody
drove past that crew from nine in the morning *until* two cop
cars, an ambulance, and me came squealing in there about
half past ten. Besides that, they got an A-one loafer on that
crew and he told us there was just one old man walking a
poodle who went along the sidewalk during that hour. Not
including, of course"—heavy sarcasm here—"two little girls
about four on tricycles."

Before I could interrupt, point out that this contingent of
beady-eyed sewer repairmen certainly couldn't speak for approaches through backyards on the south side of the street or
from the footbridge used by Darrell, Don concluded briskly.
"Moreover, we've checked every house on the block and
nobody had more than a nodding acquaintance with Feder.
We've checked Feder's friends—and believe me, that guy

knew a hell of a lot of people—and we haven't picked up any quarrels, any disputes that might lead to murder."

I suppose I must have looked skeptical.

"Nope. This is on the level." He glanced longingly toward the thermos, and I refilled his mug. "This guy was Mr. Popularity."

But Paul might have had secret images and passions no one knew about it. Don was a good cop. He would have asked the right questions. But people lie.

I stuck to the point. "If Darrell could cross that footbridge, so could someone else." I continued to study Don's map.

"Sure." Don sipped at his coffee, relaxed now. "But who? We don't have any candidates among Feder's friends. I mean, for Christ's sake, we're talking major motive when a killer strikes that savagely. There would have to be some kind of indicator, as many people as we've interviewed. Are you postulating a vagrant killer? Somebody who came across that bridge and thought, 'Hey, why don't I break into that garage apartment? Never mind there's a car in the drive and somebody's obviously washing it, but I'll break in and kill whoever's there.' No way, Henrie O."

The session with a red-eyed, haggard Darrell Meriwether almost broke my heart. He was unshaven, in too-large orange dungarees, and his voice sounded hollow through the mesh in the plate glass that separated us. He tried manfully to keep his mouth from trembling, but couldn't quite. He kept shaking his head. "Nobody would've killed Paul. I tell you, Mrs. Collins, he was a great guy. Everybody liked him. And he didn't have anything worth stealing. I mean, we didn't have any money, either of us. Grad students. That's why we roomed together. As for what the police"—his pale face flushed—"that's crap. Pure crap." Then his face crumpled. "Barbara—oh God, Barbara doesn't—"

"No, she doesn't. That's why she asked me to see what I could do."

For an instant hope flared in his eyes, then died. He buried his face in his hands. "I didn't do it. Oh God, I didn't do it."

• • • •

I didn't get much sleep that night. Much of the ground I covered was old. I fed the last of my information into my computer about half past two. I slept until six, then struggled up, lusting for coffee.

I read the morning papers during breakfast, of course. My day can't start any other way. Feder's murder and Meriwether's arrest were the lead story. I read it carefully, but didn't learn anything new. The latest Middle East crisis was the second lead and the bottom of the page was filled with the fourth in a series on the origins of animals used in research, including kidnapped pets. A small story at the bottom of the page caught my eye:

POLICE SEEKING BANK EMPLOYEE

Police are seeking Hazel Dublin, an employee in the customer service department of the First National Bank, for questioning in the disappearance Thursday morning of an unspecified number of bearer bonds from the bank.

I didn't see a sidebar interview with an acquaintance or coworker of Hazel Dublin. If it were my story . . . But those were other days. After breakfast, a dull ache in my temples, I reviewed all of my notes on Darrell Meriwether and Paul Feder.

If the seeds of murder were buried in the past of either young man, they were too well hidden for me to find. And if I couldn't find them, no one could.

I don't intend to sound arrogant. Merely factual. I know of no investigative reporter better than I.

So, it didn't look to me as though it was a personal murder.

What was left?

Happenstance.

Paul Feder was in the wrong place at the wrong time, like the customer who walks into the gas station when a robbery's in progress.

I could imagine Don Brown's shrug and offhanded response. "In the wrong place at the wrong time? Henrie O, he was in his own damn driveway!"

·   ·   ·

April is fickle. Friday morning was gray, and a sharp wind rustled the leaves of the big magnolia. I studied Paul Feder's half-washed car. No one would have chosen to wash a car this morning. I shivered. Not simply from the raw day. If yesterday had been like this, Paul Feder might have gone to the mathematics building and he might be alive today.

If my premise was correct.

And I felt it had to be.

Something happened within Paul Feder's view after he started washing his car at 9:00 A.M. that made his murder imperative.

What?

A *Saturday Evening Post* cover during Norman Rockwell's heyday couldn't have exuded more small-town charm: two Victorian frame houses on large lots, a chat driveway, several oaks, the glorious magnolia, two blooming red buds, a screened-in porch on the house next door, a hedge-lined path to the footbridge over the gully, daffodils budding.

Here's where Paul Feder stood. I glanced at my watch. Half past nine.

I surveyed it all once again, noting this time the fenced backyards. This wasn't to say that those fences couldn't have been scaled. Certainly they could have. And certainly someone climbing those fences would have attracted Feder's attention.

But so would someone coming from the path to the footbridge.

In fact, any such person would pass within only a few feet of Feder.

If someone crossed that footbridge on Thursday morning between 9:00 and 10:00 A.M., the destination had to be either the Murray house or the house next door. That observant, effort-allergic worker among the sewer repair crew would have mentioned anyone coming out of the drive by the Murray house.

So no one had.

The wind rustled a stand of cane near the footbridge. It sounded almost like light, swift footsteps. I shivered.

No one answered my knock at either the Murray house, 1205 N. Calhoun, or at the house next door, 1207 N. Calhoun. I walked slowly up the drive to the street, the chat crackling beneath my Rockports. A boom box next to the excavated hole in the street twanged country music. Two workmen knee-deep in a pit shoveled dirt. A third leaned against his shovel.

Such would have been the scene Thursday morning. I didn't bother to approach the sewer repairmen. Don Brown was a good cop. No point in retraveling that ground. Instead, I glanced up and down the street. Most of the houses had that shuttered, somnolent air of houses whose occupants are elsewhere.

But across the street and two houses down, an elderly woman sat on the wooden front porch with one shawl around her shoulders, another over her lap.

As I came briskly up her walk she smiled, but her eyes were sharp and curious. "Good morning."

"Hello. I'm considering buying a house here." I pointed down the street at a For Sale sign. "I believe in finding out what I can about a neighborhood before I move into it."

"Oh, this is a wonderful neighborhood." Then her smile fled and her eyes darkened and she looked toward the Murray house. "Even though—I saw you down there. I suppose you know—"

"Yes. And I'll have to admit that's made me nervous."

She gestured for me to join her. "Forgive me for not getting up." It was brisk, not self-pitying. I saw then that the bottom shawl didn't quite obscure the tires of her wheelchair.

I dropped into the wicker chair beside her. "Yesterday—"

"I wasn't here. A doctor's appointment. I left just before nine." She looked across the street again. "I didn't know those boys, but I've watched them come and go. They're nice boys. I find it hard to believe—" She shook her head.

Reporters have to ask a lot of questions. Sometimes they get half answers, fake answers, stupid answers. Sometimes they ask and ask and ask and never find the facts that they need. And sometimes they get lucky. It was my day for luck. The kind of luck, however, that springs directly from effort. If I had not come to the site, if I had not looked for a witness, etc. As I am fond of telling students, "Nothing ventured, nothing gained" is perhaps the most profound adjuration refined through time by our species. I am enormously dismayed by the passivity that rules—and ruins—so many lives.

Olivia Briley had lived all of her life on this block, and the past five years, since a car wreck injured her spine, much of her days had been spent on her front porch.

"I don't feel so trapped, you see, when I'm outside."

"What do you think happened over there yesterday?" I gazed across the street, but I have excellent peripheral vision and I caught the uneasy look on her face.

"I don't know," she said slowly. "The paper said they'd arrested the other boy. I—it seems so unlikely."

"Who else could have done it? A tramp from the park?" I tried to appear candid, not, I know, an expression that sits easily on my rather world-weary countenance.

"Oh, maybe that's what happened. Oh, maybe so."

A child could have detected the false note of eagerness in her voice.

"And they'll catch him and then our neighborhood will be safe, just as it's always been."

Oh, sure. And our preppy president's Points of Light will burst into a radiance that will succor the thousands of mentally ill expelled from institutions to enjoy their freedom to roam America's seediest streets. And if you can buy that, I have some excellent oceanfront property in Arizona. . . .

I made encouraging noises and drew her out about this wonderful neighborhood. It took a while to gently maneuver her back to the houses that interested me, 1205 N. Calhoun and 1207 N. Calhoun.

Suddenly that false note was back in her voice. "Zenia Murray's a perfect neighbor. Just look at her tulips. Have you ever seen anything so glorious? Now, that's the kind of neighbor who helps property appreciate." Faded brown eyes stared at me earnestly.

"And Mr. Murray?" I asked.

"Oh, he's been dead for years."

"So Mrs. Murray lives alone and rents out her garage apartment?"

She was a definite beat too long in answering, but I merely stared blandly across the street as if this were the most inconsequential chatter, just a curious woman wanting to know about prospective neighbors.

"No. Her nephew lives with her." Her lips firmed in disapproval. "But she has to do everything herself, that good-for-nothing nephew of hers never lifts a hand. He never holds a job for more than a few months, then he goes on unemployment. Shiftless, that's what Rex Timmons is. And slamming out of the house when something doesn't suit him, going over to the park to work out. Shows off his muscles and picks up girls, that's what he does. I've told Zenia she's a fool to put up with it, but she says Rex is her dead sister's son and she just can't turn him out. I've seen those young men hanging around the park. Up to no good. Buying, selling drugs. Thursday morning? I'm sure he wasn't out of bed yet. Not Rex. As for Zenia, she's a teacher and I saw her leave for school just a few minutes before the cab picked me up to go to the doctor's office."

"And the house next door . . ."

"Oh, he's such a *nice* young man. He went up in my maple and rescued Sweetie Pie, my new kitten. She was just a little thing and last winter she got out and the first thing you know I heard this terrible mewing and Sweetie Pie was way up in the tree and too scared to come down. Burt Samson's his name. Friends? Why, you know, I never thought about it, but I don't think I've ever seen anyone visit him. Now, isn't that funny? Because he's such a nice young man. But perhaps he's shy. He's tall and gangling, you know, with brown hair and he wears horn-rims. So civilized in his appearance. Now, as for friends—those two young men—the ones in the garage apartment, they had people over all the time. Sometimes they'd play basketball for hours with that hoop on the garage. And to think—" She pressed a suddenly trembling hand to her cheek. She stared across the street. "Oh, I should have said something. I should have *done* something!"

I scarcely dared to breathe.

Then she did look at me, her faded brown eyes stubborn and sad. "I knew something was wrong—over there." She gestured with a wrinkled, ringless hand. "But people won't believe me when I tell them—I saw blood against the moon the other night and I *felt* evil, felt it. But who would have believed me?"

The first call I made when I reached the campus was to my favorite police lieutenant. After a long, thoughtful pause, Don responded affirmatively to my request for information in re criminal activities in Derry Hills within the past forty-eight hours. Then I settled down to my modem-equipped

computer. I have some very interesting access codes, quite
illegal to use, to credit bureaus, college records, hospitals,
banks, and other entities, which make the gathering of information simplicity itself. Most software safeguards wouldn't
give pause to a computer-literate ten-year-old. I supple-
mented the data retrieval with a number of old-fashioned
phone calls. It's amazing what people will reveal to strangers
over the telephone to a voice of authority.

In less than an hour, I'd gathered and printed out a good
deal of information on Rex Timmons and Burt Samson.

REX TIMMONS—B. April 26, 1966, Jefferson City,
Missouri, son of Byron Timmons and Cecily Murray Timmons. Only child. Father a fireman, died when struck by
falling masonry in a house blaze in 1970. Mother a clerk at a
local department store, died of breast cancer in 1980. Rex
came to live with his Aunt Zenia. A "C" student in high
school, he took a business course from the local junior college but dropped out during his second year. Employed spo-
radically. Heavy into physical fitness and war games. Hangs
around the Tenkiller Gym, dates girls he meets there. No
lasting relationships. Most recently worked at a rental car
agency, cleaning up cars. Fired last week for telling a super-
visor to fuck off when he was told to redo a car. No credit
record, no bank account.

BURT SAMSON—Born in Little Rock, Arkansas, November 3, 1963. Father Harold T. Samson, independent insurance agent, mother Aline, high school counselor. Youngest
of four sons. Football, track athlete in high school. BBA in
accounting from the University of Arkansas, 1984. Employed
as auditor by small accounting firm in Little Rock until moving to Derry Hills last winter. Financial officer at local software plant. Plays outfield in a softball league. An
accomplished rock climber. Excellent credit. Combined
credit-card debt presently $6,984.82, monthly payments to
GMAC for car loan, balance in checking account at First
National Bank in Derry Hills, $398.36; savings account,
$4,678.21.

Then I studied a copy of two black-and-white photos
from college yearbooks at a local library (fax machines are so
helpful).

Rex Timmons crouched like Rambo assaulting a hill, an
AK-47 replica (I hoped) cradled in his arms. He looked comfortable in the jungle-issue camouflage uniform—and reck-

less. His hair was cropped short. He had muscular arms, a rugged face, and a wild look in his eyes.

Burt Samson gripped a slim coil of rope and looked up at a granite overhang. (No glasses; contact lenses for climbing?) His face had the finely honed look of a man on a quest, total absorption, rapt concentration. Of course, it focused the mind wonderfully when an incorrect choice might bounce you against cliff walls to your death.

Two agile, strong, physically attractive young men.

Don Brown slumped into the chair opposite my desk and eyed me quizzically. "I thought you were working on the Feder kill."

"I am."

He waggled a file folder. "So why the inquiries in re unsolved crimes in the twenty-four hours preceding Feder's murder and missing person reports filed after his murder?"

"I have a wide-ranging interest in my community."

He didn't say bullshit. He merely looked it.

But he had the information for me. I eagerly reached for the sheet of paper he held out. I didn't, as he later told a mutual friend, "snatch" it from him.

CRIMES

Nick's Pizza, 312 N. Broadway, robbed after closing Wednesday night by an armed man (white, skimpy blond beard, midtwenties, six feet tall, thin), $436 in cash taken.

Clint's Texaco, 584 S. Porter, robbed shortly after 9:00 A.M. Thursday by knife-armed teenagers (one white, short, fat; one black, tall, muscular), $215 taken.

First National Bank, 105 Main Street, twenty ten-thousand-dollar bearer bonds reported missing at 10:00 A.M. Thursday. The bonds were checked out of the vault at 8:30 Thursday morning by Hazel Dublin, who delivered the folder to the desk of Margot Wood, vice-president, soon after. Wood opened the folder shortly before ten; it was filled with obviously fake bonds. Dublin was called for, but had left the bank sometime earlier. She was last seen going into the women's rest room about nine o'clock. Her apartment has been under a stakeout since the alarm, but she has not returned there. Coworkers expressed shock at the suggestion Dublin might have absconded with the bonds.

MISSING PERSONS

Hazel Dublin, 27, reported missing by E. P. Dunlap, a vice-president of First National Bank. Apprx. five feet seven inches tall, 130 pounds, medium-length blond hair (perhaps dyed), brown eyes. Oval face. No distinguishing scars, so far as known.

Lily Raymond, 45, reported missing by her husband, Jack Raymond. Didn't come home from work (Waitress, afternoon shift, Stars and Bars Grill, 2834 W. Council). Raymond admitted they'd quarreled that morning, says she may have gone to Kansas to her mother's.

Don Brown folded his arms across his chest. "Missing Persons isn't my bailiwick but I talked to the detective in charge. The bank employee's fade is one for the books, Henrie O. You'll never guess what's turned up." He waited with the air of a magician about to perform a dazzling trick.

Richard always told me showing off was bad form. But sometimes I can't resist.

"Oh, I might have an idea or two," I said casually. "Such as, she's only worked there for six months or so, and she never had much to do with anyone. Polite, pleasant, competent, boring. And I'll bet Hazel Dublin isn't her name, but the name of a bona fide bank employee who left employment in a midwestern bank about the time this 'Hazel Dublin' came to Derry Hills. I've no doubt the real Hazel Dublin was astonished at the suggestion she had moved to Derry Hills and gone to work for the First National Bank."

Don Brown's blue eyes widened. He sat up very straight. "Hey, wait a minute, Henrie O, how did you know?"

"I'm right, then."

And one step closer to the murderer of Paul Feder.

Of course, Don pressed me for details, but I wasn't ready yet. I promised to share the results of my investigation by the next morning.

"Why not now?" It was his tough cop voice.

I told him I had yet to hear from some sources and I couldn't quite prove my case.

"Your case?" he sputtered. "Now, wait a minute; if you know anything at all about this woman it's your duty to share it with the authorities immediately. As in, right now."

"I don't *know* anything," I retorted crisply. "I am merely making deductions that any reasonable person might make from information we've shared." I should have left well enough alone, but I was, I admit, irritated by his attitude. "It's obvious that the Derry Hills Hazel Dublin was a temporary creature created for the sole purpose of obtaining a job at the First National Bank, a simple matter when the persona offered was that of a trusted employee with several years' experience at a bank in a midwestern city. Am I not correct?"

"Peoria," he said finally, in a strained tone.

"Further, upon examination, I am sure that the Derry Hills police, under a duly authorized search warrant, have discovered that 'Hazel Dublin's' apartment is empty and contains nothing which might indicate her true identity."

"Plenty of prints," Don snapped.

My smile was not quite pitying. "So few young women have ever had occasion to be fingerprinted, and, of course, the lack of fingerprints on record was quite important in her selection."

"Selection? Wait a minute. You're talking criminal conspiracy." He leaned forward, his intelligent blue eyes intent and demanding. "Selection—who selected her?"

"I have some thoughts on that, but I can't share them yet. And the sooner you depart, the sooner I will be able to pursue my investigations."

Reluctantly, he stood. "Taxpayers pay us to investigate crimes, Henrie O."

I smiled cheerily. "I always sleep well at night, knowing that the stalwart enforcers of the law in Derry Hills are shielding its citizens from the forces of evil."

My office door has an automatic stopper on it, so he was foiled in his effort to slam the door behind him.

Dear Don.

I spent a half hour or so at my computer, but I wasn't surprised when I pulled up nothing of interest about Hazel Dublin. No credit record, no local involvement, no circle of friends.

I was just hooding my computer when the phone rang.

Don didn't bother with a salutation. "So I'm not stupid, Henrie O. You've got some kind of wild idea our disappearing bank employee is hooked up with either the Murray house or the house next door, and Feder saw her—or saw something—that could tip us off about the bonds. I mean, I won't go into the psychology of the deal—what kind of woman—even a thief—is going to batter some guy's brains out? And Feder was a good-sized man. But, cops have to investigate all kinds of wild tips."

My hand tightened on the receiver. "Have you talked to Timmons or Samson?"

"Sure. But don't sweat. Just in case you're on the right track, I didn't mention Dublin. Pressed 'em both on where they were when Feder was killed. Timmons still claims he was asleep. Samson got edgy, said he'd told us he was at his office—but nobody can prove he didn't slip out the back way."

I sighed in quick relief. I didn't want either of the chickens to know a fox was sniffing about.

"Although Timmons is no angel. Slouchy guy. I can see why you might suspect him of some kind of crooked deal. Be nice to know where he gets some of his spending money. But he and the guy next door"—a rustle of papers—"Burt Samson—are clean as a whistle on this Dublin character. Neither one of them has any connection to Dublin at all."

"Of course not."

He breathed deeply.

"The first requisite, of course, was that Dublin avoid contact with whichever one is involved."

"Henrie O, I'm telling you you're on the wrong track. There isn't any link."

"Oh, my dear, of course there is. But don't worry, in the morning I'll be able to tell you which one it is. I'll give you a call and you can get the search warrant."

"I'd have to have probable cause." His voice was tight.

"Dear Don, I know you can persuade the judge. You see, you're going to get an anonymous tip over the phone. 'Bye now." I hung up on what sounded very much like a roar. Perhaps the abrupt cessation of our call was a bit rude on my part, but I didn't want to tell Don I had one further investigative foray yet to make, one that was absolutely essential.

He wouldn't have approved. He has such strong feelings about legality.

I ignored the shrill of the telephone as I locked my office door and departed.

I was careful, of course.

I dressed in dark gray sweats and wore a cap. I rode my bike to the park and left it well hidden among the fronds of a densely grown weeping willow. Willows are among the earliest trees to green. So convenient. I carried a useful implement in one pocket that makes it quite easy to open almost any door unless it has a very sophisticated lock. My other pocket bulged a bit from the container of mace. The mace was just in case, but I expected no trouble. I'd done some checking. Zenia Murray wasn't due home from school until 5:30, which gave me thirty-five minutes clear. Much more than I needed. Rex Timmons was at the Tenkiller Gym pumping iron. Burt Samson was on his way from the software plant to the Derry Hills softball fields. His team had a game scheduled at 5:15.

It took me eight minutes to check out both cellars.

I'd never doubted what I would find.

I did have one other useful tool with me, a squeeze bottle filled with water.

The patch of earth that had been disturbed in one of the basements showed up clearly, six feet long, two feet wide. Recently disturbed earth absorbs water quickly. Hard-packed earth is almost impervious.

Now I knew.

I didn't wait until morning, of course. I'd told Don Brown morning because I didn't want a policeman sticking to me like glue. I punched in the numbers to his office (the dear young man works such long hours, but I knew I could catch him before he left for his night law class). "This is an anonymous phone call."

"Very funny, Henrie O."

"Is something wrong? You sound quite grim."

"I am not amused, as Queen Victoria once remarked."

"I do so admire literate policemen. But there is work to be done. You can get Judge Crowe on the phone." I told him the address for which he needed a search warrant.

"Look, there has to be probable cause—"

"As I said, this is an anonymous phone call from an informant: On Thursday morning, the missing bank employee, aka Hazel Dublin, came across the bridge over the ravine and was seen by Paul Feder, who was washing his car. She entered . . ."

Of course, Don Brown got the search warrant and found the grave, just where the anonymous informant reported it would be, and the body of a young woman, who was identified as the missing bank employee. The bearer bonds were found secreted in the lining of a backpack in a second-floor closet.

The *Clarion* ran a superb story, written by one joyous young woman reporter, Barbara Hamish:

> Reconstructing what is now seen as a double crime, police theorize that Rex Timmons, who has been arrested for murder, conspired with an unknown young woman to steal bearer bonds from the First National Bank, Timmons intending all along to murder the missing bank employee and enjoy the fruits of the crime by himself. Unfortunately for Timmons's scheme, police believe 'Hazel Dublin' was seen entering the back door of Timmons's home by Paul Feder. Police believe that sighting sealed Feder's fate. After killing 'Dublin,' police theorize that Timmons went outside and told Feder he had arranged earlier to borrow Feder's roommate's golf clubs. Going upstairs with Feder, Timmons took a club and battered Feder to death.

I accepted, of course, when Don asked me out for a celebratory steak. One of the many pleasures of living in the Midwest after so many years of food on the run is the availability of the best beef in the world. As for the cholesterol mania, mankind has thrived on beef for millennia, and that's good enough for me.

Don was excited. Knowing where to look, the police had discovered much. Timmons had met "Dublin" at a wargames competition in Chicago. "Dublin" was identified as Miriam Ventriss, who had lived in the same apartment complex in Peoria with the real Hazel Dublin. Don described the swift compilation of detail as soon as the basic form of the crime became apparent. But finally, he ran down and looked at me quizzically. "Okay, Henrie O, just between the two of us, how the hell did you know which guy did it? It could have been either one of them. God, I had cold chills—I could just see the wrongful search suit if you'd been wrong! How the hell did you know it was Timmons?"

I hadn't known, of course. In fact, I'd expected to find the grave in Samson's cellar—after all, he'd been an auditor. So, of course, it was a very good thing indeed that I'd made my illegal entries. But I had no intention of revealing my prefatory survey to Don.

"I wish," I said sincerely, "that I could reveal my sources. But you know how it is—"

He gave me a startled look. "There really is an anonymous tipster? Who the hell?"

But he knew better than to pursue it. An old reporter never confides.

whatever has to be done

JAN GRAPE

Jan Grape is a new voice in private-eye fiction, but she is not new to the scene. She has been an important member of PWA for several years and is currently editor of the PWA newsletter, Reflections in a Private Eye. *She and her husband, Elmer, own and operate Mysteries & More, the only mystery bookstore in Austin, Texas.*

With this, only her second published PI story, she proves herself a strong addition to the PI ranks, and in Texas-based partners Jenny Gordon and C. J. Gunn she has created a fresh new voice—make that two fresh new voices. Much of the strength of "Whatever Has to Be Done" comes from the friendship and working relationship of these two new female PIs. Jan Grape is here, and she is most welcome. See if you don't agree that this "Texas bro-o-ad"—as she describes herself as only a true Texan can—has a future.

———————

A fierce lightning and thunder storm jarred me awake at 5:12 A.M. Autumn storms in Houston, Texas, often give the impression the end of the world is near. The dream I'd been immersed in had been pleasant, but try as I might, I couldn't remember it. The brilliant streaks flashed a sesquicentennial fireworks display and seeped through the top edge of the miniblinds as Mother Nature declared a moratorium for sleepers.

It's not in my emotional makeup to wake up early; neither alert nor cheerful. Maybe it has to do with one of my past lives or blood pressure slowdown or something. Anyway, I tossed around trying to will myself back to sleep, knowing all the time it wouldn't work. But I waited until seven to crawl out to the shower. "Damn Sam," I said aloud while dressing and wishing I could have my caffeine intravenously. "Lousy way to start a Friday."

The pyrotechnics were over, but the rain continued steadily, steaming the interior of my car and making the rush-hour drive to the LaGrange Building hazardous and hair-raising. Determined to shake off frustration at the lack of sleep and the Gulf Coast monsoon, I paused in front of the fourth-floor door and felt a sense of pride as I read the discreet sign: G&G INVESTIGATIONS. My partner, Cinnamon Jemima Gunn, and I could be proud, we'd turned a profit the last three months. No one expected it to last. Sometimes even we had doubts.

There was a message from C.J., as she was known to all except a few close friends, on the answering machine. "Gone to Dallas for the weekend, Jenny. Work today and play tomorrow. Keep outta trouble, Girlfriend." She had a legitimate reason to go, a dying client wanted to find a missing niece and a good lead led to "Big D," but once the work was done, she had a friend playing football for the Cowboys who would show her a fun weekend.

Lucky sister, I thought, ready to feel sorry for myself,

"but wait—there's only a half day's work here," I said aloud, "and it's rainy—and besides it's Friday." It only took two seconds to decide to finish the paperwork and to blow this joint. I put myself in high gear and was ready to leave by noon.

I had straightened up the lounge/storeroom, grabbed my purse, and reset the phone machine when the outer door opened.

"Oh. No. Don't tell me you're leaving?" the woman said. "Are you Jenny Gordon?"

She was slender with reddish-blond hair, not really pretty, her eyes were too close together and her mouth too thin, but there was something about her. Vulnerability? She had a voice that rose into a whine and grated like fingernails on glass. I hate voices like that. She dropped her dripping umbrella, one of those bubble see-through ones, onto the floor. Her raincoat, after she peeled it off to reveal a blue velour jogging suit, hit the sofa and slid to the floor. I hate slobs, too. As if your things are not good enough. Maybe people like that just don't care. Or maybe she was used to someone picking up after her.

"I am Jenny Gordon and I was leaving, but what may—"

"Well, great. That's the way my whole life has been the past twenty-four hours. All screwed up." She walked over and sat on one of the customer chairs, rummaged in her purse for a cigarette, and pulled out a lighter encased in a silver-and-turquoise case. "It's really the shits, you know. Me needing a PI." She burst out laughing in a high-pitched nervous tone.

I tried to figure out what was going on without much luck.

She stopped laughing long enough to say, "And who does he send me to? A woman, for Christ's sake." She laughed some more and finished with a cough, then flicked the lighter and lit the cigarette without asking if I minded. I smoke, and didn't mind, yet it's nice to be asked.

I'm not the happy-homemaker type, but I couldn't stand the spreading, staining puddles. The woman really was a slob, I thought, picking up her raincoat. I hung it on the coatrack, folded her umbrella, and stood it in the wastebasket near the door. There was no sign she noticed what I did and no thanks either. Some people should just stay in their own pigpens and not run around spreading their muck.

I headed across the room, intending to get some paper towels to soak up the mess. "As I started to ask a moment ago, is there something I can do, Miss . . . ?"

"Ms. Loudermilk. Voda Beth Loudermilk."

"Ms. Loudermilk, why do you need an investigator?" I paused momentarily in the doorway. Her answer stopped me cold.

"I killed my husband last night. Emptied his own gun into him." The whine was gone, and the words came out in monotone as if she were describing a grocery list. "He died on me." She smashed the cigarette into an ashtray. "Isn't that the silliest thing you ever heard?" She laughed, but sounded close to tears.

If I was surprised because she didn't throw the butt onto the floor, I was totally wiped out by what she said. I was so intent, I didn't notice someone else had opened the outer door and entered. I blurted out, "Perhaps you need a lawyer, Ms. Loudermilk, not a detective."

"It was time he hurt some instead of me."

A quiet voice interrupted, "Voda Beth. Shut your mouth and keep it shut." He spoke in a quiet even tone.

The speaker was a short wiry man I recognized immediately from his many newspaper photos and television appearances. A shock of steel-gray hair, brushed back to emphasize the widow's peak, the piercing blue eyes and every one of his seventy-eight years etched on his face. I'd never met him, of course, but I knew who he was. Hell, everyone knew who "Bulldog" King Porter was—the best criminal lawyer money could buy.

"Oh shit, Bulldog," Voda Beth said. "You know a PI's like a priest. They can't reveal the confidences their clients tell them."

He was dressed like a lawyer would have dressed forty or fifty years ago. Dark charcoal, pinstripe, three-piece suit, white shirt with French cuffs peeking out the prerequisite amount, big gold cuff links. The tie, a shade lighter than the suit, was not a clip-on and tied with a perfect Windsor knot. A heavy gold-link watch chain had a gold Phi Beta Kappa key dangling from one end. "That only applies to PIs in dime-store novels." Bulldog walked over to me and held out his hand. "Ms. Gordon, I've heard a lot about you. I'm Bulldog Porter."

His hand was soft, but the grip firm. "I'm honored to

meet you, sir, I've heard a lot about you, too." Porter had begun his practice in Galveston during the thirties, when the island city considered itself a free state, allowing drinking, gambling, and prostitution. He had even defended members of the "beach gang" who smuggled Canadian booze into the Gulf port and shipped it to places like Chicago and Detroit.

"I'll just bet you have, Ms. Gordon." He chuckled. "And let me tell you up front, most of it is true."

Ms. Loudermilk stood up. Her curly hair framed a sharp-angled face that twisted in anger. "Bulldog . . ."

"Voda Beth, just sit right back down there and keep quiet for a minute."

She glared, but did as he said.

"Now, Ms. Gordon . . ."

"Please call me Jenny, Mr. Porter."

"Only if you call me Bulldog."

"Deal. Now, I'm assuming you have a special reason to be here."

"Good. I like that. Cut the crap and right down to brass tacks." He nodded to our storage/lounge area. "Let's go in there and have a little chat. Voda Beth, you stay put." The woman sent him a lethal look, but didn't get up.

"My client," he said as we sat at the kitchen-style table, "was mouthing off when I came in. Let's chalk that up to her current emotional state. To her grief, if you will. You see, her husband was shot and killed around eight P.M. last night. She was questioned for hours, eventually charged by the police and locked up in women's detention over at Sixty-one Reisner, just before dawn. She's been without food or sleep for over twenty-four hours."

"Her lack of sleep," I said, "plus the grief and trauma she's experienced has rendered her incapable of acting correctly or speaking coherently."

"Exactly. I heard you were sharp." He took out a pipe and, within seconds, had asked if I minded and got it lit. Bulldog Porter wasn't known as the plodding, methodical type. "We have great need of an investigator and you were highly recommended by Lieutenant Hays of HPD homicide department."

The fact that Larry Hays sent Porter to me was a surprise. Larry was a good friend, but he still thought it was laughable my being a private detective. My background is medical; an X-ray technologist. I worked ten years detecting the mystery of the human body and knew nothing about real mysteries. Luckily, C.J. had the necessary police experience and I'd been a willing pupil.

If what Bulldog said about the woman was true, she needed help. Maybe I was wrong to condemn her casual attitude about her wet things. If I'd just spent the night in jail, I sure as hell wouldn't be worrying about neatness. Besides, the chance to do a job for Porter was worth considering. G&G Investigations wasn't doing so well that we could turn down someone with his clout. "Did she kill her husband?"

He didn't answer immediately. "Her father and I were old school chums and I agreed to take her case because of him. Voda Beth says she has been physically, sexually, and emotionally abused her whole married life. That she pulled his own gun out from under the mattress and emptied it into him because he was hitting on her and she couldn't take it any longer. Actually, it shouldn't be hard to prove diminished capacity." He leaned back, and his eyes zeroed on mine like an electron beam. "What I need from you, Jenny"—he smiled—"is to discover if her story of abuse is true."

"Is there any physical evidence of her being beaten, like bruises or anything?"

"Not to my knowledge."

"Has she ever reported to a doctor or to anyone that she was abused?"

"I don't think so. But I'd like you to find out."

"What do you know about Mr. Loudermilk?"

"Another thing for you to look into. J. W. Loudermilk owned a development and construction company which was doing quite well until Houston's oil bust. But you'd need to do a thorough background check on him. I do know he was married before and he has a daughter from that first marriage. The daughter lived with him until recently, and she'd be the first place to start."

"And next, the ex-wife?"

"Precisely. Her name is Elwanda Watson. Had a second marriage which also didn't last. Four children by Watson. I have addresses and phone numbers for you." He placed the pipe in the ashtray I'd placed near him, reached into his inner coat pocket, and held out an index card. "I believe you've already decided to work for me?"

I smiled as I took the card. "I have indeed." I went to get

a copy of our standard contract for his signature. Voda Beth didn't look up when I passed through. When I returned, Porter had written out a check and handed it to me. He'd not inquired about fees. I nearly gasped; it was made out for five thousand dollars.

"I need to have as much information as possible by next Tuesday morning for the preliminary hearing," Bulldog said. "That means working through the weekend if necessary. If you can find out the truth about the Loudermilks' relationship, I might be able to get the charges dropped and we won't have to go to trial."

"If the truth is as she says it is."

"Oh. Naturally. But I believe it is." Mr. Porter spent a few seconds with *our* client and left.

It was time to interview the widow. I walked in and sat behind the desk, searching her face. A neon sign flashing NOT GUILTY did not appear on her forehead.

"Why don't you tell me what happened, Voda Beth?"

Her eyelids were red-rimmed and the pale blue eyes were devoid of life or light. She was holding her body rigid and her mouth tight as if to keep herself from flying apart.

"Look," I said, "I know you're exhausted, you need food and rest; how about telling me a few brief details, and if I need something else, we can talk later."

"J.W. and I had been arguing all evening. If I said black, he said white. I can't remember what started this particular one. Finally, I told him I couldn't take any more tonight, that I wanted to go to bed. I went to our bedroom, took a shower, and he sat in the den and drank."

"Did he drink a lot?"

"Sometimes, and even more lately."

"Why lately?"

"Things were bad financially, really bad the past few months." Voda Beth pressed her hands to her temples, then rubbed them slowly. "I remember now. That's what started the argument. Money. I'd bought two new bras yesterday, the underwire on my last one broke that morning."

My partner, C.J., had been a policewoman in Pittsburgh for eight years and one thing she'd taught me about interviewing someone is it's usually best to not say anything once the person is talking. If you interrupt you can lose them, they'll clam up.

"I had just finished brushing my hair and was ready to

get into bed when J.W. came in, yelling about how stupid I was for spending money we didn't have. He was furious. He'd sat in there and drank and got madder and madder.

"He got right in my face, screaming, and when I tried to ignore him, he got even madder. He slapped me. Twice at least, and the third time he knocked me onto the bed. He kept hitting with his open hand. One blow made me bite my lip, see?"

She showed me a large blood hematoma inside her cheek. I made appropriate noises of sympathy. "What happened next?"

"He straddled me and started punching me in the stomach and breast with his fists. A blackness came over me —slowly, at first. It got darker and redder. Somehow—I really don't know how—I got my hand under the mattress and got hold of his gun. The next thing I knew, he was laying across the bed and . . . and I remembered hearing the gun and there was blood everywhere and . . ."

She began crying, great shuddering sobs. I walked around the desk, handed her a box of Kleenex, and patted her shoulder, not really knowing what to say or do. She kept trying to say she didn't mean it, but it was a long time before she got it all out.

When she'd calmed down, and blew her nose, I sat down behind the desk. "This wasn't the first time your husband beat you?"

"No. He didn't do it often and he'd always apologize, say he was sorry and he'd never do it again. That he loved me and didn't want to hurt me. Months would go by and I'd believe everything was fine, then *wham.*" She was back to her monotone voice.

"Did you ever tell anyone? Your doctor maybe?"

"No. I was too ashamed. Besides, whatever I'd done to set him off was all my fault. I was the one who—"

"Voda Beth. Whatever you did was no reason to be battered or beaten. But my telling you won't help or make any difference to you. You need to get professional help."

"I will. Bulldog is setting it up."

I walked around to her again and patted her shoulder once more. "It's time you went home. You didn't drive over here, did you?"

"Bulldog brought me. He said he'd send someone to pick me up."

"Come on then, I'll go downstairs with you."

A white stretch limo was waiting in the front circular drive when we reached the lobby and a driver lounging against the front passenger fender saw us and walked over. "Ms. Loudermilk?" He helped her in and she waved one finger as he closed the door.

I walked to the parking garage. Lowly private investigators have to drive themselves home.

"If that tight-assed bitch thinks she can kill my father and get away with it, she's crazy."

J. W. Loudermilk's daughter was two months over eighteen, but looked twenty-five. Her name was Elizabeth, but she preferred to be called Liz, she said, after inviting me into her condo in far southwest Houston. She mentioned that she was scheduled for a tennis lesson at the nearby YWCA, but said she could spare a few minutes.

I'd been unable to reach her the evening before and had secretly been glad. Voda Beth's story had unnerved me. With a good night's sleep, I'd hoped to be able to think more rationally. Silly me. My dreams had been filled with a faceless someone who punched and slapped me half the night. It was three o'clock before I finally slid into a dreamless sleep.

I showered and dressed in my weekend office attire— Wrangler jeans and a T-shirt—but since it was a cool forty-nine degrees this morning, I pulled on a sweater. My hair had been short and curly-permed for summer, and as I combed through the tangled dark mop I decided to let it grow for the cooler weather. I checked out a new wrinkle at one corner of my right eye. "Damn Sam. At thirty-three, you shouldn't be having wrinkles," I said. "Someday you'll have to pay more attention to such things, but not today."

A tiny smudge of cocoa-frost eye shadow added depth to my dark eyes, and a quick swipe of powder was easy and fast and completed my bow to cosmetics. Spending time with creams and moisturizers was not my idea of fun, and I intended to fight it as long as possible.

I'd arrived for my appointment with J.W.'s daughter at 10:30 A.M. on the dot.

She had offered a cold drink. I accepted a diet Coke and sat down as she bustled around in the kitchen. Her living room was a high-beamed-ceiling affair, all mirrors, posters, and wicker furniture from Pier One Imports. There wasn't a sofa, just two chairs, and a lamp table between them, set before a fireplace. As a young woman out on her own, she probably couldn't afford much.

I studied her as she brought in the drinks. She was lovely, self-assured and poised. She had a heart-shaped face, blue-black hair, cut shoulder length and curly-permed. Her eyes were such a deep indigo they looked violet, and there was no doubt her resemblance to a young Liz Taylor was often mentioned. She was dressed in a white tennis skirt and top, showing off her golden tan to great advantage. Oh, to be eighteen again, I thought. But only for a brief second.

"Mrs. Gordon?" She seated herself opposite me.

"Jenny, please."

"Okay, Jenny. Let's get one thing cleared up right now. I never did like Voda Beth. She's a coke-snorting, greedy slut who married my father for his money."

"You know all this for a fact?"

The violet eyes narrowed briefly, before looking at me head-on. Maybe she was sincere, but her clichéd words sounded like the old evil stepmother routine. "My father owned his own construction and development company. He built office buildings and shopping malls. When his business suffered reverses, she couldn't stand it."

Liz sat her glass down on the end table next to her chair, picked up a nail file, and began filing her nails. "They argued all the time. Mostly about money. She was always wanting this new dress or that new piece of furniture. Now, with Dad dead, I guess she'll be in high cotton."

"Were their arguments ever violent? Did you see or hear your father hitting her?"

Liz finished the nail she was working on, put that finger to her mouth, and began chewing on the cuticle. She shook her head, "Dad did have a temper, but I don't think he ever so much as slapped the bitch."

I sipped on the diet Coke. "What gave you the idea she'll be in high cotton now? Insurance?"

"She talked him into taking out a policy for two million a few months ago. She killed him to get that money, there's no doubt in my mind."

I made a mental note to check out the insurance. "How did you find out about this policy?"

"*She* flaunted it in my face. It's one of those big companies, something Mutual. I'm sure you can find a record of it someplace."

"You mentioned she used coke?"

"I've known ever since I was sixteen and she offered it to me." Liz's face contorted with fury. "That bitch came along, turned my father against me, but it only worked a short time."

"What else did they argue about besides the money?"

"The drugs and the men she slept with."

"She slept around?"

"He said she did. I have no knowledge of that personally."

The picture the girl painted was certainly not something to help Mr. Porter. In fact, it was more likely to hang Voda Beth Loudermilk. But it did strike me strange that the girl didn't have one kind word to say about her stepmother. "How old were you when they married?"

"Thirteen." She drained her glass. "My mother couldn't hold on to Dad. She's a silly bitch, too. Sometimes she doesn't have the sense God gave a goose." She stood. "Sorry, Jenny. I do have to get to the Y for my tennis lesson. My fondest hope is that Voda Beth rots in jail."

Thirteen is a difficult age. I knew from losing my own mother when I was twelve that I would have resented it tremendously if my father had remarried. Her remarks about her own mother seemed strangely out of place. Didn't this girl like anyone? I wondered. Placing my unfinished drink on the table, I got up. "Appreciate your talking to me, Liz." I handed her one of my cards. "If you think of anything else I should know, please call."

Liz preceded me to the door and opened it. "If it's something that'll help convict her, you'll hear from me."

It would be easier to make notes of my interview at my office. When I arrived, I was surprised to find C.J. at the front desk, hacking away at the computer. "It's good to see you, but weren't you supposed to stay in Dallas all weekend?"

"Yes, but don't ask any questions, okay?" Her tone indicated she wasn't kidding. C.J.'s face, which always reminded me of a darker-skinned Nichelle Nichols, the *Star Trek* actress, was marred by a deep frown of concentration. The new computer we'd recently bought was giving her fits. She continued hitting the buttons and keys like she was working out on a punching bag.

The fun with the football player obviously hadn't worked out. "Ooo . . . kay," I said, and told her about our new client, Voda Beth Loudermilk, brought in by Mr. Bulldog Porter himself. She nodded without comment and I began telling of my interview of Liz Loudermilk. "Liz tried to look and sound sincere, but I'm having a hard time believing her. The hate this girl had was so thick in the room it nearly smothered me."

She paused and turned to listen. "Sounds like she's definitely jealous of the second wife."

"I've tried to imagine how I would feel in that situation. I'm sure I would have resented any woman *my* father brought in to take my mother's place."

"Five years is a long time to nurse a grudge. Didn't Voda Beth ever do anything nice for Liz?" C.J. looked down at herself and tried to brush off a minute piece of something white from her bright green sweater, gave up and plucked it with her fingernails, and tossed it away. The sweater, trimmed in brown and gold leather, was worn over a slim dark brown skirt, and she'd added a bright green leather belt. She was also wearing green-tinted panty hose and dark brown boots. At her six-foot height, she looks great in whatever she wears, but a couple of years as a model in Manhattan had set her style forever into the high-fashion look.

My taste usually runs to Levi's or sweats. Of course, no matter what I wore, I still looked just like me, Jenny Gordon, of Houston, Texas. "Liz Loudermilk will cheerfully push the plunger on the syringe if her stepmother is sentenced to die by injection. She ain't too crazy about her own mother, either."

"Maybe she's got a fixation on her father and anyone else is just a big zero in her mind."

"You're probably right, I was madly in love with my father when I was fourteen." I added, thinking back, "About six months later, I hated him."

"That was a normal growing-up process. I did about the same thing." She smiled and leaned the chair back, folding her hands across her stomach. "Girlfriend, you know what strikes me about your conversation with that girl?"

"That insurance policy?"

"Yes. But besides that. She called Voda Beth a tight-assed bitch. That describes someone uptight or morally rigid. It's not something I normally would associate with a woman who used drugs and slept around."

"You're right. It's total contradiction, isn't it?" I lit a cigarette, forgetting for a moment how much C.J. disliked my smoking.

She fanned the smoke with an exaggerated flip of her black hand. "Get out of here with that thing." She turned back to the computer. "Besides, until I figure out how to trace that insurance policy, I don't need you in my hair." She picked up the telephone receiver. "I guess I'd better call the 'old pro' over at Intertect first and find out where to start."

C.J. had a good working relationship with the private investigators over at Intertect, an office that specialized in computers and data bases. Good thing. Computers blow my mind completely. I'd probably never figure this one out.

I went into the lounge and turned on the air purifier and thought about my client. Bulldog Porter had wanted me to find "something" to prove wife abuse. Unfortunately, the talk with Liz Loudermilk had only tightened the noose.

I'd felt sorry for Voda Beth when she told of being beaten. She might even be a greedy slut, but I doubted she was as bad as the girl had tried to make her appear. It's easy to use pop psychology to categorize people, yet the girl did sound like the classic example of a jealous daughter.

I walked back through to the back office to my desk, taking care not to disturb C.J. as she punched keys on the computer and numbers on the telephone. I called to make a late-afternoon appointment with the ex-wife, Elwanda Watson. She worked as a waitress at a seafood restaurant out in the Heights area and said we could meet there. I typed up notes of the "Liz" interview on my old IBM Selectric and placed them in the Loudermilk file. I'd never let that machine go, even if I did learn things like Word Perfect programs and networking with modems.

Just before 5:00 P.M., Elwanda Watson called and changed our meeting to her home. I stacked the paperwork on my desk, told C.J. I'd see her tomorrow, not that she heard me—she was still wrestling with the computer. Just before the door closed, however, she called out, "Sunday brunch at my house, okay?"

Saturday-afternoon traffic around the LaGrange Building

was thicker than bees around molasses—maddening, but normal. The building is located two and a half blocks from the Galleria. Only twenty years ago, this whole area was still part of a dairy farm. Now, a six-block-square area of high-dollar shopping malls, department and specialty stores, hotels and high-rise office buildings, including developer Gerald Hines's sixty-five-story Transco Tower, filled the land where crimson clover used to grow and cows got fat. From the air, the whole area was filled with concrete, steel, and bronzed glass and looked like a city skyline, but it's six miles from downtown Houston in suburbia-land. The lack of zoning laws here makes for some unusual building developments.

Elwanda Watson lived in a story-and-a-half house made of white brick and wood and cedar shakes, four miles west of my office. An older neighborhood built in the late fifties before contractors and architects took a notion to make suburban houses all look alike. These were in a wide range of individual styles and colors. A huge magnolia tree stood sentinel in front and a pink bicycle lay on its side in the St. Augustine grass. Four baskets of white-and-burgundy impatiens hung from the eaves.

The woman who answered the door was short, overweight, with ponderous breasts and hips almost scraping the doorway. She had short, dark hair streaked heavily with gray and a startled expression that seemed to be permanent. She wore a dingy white sweatsuit, no makeup, and said she was Elwanda Watson. It would be difficult to believe Liz Loudermilk came from this woman's womb, if it had not been for the eyes. That unique shade of blue, tingeing to violet. Either Elwanda had lost her beauty long ago, or Liz got her looks from her father.

She led me to a large kitchen/den area, both paneled in knotty pine; there were children's play noises coming from the backyard. She indicated I should sit in the chair across from the sofa and brought tall glasses of iced tea before settling on the Early American–style sofa.

I glanced around. The room had the look of having been hastily picked up. A large entertainment cabinet stood against one wall. Wires and plugs stuck out and dangled from the front and one side, indicating sound and electronics had once been installed and then removed. A small TV set was alone on a shelf. Newspapers, magazines, books, and games;

Monopoly, Scrabble, Ninja Turtles, Yahtzee, Parcheesi, dominoes, and cards were piled on and in the cabinet. The drapes hung loose from the rod on one side and dragged on the floor. It was an I-don't-care look, much like the woman herself. Two failed marriages had taken their toll. "Ms. Gordon, what—" she said.

Smiling at her, I said, "Call me Jenny, please."

"And I'm Elwanda. Well, Jenny, what is it you wish to know? This whole horrible thing is too, too weird. Poor old J.W. dead. And Voda Beth accused of killing him. Unbelievable, I tell you. It just boggles my mind."

"It's hard to believe Voda Beth killed J.W.?"

"I'd just never figure her to do something so awful. She seems like such a nice person. Gracious and polite to me, and she's been really kind and generous to my Liz."

"Really? Liz doesn't share your feelings."

"Oh that Liz. She *can* act like a spoiled brat. The things I could tell you would take half the night. But you don't have time for that. She mouths off about Voda Beth something terrible sometimes, but deep down I know she likes her stepmom."

"That wasn't the impression I got this morning."

"Oh, I know," said Elwanda. "Liz told me how tacky she was this morning and asked me to apologize for the things she said."

"She doesn't owe *me* an apology."

"Well, she did mislead you. Made it seem like Voda Beth was a wicked person when she's not." She rubbed both eyes like a person just waking up. "My daughter is beautiful and brilliant, but she can also act like a two-year-old when she doesn't get her way. Sooner or later you have to give in. Of course, she's always sorry afterward and will make up for it a hundred ways."

Despite Elwanda's trying to make Liz sound like nothing more than a rebellious and rambunctious child, I had seen the rage Liz had toward Voda Beth. It wasn't just a temper tantrum. I'd hate to see that rage turned on anyone. Elwanda was maternally blind to her child's faults. She didn't want to think otherwise, and I thought it best to get off that subject.

"Voda Beth claimed J.W. was beating her when she killed him. Was he ever abusive to you?"

"Oh my. No. I was married to the man for ten years and he never raised a hand to me." She looked directly at me and her wide-eyed look of astonishment was more pronounced. "And I don't see him abusing Voda Beth, either. He worshiped her. He was always a kind and wonderful husband. And father. Always."

If that was true, I wondered, then why did she divorce this Boy Scout? I had to ask. "Why did you—"

"Divorce him? He left me. For another woman. Not Voda Beth, it was over long before he met her. There were lots of other women. Some men are born womanizers, and J.W. was one. That is, until Voda Beth caught him. I don't think he ever strayed from her." Tears welled up in those big violet eyes, and this overweight, throwaway wife's voice held a wistful note.

"What about his low boiling point?"

It took her a moment to speak. "He could get angry, real easylike when he was young, but he'd mellowed out. Even so, his anger never, ever, led to violence."

"Did Voda Beth ever go out on him?"

"I don't think so. He probably would've told me if she had."

I raised an eyebrow.

"It sounds funny, I guess, but after he married her, J.W. and I got real friendlylike. I mean, like close friends. He apologized for hurting me in the past. He was so good when my marriage with Don Watson broke up. Offered me money because he knew I was having a hard time with four little kids."

At their mention, the children's voices outside reached a crescendo and she walked to the patio door to check. Evidently, it was nothing that needed her presence. Motherlike, however, she stuck her head out and told them to stop whatever they were doing and find something else to do. She came back to the sofa and sat. "I think, it was because he was finally happy. He said once, Voda Beth had taught him the right way to treat a woman and he'd learned his lesson."

Obviously, Elwanda still had deep feelings for J. W. Loudermilk and she wasn't going to say anything against him. Unfortunately, what she said was detrimental to my client. If J.W. didn't have a history of abusing women, it looked like Voda Beth had lied. I stood. "I appreciate your talking to me."

"Sorry I wasn't more help." We headed to the front door and she said, "Oh, I just thought of something. It's possible they had some fights over Liz. That was one thing he could get angry enough to come to blows over. Although I still don't see it."

"Why not?"

"Liz would have told me about it."

After the way the girl had talked about her mother, I was not sure she'd confide in Elwanda, but what do I know about daughters? Especially teenage ones.

"Liz was very angry with her father the past few years—for breaking up our marriage, for marrying Voda Beth. For what she saw as him neglecting her. She would gripe and complain how he didn't pay any attention to her, how he was always fawning over Voda Beth. Now that I think on it, she must have been jealous of her father."

That could explain the rage I saw in the girl. "I guess that's normal in young girls who want their father all to themselves."

"She could get all worked up about it. Throw fits and scream at him. That's one reason he made her move out of the house."

"He made his own daughter leave?"

"About three months ago. She was working and making good money, but she would stay out all hours and do things to aggravate him—like smoking pot in the house. Anyway, he got fed up, and although Voda Beth tried to stop him, he made Liz get a place of her own. She was really bent all out of shape over that for a while."

"I guess it's hard to be a parent these days." I thanked her again and left.

I headed back to my apartment, grateful the traffic had slacked off; it gave me time to wonder about my client. Whatever had happened that night in the Loudermilks' home was still muddled, but it looked as if my client had lied through her teeth.

I ate a light dinner, grilled chicken and a big salad, and spent the rest of the evening reading a PI novel by one of my favorite women writers.

I went to bed, and just before drifting off to sleep, I decided tomorrow I'd call Lieutenant Larry Hays of Houston's homicide department. Maybe the police and autopsy reports would give me some fresh insights.

•   •   •   •

I called Larry Hays on his car phone and caught him as he was driving away from headquarters to go have breakfast. "No rest for the wicked, huh?"

"Not on Sunday," he said. "Meet me at Kay's in twenty minutes."

Kay's was a favorite hangout of law enforcement personnel. The restaurant's owner, Bert DeLeon, had a thing about listening to the cops' war stories. He really got into that stuff. He'd been especially fond of my late husband, and when Tommy introduced me to him, I figured if Bert had not approved, Tommy would not have proposed. Kay's served family-style food and gave better service than the high-priced restaurants.

Lieutenant Hays sat at the back booth on the west side and a mug of coffee was waiting for me. "Are you eating?" he asked.

"Just an English muffin and half a grapefruit."

"Watching your weight again?"

"Always. I weighed a hundred twenty-five this morning."

"That's about your normal, isn't it?"

"Yes, but you know how I love chicken-fried steak and Mexican food, and the only way I can indulge is to keep this five-feet-six-inch woman on that one twenty-five."

"Poor baby."

Larry is six three and weighs about one eighty-five and never has to watch his weight because he has a great metabolism. It was frustrating and I tried not to think about it. "Just shut up and eat your cholesterol-filled eggs and pancakes and bacon."

"I intend to."

Larry had been my husband's partner and friend from the day they were rookies, until politics caused Tommy to resign and become a private detective. Larry had taken on a self-appointed task of watching out for me after my husband was killed, and sometimes it was stifling. We'd had several arguments about it, but recently he had weakened. Mostly because I'd learned from C.J. how to handle myself. He was a damn good cop and I respected his opinions. It was easier when he respected mine.

After we'd eaten, he answered my questions about the Loudermilk case. "The medical examiner has some doubts about your client's story."

"Like what?"

"The angle of the shot for one thing. Mrs. Loudermilk says she was crouched on the bed when she shot him. That doesn't wash. The ME says the shooter was standing. If she were as close to him as she says, there would have been powder burns on his body. The ME says the shooter had to be standing at least twelve to fourteen feet away."

"Wow. Bulldog's not going to like that."

Larry ran a big hand through his sandy hair. "Probably a good thing. I don't think he can prove she was abused."

"Why not?"

"I talked to our police psychologist, and although he didn't talk to her, he says she doesn't display the attitude of a battered woman. Immediately after a battering, most women usually act meek and acquiescent. She came in there full of self-confidence. Almost daring us to believe her." Larry signaled the waitress to bring him more coffee. "She's got all the buzzwords and phrases down pat. Like how he got boozed up and how he used his open hand on her face and his fists on her breasts and abdomen."

"Yeah, she gave me those classic statements, too, the ones I've read about; like how he'd say he was sorry and how she deserved it."

His hazel eyes narrowed. "At one point Thursday night, the sex crimes unit took her over to get a medical exam. No evidence of sexual intercourse. They noticed a couple of bruises on her torso, but thought they could have been self-inflicted. She gave us a pretty good story, but she hasn't given us the truth yet."

"Could she be covering for someone? Like maybe the daughter?"

"Possibly, but the captain and the DA want to go ahead with the indictment anyway. The physical evidence and her confession wraps everything up in a nice neat package with a big bow. I just never have liked neat packages."

"The daughter is seething with rage against the step-mother."

"Rage isn't evidence. Lots of daughters hate their step-parents. You don't have to worry. Bulldog will plead Voda Beth on diminished capacity and get her off or he'll plea-bargain." He absently stirred the coffee and then realized he hadn't added the sugar yet. "I do have a funny feeling there's something else."

"I guess I'd better talk to Bulldog. He's not going to be too happy with this."

"Likely not." He grabbed the check and stood. "I hate to eat and run, but I've got to go interrogate witnesses in a drive-by shooting last night."

"Have fun."

"Oh, yeah," he said harshly, his mind already to the task that lay ahead.

I headed for the office and, for once, the traffic wasn't a problem. Sunday morning is one of the rare good times to drive in this congested bayou city.

I had talked with C.J. before leaving home and canceled our brunch date. She said she'd go to the office and see what she could turn up on the computer. She wanted to run credit records on all three women, Voda Beth and Liz Loudermilk and Elwanda Watson; and throw in J. W. Loudermilk, too.

She'd made coffee. I poured a cup and sat down next to her desk. She had not found anything unusual on the women's credit records, and the daughter hadn't established any credit yet. We discussed my interview with Elwanda and I told her what Larry had said. "I'd better call Bulldog. I don't have one solitary thing to help him. He'll probably want to fire us."

"Okay," C.J. said, "but I've got a couple more checks to make while you're getting us fired."

I walked back to my desk and called Bulldog Porter's office. His answering service said he'd call me back within the hour or, if he didn't, for me to call again.

Twenty minutes later, C.J. came in my office and a gleam was in her dark eyes. "I got it."

"What?" I was still waiting on Bulldog to return my call and was trying to get my reports ready for him and figure out how much I could deduct from the five thousand he had given me.

"Remember Liz Loudermilk told you about a big insurance policy?" I nodded. "She was right. You're going to love this."

"Uh-oh. Don't tell me you've found another motive for Voda Beth."

"Our client isn't the only one with a motive. Little Miss Liz could inherit it all. All by herself."

"Oh yeah? How?"

"If Voda Beth dies first or is disqualified, it all goes to the loving daughter."

"Allll riiiight. And I guess if ole Voda Beth goes to prison for killing her husband, she'll be disqualified?"

"You got that right, Ms. Gordon, and to help put Liz to the top of the suspect list, you won't believe this, she put money down yesterday on a brand-new, fiery-red Miata."

"You have got to be kidding."

"If I'm lying, I'm dying. But just don't *forget* one important thing—stepmommy's told you and the police a big lie."

"That's okay. Old Bulldog will say she made that statement under duress," I said. "This is just what he needed. It gives him some ammunition for his reasonable doubt."

"Wonder what the lovely Liz was doing that night?"

I called Lieutenant Hays, knowing he'd need to know what we'd found. Luckily, he was near his car phone and I filled him in on Liz. He wasn't too happy. The case was closed as far as he was concerned, but after he grumbled, he said he'd talk with the daughter tomorrow, to see if she had an alibi for the night in question. He hung up.

"C.J.," I said, "I think Liz did it and our client confessed, all under some misguided idea to protect Liz. Bulldog can take this and run with it."

"When do I get to meet this mouthpiece anyway?"

"Anytime you say. You'll like him, he's positively charming."

"Uh-uh. No way I'm gonna like a shyster who use ta work fo' de mob. Those guys ain't nobody for this li'l black girl to mess wid." As usual, her slipping into southern black street talk cracked me up. Coming from such a smart and beautiful woman, it was funny.

As I laughed she said, "By the way, while running those credit-card histories I did find a few interesting tidbits on old J.W. himself." She handed me the printout of J. W. Loudermilk's Visa and American Express statements for the past year.

I flipped through them. "Holy shit, this is scary. You don't expect any old Jane Blow to be able to run a credit-card-account check."

"Oh hell"—her voice full of pride—"not just any old Jane Blow can do it. It takes a few brains and persistence. I took what I learned from my investigator pals and played around for a while and was able to come up with a password for a security code."

"My partner—the smart-ass computer hack." I was scanning the account statements and something caught my attention. Loudermilk had visited three different doctors in the past month and had charged his visits to his AmEx. "Wonder what this medical stuff is all about?"

"Give that girl a gold star. That's what I thought was so interesting."

"I happen to know this Dr. Gaudet is a neurosurgeon. I'm not sure about the other two."

She said, grinning, "Think I should check them out?"

"Holy shit. Why didn't I think of that?"

"Because you hired me to think for you."

"Someone has to do the important stuff," I said. "I don't want to talk to Voda Beth again. It makes me mad when a client lies to me, but I could go talk to Elwanda Watson again. Maybe J.W. confided some medical problem to her. It's probably not important, though."

"Fine. But do it tomorrow. I make a motion we get out of here. Sunday's almost over and we need a little R and R."

"Honey," I said, using one of her favorite expressions, "you ain't never lied."

Monday morning dawned with Houston shrouded in fog. Not unusual this time of year. With cooler air sweeping down across Texas and meeting the warm Gulf air, it was inevitable. It looked like the sun would burn it off around ten, and sure enough, I was right. When I left for Elwanda's around 10:30, there were only a few pockets of misty stuff, although the sky was still hazy.

I had not called first for an appointment; sometimes it's better to catch people when they're not on guard. Turns out Elwanda was not the only one to be surprised. I found my client, Voda Beth Loudermilk, visiting Elwanda. Neither seemed pleased to see me. They were both dressed in gowns and robes, but it looked as if neither had slept. What was going on between these two? I wondered.

They sat on the sofa next to each other and I sat in a platform rocker that angled off to their right. After exchanging a few politenesses, I mentioned Homicide was interviewing Liz this morning, setting off quite a reaction.

Voda Beth practically yelled at me. "Liz didn't have anything to do with anything. I'm the one who shot J. W. The police already have my statement." She burst out crying and Elwanda moved closer to put her arms around her, making soothing sounds as if comforting a baby.

"I resent someone accusing my daughter," Elwanda said. "Was that your idea, Ms. Gordon?"

"Not exactly. But some new information about Liz did come to my attention. Naturally, I had to tell the lieutenant in charge."

"What information?" she demanded.

"I'm not at liberty to say."

Voda Beth was crying so hard she began coughing and Elwanda got up to get a glass of water. As she moved to the kitchen the telephone rang. The receiver was a few feet from her, but when Elwanda shot a quick look at Voda Beth, the plump woman turned and said, "Jenny, would you mind getting that?"

I walked into the kitchen as Elwanda hurried back to the sofa. "Watsons' residence," I said.

"Jenny, is that you? Good. I thought you should know what I found out from Dr. James Gaudet. Seems that Loudermilk had a deep-seated, inoperable brain tumor."

I turned my back to the two women and kept my voice low. "Neuroblastoma?"

"Some big long name," she said. "I'm not sure if that was it, but the doctor said it was bad. Real bad. That he'd never seen a malignancy grow so fast. The man was only weeks away from blindness, paralysis, and death."

"Sounds like Loudermilks' luck turned . . . wait a minute."

"Now. Now you're thinking. This may have been planned."

"A mercy killing . . . maybe."

"Bingo. Something else you should know. Larry called. Daughter Liz has a strong alibi. She and a girlfriend were baby-sitting for her younger brothers and sisters at her mom's house."

"Where did Elwanda go?"

"Liz says she doesn't know, but maybe . . ."

"The Loudermilks'," C.J. and I said in unison. I thought for a moment, then said, "Why don't you call Bulldog Porter? Ask him to come over here immediately. This may get interesting." I hung up the receiver, walked to the coffeepot, and poured a cup, but it was bitter.

I could see Elwanda and Voda Beth still huddled together. It looked as if both had been crying, but there were signs of recovery. I rinsed out the coffeepot. The coffee canister was empty, and it took me a few minutes to locate a new can, open it, and get the pot dripping. I'd just poured three cups when the front doorbell rang.

Elwanda answered it and led Bulldog back into the den. Both women were definitely not expecting him. They wanted to know what was going on, would someone please tell them?

I handed the coffee around and then stood near the glass patio door and began. "I'm presenting a hypothetical case here, Bulldog. If you ladies will please listen." They turned tear-streaked faces to me. Elwanda's permanent look of astonishment was even more pronounced. Voda Beth looked tired. Bone-tired.

"I think there was this nice man, who had a nice wife and a nice ex-wife and a not so very nice brain tumor. He knows he doesn't have much time before he will be totally incapacitated, and a short time after that, he will die. He doesn't want to die like that. The man also had some business losses. There's the wife and an eighteen-year-old daughter to think about." You could have heard an eye blink, they were so quiet.

"I think this very nice man decided to commit suicide. Everything is planned, but that night for some reason, maybe fear, he was unable to do this alone. He asked his wife for help. She refused. He was on somewhat friendly terms with his ex-wife and he calls her. The ex comes over. He convinces the women time is running out. That the job must be done. The discussion continues, he is adamant, he begs and cajoles, and one of them is convinced to help. Maybe it was the ex. But the wife says to the ex-wife no, if anything goes wrong what will happen to your children? You can't go to prison. I won't allow it. But I can't kill the man I love, either. Finally, one woman does it and the wife calls the police."

I looked at each woman, but was unable to read the truth. "How does that sound to you ladies? Bulldog?"

No one said anything and I saw big tears running, first down Voda Beth's face and then Elwanda's. Silent tears that quietly dripped into their laps, leaving traces on the robes. Their hands were clasped tightly together.

Elwanda was the first to speak. "I'm the one who shot him first. Voda Beth took the gun then and emptied it into him so if the police tested her hands, there would be gunpowder traces and her fingerprints would be on the gun."

"No." The anguish was clear and strong in Voda Beth's voice. "I'm the one who fired the gun. She had nothing to do with it. I killed him and I'll take the punishment."

"Bulldog," I said. "Looks like you've got your hands full."

"Oh no," he said, "this one is already won. I doubt there will even be a trial. And if there is, plea bargaining is still an option. Thank you for your help, Jenny. You can expect business from me now and then, when I have the need of an investigator. Send me an invoice for your expenses."

I walked out of Elwanda Watson's house and drove to the LaGrange, parked, and walked inside. When I reached our office, C.J. asked, "Which one did it? Who fired the gun?"

"I don't think it really matters. They just did what they thought had to be done."

Suppose prospective parents had to take vows like the ones a bride and groom exchange. It's likely that some of the words would remain the same: they'd probably pledge to love and to cherish, in sickness and in health, for richer and for poorer. Certainly, new promises would have to be added; perhaps they'd agree to protect and to nurture. Max Allan Collins's "Louise" and Sara Paretsky's "Strung Out" present test cases investigating the limits of parental love.

louise

A MS. TREE SHORT STORY

MAX ALLAN COLLINS

To list all of Max Collins's credits would take more time and more pages than we have here. Ah, what the heck. We'll give it a shot.

Max Collins is the writer of the "Dick Tracy" comic strip, having taken that job over from Tracy creator Chester Gould fifteen years ago. Recently he authored the novelization of the Dick Tracy *movie, which starred Warren Beatty and Madonna. Mr. Collins attended the world premiere of the* Tracy *film, but the rumors about him and Madonna are just that . . . rumors.*

He is a past winner of the Shamus Award for his Nathan Heller novel True Detective *and has been nominated three other times, also with Nathan Heller novels. He is also the author of* The Dark City *and two other novels featuring Eliot Ness.*

He is . . .

No, see, I told you. Not enough time, or room.

"Louise" is one of the rare prose stories to feature Max Collins and Terry Beatty's comic-book lady PI, Ms. Tree. We believe that a rose is a rose is a rose, and by any other name, or in any form, Ms. Tree is formidable.

———————

Her face was pretty and hard; her eyes were pretty and soft.

She was a waif in a yellow-and-white peasant dress, a Keane-painting child grown up, oval freckled face framed by sweeping blond arcs. She wore quite a bit of makeup, but the effect was that of a schoolgirl who'd gotten into Mommy's things. She stood with her purse held shyly before her, a guilty Eve with a brown patent-leather fig leaf.

"Miss Tree?" she asked tentatively, only half stepping inside my private office, despite the fact that my assistant had already bid her enter.

I stood, paying her back the respect she was showing, and tried to put her at ease with a smile. "I prefer 'Ms.,' " I told her, sitting back down, and gestured toward the chair opposite me.

She settled gradually into the chair and straightened her skirt primly, though her manner was at odds with the scoop neck that showed more bosom than modesty would allow.

"I never been to a office on Michigan Avenue before." Her big blue eyes took in the stark lines of my spacious but austere inner chamber. "You sure have a nice one."

"Thank you, Miss Evans."

Pretty as she was, she had the sort of countenance that wore more suffering than even heavy makeup could hide; so it was kind of a shock when her face brightened with a smile.

"Louise," she said, and she extended her tiny hand across the desk, with a deliberation that revealed the courage she'd had to summon to behave so boldly, "call me Louise. Please."

"My assistant tells me you were quite insistent about seeing me personally."

She nodded and lowered her head. "Yes. I'm sorry."

"Don't be sorry, Miss Evans."

"It's Mrs. Evans. Excepting, I'd like you to call me Louise. I need us to be friends."

"All right," I said. This wasn't going to be easy, was it? "You said this is about your daughter. That your daughter is in trouble."

I was too busy for this, with Gold Coast divorce cases, legal work, and corporate accounts, but hers hadn't been the kind of plea you could turn down.

"Terrible trouble," she said, and her lower lip trembled; the blue eyes were filling up. "My husband . . . I'm afraid of what he might—"

Then she began to weep.

I got up, came around, and bent beside her as she dug embarrassedly for Kleenex in her purse. She was so much smaller than me, I felt like an adult comforting a child as I slipped an arm around her.

"You can tell me," I said. "It'll be all right."

"She's gone," she said. "He took her."

"Your husband took your daughter?"

"Months ago. Months ago. God knows what he done to her, by this time."

"Tell me about it. Start at the beginning. Start anywhere."

But she didn't start. She grabbed my arm and her tiny fist gripped me hard. As hard as the life that had made the sweet features of her young face so old.

"I wish I was like you," she said. Her voice had an edge. "Louise . . ."

"I've read about you, Ms. Tree. You're a strong woman. Nobody messes with you. Nobody pushes you around."

"Please . . ."

"You're big. You killed bad men before."

That was me—a cross between King Kong and the Lone Ranger, in a dress. Frankly, this petite if buxom woman did make me feel big; at five ten, one hundred forty pounds, I sure wasn't small. My tombstone would likely read: "Here Lies Michael Tree—She Never Did Lose That Ten Pounds."

And so I was to be Louise's savior; her avenger. I sighed, smiled, and said, "You really should tell me about your daughter, Louise—and your husband."

"That's why I come here. I need somebody like you to go get Maggie back. He took her, and the law can't do nothing."

I got a chair and sat next to her, where I could pat her reassuringly when necessary, and, finally, she told me her story.

Her husband Joe was "a good man, in lots of ways," a worker in a steel mill in Hammond. They met when she was working in a McDonald's in South Chicago, and they'd been married six years. That was how old Maggie, their only child, was.

"Joey's a good provider," she said, "but he . . . gets rough sometimes."

"He beat you?"

She looked away, nodded. Battered women feel ashamed, even guilty, oftentimes; it makes no logical sense, but then neither does a man beating on a woman.

"Has he beaten your daughter, too?"

She nodded. And she started to weep again.

She was out of Kleenex; I got up and got her some.

"But that . . . that's not the worst part," she said, sniffling. "Maggie is a pretty little girl. She got blond hair, just like mine. And Joey was looking at her . . . you know. *That* way. The way my daddy done me."

"Do you think your husband ever . . . ?"

"Not while I was around. But since he runned off with her, that's what I'm afraid of most."

I was a little confused; I had been assuming that this was a child custody situation. That the divorced husband had taken advantage of his visitation rights to disappear with his daughter.

"You haven't said anything about divorce," I said. "You and your husband *are* divorced?"

"No. We was talking about it. I think that's why he done it the way he done."

"What do you mean, Louise?"

"He knew that if we was divorced, the courts'd give Maggie to me. And he didn't want me to have her. Ms. Tree, when I was Maggie's age, my daddy beat on me. And he done other things to me. You know what kind of things."

I nodded.

"Ms. Tree, will you take my case? All I got is two hundred dollars I saved. Is that going to be enough?"

"It's going to be like McDonald's, Louise," I said.

"Huh?"

"You're going to get back some change."

Louise had reported her husband's disappearance to the police, but in the five months since Joey Evans and his daughter vanished, there had been little done. My contact at the police department confirmed this.

"The Missing Persons Bureau did what they could," Rafe Valer said, sitting on the edge of his desk in his small, cluttered office at Homicide.

"Which is what, exactly?"

Rafe shrugged. Darkly handsome describes him, but considering he's black, saying so may be in poor taste. Thirty, quietly ambitious, and as dependable as a pizza at Gino's, Lieutenant Valer had been my late husband Mike's partner, before Mike went private.

"Which is," he said, "they asked around Hammond, and South Chicago, talking to his relatives and friends. They found that one day, five months ago, Joe Evans quit his job, sold his car for cash, packed his things, and left."

"With his six-year-old daughter."

"With his six-year-old daughter. The assumption is, Evans has skipped the state."

I almost shouted. "Then this is an FBI matter!"

"Michael," Rafe said, calmly, smoothly, brushing the air with a gentle hand as if stroking an unruly pet, "it isn't kidnapping when a natural parent takes a child along when they take off."

"This is a case of child abuse, Rafe. Possibly sexual abuse!"

"I understand that," Rafe said, his voice tightly patient, "but Louise Evans never filed charges of any kind against her husband, before or after he ran off. Nor has she filed for divorce."

"Goddammit. So what does that leave her with?"

"You," Rafe said.

As if I were dealing a hand of cards, I tossed a photo of rugged, weak-jawed Joe Evans onto the conference-room table; then a photo of blond little Maggie, her mother's cute clone; then another of the family together, in what seemed happier times, unless you looked close and saw the strain in the faces of both adults.

"Sweet-looking child," Dan Green said, softly, prayerfully.

Dan, not yet thirty, was the younger of my two partners, a blond, mustached, good-looking kid whose regular features were slightly scarred from a fire an arsonist left him to die in. He'd lost an eye in that fire, too, and a hand; a glass eye and a hook took their place.

"Right now," I said, "she's very likely enduring hell on earth."

"Sexual abuse at any age is a tragedy," Roger Freemont said, taking Maggie's photo from Dan. His deep voice was hollow. "At this age, no word covers it."

Roger, balding, bespectacled, with a fullback's shoulders, was the rock of Tree Investigations, Inc. He'd been my husband's partner in the business; like Rafe Valer, Roger had worked with Mike in the Detective Bureau.

"I accepted a retainer of fifty dollars from Louise Evans," I said.

The two men gave me quick, searching looks, then shrugged and gave their attention back to the photos spread before them.

"Of course I did that for the sake of her self-respect," I said. "She works at a White Castle. She had two hundred bucks she'd saved and wanted to give it all to me."

"Fifty bucks will cover it," Roger said.

"Easily," Dan said. "So—where do we start?"

"They've been gone five months," Roger said, "and that's in our favor."

"Why?" Dan asked.

Roger shrugged. "He's settled in to his new life. Enough time has passed for him to think he's gotten away with something. So he gets careless. Enough time has passed for him to start seriously missing family and friends. So he makes phone calls. Writes letters."

Dan was drinking this in.

"Evans has a big family," I said, referring to my notes from several conversations with Louise. "They're a tight-knit working-class bunch. Two brothers and three sisters, all grown adults like Joey. One brother and two of the sisters live in the area—Hammond, Gary, South Chicago. Another brother lives in Dallas."

"*That* sounds like a good bet," Dan said. "I bet Joey's deep in the heart of you-know-where."

"Maybe. He also has a sister in Davenport, Iowa."

Roger perked up. "What is that? A three-hour drive?"

"Around," I said.

"Close to home," Roger said, eyes narrowing, "but far enough away."

"Where do we start?" Dan asked.

"You're going to go by the book, Dan. And Roger—you aren't."

Dan said, "Huh?" while Roger only nodded.

I assigned Dan to check up on Evans's last place of employment—the steel mill—to see if Evans used the place as a reference for a new job; ditto Evans's union—that union card would be necessary for Evans to get a similar job elsewhere.

"If Evans wanted to drop out," Dan said, "he wouldn't have used the mill as a reference, or maintained his union card. . . ."

"Right," I said. "But we can't assume that. He may not be using an assumed name. Maybe he's still living as Joe Evans, just somewhere else. Also, Dan, I want you to go over Louise Evans's phone bills for the six months prior to her husband leaving. Find out what, if any, out-of-town calls he was making."

Dan nodded.

"Any credit-card trail?" Roger asked.

I shook my head. "The only credit card the Evanses had was an oil company card, and Louise received no bills incurred by her husband after he took off."

"Any medical problems, for either the father or child?" Roger asked.

"No."

"Damn," Roger said.

"Why 'damn'?" Dan asked him.

"Prescription medicine would give us a trail," Roger said. "And we could check the hospitals and clinics in areas where we suspect they might be staying."

"They're both in fine health," I said. "Except, of course, for whatever physical and mental traumas the son of a bitch is inflicting on that child."

The two men shook their heads glumly.

"Roger," I said, "you talk to Evans's family members—his father's deceased, but mother's still alive. She may be the best bet. Anyway, after you've talked to them all, keep Ma under surveillance. Go through all their trash, of course— phone bills, letters."

Roger nodded, smiled a little. This was old hat to him, but Dan was learning.

"Better cook up some jive cover story for when you talk to the family," Dan advised him. "Don't tell them you're a detective."

Roger smirked at him. But he let him down easy: "Good idea, kid." There was no sarcasm in his voice; he liked Dan. "I'll tell 'em I'm trying to track Joey down for a credit union refund. They'll want to help him get his money."

Dan grinned. "I like that."

"Make it a fifty-dollar refund check," I said.

"I like that figure, too," Roger said.

Dan made it unanimous.

Three days later, we had something.

It hadn't come from Dan, not much of it anyway. The by-the-book route had only confirmed what Missing Persons found: one day, Joe Evans quit and took off, abandoning if not quite burning all his bridges behind him. His boss at the steel mill had not been called upon for a reference, nor had his union card been kept active. And his friends at the mill claimed not to have heard from him.

"None of his pals saw it coming," Dan said. "Or so they say."

"What about the phone records Louise provided?"

Dan checked his notes. "Joey talked to both his brother in Dallas and his sister in Davenport a number of times in the six months prior to his disappearance. They're a close family."

"Which sibling got the most attention? Texas or Iowa?"

"Iowa. That's where little sister is. Agnes, her name is. He must've called her twenty times in those six months."

Roger fleshed out the picture.

"They're a close family, all right," he said. "Even when a businesslike stranger comes around with fifty bucks for their brother, they clam up. Nobody wanted the refund check ex-cept the gal in charge—Loretta Evans, the matriarch, a tough old cookie who could put the battle in battle-ax. Come to think of it, she could put the ax in, too."

"She took the check?"

"She did. And she mailed it out the same day. I saw her do it. Speaking of mail, I checked trash cans all over Indiana, seems like. I got to know the Evanses better than the Evanses know the Evanses. I could save 'em some money."

"How's that?"

"They should share a copy of the *National Enquirer*. Just pass one around, instead of all picking it up."

"Speaking of inquiring minds, what did yours find out?"

"Exactly what it wanted to know," Roger said. "The family seems close in general, but in particular, they seem to want to keep in touch with Agnes."

"Joe's sister."

"His baby sister. She's only twenty-two. Anyway, they been calling her a lot. All of 'em."

"Interesting."

"There's also a bar in Davenport, called Bill's Golden Nugget, where they call from time to time. Maybe she works there."

"It's a lead, anyway," I said. "Damn—I wish I knew where that letter Loretta Evans mailed went to."

"It went to Agnes," Roger said. He was smiling smugly.

"How do you know?"

"Because I waited around on the corner where she mailed it till a postman came around to empty the box and told him I slipped an important letter in that I thought I forgot to put a stamp on. I had a hysterical expression on my face and a stamp ready in my hand, and the bastard took pity on me and let me sort through, looking for my letter."

"And you found one addressed to Agnes Evans."

"Sure."

"What did you do with it?"

"Left it right there," he said. "You don't think I'd tamper with the U.S. mail, do you?"

A foul, pungent odor from Oscar Mayer permeated the working-class neighborhood the massive plant bordered; but nobody seemed to notice, on this sunny June afternoon, or anyway to care. Ragamuffin kids played in the streets and on the sidewalks, wearing dirt-smudged cheeks that knew no era, and housewives hung wash on lines strung across porches, apparently enjoying a breeze that to me only emphasized the slaughterhouse stench.

The address I had for Agnes Evans was 714 1/2 Wundrum; it turned out to be a paint-peeling clapboard duplex in the middle of a crowded block.

My Buick was dirty enough to be at home in the neighborhood, and in my plaid shirt, tied into a halter top, and snug blue jeans, I fit in, too. I felt pretty much at home, actually; with a cop for a father, I had grown up in neighborhoods only a small step up from this—minus the slaughterhouse scent, thankfully.

I knocked at 714 1/2 and then knocked again. The door opened cautiously and a round-faced woman in her early twenties peeked out at me. She had permed dishwater-blond hair, suspicious eyes, and her brother's weak jaw.

"Yeah?"

Pleasant, not at all pushy, I said, "I'm looking for Doris Wannamaker."

"No Doris anybody here," Agnes Evans said. She eased the door open somewhat; not all the way, but I could get a better look at her. She wore tight jeans with fashion-statement holes in the knees and a blue T-shirt with "Quad Cities USA" in flowing white letters. She was slim, attractive, and wore no makeup.

I said, "Isn't this 714 1/2?"

"Yeah."

I could hear a TV inside; a cartoon show.

"Wundrum Street?"

"That's right."

I sighed. "She's gone, huh. I guess that's the way it goes these days. Wonder how much I missed her by."

"I lived here six months," she said. "I don't know who lived here before me."

I shrugged, smiled. "We was in beauty school together, Doris and me. I was just passing through town and wanted to surprise her. Sorry to bother."

Agnes Evans finally smiled. It was an attractive smile. "I went to beauty school. At Regent."

Of course I'd known that.

I said, "I went to the University of Beauty Science in Cedar Falls."

"Supposed to be a good school," Agnes allowed. "I graduated Regent. I didn't keep my certificate up, though."

"Me neither," I said.

The door was open wider. I could see the little girl, wearing a red T-shirt and underpants, sitting like an Indian in front of the TV, watching Tom bash Jerry with a skillet.

"Sure sorry I bothered you," I said.

"No problem."

"Look, uh . . . is there any chance I could use your phone? I want to try to catch my boyfriend at the motel, before he goes out."

"Well . . ."

"I thought I was going to have the afternoon filled with seeing Doris and talking old times, but now . . . could I impose?"

She shrugged, smiled tightly, but opened the screen and said, "Come on in."

The house was neat as a pin; neater. The furniture was the kind you rented to own, but it was maintained as if owning it was the plan. The TV was a big portable on a stand, and there was a Holiday Inn–type landscape over the plastic-covered sofa. A window air conditioner chugged and the place was almost chilly, and the smell of whatever-goes-into-weenies wasn't making it inside.

"Hi, honey," I said, stopping near the little girl.

She didn't look up at me; she was watching Jerry hit Tom with a toaster. "Hi," she said.

Maggie looked older than her picture, but not much. A little child with almost white-blond hair, and a lot of it, a frizzy frame around a cameo face that was blank with TV concentration.

I pretended to use the phone in the kitchen—which was tidy and smelled of macaroni and cheese—while Agnes stood with her arms folded and studied me as she smoked a cigarette. She was still just a little suspicious.

"I'll see you later, then," I told the dial tone, and hung up and smiled at Agnes and shrugged. "Men," I said.

She smirked and blew smoke and nodded in mutual understanding.

As I walked out she followed. I said, "So you're not in hair anymore?"

"No. My boyfriend Billy runs a bar. I work there most evenings."

"Really? Who looks after your little girl?"

"That's not my little girl. Cindy is, uh, a friend of mine's kid. I look after her, days."

"Sweet little girl," I said.

"She's a honey," Agnes said.

I left them there, in the neat house in the foul-smelling neighborhood. I wasn't worried about leaving Maggie in Agnes's care. It was someone else's care I was worried about.

The someone who was with Maggie, nights.

Bill's Golden Nugget was a country-western bar on Harrison, a one-way whose glory days—at least along this saloon-choked stretch—were long gone. I parked on a side street, in front of a natural-food co-op inhabited by hippies who hadn't noticed the sixties were over. The Nugget was between a pawnshop and a heavy-metal bar.

It was midafternoon and the long, narrow saloon was sparsely populated—a few out-of-work blue-collar urban cowboys were playing pool; a would-be biker played the Elvira pinball machine; a couple of guys in jeans and work shirts were at the bar, having an argument about baseball. Just enough patrons to keep the air smoky and stale. A Johnny Paycheck song worked at blowing out the jukebox speakers. The room's sole lighting seemed to be the neon and/or lit-up plastic signs that bore images of beer, Marlboro men, and *Sports Illustrated* swimsuit models, none of which had the slightest thing to do with the Nugget. Except for the beer.

A heavyset, bearded, balding blond man in his late twenties was behind the bar. He wore a plaid shirt that clashed with mine and red suspenders that clashed with his. I heard somebody call him Bill.

He seemed pleasant enough, but he was watching me warily; I was new, and maybe I was a hooker.

I took a stool.

"What'll it be, sweet thing?" he said. There was nothing menacing about it. Not even anything condescending. But he was eyeing me carefully. Just a good on-top-of-it bar owner who was probably his own bouncer.

"What have you got on tap that I'd like, big guy?"

"Coors," he said, and it was sort of a question.

"You kidding, Bill? Drinking that stuff is like makin' love in a boat."

"Huh?"

"Fucking close to water," I said, and I grinned at him. He liked that.

"I also got Bud," he said.

"Bodacious," I said.

He went away smiling, convinced I was not a hooker, just available. Even a guy with a good-looking girl like Agnes at home has his weaknesses.

I milked the Bud for fifteen minutes, tapping my toes to the country music, some of which was pretty good. That Carlene Carter could sing. Nobody hit on me, not even Bill, and that was fine. I just wanted to fit in.

There was a room in back that was at least as big as the front, with tables and a dance floor and a stage for a band and a second bar; it wasn't in use right now, but some beer-ad lighting was on and somebody was back there working, loading in boxes of booze or whatever, through the alley door.

When the guy finished, he came up front; he was in a White Sox sweatshirt with cutoff sleeves and blue jeans. He was a brawny character, maybe twenty-five, good-looking except for a weak chin.

He was Joey Evans.

I had a second Bud and eavesdropped as Evans—whose voice was high-pitched and husky, not suited to his rather brutish build—asked if he could take a break.

"Sure, Freddy," Bill said. "Take five, but then I need you with me behind the bar. It's damn near happy hour, kid."

Freddy/Joey went behind the bar and got himself a can of diet Coke. He went to a table, away from any patrons, and sat quietly sipping.

I went over to him. "You look like you could use some company. Hard day?"

"Hard enough," he said. He took my figure in, trying to be subtle; it was about as successful as McGovern's run at the presidency.

"Have a seat," he said, and stood, and pushed out a chair.

I sat. "Hope you don't mind my being so forward. I'm Becky Lewis." I stuck out my hand. We shook; his grip was gentle. Right.

"You're from Chicago, aren't you, Becky?" he said. He

smiled boyishly; his eyes were light faded blue, like stonewashed denims.

I was supposed to be the detective. "How did you gather that?"

"The accent," he said. "I'd know that flat nasal tone anywhere."

He should: he had it himself.

"I figured you for Chicago, too. South side?"

"Close," he said. "How . . . ?"

"You're not wearing a Cubbies sweatshirt, now, are ya?"

He grinned. "Hell, no! Screw them and their Yuppie fans."

"You got that right. Let me buy you a beer . . . Freddy, is it?"

"Freddy," he said. "No thanks. I'm workin'. But I'll buy you one."

"I already got one. Let's just get to know each other a little."

There was not much to know, he said. He was fairly new to the area, working as a bartender for Bill, who was a friend of a friend.

"You got strong hands, Freddy," I said, stroking one. "Working hands. Steel-mill hands."

His eyes flared. Maybe I'd gone too far.

"I . . . I got tired of factory life. Just too damn hard. I need to be sharp, not wasted, when I spend time with my kid. I'm a single parent, you know. I'm trying for that quality-time thing, you know."

I bet he was.

"How many kids you got, Freddy?"

"Just the one. Sweet little girl. Cindy. Starts first grade next year. You got any kids?"

"I'm divorced, but I never had any kids. Didn't think I was cut out for it."

"Oh, you should reconsider. There's nothing like it. Being a parent—it's the best thing that ever happened to me."

Really.

"I don't know," I said, "I'm afraid I might lose my temper around 'em or something."

"That can be a problem," he admitted. "But I'd never lay a hand on Cindy. Never."

"Spare the rod and spoil the child, Clyde."

His brow knit. "I don't believe in that shit. Look—I used

to have a bad temper. I'll be honest with you, Becky. I used to . . . well, I used to get a little rough with the ladies sometimes."

I stroked his hand, and almost purred, "I like it a little rough."

Gag me, as they say, with a spoon.

"I don't mean that. I don't mean horseplay or nothing. I mean, I hit women before. Okay? See this diet Coke? It's not just 'cause I'm workin'. I don't drink anymore. I get nasty when I drink, so I don't drink."

"It's a little rough, being a recovering alcoholic, isn't it, working in a bar?"

"Being somebody who don't drink is a valuable commodity when you work in a bar-type situation. That's what Bill likes about me."

"You're not . . . tempted?"

"No. I haven't had a drink in five years."

"Five years?" Was he lying, or crazy? Or both? Was this a trick question?

He swirled the diet Coke in the can. "Five years sober. Five years dry. Besides, Becky—this job was all I could get."

"A strapping boy like you?"

His expression darkened. "I got my reasons. If you want to be my friend, you got to respect my privacy, okay?"

Funny, coming from a guy I just met who already had admitted he was a reformed drunk and supposedly reformed woman-beater. Was there something psychotic in those spooky faded blue eyes?

"Sure, honey," I said, "I'll respect your privacy. If you respect me in the morning."

He grinned again, shyly. "I got to get behind the bar, 'fore Bill tears me a new you-know-what."

"Can we get together after you get off work?"

"I got to spend the evening with my little girl."

"Right. Quality time."

"That's it. But I ought to have her in bed by nine o'clock."

I bet.

"You could stop over after that," he said. "I can give you the address. . . ."

•   •   •   •

Louise sat next to me in the front seat. She wore the same peasant dress she'd worn to my office; clutched the same patent-leather purse. Her heavy makeup, in the darkness as we sat in the car at the curb, gave her a Kabuki-like visage.

I had phoned her long distance, right after my encounter with Joey at the Nugget. She'd been standing by for my call, as I'd primed her that if I found Maggie, I'd need her to come immediately. I couldn't take Maggie without Louise present, and not just because the child would rightfully resist going with a stranger.

The fact was, with Louise along, taking Maggie would not be kidnapping. Without her, it would.

"Are you all right, Louise?"

She nodded. We were in my Buick; we had left her Datsun in a motel parking lot near the interstate. That's where we had met, after she made the three-hour drive in two and a half hours. It was now approaching 9:30 and the sky was a brilliant dark blue with more stars than any child could ever hope to dream upon. Moving clouds seemed to rise cotton-candy-like, but it was only smoke from Oscar Mayer.

We were several blocks from Agnes Evans's duplex, but the meat-packing smell still scorched the air. Joey Evans and his daughter lived in a single-family, single-story clapboard, smaller and newer than his sister's place. Built in the fifties sometime. I lived in a house like this when I was six.

"He's expecting me," I told her. I'd already told her this, but I'd been telling her a lot of things and I wasn't sure anything was sticking.

She nodded.

"I'll go up, and knock, and after he lets me in, I'll excuse myself to go to the rest room, I'll find the back door, unlock it, and you come in and I'll keep him busy while you find your way to Maggie's room."

She nodded.

"Then you slip out the back door with her. When you're in the car with her, safe, honk twice. Short honks. Then I'll get out of there on some excuse, and we're outta here. You girls will be on your way home."

She smiled wanly. "Ms. Tree—thank you. Thank you so very much. I knew you could do it. I knew you could."

"I haven't done it yet. *We* haven't. Now, you need to have a clear head about you, Louise! I want to get you in and out, with Maggie, without him knowing till we're taillights. I don't want *any* violence going down—that husband of yours looks like he could bench-press a grand piano."

She nodded.

"Wait five minutes after I go to the door; then go around behind the house and find the back door. How long?"

"Five minutes."

"When you're safe in the car, how many times will you honk?"

She raised two fingers, as if making the peace sign. "Short honks."

"Good, Louise." I patted her shoulder. I felt confident about this. About as confident as you feel when you make your first dental visit in five years.

He answered my first knock. He was wearing a blue-and-white-checked sport shirt and jeans; he looked nice. He asked me to come in, and I did. He smelled like Canoë cologne; I didn't even know they still made that stuff.

"It's not much, Becky," he said, gesturing about, "but it's enough for Cindy and me."

Whether he and his sister had similar decorating styles, or whether one of them had done the other's home, I couldn't say; but it was the same rent-to-buy decor, just a tad sparser than sis's place. The TV was a console, apparently an old used model, with a Nintendo unit on the floor in front representing the only visible extravagance. Over the couch was another discount-store oil painting, this one a sad-eyed Gacy-like clown handing a red balloon to a little girl who looked disturbingly like Maggie.

"You really keep the place neat," I said, sitting on the couch.

"Cindy helps me. She's really the strong one in the family."

"I'd love to meet her."

"Maybe next time. She's asleep. Besides, I don't like her to see me with other ladies."

"Other ladies?"

"Other than her mommy."

"But you're divorced."

"I know. But she's only six. She doesn't understand stuff like that. Of course, then, neither do I."

What sort of sick relationship did this son of a bitch have with little Maggie? Had he turned her into a "wife"? A six-year-old wife? This guy was lucky I wasn't armed.

"Look," I said, smiling, trying to maintain the pretense of warmth, "I need to use the little girls' room. Where . . . ?"

He pointed the way. It was through a neat compact kitchen, which connected to a hall off of which was Maggie's room. Or Cindy's room. At least she didn't sleep with her daddy.

She sure looked angelic right now, blond hair haloing her sweet face on the overstuffed pillow. Her room was the only one that wasn't spare—even in the meager glow of the night-light, I could see the zoo of stuffed animals, the clown and circus posters, the dolls and their little dresses. Daddy gave her everything.

The sick bastard.

When I returned, having flushed a toilet I really had had to use, I left the back door, off the kitchen, unlocked.

I sat down next to Joey—keeping in mind I needed to call him Freddy—and he said, "I can get you a beer, if you like."

The last thing in the world I wanted was for him to go traipsing through the kitchen while Louise was sneaking in.

"No thanks, I'm fine. I just got *rid* of a beer, honey."

He laughed embarrassedly.

I nudged him with an elbow, gently. "What are you doing with beer in the house, anyway? You haven't had a drink in five years, right?"

A smile creased his pleasant face. "You're sure a suspicious girl. I keep a few brews in the fridge for company."

"You entertain a lot?"

"Not much. My si—"

He started to say "sister," I think; then shifted gears.

"My friends Bill and Agnes both like their beer. In fact, Bill sometimes likes it too much." He shook his head. "A guy who runs a bar shouldn't drink up the profits."

"He's lucky to have you around."

"Actually, he is. I only hope he can stay in business. I sure need this job."

The child's scream shook the house.

Evans and I both bolted off the couch, and then, framed in the archway of the hall leading to the kitchen, there was Louise, pulling the unwilling little girl by the arm. The child, wearing an oversize, man's white T-shirt with Bart Simpson on it, was screaming.

Louise, her eyes crazed, her Kabuki face frozen with

rage, slapped the little girl savagely; it rang like a gunshot off the swirl-plaster walls.

That silenced the little girl's screams, but tears and whimpering took their place.

"Louise!" Evans said, face as white as a fish's underbelly. "What—"

Her purse had been tucked under one arm. Now, still clinging to the little girl with one hand, she dug her other hand into the brown patent leather bag and came back with a snout-nosed black revolver.

"You bastard," she said, "you sick bastard . . ."

Those had been my thoughts, exactly, earlier, but now I was having new thoughts. . . .

"Louise," I said, stepping forward. "Put the gun down."

"You did it to her, didn't you?" she said to him. "You did it to her! You fucked her! You've been fucking her!"

The little girl was confused and crying.

Evans stepped forward, carefully; he was patting the air gently. "Louise—just because your father—"

"Shut up!" she said, and she shot at him. He danced out of the way as the shot rang and echoed in the confined space; the couch took the slug.

I wasn't waiting to see who or what took the next one: I moved in and slapped the gun out of her hand; then I slapped her face, hard.

I had a feeling I wasn't the first one to do that to Louise.

She crumpled to the floor and she wept quietly, huddling fetally; her little girl sat down close to her, stroking her mother's blond hair.

"Mommy," Maggie said. "Don't cry, Mommy. Don't cry."

I picked up the gun.

Evans was standing looking down at his wife and child. He looked at me sharply, accusingly.

"I'm a private detective," I explained. "She hired me to get Maggie back."

"She told you I beat Maggie, right?" he snapped. "And worse?"

I nodded.

"Why the hell do you think I ran from her?" he said, plaintively; his face was haunted, his eyes welling. "*I* wasn't the one beating Maggie! But the courts would've given Maggie to her mommy. They would never have believed me over her. How *else* could I have stopped this?"

I didn't have an answer for him; he wasn't necessarily
right—the courts might have realized Louise was the abusing parent. But they might not have. I sure hadn't.

He knelt beside his wife; the little girl was on one side of
her, and he was on the other. They were mostly in the
kitchen. Louise didn't seem to notice them, but they tried to
soothe her just the same.

"Her father did terrible things to her," he said softly.
"She got me all confused with him. Looked at me and saw
her daddy—thought I'd do the same things to Maggie he
done to her."

"But the only one imitating her father," I said, "was Louise."

"Mommy doesn't mean to hurt me," the little girl said.
"She loves me." It was almost a question.

Sirens were cutting the air; responding to the gunshot.

"I was wrong," he said, looking at me with eyes that
wanted absolution. "I shouldn't have run. I should have
stayed and tried to fix things."

Who could blame him, really?

Something in Louise had been broken so very long ago.

But as I watched them there, the little family huddling on
the cold linoleum, I had to hope that something at long last
could start being mended.

strung out

A V. I. WARSHAWSKI STORY

SARA PARETSKY

For Betty Nicholas, who provided essential technical
advice—and made important connections

*Sara Paretsky, named one of thirteen Women of the
Year in 1987 by* Ms. *magazine, and the founder and
first president of Sisters in Crime, is the creator of
V. I. Warshawski, featured in the movie of the same
name. V.I., like Sara, is "interested in singing and
has the misfortune to be a fan of the Chicago Cubs."
A tough, Chicago-based private investigator with a
penchant for silk blouses, V.I., who isn't intimidated
by mobsters, longshoremen, or corporate criminals,
is featured in six books, including* Bitter Medicine,
Blood Shot *(winner of a 1989 British Crime Writers*

Silver Dagger Award and an Anthony nominee) and
Burn Marks. *Sara is also the editor of* Eye of a
Woman, *an anthology of short stories by women,*
featuring female investigators.

In "Strung Out," V.I. is quick to learn the score
in a game in which love means nothing.

1

People born near the corner of 90th and Commercial used to
have fairly predictable futures. The boys grew up to work in
the mills; the girls took jobs in bakeries or coffee shops. They
married each other and scrimped to make a down payment
on a neighborhood bungalow and somehow fit their large
families into its small rooms.

Now that the mills are history, the script has changed.
Kids are still marrying, still having families, but without the
certainty of the steel industry to buoy their futures. The one
thing that seems to stay the same, though, is the number who
stubbornly cling to the neighborhood even now that the jobs
are gone. It's a clannish place, South Chicago, and people
don't leave it easily.

When Monica Larush got pregnant our senior year in
high school and married football hero Gary Oberst, we all
just assumed they were on their way to becoming another
large family in a small bungalow. She wasn't a friend of mine,
so I didn't worry about the possible ruin of her life. Anyway,
having recently lost my own mother to cancer, I wasn't too
concerned about other girls' problems.

Monica's and my lives intersected only on the basketball
court. Like me, she was an aggressive athlete, but she clearly
had a high level of talent as well. In those days, though, a
pregnant girl couldn't stay in school, so she missed our
championship winter. The team brought her a game ball. We
found her, fat and pasty, eating Fritos in angry frustration in
front of the TV in her mother's kitchen. When we left, we

made grotesque jokes about her swollen face and belly, our only way of expressing our embarrassment and worry.

Gary and Monica rewrote their script, though. Gary got a job on the night shift at Inland Steel and went to school during the day. After the baby—Gary Junior—was born, Monica picked up her GED. The two of them scrimped, not for a down payment, but to make it through the University of Illinois's Chicago campus. Afterward Gary took a job as an accountant with a big Loop firm, Monica taught high school French, and they left the neighborhood. Moved north was what I heard.

And that was pretty much all I knew—or cared—about them before Lily Oberst's name and face started popping up in the papers. She was apparently mopping up junior tennis competition. Tennis boosters and athletic-apparel makers were counting the minutes until she turned pro.

I actually first heard about her from my old basketball coach, Mary Ann McFarlane. Mary Ann's first love had always been tennis. When she retired from teaching at sixty, she continued to act as a tennis umpire at local high school and college tournaments. I saw her once a year when the Virginia Slims came to Chicago. She umpired there for the pittance the tour paid—not for the bucks, but for the excitement. I always came during the last few days and had dinner with her in Greek Town at the end of the finals.

"I've been watching Lily Oberst play up at the Skokie Valley club, Vic," Mary Ann announced one year. "Kid's got terrific stuff. If they don't ruin her too young she could be—well, I won't say another Martina. Martinas come once a century. But a great one."

"Lily Oberst?" I shook my head, fishing for why the name sounded familiar.

"You don't remember Monica? Didn't you girls keep in touch after your big year? Lily is her and Gary's daughter. I used to coach Monica in tennis besides basketball, but I guess that wasn't one of your sports."

After that I read the stories in detail and got caught up on twenty years of missing history. Lily grew up in suburban Glenview, the second of two children. The *Herald-Star* explained that both her parents were athletic and encouraged her and her brother to go out for sports. When a camp coach brought back the word that Lily might have some tennis aptitude, her daddy began working with her every day. She had just turned six then.

Gary put up a net for her in the basement and would give her an ice cream bar every time she could hit the ball back twenty-five times without missing.

"He got mad when it got too easy for me," Lily said, giggling, to the reporter. "Then he'd raise the net whenever I got to twenty-four."

When it became clear that they had a major tennis talent on their hands, Monica and Gary put all their energy into developing it. Monica quit her job as a teacher so that she could travel to camps and tournaments with Lily. Gary, by then regional director for a pharmaceutical firm, persuaded his company to put in the seed money for Lily's career. He himself took a leave of absence to work as her personal trainer. Even now that she was a pro Monica and Gary went with her everywhere. Of course Lily had a professional coach, but her day always started with a workout with Daddy.

Gary Junior didn't get much print attention. He apparently didn't share the family's sports mania. Five years older than Lily, he was in college studying for a degree in chemical engineering, and hoping to go off to Procter & Gamble in Cincinnati.

Lily turned pro the same year Jennifer Capriati did. Since Capriati was making history, joining the pros at thirteen, Lily, two years older, didn't get the national hoopla. But Chicago went wild. Her arrival in the Wimbledon quarterfinals that year was front-page news all over town. Her 6–2, 6–0 loss there to Monica Seles was shown live in every bar in the city. Fresh-faced and smiling under a spiky blond hairdo, she grinned through her braces and said it was just a thrill to be on the same court with players like Seles and Graf. The city fell in love.

So when it was announced that she was coming to Chicago to play in the Slims in February the tournament generated more publicity than it had ever known. After a year and a half on the pro circuit Lily was ranked eighth in the world, but the pictures of her arrival at the family home still showed an ingenuous grin. Her Great Dane, standing on his hind legs with his paws on her shoulders, was licking her face.

Mary Ann McFarlane called me a few days after the Obersts arrived back in town. "Want to come up to Glenview and watch the kid work out? You could catch up with Monica at the same time."

That sounded like a treat that would appeal to Monica about as much as it did to me. But I had never seen a tennis prodigy in the making. I agreed to drive out to Glenview on Friday morning. Mary Ann and I would have lunch with Monica after Lily's workout.

The Skokie Valley Tennis Club was just off the Edens Expressway at Dempster. Lily's workout started at eight but I hadn't felt the need to watch a fifteen-year-old, however prodigious, run laps. I arrived at the courts a little after ten.

When I asked a woman at the reception desk to direct me to Lily, she told me the star's workout was off-limits to the press today. I explained who I was. She consulted higher authority over the phone. Mary Ann had apparently greased the necessary skids: I was allowed past a bored guard lounging against a hall door. After showing him my driver's license, I was directed down the hall to the private court where Lily was practicing. A second guard there looked at my license again and opened the door for me.

Lily had the use of three nets if she needed them. A small grandstand held three people: Mary Ann and Monica and a young man in a workout suit with "Artemis" blazoned across the back. I recognized Monica from the newspaper photos, but they didn't do justice to her perfectly styled gold hair, the makeup enhancing her oval face, or the casual elegance of her clothes. I had a fleeting memory of her fat, pasty face as she sat eating Fritos twenty years ago. I would never have put those two images together. As the old bromide has it, living well is the best revenge.

Mary Ann squeezed my hand as I sat on her other side. "Good to see you, Vic," she whispered. "Monica—here's Vic."

We exchanged confused greetings across our old coach, me congratulating her on her daughter's success, she exclaiming at how I hadn't changed a bit. I didn't know if that was a compliment or not.

The man was introduced as Monte Allison, from Artemis Products' marketing department. Artemis supplied all of Lily's tennis clothes and shoes, as well as a seven-figure endorsement contract. Allison was just along to protect the investment, Mary Ann explained. The equipment maker heard her and ostentatiously turned his left shoulder to us.

On the court in front of us Lily was hitting tennis balls. A kid in white shorts was serving to her backhand. A dark man in shabby gray sweats stood behind her encouraging her and critiquing her stroke. And a third man in bright white clothes offered more forceful criticisms from the sidelines.

"Get into the shot, Lily. Come'n, honey, you're not concentrating."

"Gary," Mary Ann muttered at me. "That's Paco Callabrio behind her."

I don't know much about tennis, but even I'd heard of Callabrio. After dominating men's tennis in the sixties he had retired to his family home in Majorca. But five years ago he'd come out of seclusion to coach a few selected players. Lily had piqued his interest when he saw her at the French Open last year; Monica had leaped on the opportunity to have her daughter work with him. Apparently Gary was less impressed. As the morning wore on Gary's advice began clashing with Paco's more and more often.

In the midst of a heated exchange over Lily's upswing I sensed someone moving onto the bench behind me. I turned to see a young woman leaning at her ease against the bleacher behind her. She was dressed in loose-fitting trousers that accentuated the long, lean lines of her body.

Lily saw the newcomer at the same time I did. She turned very red, then very white. While Paco and Gary continued arguing, she signaled to the young man to start hitting balls to her again. She'd been too tired to move well a minute ago, but the woman's arrival infused her with new energy.

Mary Ann had also turned to stare. "Nicole Rubova," she muttered to me.

I raised my eyebrows. Another of the dazzling Czech players who'd come to the States in Martina's wake. She was part of the generation between Martina and Capriati, a year or so older than Graf but with time ahead of her still to fight for the top spots. Her dark, vivid beauty made her a mediagenic foil to Graf's and Lily's blondness, but her sardonic humor kept her from being really popular with the press.

"Gary's afraid she's going to rape his baby. He won't let Lily go out alone with any of the women on the circuit." Mary Ann continued to mutter at me.

I raised my brows again, this time amazed at Mary Ann's

pithy remarks. She'd never talked so bluntly to me when she was my basketball coach.

By now Gary had also seen Rubova in the stands. Like Lily he changed color, then grew even more maniacal in his demands on his daughter. When Paco advised a rest around eleven-thirty, Gary shook his head emphatically.

"You can't spoil her, Paco. Believe me, I know this little girl. She's got great talent and a heart of gold, but she's lazy. You've got to drive her."

Lily was gray with exhaustion. While they argued over her she leaned over, her hands on her knees, and gasped for air.

"Mr. Oberst," Paco said, his chilly formality emphasizing his dislike, "you want Lily to be a great star. But a girl who plays when she is this fatigued will only injure herself, if she doesn't burn out completely first. I say the workout is over for the day."

"And I say she got to Wimbledon last year thanks to my methods," Gary yelled.

"And she almost had to forfeit her round of sixteen match because you were coaching her so blatantly from the seats," Paco shouted back. "Your methods stink, Oberst."

Gary stepped toward the Catalan, then abruptly turned his back on him and yelled at his daughter, "Lily, pick up your racket. Come on, girl. You know the rules."

"Really, Oberst," Monte Allison called tentatively down to the floor from the stands. "We can't injure Lily—that won't help any of us."

Monica nodded in emphatic agreement, but Gary paid no attention to either of them. Lily looked imploringly from Paco to Gary. When the coach said nothing else, she bent to pick up her racket and continued returning balls. She was missing more than she was hitting now and was moving leadenly around the court. Paco watched for about a minute, then turned on his heel and marched toward a door in the far wall. As he disappeared through it, Monica got up from Mary Ann's left and hurried after him.

I noticed a bright pink anorak with rabbit fur around the hood next to where she'd been sitting, and two furry leather mittens with rabbits embroidered on them.

"Those are Lily's," Mary Ann said. "Monica must have forgotten she was holding them for her. I'll give them to the kid if she makes it through this session."

My old coach's face was set in angry lines. I felt angry, too, and kept half rising from my seat, wondering if I ought to intervene. Paco's departure had whipped Gary into a triumphant frenzy. He shooed the kid serving balls away and started hitting ground strokes to his daughter at a furious pace. She took it for about five minutes before collapsing on the floor in tears.

"I just can't do it anymore, Daddy. I just can't."

Gary put his own racket down and smiled in triumph.

A sharp clap came from behind me, making me jump. "Bravo, Gary!" Nicole cried. "What a man you are! Yes, indeed, you've proved you can frighten your little girl. Now the question is: Which matters more to you? That Lily become the great player her talent destines her to be? Or that you prove that you own her?"

She jumped up lightly from the bench and ran down to the court. She put an arm around Lily and said something inaudible to the girl. Lily looked from her to her father and shook her head, flushing with misery. Nicole shrugged. Before leaving the court she and Gary exchanged a long look. Only an optimist would have found the seeds of friendship in it.

2

The Slims started the next Monday. The events at the Skokie Valley Tennis Club made me follow the newspaper reports eagerly, but the tournament seemed to be progressing without any open fireworks. One or two of the higher seeds were knocked out early, but Martina, Rubova, Lily, and one of the Maleeva sisters were all winning on schedule, along with Zina Garrison. Indeed, Martina, coming off knee surgery, seemed to be playing with the energy of a woman half her age.

I called Mary Ann McFarlane Thursday night to make sure she had my pass to the quarterfinal matches on Friday. Lily was proving such a hit that tickets were hard to get.

"Oh, yes," she assured me. "We umpires don't have much leverage, but I got Monica to leave a pass for you at the will-call window. Dinner Sunday night?"

I agreed readily. Driving down to the Pavilion on Friday,

I was in good time for the noon match, which pitted Martina against Frederica Lujan.

Lujan was seeded twelfth to Martina's third in world rankings, but the gap between their games seemed much wider than those numbers. In fact, halfway through the first set Martina suddenly turned her game up a notch and turned an even match into a rout. She was all over the court, going down for shots that should have been unhittable.

An hour later we got the quarterfinal meeting the crowd had come to see: Lily against Nicole Rubova. When Lily danced onto the court, a vision in pink and white with a sweatband pulling her blond spikes back from her face, the stands roared with pleasure. Nicole got a polite round of applause, but she was only there to give their darling a chance to play.

A couple of minutes after they'd started their warmup, Monica came in. She sat close to the court, about ten rows in front of me. The man she joined was Paco Callabrio. He had stood next to Lily on the court as she came out for her warmups, patted her encouragingly on the ass, and climbed into the stands. Monica must have persuaded him not to quit in fury last week.

At first I assumed Gary was boycotting the match, either out of dislike of Paco or for fear his overt coaching would cause Lily to forfeit. As play progressed, though, I noticed him on the far side of the court, behind the chair umpire, making wild gestures if Lily missed a close shot, or if he thought the line umpires were making bad calls.

When play began Rubova's catlike languor vanished. She obviously took her conditioning seriously, moving well around the court and playing the net with a brilliant ferocity. Mary Ann might be right—she might have designs on Lily's body—but it didn't make her play the youngster with any gentleness.

Lily, too, had a range of motion that was exciting to watch. She was big, already five-ten, with long arms and a phenomenal reach. Whether due to Gary's drills or not, her backhand proved formidable; unlike most women on the circuit she could use it one-handed.

Lily pushed her hard but Rubova won in three sets, earning the privilege of meeting Navratilova the next afternoon. It seemed to me that Lily began hitting the ball rather tentatively in the last few games of the final set. I wasn't knowl-

edgeable enough to know if she had reached her physical
limit, or if she was buckling under Rubova's attack.

The crowd, disappointed in their favorite's loss, gave the
Czech only a lukewarm hand as she collected her rackets and
exited. Paco, Monica, and Gary all disappeared from the
stands as Lily left the court to a standing ovation.

Mary Ann had been umpiring the far sideline during the
Rubova match. Neither of the players had given the referee a
hard time. Rubova at one point drew a line on the floor with
her racket, a sarcastic indicator of where she thought Mary
Ann was spotting Lily. Another time Lily cried out in frustration to the chair umpire; I saw Monica's shoulders tense and
wondered if the prodigy was prone to tantrums. More likely
she was worried by what Gary—turning puce on the far side
—might do to embarrass her. Other than that the match had
gone smoothly.

Doubles quarterfinals were on the agenda for late afternoon. I wasn't planning on watching those, so I wandered
down to the court to have a word with Mary Ann before I
left.

She tried to talk me into staying. "Garrison has teamed
up with Rubova. They should be fun to watch—both are real
active girls."

"Enough for me for one day. What'd you think of the kid
in tournament play?"

Mary Ann spread her hands. "She's going to go a long
way. Nicole outplayed her today, but she won't forever. Although—I don't know—it looked to me in the last couple of
games as though she might have been favoring her right
shoulder. I couldn't be sure. I just hope Gary hasn't got her
to injure herself with his hit-till-you-drop coaching methods.
I'm surprised Paco's hanging on through it."

I grinned suggestively at her. "Maybe Monica has wonderful powers of persuasion."

Mary Ann looked at me calmly. "You're trying to shock
me, Vic, but believe me, I was never a maiden aunt. And
anyway, nothing on this circuit would shock me. . . . They
have free refreshments downstairs for players and crew. And
press and hangers-on. Want to come have some coffee before
you go? Some of the girls might even be there."

"And be a hanger-on? Sure, why not?" Who knows,
maybe Martina would see me and remember an urgent need
for some detective work.

A freight elevator protected by guards carried the insiders to the lower depths. Mary Ann, in her umpire's uniform, didn't need to show any identification. I came in for more scrutiny, but my player's-guest badge got me through.

The elevator decanted us onto a grubby corridor. Young people of both sexes hurried up and down its length, carrying clipboards at which they frowned importantly.

"PR staff," Mary Ann explained. "They feed all the statistics from the match to different wire services and try to drum up local interest in the tournament. Tie-ins with the auto show, that kind of thing."

Older, fatter people stood outside makeshift marquees with coffee and globular brownies. At the end of the hall I could see Paco and Monica huddled together. Gary wasn't in sight.

"Lily may have gone back in for a massage; I think she already did her press interview. Gary must be inside with her. He won't let her get a workover alone."

"Inside the locker room?" I echoed. "I know she's Daddy's darling, but don't the other women object to him being there while they're changing? And can she really stand having him watch her get massaged?"

"There's a lounge." Mary Ann shepherded me into the refreshment tent—really a niche roped off from the cement corridor with a rather pathetic plastic canopy overhead. "Friends and lovers of the stars can sit there while the girls dress inside. I don't expect he actually hangs around the massage table. Don't go picturing some fabulous hideaway, though. This is a gym at a relatively poor university. It's purely functional. But they do have a cement cubbyhole for the masseuse—that sets it apart from the normal school gym."

I suddenly realized I was hungry—it was long past lunchtime. The Slims catering was heavy on volume and carbohydrates. I rejected fried chicken wings and rice and filled a plastic bowl with some doubtful-looking chili. Mary Ann picked up a handful of cookies to eat with her coffee.

We settled at an empty table in the far corner and ate while Mary Ann pointed out the notables to me. Zina Garrison's husband was at the buffet next to Katerina Maleeva. The two were laughing together, trying to avoid a fat reporter who was unabashedly eavesdropping on them.

A well-groomed woman near the entrance to the mar-

quee was Clare Rutland, the doyenne of the tour, Mary Ann
explained. She had no formal title with the Slims, but
seemed to be able to keep its temperamental stars happy, or
at least functioning.

As I ate my chili, six or seven people stopped to talk to
Rutland. They'd nod at her remarks and race off again. I
imagined tennis stars' wishes, from lotus blossoms to Lotus
racers, being satisfied at the wave of her hand.

Mary Ann, talking to acquaintances, began picking up
some of the gossip buzzing the room: Lily might have
strained her shoulder. Maybe torn her rotator cuff. In this
kind of environment the worst scenarios are generated rapidly from the whiff of an idea. And Gary apparently had been
thrown out of Lily's press conference and was now sulking in
the women's lounge.

A collective gasp from the other side of the room made
me jerk my head around. Nicole Rubova was sprinting down
the hall, wet, with a towel haphazardly draping her midriff.

"Clare," she gasped.

Clare Rutland was on her feet as soon as she heard the
outcry, almost before Rubova came into view. She took off
her cardigan and draped it across the player's shoulders.
Rubova was too far from us for me to be able to hear her, but
the reporters in the room crowded around her, tournament
etiquette forgotten. It only took a minute for Mary Ann to get
the main point of the story from one of them: Gary Oberst
was on the couch in the players' lounge. Someone had
wrapped a string from a tennis racket around his neck a few
times. It was only later that everyone realized Lily herself
had disappeared.

3

Clare Rutland curled one foot toward her chin and massaged
her stockinged toes. Her face, rubbed free of makeup,
showed the strain of the day in its sharply dug lines.

"This could kill the Slims," she remarked to no one in
particular.

It was past midnight. I was in the windowless press room
with her, Mary Ann, and a bunch of men, including Jared
Brookings, who owned the PR firm handling the Slims in

Chicago. Brookings had come in in person around nine, to see what could be done to salvage the tournament. He'd sent his fresh-faced minions packing long ago. They'd phoned him in terror when the police arrested Nicole Rubova, and clearly were not up to functioning in the crisis.

Arnold Krieger was there, too, with a handful of other reporters whose names I never learned. Krieger was the fat man who'd been listening in on Zina Garrison's husband earlier in the dining area. He covered tennis for one of the wire services and had made himself at home in the press room when the cops commandeered it for their headquarters.

"She'll be out on bond in the morning, right?" Krieger palmed a handful of nuts into his mouth as he started to talk, so his words came out clogged. "So she can play Martina at one, per the schedule."

Clare looked at him in dismay but didn't speak.

Brookings put his fingertips together. "It all depends, doesn't it? We can't be too careful. We've spent two decades building these girls up, but the whole fabric could collapse at any minute."

I could see Mary Ann's teacher instincts debating whether to correct his mixed metaphors and deciding against it. "The problem isn't just having one of the stars arrested for murder," she said bluntly. "Lily Oberst is a local heroine and now everyone is going to read that an evil lesbian who had designs on her killed her father because he stood between them. Chicago might rip Nicole apart. They certainly won't support the tournament."

"Besides," Clare Rutland added in a dull voice, "Martina withdrew as soon as she heard about Rubova's arrest. She's gone off to locate a lawyer to handle the defense. And she may not play any more Slims this year if a cloud hangs over Rubova. Neither will Freddie Lujan. If those two drop out, others may follow suit."

"If a cloud hangs over Rubova, it's over the whole tour." Monte Allison, the Artemis Products representative, spoke for the first time. "We may withdraw *our* sponsorship for the rest of the year—I can't speak for Philip Morris, of course. That's a corporate decision, naturally, not mine, but we'll be making it tomorrow or—no, tomorrow's Saturday. We'll make it Monday. Early."

I'd never yet known a corporation that could make an important decision early Monday just because one of its vice-presidents said so in a forceful voice. But Allison was fretful because none of the tennis people was paying attention to him. Since Artemis also helped Philip Morris promote the tour, Allison was likely to urge that they withdraw their sponsorship just because he didn't like the way Clare Rutland kept snubbing him.

I muttered as much to Mary Ann.

"If they have to make a decision Monday, it gives you two days to solve the crime, Vic," she said loudly.

"You don't believe Rubova killed Oberst?" I asked her, still *sotto voce*.

"I believe the police wanted to arrest her because they didn't like her attitude," Mary Ann snapped.

The investigation had been handled by John McGonnigal, a violent crimes sergeant I know. He's a good cop, but a soignee, sardonic woman does not bring out the best in him. And by the time he'd arrived Nicole had dressed, in a crimson silk jumpsuit that emphasized the pliable length of her body, and withdrawn from shock into mockery.

When McGonnigal saw me slide into the interrogation room behind Rubova, he gave an exaggerated groan but didn't actively try to exclude me from his questioning sessions. Those gave me a good sense of where everyone claimed to have been when Gary was killed, but no idea at all if McGonnigal was making a mistake in arresting Nicole Rubova.

I couldn't help thinking traditional police repugnance at female-female sexuality had helped him interpret evidence so that it pointed at her. I hadn't been able to get the forensic data, but the case against her seemed to depend on two facts: She was the only person known to be alone with Gary in the locker room. And one of her rackets had a big section of string missing from it. This last seemed to be a rather slender thread to hang her on. It would have taken a good while to unthread enough string from a racket to have enough for a garotte. I didn't see where she'd had the time to do it.

McGonnigal insisted she'd spent Lily's press conference at it, dismissing claims from Frederica Lujan that she'd been talking to Nicole while it was going on. Some helpful person had told him that Frederica and Nicole had had an affair last year, so McGonnigal had decided the Spanish player would say anything to help a friend.

None of the Slims people had questioned my spending

the day there—they were far too absorbed in their woes over
the tournament. The men didn't pay any attention to Mary
Ann's comment to me now, but Clare Rutland moved slightly
on the couch so that she was facing my old coach directly.
"Who is this, Mary Ann?"

"V. I. Warshawski. About the best private investigator in
the city." Mary Ann continued to speak at top volume.

"Is that why you came to the matches today?" The large
hazel eyes looked at me with intense interest. I felt the
power she exerted over tennis divas directed at me.

"I came because I wanted to watch Lily Oberst. I grew
up playing basketball with her mother. Mary Ann here was
our coach. After watching Gary train Lily last week I would
have thought the kid might have killed him herself—he
seemed extraordinarily brutal."

Clare smiled, for the first time since Nicole Rubova had
come running down the hall in her towel ten hours ago. "If
every tennis kid killed her father because of his brutal coaching, we wouldn't have any parents left on the circuit. Which
might only improve the game. But Oberst was one of the
worst. Only—why did she have to do it *here*? She must have
known—only I suppose when you're jealous you don't think
of such things."

"So you think Rubova killed the guy?"

Clare spread her hands, appealing for support. "You
don't?"

"You know her and I don't, so I assume you're a better
judge of her character. But she seems too cool, too poised, to
kill a guy for the reason everyone's imputing to her. Maybe
she was interested in Lily. But I find it impossible to believe
she'd kill the girl's father because he tried to short-circuit
her. She's very sophisticated, very smart, and very cool. If
she *really* wanted to have an affair with Lily, she'd have
figured out a way. I'm not sure she wanted to—I think it
amused her to see Lily blush and get flustered, and to watch
Gary go berserk. But if she did want to kill Gary she'd have
done so a lot more subtly, not in a fit of rage in the locker
room. One other thing: If—*if*—she killed him like that, on
the spot, it must have been for some other reason than Lily."

"Like what?" Arnold Krieger had lost interest in Monte
Allison and was eavesdropping on me, still chewing cashews.

I hunched a shoulder. "You guys tell me. You're the ones
who see these prima donnas week in and week out."

Clare nodded. "I see what you mean. But then, who did kill Oberst?"

"I don't know the players and I don't have access to the forensic evidence. But—well, Lily herself would be my first choice."

A furious uproar started from Allison and Brookings, with Clare chiming in briefly. Mary Ann silenced them all with a brief whistle—she still could put her fingers in her mouth and produce a sound like a steam engine.

"She must have been awfully tired of Gary sitting in her head," I continued when Mary Ann had shut them up. "She could hardly go to the bathroom without his permission. I learned today that he picked her clothes, her friends, ran her practice sessions, drove away her favorite coaches. You name it."

The police had found Lily quickly enough—she'd apparently had a rare fight with Gary and stormed away to Northwestern Hospital without telling him or Monica. Without her entourage it had taken her a while to persuade the emergency room that her sore shoulder should leap ahead of other emergencies. Once they realized who she was, though, they summoned their sports medicine maven at once. He swept her off in a cloud of solicitude for X rays, then summoned a limo to take her home to Northbrook. There still would have been plenty of time for her to kill Gary before she left the Pavilion.

"Then there's Monica," I went on. "She and Paco Callabrio have been pretty friendly—several people hinted at it during their interviews this afternoon. She and Gary started dating when they were fifteen. That's twenty-four years with a bully. Maybe she figured she'd had enough.

"I don't like Paco for the spot very well. He's like Nicole —he's got a life, and an international reputation; he didn't need to ruin it by killing the father of one of his pupils. Although apparently he came out of retirement because of financial desperation. So maybe he was worried about losing Lily as a client, and his affair with Monica deranged him enough that he killed Oberst."

"So you think it's one of those three?" Clare asked.

I shrugged. "Could be. Could be Allison here, worried about his endorsement contract. He watched Gary driving Lily to the breaking point. Artemis could lose seven, eight million dollars if Lily injured herself so badly she couldn't play anymore."

Allison broke off his conversation with Brookings when he heard his name. "What the hell are you saying? That's outrageous. We're behind Lily all the way. I could sue you—"

"Control yourself, Monte," Clare said coldly. "No one's accusing you of anything except high-level capitalism. This detective here is just suggesting why someone besides Nicole might have killed Gary Oberst. Anything else?"

"The hottest outsider is Arnold Krieger here."

Two of the anonymous reporters snickered. Krieger muttered darkly but didn't say anything. The tale of Lily's interview with him had come out very early in McGonnigal's questioning.

Tennis etiquette dictates that the loser meet journalists first. The winner could then shower and dress at her leisure. Lily had come bouncing out, surrounded by Paco, Gary, and Monica. She'd giggled with the press about her game, said she didn't mind losing to Nicole because Nicole was a great player, but she, Lily, had given the game her best, and anyway, she was glad to have a few extra days at home with Ninja, her Great Dane, before flying off to Palm Springs for an exhibition match. People asked about her shoulder. She'd said it was sore but nothing serious. She was going over to Northwestern for X rays just to be on the safe side.

Arnold Krieger then asked whether she felt she ever played her best against Rubova. "After all, most people know she's just waiting for the chance to get you alone. Doesn't that unnerve you?"

Lily started to giggle again, but Gary lost his temper and jumped Krieger on the spot. Security guards pried his hands from the journalist's throat; Gary was warned out of the press room. In fact, he was told that one more episode would get him barred from the tour altogether.

The cops loved that, but they couldn't find anyone who'd seen Krieger go into the locker room afterwards. In fact, most of us could remember his staying near the food, playing tag-team with Garrison's husband.

"Don't forget, it was Rubova's racket the string was missing from," Krieger reminded me belligerently.

Clare eyed Krieger as though measuring him for an electric chair, then turned back to me. "What do you charge?"

"Fifty dollars an hour. Plus any unusual expenses—things above the cost of gas or local phone bills."

"I'm hiring you," Clare said briskly.

"To do what? Clear Nicole's name, or guarantee the tour can go on? I can only do the first—if she's not guilty. If it turns out to be Lily, or any of the other players, the Slims are going to be under just as much of a cloud as they are now."

Clare Rutland scowled, but she was used to being decisive. "Clear Nicole for me. I'll worry about the Slims after that. What do you need me to do to make it official?"

"I'll bring a contract by for you tomorrow, but right now what I really want is to take a look at the women's locker room."

"You can't do that," one of the anonymous reporters objected. "The police have sealed it."

"The police are through with it," I said. "They've made their arrest. I just need someone with a key to let me in."

Clare pinched the bridge of her nose while she thought about it. Maybe it was the objections the men kept hurling at her that made her decide. She stood up briskly, slipped her feet into their expensive suede pumps, and told me to follow her. Mary Ann and I left the press room in her wake. Behind us I could hear Allison shouting, "You can't do this."

4

I tore the police seal without compunction. If they'd been in the middle of an investigation I would have honored it, but they'd had their chance, made their arrest.

The locker room was a utilitarian set of cement cubes. The attempt to turn the outermost cube into a lounge merely made it look forlorn. It held a few pieces of secondhand furniture, a large bottle of spring water, and a telephone.

Gary had been sitting on a couch plunked into the middle of the floor. Whoever killed him had stood right behind him, wrapping the racket string around his throat before he had time to react—the police found no evidence that he had been able even to lift a hand to try to pull it loose. A smear of dried blood on the back cushion came from where the string had cut through the skin of his neck.

Whoever had pulled the garotte must have cut her—or

his—hands as well. I bummed a pad of paper from Clare and made a note to ask McGonnigal whether Nicole had any cuts. And whether he'd noticed them on anyone else. It was quite possible he hadn't bothered to look.

The lounge led to the shower room. As Mary Ann had warned, the place was strictly functional—no curtains, no gleaming fittings. Just standard brown tile that made my toes curl inside my shoes as I felt mold growing beneath them, and a row of small, white-crusted shower heads.

Beyond the showers was a bare room with hooks for coats or equipment bags and a table for the masseuse. A door led to the outer hall.

"It's locked at all times, though," Clare said.

"*All* the time? I expect someone has a key."

She took the notepad from me and scribbled on it. "I'll track that down for you in the morning."

A barrel of used towels stood between the showers and the massage room. For want of anything better to do I poked through them, but nothing unusual came to light.

"Normally all the laundry is cleared out at the end of the day, along with the garbage, but the maintenance crews couldn't come in tonight, of course," Clare explained.

The garbage bins were built into the walls. It was easy to lift the swinging doors off and pull the big plastic liners out. I took them over to the masseuse's corner and started emptying them onto the table piece by piece. I did them in order of room, starting with the lounge. Police detritus—coffee cups, ashes, crumpled forms—made up the top layer. In the middle of the Styrofoam and ash, I found two leather mittens with bunnies embroidered on them. The palms were cut to ribbons.

I went through the rest of the garbage quickly, so quickly I almost missed the length of nylon wrapped in paper towels. One end poked out as I perfunctorily shook the papers; I saw it just as I was about to sweep everything off the massage table back into the bag.

"It's racket string," Mary Ann said tersely.

"Yes," I agreed quietly.

It was a piece about five inches long. I unrolled all the paper toweling and newsprint a sheet at a time. By the time I finished I had three more little pieces. Since the garotte that killed Gary had been deeply embedded in his throat, these might have been cut from Nicole's racket to point suspicion at her.

"But the mittens . . ." My old coach couldn't bring herself to say more.

Clare Rutland was watching me, her face frozen. "The mittens are Lily's, aren't they? Her brother got them for her for Christmas. She showed them off to everyone on the tour when we had our first post-Christmas matches. Why don't you give them to me, Vic? The string should be enough to save Nicole."

I shook my head unhappily. "It *could* be. We'd have to have the lab make sure these pieces came from her racket. Anyway, I can't do that, Clare. I'm not Gary Oberst's judge and jury. I can't ignore evidence that I've found myself."

"But, Vic," Mary Ann said hoarsely, "how can you do that to Lily? Turn on her? I always thought you tried to help other women. And you saw yourself what her life was like with Gary. How can you blame her?"

I felt the muscles of my face distort into a grimace. "I don't blame her. But how can you let her go through her life without confronting herself? It's a good road to madness, seeing yourself as above and beyond the law. The special treatment she gets as a star is bound to make her think that way to some degree already. If we let her kill her father and get away with it, we're doing her the worst possible damage."

Mary Ann's mouth twisted in misery. She stared at me a long minute. "Oh, *damn* you, Vic!" she cried, and pushed her way past me out of the locker room.

The last traces of vitality had left Clare Rutland's face, making her cheeks look as though they had collapsed into it. "I agree with Mary Ann, Vic. We ought to be able to work something out. Something that would be good for Lily as well as Nicole."

"No," I said.

She lunged toward me and grabbed the mittens. But I was not only younger and stronger, my Nikes gave me an advantage over her high heels. I caught up with her before she'd made it to the shower-room door and gently took the mittens from her.

"Will you let me do one thing? Will you let me see Lily before you talk to the police?"

"What about Nicole?" I demanded. "Doesn't she deserve to be released as soon as possible?"

"If the lawyer the other women have dug up for her doesn't get her out, you can call first thing in the morning. Anyway, go ahead and go to them with the string now. Won't that get her released?"

"I can't do that. I can't come with two separate pieces of evidence found in the identical place but delivered to the law eight hours apart. And no, I damned well will not lie about it for you. I'll do this much for you: I'll let you talk to Lily. But I'll be with you."

Anyway, once the cops have made an arrest they don't like to go back on it. They were just as likely to say that Nicole had cut the string out herself as part of an elaborate bluff.

Clare smiled affably. "Okay. We'll go first thing in the morning."

"No, Ms. Rutland. You're a hell of a woman, but you're not going to run me around the way you do the rest of the tour. If I wait until morning, you'll have been on the phone with Lily and Monica and they'll be in Majorca. We go to-night. Or I stick to you like your underwear until morning."

Her mouth set in a stubborn line, but she didn't waste her time fighting lost battles. "We'll have to phone first. They're bound to be in bed, and they have an elaborate security system. I'll have to let them know we're coming."

I breathed down her neck while she made the call, but she simply told Monica it was important that they discuss matters tonight, before the story made national headlines.

"I'm sorry, honey, I know it's a hell of an hour. And you're under a hell of a lot of strain. But this is the first moment I've had since Nicole found Gary. And we just can't afford to let it go till morning."

Monica apparently found nothing strange in the idea of a two A.M. discussion of Lily's tennis future. Clare told her I was with her and would be driving, so she turned the phone over to me for instructions. Monica also didn't question what I was doing with Clare, for which I was grateful. My powers of invention weren't very great by this point.

5

A single spotlight lit the gate at Nine Bob-O'-Link Lane. When I leaned out the window and pressed the buzzer, Monica didn't bother to check that it was really us: She released the lock at once. The gate swung in on well-oiled hinges.

Inside the gate the house and drive were dark. I switched my headlights on high and drove forward cautiously, trying to make sure I stayed on the tarmac. My lights finally picked out the house. The drive made a loop past the front door. I pulled over to the edge and turned off the engine.

"Any idea why the place is totally dark?" I asked Clare.

"Maybe Lily's in bed and Monica doesn't want to wake her up."

"Lily can't sleep just knowing there's a light on somewhere in the house? Try a different theory."

"I don't have any theories," Clare said sharply. "I'm as baffled as you are, and probably twice as worried. Could someone have come out here and jumped her, be lying in ambush for us?"

My mouth felt dry. The thought had occurred to me as well. Anyone could have lifted Lily's mittens from the locker room while she was playing. Maybe Arnold Krieger had done so. Gotten someone to let him in through the permanently locked end of the women's room, lifted the mittens, garotted Gary, and slipped out the back way again while Rubova was still in the shower. When he realized we were searching the locker room, he came to Northbrook ahead of us. He'd fought hard to keep me from going into the locker room, now that I thought about it.

My gun, of course, was locked away in the safe in my bedroom. No normal person carries a Smith & Wesson to a Virginia Slims match.

"Can you drive a stick shift?" I asked Clare. "I'm going inside, but I want to find a back entrance, avoid a trap if I can. If I'm not out in twenty minutes, drive off and get a neighbor to call the cops. And lock the car doors. Whoever's in the house knows we're here: They released the gate for us."

The mittens were zipped into the inside pocket of my parka. I decided to leave them there. Clare might still destroy them in a moment of chivalry if I put them in the trunk for safekeeping.

I took a pencil flash from the glove compartment. Using it sparingly, I picked my way around the side of the house. A dog bayed nearby. Ninja, the Great Dane. But he was in the house. If Arnold Krieger or someone else had come out to get a jump on us, they would have killed the dog, or the dog would have disabled them. I felt the hair stand up on the back of my neck.

A cinderblock cube had been attached to the back of the house. I shone the flash on it cautiously. It had no windows. Apparently they had built a small indoor court for Lily, for those days when she couldn't get to the club. It had an outside door that led to the garden. When I turned the knob, the door moved inward.

"I'm in here, Vic." Monica's voice came to me in the darkness. "I figured you'd avoid the house and come around the back."

"Are you all right?" I whispered loudly. "Who's inside with Lily?"

Monica laughed. "Just her dog. You worried about Paco interrupting us? He's staying downtown in a hotel. Mary Ann called me. She told me you'd found Lily's mittens. She wanted me to take Lily and run, but I thought I'd better stay to meet you. I've got a shotgun, Vic. Gary was obsessive about Lily's safety, except, of course, on the court. Where he hoped she'd run herself into early retirement."

"You going to kill me to protect your daughter? That won't help much. I mean, I'll be dead, but then the police will come looking, and the whole ugly story will still come out."

"You always were kind of a smartmouth. I remember that from our high school days. And how much I hated you the day you came to see me with the rest of the team when I was pregnant with little Gary." Her voice had a conversational quality. "No. I can persuade the cops that I thought my home was being invaded. Someone coming to hurt Lily on top of all she's already been through today. Mary Ann may figure it out, but she loves Lily too much to do anything to hurt her."

"Clare Rutland's out front with the car. She's going for help before too long. Her story would be pretty hard to discount."

"She's going to find the gate locked when she gets there. And even Clare, endlessly clever, will find it hard to scale a ten-foot electrified fence. No, it will be seen as a terrible tragedy. People will give us their sympathy. Lily's golden up here, after all."

I felt a jolt under my rib cage. "*You* killed Gary."

She burst out laughing. "Oh, my goodness, yes, Vic. Did you just figure that out, smartass that you are? I was sure you were coming up here to gun for me. Did you really think little Lily, who could hardly pee without her daddy, had some sudden awakening and strangled him?"

"Why, Monica? Because she may have hurt her shoulder? You couldn't just get him to lay off? I noticed you didn't even try at her practice session last week."

"I always hated that about you," she said, her tone still flat. "Your goddamned high-and-mightiness. You don't—didn't—ever stop Gary from doing some damned thing he was doing. How do you think I got pregnant with little Gary? Because his daddy said lie down and spread your legs for me, pretty please? Get out of your dream world. I got pregnant the old-fashioned way: He raped me. We married. We fought —each other and everything around us. But we made it out of that hellhole down there just like you did. Only not as easily."

"It wasn't easy for me," I started to say, but I sensed a sudden movement from her and flung myself onto the floor. A tennis ball bounced off the wall behind me and ricocheted from my leg.

Monica laughed again. "I have the shotgun. But I kind of like working with a racket. I was pretty good once. Never as good as Lily, though. And when Lily was born—when we realized what her potential was—I saw I could move myself so far from South Chicago it would never be able to grab me again."

Another *thwock* came in the dark and another ball crashed past me.

"Then Gary started pushing her so hard, I was afraid she'd be another Andrea Jaeger. Injured and burned out before she ever reached her potential. I begged him, pleaded with him. We'd lose that Artemis contract and everything else. But Gary's the kind of guy who's always right."

This time I was ready for the swish of the ball machine. Under cover of its noise, I rolled across the floor in her direction. I didn't speak, hoping the momentum of her anger would keep her going without prompting.

"When Lily came off the court today favoring her shoulder, I told him I'd had it, that I wanted him out of her career. That Paco knew a thousand times more how to coach a girl with Lily's talent than he did. But Mr. Ever-right just laughed and ranted. He finally said Lily could choose. Just like she'd chosen him over Nicole, she'd choose him over Paco."

I kept inching my way forward until I felt the net. One of the balls had stopped there; I picked it up.

Monica hadn't noticed my approach. "Lily came up just then and heard what he said. On top of the scene he'd made at her little press doohickey it was too much for her. She had a fit and left the room. I went down the hall to an alcove where Johnny Lombardy—the stringer—kept his spool. I just cut a length of racket string from his roll, went back to the lounge, and—God, it was easy."

"And Nicole's racket?" I asked hoarsely, hoping my voice would sound as though it was farther away.

"Just snipped a few pieces out while she was in the shower. She's another one like you—snotty know-it-all. It won't hurt her to spend some time in jail."

She fired another ball at the wall and then, unexpectedly, flooded the room with light. Neither of us could see, but she at least was prepared for the shock. It gave her time to locate me as I scrambled to my feet. I found myself tangled in the net and struggled furiously while she steadied the gun on her shoulder.

I wasn't going to get my leg free in time. Just before she fired, I hurled the ball I'd picked up at her. It hit her in the face. The bullet tore a hole in the floor inches from my left foot. I finally wrenched my leg from the net and launched myself at her.

6

"I'm sorry, Vic. That you almost got killed, I mean. Not that I called Monica—she needed me. Not just then, but in general. She never had your, oh, centeredness. She needed a mother."

Mary Ann and I were eating in Greek Town. The Slims had limped out of Chicago a month ago, but I hadn't felt like talking to my old coach since my night in Grenview. But Clare Rutland had come to town to meet with one of the tour sponsors, and to hand me a check in person. And she insisted that the three of us get together. After explaining how she'd talked the sponsors and players into continuing, Clare wanted to know why Mary Ann had called Monica that night.

"Everyone needs a mother, Mary Ann," I said. That's the weakest damned excuse I ever heard for trying to help someone get away with murdering her husband."

Mary Ann looked at me strangely. "Maybe Monica is right about you, Victoria: too high-and-mighty. But it was Lily I was trying to help. I wouldn't have done it if I'd known Monica was going to try to kill you. But you can take care of yourself. You survived the encounter. She didn't."

"What do you mean?" I demanded. "All I did was bruise her face getting her not to shoot me. And no one's going to give her the death penalty. I'd be surprised if she served more than four years."

"You don't understand, Vic. She didn't have anything besides the . . . the scrappiness that got her and Gary out of South Chicago. Oh, she learned how to dress, and put on makeup, and what kinds of things North Shore people eat for dinner. Now that the fight's gone out of her she doesn't have anything inside her to get her through the bad times. You do."

Clare Rutland interrupted hastily. "The good news is that Lily will recover. We have her working with a splendid woman, psychotherapist, I mean. She's playing tennis as much as she wants, which turns out to be a lot. And the other women on the circuit are rallying around in a wonderful way. Nicole is taking her to Maine to spend the summer at her place near Bar Harbor with her."

"Artemis dropped their endorsement contract," I said. "It was in the papers here."

"Yes, but she's already made herself enough to get through the next few years without winning another tournament. Let's be honest. She could live the rest of her life on what she's made in endorsements so far. Anyway, I hear Nike and Reebok are both sniffing around. No one's going to do anything until after Monica's trial—it wouldn't look right. But Lily will be fine."

We dropped it there. Except for the testimony I had to give at Monica's trial I didn't think about her or Lily too much as time went by. Sobered by my old coach's comments, I kept my time on the stand brief. Mary Ann, who came to the trial every day, seemed to be fighting tears when I left the courtroom, but I didn't stop to talk to her.

The following February, though, Mary Ann surprised me by phoning me.

"I'm not umpiring this year," she said abruptly. "I've seen too much tennis close up. But Lily's making her first public appearance at the Slims, and she sent me tickets for all the matches. Would you like to go?"

I thought briefly of telling her to go to hell, of saying I'd had enough tennis—enough of the Obersts—to last me for-ever. But I found myself agreeing to meet her outside the box office on Harrison the next morning.

This pair of stories by Sandra Scoppettone and Robert J. Randisi deals with families, and how justice ultimately comes to the family members, no matter how long it might take.

Of course, there are families, and then there are "families."

---

like father,
like daughter

SANDRA SCOPPETTONE

*Sandra Scoppettone, nominated for an Edgar for her
young adult novel,* Playing Murder, *has made the
streets of New York City her special province. Her
incisive renderings of the contemporary urban scene
and of the currents that lie beneath the surface of
human interactions give her crime novels for adults*
(Some Unknown Person, Such Nice People, Innocent Bystanders, *and most recently,* Everything You
Have Is Mine) *the crackle of brisk authenticity. An
astute observer of people and the passions that move
them, she has also written several mysteries under a
pseudonym, the first of which earned her an Edgar
nomination.*

*We learn much more from our parents than we
realize, as the narrator of "Like Father, Like Daughter" finally admits.*

I notice it for the first time while looking in the mirror as I brush the left side of my hair. "Swoon" is the word that comes to mind. I have no explanation for this. I've been brushing my hair for forty years and this has never happened. With the fainting feeling, I experience a frisson of fear. I stare, brush in hand. All is well again. Have I imagined it? I'm unwilling to test this out and put the brush back in its place.

I walk up Sixth Avenue in the Village and as I pass a man coming toward me, without turning my head, I glance to the left and it happens again. Envision an elevator that stops too suddenly; picture rising too quickly from a sitting position. Though fleeting, perhaps a tenth of a second, it's disconcerting. More. Anxiety is definitely an attendant.

When June awakens she doesn't know where she is and she's terrified. This isn't her bedroom. Bosworth, her teddy, isn't in the bed with her. And then she sees her father. He looks sad but he smiles at her. Smiles funny. Crooked.

"Hi, Junie," he says. His voice sounds as if it's far away.

"Daddy."

And then he's gone. Two strange people hover over her. One is a nurse. June can tell because she's seen pictures of nurses in her storybooks. The man must be a doctor. He has that thing around his neck. The doctor puts two ends in his ears and one end on her chest. She knows from visiting Doctor Wayne that she shouldn't talk while he does this. Also, she knows she's in a hospital. June's never been in one before because she's only six and they won't let kids her age visit. Still, this has to be a hospital. She's seen pictures. And where else could it be?

But why is she here?

June searches her mind. She doesn't remember being sick. Yesterday, after school, she played cowboys with Billy Bishop and Bobby Mander. When Daddy came home from work he played a game of Parcheesi with her. Then she ate dinner. Mommy made macaroni and cheese, her favorite. After that she had her bath and went to bed as always. Daddy read her another chapter of *Winnie the Pooh.* Then both Mommy and Daddy kissed her good night, left the door open and the light on in the hall. Soon she went to sleep.

Now she's here.

The doctor and nurse stop poking and prodding.

"How do you feel, June?" the doctor asks.

She doesn't know how to answer so she stares at him.

"Stomach a little upset, hmmm?"

June realizes when he says that, that it's true. But she doesn't feel like she's going to vomit. She hates to vomit more than anything. She nods.

"That'll pass," the doctor says. He smiles at her and it makes her think of the jack-o'-lantern Mommy made for Halloween. Where is Mommy?

"Do you know where you are?" the doctor asks.

She's afraid to answer. What if she says the wrong thing?

"Cat's got her tongue," says the nurse.

June wonders what this means. What cat? People always say this, but it never makes sense to her.

The doctor asks her again if she knows where she is.

"A hospital," she says tentatively.

"Very good," he says, as if she's won a spelling bee.

June's relieved that she hasn't made a mistake.

"Do you know *why* you're here, June?" he asks.

Now she feels her father's hand on hers. She turns to look at him. He frowns, his eyes droop like old flowers.

"Do you, Junebug?" Daddy asks. "Do you know why you're here?"

She feels like crying. Daddy will be mad if she gives the wrong answer. But he won't hit her, he never hits her. He'll go far away, though he'll still be there. Where's Mommy? Can she ask this? she wonders.

"Junie," Daddy encourages. "Tell us why you're here."

Her breath comes in short little stabs. She has to say something. This funny breathing makes her feel dizzy.

"Sick," she finally manages.

The doctor and nurse look at each other and then at her father.

"That's a good girl," the doctor says. June decides she hates him.

"You get some rest now, young lady, and I'll see you later."

"Want anything?" the nurse asks.

Slowly she rolls her head from side to side and realizes that it hurts. It's like when she has a fever and Mommy puts wet cloths on her forehead.

The doctor and nurse leave. Daddy sits down by the bed, holds her hand.

"Daddy? Where's Mommy?"

Daddy's lips fold in and she can't see his mouth. Twitches in his cheeks make his dimple go on and off like a blinking light. He takes a deep breath, says, "She's resting, Junie."

What does this mean?

"Try to sleep now, okay? You need to sleep."

She wants to ask why, and where Mommy is resting, but it's true that she's tired. Her eyes close and open. Close and open. *Mommy's resting,* she thinks. It's her last thought before sleep overtakes her.

I'm watching a television movie and a man hits a woman. A mind picture presents itself to me. I see my mother's face, though blurred. Often I cannot recall the way she looked, now I do. I see her brown hair worn softly around her heart-shaped face. Crimson lipstick. Her hazel eyes look sad. And there's another thing. The skin around the right eye is discolored, blue and purple, and is smaller than the other one.

I don't remember the reason she gives me for this, but the feeling I experience, then and now, is that she's lying.

The image recedes and I cannot bring it back no matter how I try. Still, the feeling of sinking, sliding into a black pit stays with me. Depression. I feel immobile. I don't want to ask myself about the memory but I know I must confront it, ask the all important questions: How did my mother get that black eye? Why did I know at five or six that what she told me wasn't true?

These inquiries frighten me and I can't formulate them into memory searches. I want to know but I don't want to know. I continue to look at the movie on television, drift back into the comfortable world of denial. What appears on the screen lacks relevance for me. It's entertainment. Entertainment. Oh yes. Let me be entertained, let me live today in the day. I don't want to think about her. I don't know why. I've never known. Until now it hasn't mattered.

When Daddy takes June home from the hospital, she runs from room to room looking for Mommy, but she isn't there. June feels frightened and ready to cry. Daddy sits in the living room on the couch. He pats the cushion beside him, invites her to sit. She feels wary.

June approaches him cautiously, as though he's a stranger, someone she's been warned against. This confuses her. Daddy's not a stranger, not some man on the street who Mommy said might offer her candy or a ride in a bright shiny car. So why does she feel afraid? Why does her heart run riot in her chest?

"Junebug," Daddy says, "sit down. I have something to tell you." He pats the cushion again.

She tells herself that this is *Daddy,* that there's nothing to fear. Not quite trusting this information she joins him on the couch anyway.

Daddy puts his arm around her small shoulders and June tries not to flinch, succeeds. It feels hot, heavy, his fingers on her arm dance like spider legs. June wishes he'd stop drumming on her. And she wants to ask where Mommy is, but the words won't form.

Daddy speaks again. "I want to tell you something," he says.

June has a bad feeling. She doesn't want to hear what Daddy wishes to say. Tempted to put her fingers in her ears, she finds she can't because Daddy has his arm around her like a vise.

"Junebug?" he says.

She feels his warm breath on her cheek.

"Look at me, honey."

Why doesn't she want to look at him? she wonders. If she doesn't see his face then it won't be real. But *what* won't be real?

"Junebug," he says again in a coaxing tone.

"What?" she asks, staring at the skirt of her blue-and-white dress that ends above her knees.

"Look at me."

Slowly, she turns her head and gazes up into his eyes. They are brown, like hers. June thinks she can see herself reflected in them and feels she may disappear, drown, die.

"I want to tell you about Mommy," he says in a serious tone.

His words cause her to feel apprehension, panic. She says nothing but continues to stare at him as if she's frozen into position, the way you are when you play statue. No part of her moves, she believes, not even her eyes make a blink.

"You want to know about Mommy, don't you, June?"

It seems a stupid question and yet she can't bring herself to say yes. Or no. She can't move her lips.

Daddy lets out a long sigh. "June, you don't remember, do you?"

Remember what? She's been asked this question over and over in the last three days. Doctors, nurses, Daddy, Mommy's sister, Aunt Mary. Everyone has asked her if she remembers, but they don't say what it *is* she's supposed to remember. And she's told them all, so many times, that, no, she doesn't. How often does she have to tell them? Tell Daddy? She feels annoyed.

"No," she says definitely. "I told you."

"I just wanted to make sure," he says, the voice unruffled, like cool clouds.

"Don't ask me again," she orders, surprises herself.

Daddy's brows rise for an instant. "All right, Junebug, don't be upset."

"I'm not," she lies.

"What I want to tell you about Mommy is that she's gone away."

These are the words she's been afraid to hear. Her heart vaults as though jumping a hurdle. *Mommy has gone away.* Away, where? June can't bring herself to ask.

But she needn't because Daddy goes on. "She was in an accident, sweetheart."

"Accident?" she whispers.

"Yes."

She doesn't ask what kind of accident. If she doesn't know, she believes, it won't be true. Daddy continues to speak, though she doesn't want him to.

"Mommy's gone to be with God in heaven."

June knows what this means. Archie, her turtle, Boris, her kitten, have both gone to be with God in heaven. It means no more. It means *dead.* When Archie and Boris went to be with God in heaven, she never saw them again. Her heart sags. So this must mean she'll never see Mommy again. She feels terrified.

"It's just you and me now, Junebug," Daddy says.

I want my Mommy, she screams in her head.

"Yes," he says, "just you and me."

·   ·   ·

The swooning feeling continues each time I brush the left side of my hair. Also if I glance to the left without turning my head. It sickens me. I still don't know why. It's something I've come to accept, like getting wet when it rains.

My life is undermined. A depression, black and hollow, starts my day. When I open my eyes upon awakening, there's an infinitesimal moment of no feeling, and then despair. I lie on my back, look up at the beams on the ceiling, count them. There's always the same number.

Why do I sink into this hopelessness? My life, by all standards, is a good one. I have my work, my lover, a fine place to live, enough money. Still, a sense of despondency fills the rooms like thick fog.

Lying beside me, Anne asks, "What is it? What's going on with you?"

I feign innocence because to speak of my feelings, my odd sensations, will fashion them into something to deal with.

"June," she says, "you've been acting very, I don't know, weird lately."

I deny this, become defensive. "You're imagining it."

"No. Something's bothering you."

I get out of bed. "You're crazy," I say.

At the breakfast table we pass things back and forth: sugar, butter, milk. I can feel a distance develop between us like a cold breath of air.

She tries again. "I know you."

"I should hope so," I say brightly, pretending not to discern what she means. "After eighteen years you'd *better* know me." I smile bravely, look into her blue eyes.

"Exactly," she says. "Eighteen years, June. You think after all this time I can't tell when you're upset?"

I say nothing. I stare at her. She's lovely. Ash-blond hair, fair skin, her full mouth projecting sadness now.

She reaches across the table, puts her hand over mine.

My flood of tears surprises me.

Anne gets up, comes over, wraps her arms around me, I rest my head against her breasts.

When my crying subsides she strokes my hair, kisses the top of my head, sits down next to me. "What? Tell me."

"I don't know what it is," I say truthfully, then tell her about my hair and sideways glances, the swooning feeling, the depression.

"You have no idea what it has to do with?" Anne asks.

"My mother," I say, shocked. I feel like a ventriloquist's dummy, as though someone else has said, *my mother.*

"Your mother?"

"I don't know why I said that, Anne. I haven't a clue what it could mean." But then I recall the image of my mother with the black eye and I tell Anne about this.

"Do you think your father—"

"No," I say quickly. Too quickly.

"Look, the idea of your father hitting your mother is . . . well, it just seems absurd, but maybe . . ."

"No."

"Why are you so adamant?"

I start to defend him but as I do a new image comes to mind: I see my father with his arm raised. There's something in his hand but I can't perceive what it is. My arms reach up, my hands on his chest as though I'm pushing him, or holding him back. And there is my mother, behind me. I'm between them. The picture diminishes, is gone.

"What?" Anne asks.

I say nothing. I can't. I don't want to tell her. I shake my head, dismissive.

"June, you have to tell me."

"I don't *have* to do anything," I say childishly.

She sighs, stands up. "Okay, kid. Whatever you say."

Anne knows it's useless to push me when I get like this. I shut down as though a power switch is flicked. I'm inaccessible to her as well as to myself. Nothing has happened, I never had those swooning sensations, I saw no images, forget it. Zip.

The day after June comes home from the hospital he says to her, "We're going to move."

"Where?"

"To a different part of the state. I found us a nice house in a place called Danbury."

"Danbury," June repeats. But she doesn't want to move. This is the house where Mommy lived. She has friends here on the block. And what about school? School will start in two weeks.

"Aunt Mary will help you pack. We're moving the day after tomorrow."

"I don't want to move," June says.

"You'll like this house, Junebug. It has a swimming pool and a big playroom."

She doesn't care. She doesn't know what it means but she doesn't want to leave Mommy.

Two days later June and her daddy move to the white house in Danbury, Connecticut. Everything is new. All the people are new. When they ask her where her mommy is, she tells them that she died in an accident. When they ask what kind of accident, June says nothing and soon people stop asking.

My father lives in Danbury, Connecticut, in a house we moved to when I was six. He has lived there alone since Beatrice, his second wife, died two years ago.

Beatrice and I never liked each other. She married my father six months after my mother died. We lived with an uneasy truce. There was no abuse, either verbal or physical. We never spoke of my mother.

Since his stroke, a year ago, my father has employed a housekeeper, Mrs. Wright, who comes in daily. I gaze at the phone. Mrs. Wright will answer if I call. He may, or may not, come to the phone, depending on his health.

Forty-six years after the event I feel I must ask him how my mother died. I can't believe that I never asked before, that I've been satisfied all these years with that one word: *accident*. What could I have been thinking? Perhaps that's just it, I wasn't thinking.

I've expunged my mother's memory so adroitly that the oddness, the strangeness surrounding her death hasn't, until now, even tempted me. And I call myself a mystery writer.

I place my hand on the ebony phone. I wait, poised as if for inspiration. But I know about inspiration: it almost never comes. The hell with it. I lift the receiver and punch in the eleven numbers. After two rings Mrs. Wright picks up. We go through a desultory exchange and then she walks to my father and hands him the portable phone.

"Junebug," he says, voice hoarse, husky since the stroke.

I hate this nickname and he knows that but I ignore it. "I have to ask you something, Daddy."

My father doesn't like to be asked questions of any nature so he tries to deflect me and asks how Anne is. I answer, then go quickly into the reason I've called. "How exactly did Mommy die?"

There's a long silence.

"Daddy, did you hear me?" I know he did.

Silence. Then: "Why bring that up now?"

"I have to know."

"Accident," he mumbles.

"Yes, I know, but what *kind* of accident?"

"I'm not feeling well today," he says, whiny.

"I'm sorry."

"Blood pressure's up," he blackmails.

I press on. "What kind of accident did Mommy die in?"

After moments, with only static on the line, he says, "Why?"

"I want to know. I have a *right* to know how my mother died."

"You never cared before," he accuses.

My own blood pressure rises and the hand that holds the phone gets slick with sweat. Furious, I say, "It's not that I didn't *care*." How can I explain that in a sense, I forgot that I didn't know? It's too bizarre to voice.

"What then?"

"Look, Daddy," I try reasonably, "it doesn't matter what I did or didn't ask in the past. I want to know *now*."

This time the silence yawns endlessly, then finally in his rasping voice he says, "Car." And hangs up.

Car. I replace the handset in the cradle. *Car.* Does this mean she was in a car accident? Whose car was it? Who was driving?

I rush to the closet, where I take out an old shoe box. In here I store the pictures from my past. At the dining-room table I open the box and dump out the photographs. They spill over the oak surface like playing cards out of control.

As I shuffle through them, bits and pieces of my life flash past me. I remember now that there are none of my mother. Why haven't I ever questioned this? Was I so good, so docile, that I accepted whatever I was told? Surely pictures had been taken of her during her life, during my life with her.

And then I find it.

A photograph of the car. It's what I've been looking for. I'm not good at classifying types or years of cars, but this one is clearly from the forties. The picture is black-and-white. The car is a boxy four-door type, but only two doors show, as the picture was taken from the driver's side. I remember now that the car was gray. My father sits in the driver's seat, his hand stuck out of the open window in a wave. He's not smiling. . . . I've noted before that there are no pictures of my father smiling.

I stare at the car and try to remember. Yes, we had this car before she died. But what about afterward? I turn the photo over and suck in my breath. There, written in Beatrice's hand, is the date. A year after my mother's death.

Even if the accident *had* happened in our car, she wouldn't have been the driver because she didn't drive. I remember something about her trying to learn, a bee flying in the window and that ending her lessons.

So whose car was she in when she had the accident?

And who was driving?

I can't recall any mention of another person. Wouldn't I have heard something about this if she'd been the passenger in a car accident? Still, we'd moved so soon afterward. Why?

I turn back to the picture and stare at it. The more I look at the photo, the sicker I feel. My eyes block out my father and I see only the car. I shift my eyes to the left, and though I'm sitting down, I feel as if I might faint. I return my gaze to the picture.

The *car*. Oh, Jesus.

June is sleeping, dreaming. Something wakes her. She opens her eyes. It's dark. Her mother's bent over her, her breath smells that awful way it does when she and Daddy have their drinks. June can see Mommy's still in her dress.

"Come on, June," her mother whispers. "Get up and be quiet."

"Where are we going?" she asks sleepily.

"Shush. Hurry up."

Mommy sounds angry and June feels afraid. "But . . ."

"Shhh." She pulls back the covers and takes June by the arm; her fingers press into June's flesh.

June wants to tell Mommy that she's hurting her but something stops her. Then Mommy lets go of June's arm and takes her hand.

They tiptoe into the hallway. June notices that the light is still on in Daddy's room. They pass his door and start down the steps. June stops and looks up at her mother.

"My slippers," she says.

"That's okay." She directs her to continue down. Mommy's nylons make that swishing sound when she walks and it's then that June realizes Mommy isn't wearing shoes either.

The living room is dark, but June knows it well and they go through it and into the kitchen. She waits for Mommy to turn on the light but she doesn't. Instead, she leads June to the door that opens from the kitchen into a hallway. A broom, carpet sweeper, paper bags, some tools are kept there. From this place you can go down to the cellar or open another door to the outside.

Mommy stops and reaches up to a hook where keys hang, takes some, then opens the outside door. June doesn't understand why they are going outside in the middle of the night. For a moment they stand on the landing as Mommy closes the back door. June starts down the steps toward the yard.

"No," Mommy orders.

June stops on the second step down, looks at her. Mommy shakes her head, motions her back. There's another door at the head of the landing that leads to the garage. Mommy opens it.

Why are they going into the garage? June wonders. Her stomach drops the way it does sometimes in an elevator.

They go down two steps and Mommy closes the door, then they continue down the last three. It's dark in the garage and quiet. June hears Mommy breathing, then hears her own that is faster than usual. She smells the dark and it's bad. Mommy leads her to the car, opens the front door.

"Get in," Mommy says.

June feels frightened, it's strange. Why are they getting in the car? Mommy doesn't drive the car. She feels her mother's hands on her back pushing her forward. June climbs up until both knees are on the driver's seat. She wears shorty pajamas so she feels the nap against her skin. Mommy keeps pushing her and she bangs into the round knob on the top of the stick that comes up from the floor. She cries out.

"Be quiet, June," she says harshly.

June wants to cry but, instead, presses her lips firmly

together. She crawls around the knob and falls into the passenger seat on her back. Scared. So scared. She straightens herself around so that she sits up in the seat.

June's eyes have become accustomed to the dark and she makes out the dashboard, the place called the glove compartment. When she turns to look to her left, she sees her mother get into the driver's seat. June watches while Mommy closes the door carefully, so carefully that it barely makes a sound.

Now they are both in the car. The doors and windows are closed. And something else. The big garage door is closed, too. How will they get the car out? Is Mommy going to drive even though she doesn't know how? Is Mommy going to drive *through* the garage door? June breathes swiftly, her head feels light. She's too frightened, she has to ask.

"Mommy, what are we doing?"

Her mother looks at the windshield but doesn't answer.

"Mommy, what are we doing?"

Nothing.

Terror engulfs June but she asks again. "Mommy, what are we doing? Where are we going?"

Silence.

June's voice rises. "Mommy, Mommy, Mom—"

Her mother pulls the left side of her hair, hard.

June squeals in pain.

"*Shut up,* June. Just *shut up,*" she says through her teeth, and lets go of her hair.

June feels the pain in her scalp but her mother's voice is what hurts her more. Gingerly, she touches her hair as if to soothe it. She slides down in her seat, stares straight ahead. Afraid to have her mother see her looking at her, June glances to the left without moving her head.

Mommy sits still. Eyes face front. Then she lifts her hand and June hears a jingling sound. The keys. Horrified, June sees, from the corner of her eye, her mother put the key into the slot where Daddy puts it to start up. And then Mommy turns the key. The engine makes the starting noise. Her mother *is* going to drive through the big garage door. How else will they get out of the garage?

Daddy will be so mad, June thinks. Mommy shouldn't break through the door. She wants to tell Mommy this but she's afraid Mommy will pull her hair again, or maybe slap her, though she hardly ever does that. But this is different. Mommy's different.

June clutches the seat. If Mommy's going to smash through the door, they could get hurt.

June waits.

Again she glances to the left without moving her head. Mommy's hands are on her lap. How can she drive the car if her hands are not on the steering wheel? June wants to scream. She's never felt so frightened. But of what? Mommy doesn't move the car. They just sit there. So why is she frightened? Why does her stomach feel the way it does when she goes to the dentist? Why does she want to cry? Why does she want to scream?

I sit on a wing chair in the living room of my father's house. He's across from me, on the corner seat of the sofa, where he spends almost all his life. It's the housekeeper's day off.

I've told him I know that my mother took me with her to the car in the garage, where she tried to kill us both, but obviously only succeeded in killing herself. How horrible her life must've been to do that. And did she, misguidedly, believe she was sparing me? I've asked him to tell me what happened . . . tell me, finally, the truth.

Even with the stroke, one side of his face strangely immobile, you can see that he was once a handsome man. His black hair is now completely white, but he's amazingly devoid of wrinkles.

With all the memories that have surfaced, I still find it hard to see him differently from the way I have all my life. To me he was gentle, sensitive, and as my mother would've said, *refined*. But this man gave my mother a black eye, committed other abuses that I witnessed. It's almost impossible for me to integrate these personalities, for they're as separate as if they were two people.

"What happened?" I ask again.

His lip trembles. I know that soon he'll start to cry.

"Why can't you let it go?" he says in the strange husky voice he's developed since his stroke.

"Because it affects my life," I explain, as though to a child. "Because I find myself depressed and I *need* to know the truth."

"You said you knew the truth."

"I don't know the ending. I can't remember how I got out of the car. Why did she die and I live?"

The tears roll down his cheeks but I feel no sympathy. He's had no right to keep this from me.

"You're upsetting me," he says, hauling out the "stroke victim" defense.

"I can't help that. Tell me what happened."

There's a long, long silence and I think he isn't going to talk but then he does.

"I found you."

"And?"

"I've always . . . been . . . a light sleeper."

I say nothing.

"I heard . . . I heard the car start."

Something thumps inside me. *I heard the car start.* I wait.

My father clutches his forehead. "I don't feel well."

"Tell me the rest," I say unmercifully.

"I think . . . think you'd better . . . call the doctor."

"Not until you tell me." I refuse to fall for this.

He cries now, sucking sobs. "I . . . came . . . downstairs. I went . . . into the garage. There . . . you were, both . . . of you. I . . . saved your . . . life, Junebug."

The horror of what I suspect creeps upward from my toes like a fungus. I try not to think this way. It's too odious. Still, I have to persist, I have to know.

"And Mommy?" I ask. "What about *her* life?"

Great tormented wails.

"Well?"

"Too . . . late," he sputters. "Too . . . late."

But I know he's lying. He heard the car start.

"After you heard the car start, what did you do?"

"I . . . told you. Get me . . . my doctor, June."

"No. What did you do? How *long* did you wait after you heard it start before you came downstairs?"

He shakes his head as though he doesn't understand or doesn't remember. I know he does both but isn't going to tell. So I decide to do it for him.

"You came down pretty soon after hearing it, didn't you? I can imagine it. You're lying there, sleeping in your 'light' way. You wake up, wonder what's awakened you, recall that it was the sound of the car starting. You don't move immediately because this doesn't make sense to you. So you lie there for a while, trying to figure it out. Maybe you even wait five minutes before you get up. Then you go to Mommy's room and see that she's not in bed. Next, to mine and—"

"June . . . no . . . stop. . . ."

"Next, to mine and see that I'm not there. You hesitate for a bit, then make the connection: she doesn't drive, so why has she taken me with her to the car? There can only be one reason. How am I doing so far?" I ask.

He sobs, nods.

"So you rush downstairs and out the back door to the garage. The car's running. You open the driver's door. We're both there, unconscious. Did you go around to the other side or did you just lean across her to get me?"

"Doc . . . tor."

"I think you leaned across her and picked me up, carried me from the car back into the house. I was alive, of course. But so was she. Why didn't you go back for *her*? Hmmm? Why the hell didn't you go back for *her*?" I scream.

His eyes seem to roll upward and he shudders.

"You could've saved her but you didn't. You knew I'd be all right so you waited until she was dead to call the police and ambulance. You killed her. You murdered her," I say.

"Help . . . me," he says almost inaudibly.

"First tell me if what I've said is true?"

"Help . . ."

"Tell me," I demand.

"Yes."

A big black medal of pain attaches itself to my heart and for a moment I feel faint. But it passes.

"Str . . . o . . . ke," he says.

I stare at him, unmoving. It's clear to me now that he really *is* having a stroke. I watch, frozen.

He twitches, his body in a paroxysm. His mouth moves but no words come out.

I continue watching, as if this is a movie. But I know it's not.

He's seized in an excruciating convulsion and then just as suddenly he goes limp. His head rolls to the side, his eyes and mouth open, a thin line of saliva trails down his chin. He's still.

I wait for ten minutes.
He doesn't move, doesn't breathe.
I get up, go to the phone and dial the police.
As it rings I realize: I am my father's daughter.

t u r n a b o u t

A NICK DELVECCHIO STORY

ROBERT J. RANDISI

Bob Randisi is the editor of five PWA anthologies and the author of eight PI novels. His most recent novels are Separate Cases, *the fourth mystery featuring Manhattan PI Miles Jacoby, and* The Dead of Brooklyn, *the second novel in the Brooklyn-based Nick Delvecchio series. He is the cofounder of Mystery Scene* magazine *and its American Mystery Award, and the American Crime Writers' League; the founder of the Private Eye Writers of America, and the creator of their Shamus Award; he is also the mystery reviewer for* The Orlando Sentinel.

"Turnabout" is a Nick Delvecchio story. It shows just how dangerous it can be to get involved in other people's family squabbles.

1

Frank Cabretta looked every bit as dangerous in jail as he had looked out. The fact that he was wearing prison clothes diminished his stature not one iota. He sat in his plastic chair as if he were sitting in the leather chair behind his huge oak desk in his luxurious home in Long Island.

"Nick," he said.

"I thought I told you a long time ago not to call me that."

Cabretta smiled contemptuously.

"What are you going to do," he asked, "send me to prison?"

I gave way to a small smile and said, "You have a point."

Even here Cabretta was entitled to certain privileges, such as a private meeting room on demand that was usually reserved for lawyer/client relationships. I was a private detective, not a lawyer, and Cabretta was certainly not a client. On the contrary, five years ago I was a cop, and Cabretta was behind bars with my compliments.

That made Cabretta's "summons" even more curious.

"Have a seat," Cabretta said. "I have something I want to talk to you about."

"What makes you think I'm interested in anything you'd have to say to me?"

Cabretta, a good-looking man in his late forties, smiled and said, "The fact that you're here answers that question."

"I'm here because I was paid five hundred dollars to come."

"Five?" Cabretta said, showing mild surprise. "I told my lawyer to offer you two."

"He did," I said, and left it at that.

"I see," Cabretta said. "Will you have that seat?"

I hesitated, then said, "Why not?" and sat across the table from the ex–drug king turned prisoner.

Cabretta turned to the guard who was standing inside the door and said, "Get lost."

"I can't—"

"Beat it, screw!"

The guard looked at me and I said, "It's all right."

"I'll be right outside."

"Stay away from the door!" Cabretta called after the guard as he left. "Fuckin' walls have the biggest ears you ever saw in here," he said. "All right, then, let's get to it. I want to hire you."

"That's a laugh."

"Nevertheless," Cabretta said, "it's true."

Warily, I asked, "To do what?"

"Since I've been here my wife has either visited me or written to me at least once a week, sometimes one of each a week."

"So? She's a faithful wife."

Cabretta frowned and said, "That's what I want you to find out."

"Why?"

"I haven't seen her or heard from her in a month."

"Maybe she's sick."

"I don't think so. I think there's something else going on, and I want you to find out what."

"Why not have one of your goons outside do the job?" I asked.

"Because I want it done on the qt," Cabretta said, "and I don't trust anyone else to do it but you."

"Why's that?"

"You put me here," Cabretta said, "that means you're good at what you do. I want to hire the best."

"I'm good, but I'm not the best."

"I'll take my chances with you, Nick."

"I told you—"

Cabretta raised his hand to stay the objection and said, "Sorry . . . *Mister* Delvecchio."

"Let me get this straight," I said. "You want me to find out why your wife hasn't written or come to see you in a month."

"That's right."

"And then what?"

"And then come back here and tell me."

"You don't want me to report to your attorney?"

"He doesn't know why I'm seeing you today."

"You haven't told your attorney?" I asked, in surprise.

"I told you," Cabretta said, "I don't trust anyone on this but you."

I studied Cabretta for a few long moments. His dark hair had begun to show some gray while he'd been inside, but he looked as if he were still keeping himself in shape. He looked fit, with the build of a man ten years his junior.

"Why should I do this for you?"

"I knew you'd ask me that," Cabretta said. "You owe me."

I snorted and said, "For what?"

"For putting me here," Cabretta said, showing the first signs of agitation. "For taking away five years of my life, that's why!"

"You deserve to be in here, Cabretta," I replied casually. "You *belong* in here, and for a lot longer than five years."

Cabretta stiffened his jaw and for a moment I thought he was going to explode. I watched as the man brought his fabled temper under control, and thought that at least he had learned something during his stay here.

"All right," Cabretta finally said, "name your fee, then. You work for people for money, right? Well, I've got money. Name your price."

My regular price was two hundred and fifty dollars a day plus expenses. Things had been rough during the past year and at times the price had come down as low as *one* hundred and fifty.

"Three hundred and fifty a day, plus expenses."

Cabretta never blinked.

"Take the case and I'll have my attorney pay you a week's retainer."

"And if I don't catch her doing anything . . . wrong during that time?"

"Come and tell me, and then we're quits."

"And if I find that she is seeing someone?"

"Same thing."

I studied him for a minute and then said, "And then she ends up dead, right? Thanks, but no thanks, Frankie. I don't want that on my conscience."

Cabretta looked appalled and said, "My own wife? And even if she wasn't my wife, I don't do business that way. You know that, Ni—Delvecchio."

He was right. I did know that—but this didn't sound like business, and she *was* his wife. I was sure that all he wanted was confirmation that his wife was cheating on him, and then he'd have her taken care of. I also knew that if I didn't take the job, someone else would.

"All right, Frank," I said, finally.

"You'll work for me?"

"Sure," I said, with a shrug. "Your money's as good as anyone else's, right?"

"It's better than anyone else's . . . Nick." He spoke my name with a smug look on his face. "Can I call you Nick, now that you work for me?"

I grinned at him and said, "No."

I left the prison, knowing that I had made a decision and I had to stick to it. I didn't like it, but I knew I'd stick to it.

2

The call from Frankie Cabretta's attorney had come in early that morning. I had just stepped out of the shower and was dripping on the cheap linoleum as I picked up the receiver.

"Delvecchio," I said, holding the receiver with my right hand and drying my hair with my left. The air-conditioning from the window unit felt cold on my wet, naked flesh.

"Nick Delvecchio, please," a man's voice said. It sounded vaguely familiar, but I couldn't place it.

"This is he."

"Oh, I was expecting, er, a secretary."

"My secretary's gone out to pick up some more Sweet'n Low," I said. "We ran out. Who's calling me, please?"

"Mr. Delvecchio, my name is Walter Koenig. Do you remember me?"

"Koenig," I said, repeating the name once. It was all I need to remember the man. I stopped drying my hair and dropped my hand to my side, still holding the towel.

"Sure, Mr. Koenig, I remember you. You're Frankie Cabretta's attorney—or at least, you were five years ago." I didn't bother disguising the dislike in my tone, for both men, lawyer and client.

"I still am, Mr. Delvecchio, and that is why I am calling you," Koenig said. "Would you be able to come to my office this afternoon?"

"What for?"

"To discuss the possibility of, er, employment."

"By you? Don't you have staff investigators, counselor, or have you fallen on hard times?" I asked. I almost said, "Have you fallen on hard times, *too*," but stopped myself in time.

"Uh, I would prefer not to discuss this over the phone, Mr. Delvecchio. If you would come to my office, it would be, ah, more convenient."

"For who?"

"For, uh, me, of course," the man said. "It would also be to your benefit, however."

"How's that?"

"I would pay you two hundred dollars."

I tried to keep my tone neutral, even though my heart had leaped into my throat.

"Just to come to your office and listen?"

"That's right."

"The money would be nonrefundable?"

"Of course."

I paused a moment, then decided, what the hell!

"My fee is two hundred and *fifty* dollars a day."

There was no hesitation on Walter Koenig's part whatsoever. "Done."

The clock on my wall said it was 9:00 A.M.

"I'll be there by eleven, Mr. Koenig."

"Ten would be preferable, Mr. Delvecchio."

"Eleven, counselor."

"Ah, yes, of course," Koenig said. "I will look forward to seeing you at eleven."

I hung up the phone and kept my hand on it. I hadn't seen a full day's pay in over a month. So what if I had to suffer the company of slime like Walter Koenig for a few minutes. I'd listen to what he had to say, turn him down flat, and walk out two hundred and fifty dollars richer, without the slightest hint of guilt.

3

Koenig's office was in a building on Court Street, a healthy hike from my apartment on Sackett Street. I remember now wondering five years ago why Frank Cabretta's attorney didn't have an office on Park Avenue, across the Brooklyn Bridge in Manhattan?

The front door had gold lettering on the cherry oak wood that said WALTER KOENIG, ATTORNEY, and I entered without bothering to knock.

The woman behind the desk in the reception room looked up and gave me a professional smile—the kind that fully occupied the mouth and teeth and never invaded the eyes—and said, "May I help you, sir?"

She was in her early forties, but she was handsomely made up to hide the lines I knew had to be there. Still, she went right along with the rest of the room, which gave off the impression of class.

"I have an appointment with Mr. Koenig."

"Mr. Delvecchio?"

"That's right."

"You may go right in. He's expecting you."

When she said "He," I knew that she automatically capitalized the word.

"Thank you," I said, but the receptionist had already turned her attention back to her computer terminal.

I went to the unmarked door the receptionist had indicated and opened it, again without knocking.

Koenig was behind a cluttered desk that surprised me. For one thing it was rather small, and that and the fact that it *was* cluttered did not go along with the impression presented by the reception area, and the receptionist. This room—small, sensibly furnished, and anything but neat—seemed to reflect more of the man than the reception room did—which was, of course, only natural. After all, he spent most of his time in here.

I might have liked him for that if I hadn't known he was Cabretta's lawyer.

"Ah, Mr. Delvecchio," Walter Koenig said, rising. "I'm so glad you came."

"I'm not sure I am," I said honestly.

"Perhaps, if I were to write you a check—"

Not wishing to seem *that* mercenary, I said, "You can do that later. Why don't you tell me why I'm here?"

"Please, take a seat."

There was only one to take, a straight-backed wooden chair in front of his desk, and I took it.

Koenig was in his midforties, a tall, slender but well-built man with curly brown hair the color of shoe polish. I couldn't help but wonder if he dyed it.

"My client wishes to engage your services."

"By client you mean Frank Cabretta?"

"Yes."

I started to stand and said, "We have nothing further to talk about."

"Oddly enough," he said, "you are correct."

"What?" I asked, stopping midway out of the chair, my knees still bent.

"You see," he said sheepishly, "I know that Mr. Cabretta wishes to hire you, but I haven't the faintest idea why."

"He hasn't told you?" I asked. "His lawyer?"

"Ah, no, he hasn't."

"Isn't that rather odd?"

"I thought so," he said. "I also told him—as you mentioned on the phone—that I have my own investigators. He was quite adamant that he wanted you."

"Why?"

"Alas, I can't answer that," he said. "I've been instructed to pay you for consulting with me, and to ask you to go and see him."

"In prison?"

"Yes."

I sat back down because I was feeling silly—and my legs were getting tired.

"I don't understand."

"To be frank, I don't, either. I'm rather anxious for you to see him so that *I* can also find out what is going on."

"I put him away," I said. "At least, my testimony did. It's ludicrous that I'd go up and see him."

Koenig smiled and said, "A fascinating prospect, isn't it?"

Against my better judgment I admitted to myself that he was right. It was fascinating, and I knew that my curiosity would not allow me to pass this up.

"All right," I said. "I'll go."

"I'll write your check for the consultation," he said.

"Double it."

"What?"

"Two hundred and fifty for coming here, and another two hundred and fifty for the trip to Ossining."

"I don't think—"

"You want me to go to Sing Sing, counselor, you've got to pay my way." I shrugged, as if to say, that's the way it is, take it or leave it.

He took it.

He pulled a checkbook from his desk drawer, wrote me a check, and handed it across the desk to me. I took it, looked at it, tucked it into my wallet, and stood up.

"I suppose you'll clear the way for this," I said.

"I'll make some calls, yes."

I stared at him and then said, "You've already made them, haven't you?"

He smiled and said, "How did you guess?"

"I didn't guess," I said, "I know, just by looking at you."

"You're a very good detective."

"You're damned right I am," I said, and then added before leaving: "Just ask your client."

I wasn't a detective when I put Cabretta away, just a patrolman who happened to be in the right place at the right time, but I wasn't about to let that ruin a good exit line.

4

When I got back to Brooklyn, I went right to Koenig's office again and presented myself to his secretary.

"I'm afraid I don't have an appointment this time," I told her.

"Yes, you do," she said. "Go right in."

I went into Koenig's office and sat in his visitor's chair. There was a brown, ten-by-thirteen manila envelope on my side of his desk.

"Everything you need to know about Carla Cabretta is in there," he said. "Where she has her hair done, where she has her car serviced, where her health club is—"

"The only thing we don't know," I said, sliding her photo out of the envelope, "is who's fucking her."

"If she is having an affair," Koenig said stiffly, "that is up to you to find out."

I studied the color photo. It looked like a studio print. Just a head shot—but *what* a head! If the colors were to be believed her hair was chestnut, her eyes green. She was a beautiful woman. There was a second picture, as well. This was a candid shot of her leaving someplace, wearing a leotard. It must have been taken in front of her health club. She was tall, with long, long legs, a tiny waist, and small, high, firm breasts and wide shoulders. No body builder, Carla Cabretta, but extremely fit.

"Classy looking," I said.

"Yes, she is."

"All right, Walter," I said, using his first name to his dismay. "I'll get right on it."

"Yes," he said, "you do that." He couldn't wait for me to leave. Now that I was working for Frank Cabretta he couldn't waste his time on me. To him, I was just another employee.

That was okay with me. I didn't like him all that much, either.

"You'll notice on the back of the color photo there are two addresses," Koenig said. "One is the house in Long Island, and one is an apartment she has taken in Park Slope."

"Does Frank know about the apartment?"

"Of course," Koenig said. "If I know about it, Frank knows."

"Of course," I said, standing, "how silly of me. If he ever found out that you were keeping anything from him—"

"I wouldn't," Koenig said, "and if I were you, I wouldn't think about it, either."

"I assume I'll be reporting to you?"

"That is correct."

"Well, I'd better get to it, then."

"I would appreciate a report at the end of each day."

"By telephone all right?"

"Fine."

"Fine," I said, and he narrowed his eyes as if he suspected I was mimicking him.

And, of course, I was.

5

Carla Cabretta's Brooklyn apartment was in the Yuppified Park Slope section of Brooklyn. Her health club was also in that area, which meant that I didn't have to go very far from my own neighborhood to tail her. If and when I needed a car, I had access to a friend's mint-condition '76 Grand Prix.

I was right behind her for three straight days, and although she had met two different men for lunch, she had neither gone home with anyone, nor brought anyone home with her. I was starting to get the feeling that maybe Carla wasn't really cheating on Frank, she just wanted to get away from being Mrs. Cabretta.

I called Koenig at the end of each of the first five days

and gave him negative reports. Even if she *had* slept with someone during that time, I still would have given Koenig negative reports. It wasn't my aim to rat her out to her husband. I had loftier goals in mind.

On the evening of the sixth day I got to achieve one of those goals.

She'd had dinner with two ladyfriends, probably women she had met at the health club, from the way they looked. They were all very fit, and taut, and as a group they skillfully fended off all advances. They separated outside the restaurant, a tiny, hole-in-the-wall bistro on Atlantic Avenue, and Carla drove right home in her little blue Mercedes.

She had an apartment on the second floor of a converted brownstone, and I watched her fit her key into the front door. I always waited until she was inside before breaking off the surveillance. I watched until her light went on in front of the building and then started my motor, getting ready to leave. I took one last look at the front of the building, and abruptly shut the motor.

There was a shadow on the stairs, someone at the door, fiddling with it. It wasn't a resident, because by now I knew most of them. As I watched the door opened, illuminating for one moment a man clad in dark clothes as he entered and closed the door behind him.

It could have been anything, of course. Might even have been a simple burglar, but I didn't want to take the chance. I got out of the Grand Prix, first taking a .38 from the glove compartment, and crossed the street. I don't carry a gun as a matter of course, but all along I had the feeling I was going to need one. The .38 was my off-duty gun when I was a cop.

It was after ten and dark, and the street was empty. I already knew that there were very few kids on this block, and for the most part they rolled up the streets early.

When I reached the front door, I couldn't really see the lock well enough to tell how he had opened it. I took out my trusty lock picks and fitted them both into the lock. Unlike television and the movies, you need two hands and two instruments to properly pick a lock.

It took me a minute but I finally opened the door and slipped inside. I put the lock picks in my left pocket and took the gun out of my right.

I went through the second door and stood still a moment. I thought I could hear floorboards creaking, but that could have been from any apartment. I went to the stairs and started up. Carla's apartment was on the second floor, but the stairs were split into two flights, with a landing in between. There was supposed to be a light over the first landing, but someone had apparently unscrewed the light bulb. Either that, or it had conveniently gone out. I was on the landing when I heard her scream. My first instinct was to run up the second flight, but I held myself back. Sure enough, a shadow appeared below me, at the foot of the steps.

"Stop right there!" I said.

"Shit!" he said, and I was already on my belly when I saw the muzzle flash from his gun. His bullet went over my head. I fired and heard him cry out as the bullet struck him.

Now I ran up to the second floor and stopped when I saw her door was open a crack. I backed up two steps and leaned over so I could watch the door. Finally, the second man became impatient, and the door opened wider.

"Gino?" a voice called. "Gino, did you get him?"

"Uh," I said.

"Gino?"

"I got 'im," I said.

"Gino . . . that ain't you!"

The door started to close and I thought I'd blown it. Suddenly, though, the man staggered out into the hall, as if pushed from behind. Before he could regain his balance I was in the hall, pointing my gun.

"Don't be stupid," I called out, but obviously I was years too late. Off balance, he still squeezed the trigger of his gun. The bullet struck the wall next to me, and I fired twice, because I was taking no chances. Both bullets hit home, and he slid down the wall, leaving a bloody trail on it that tenants could either clean or talk about for years to come.

I ran down the hall, took a moment to check him, then went into the apartment. Carla Cabretta was on the floor near the door, bound hand and foot and gagged. Obviously, she had managed to hop over to the door and shove the man out into the hall.

I untied her, but kept my gun in my hand. I hadn't had time to check and make sure the first man was dead.

"Thanks for pushing him," I said.

"Thanks for being here," she said, rubbing her wrists.

I helped her to her feet, then closed and locked the apartment door.

"By the way," she said calmly, "who are you and how come you *are* here?"

She didn't strike me as the type to scream. She told me later that the man had twisted her arm so that she yelled out in pain, I suppose for my benefit. Her scream was supposed to make me rush up the steps, unaware that there was a man behind me who intended to kill me.

"Before we go into that," I said, "let's get our story straight, or we'll both be spending most of the night in a police station."

I looked at her for a moment. This was the first time I had seen her this close up. Her photos had not done her justice. Neither had watching her from across the street.

"Now that you've inspected the merchandise," she said wryly, "would you tell me what you're talking about?"

"That many shots will not go unnoticed," I said. "The police will be here soon. We've got to agree on an explanation for all of this."

"Why?" she said. "Why should I tell them anything but the truth? That I don't know any of the three of you?"

"Because I just killed two men to save our lives."

"Our lives?"

"Yes."

She frowned at me and asked, "You don't work for my husband, do you?"

I hesitated, then said, "Yes and no."

"I can't wait to hear the explanation for that one."

6

When the cops arrived, we had our story straight. Mrs. Cabretta told them who she was, and that she had hired me to be her bodyguard because she'd been getting some threatening phone calls. I showed them my PI ticket, my gun permit, and dropped some names from their precinct, the seven-seven. When the detectives arrived, I knew one of them. His name was Weinstock, and he usually partnered with Vito Matucci. At one time Matucci and I were patrol-car partners.

"Where's Vito, Weinstock?" I asked.

"You know this guy?" one of the uniformed cops asked.

"Yes, I know him," Weinstock said.

"Good," the cop said, handing Weinstock my ticket and my permit, "he's all yours."

The uniforms left, and the two bodies had been removed from the halls. All that was left behind was some blood.

"This is Simmons," Weinstock said, indicating his partner. "Matucci's got the flu." Simmons was impressive. He was the biggest black man I'd ever seen, with shoulders like the wingspan of a 747. We nodded at each other.

I didn't miss Matucci. His absence meant I didn't have to match insults with anyone.

"Tell it to me," Weinstock said.

I gave him the same story I had given the uniforms, and then Carla backed me up. Weinstock handed me back my goods.

"Come into the station in the morning, Delvecchio, and make a statement."

"Sure."

"And bring the lady."

Carla smiled at him from the sofa.

"You better save that one, Weinstock," I said. "I don't think you'll ever get one like it again."

Weinstock looked at Carla, then said, "I think you're right."

He tapped Simmons on the arm and led the way out the door.

I looked at Carla and said, "You were great. Thanks."

"Delvecchio," she said, as if tasting my name. "Aren't you the policeman whose testimony sent my husband to prison?"

"I was, yes."

"Now that that's over with," she said, "you want to tell me what's going on?"

I sat next to her on the sofa. My nostrils filled up with her perfume. It was a very nice scent. Up close like this I could see that she was about thirty-five, a good ten or twelve years younger than her husband.

"Mrs. Cabretta—"

"Please," she said, "don't call me that. After saving my life you're at least entitled to call me Carla."

"At least," I said.

We stared at each other in silence for a few moments, and then I said, "Carla, your husband hired me to follow you, and find out why you haven't come to see him during the past month."

"Why would he do that?" she asked, frowning. "He knows why I haven't come to see him. I want a divorce."

"You told him that?"

"The last time I saw him. I told him I wouldn't be back to see him, either."

"Do you have a lawyer?"

"No," she said, "Frank said that Walter would take care of everything."

"Frank agreed to the divorce?"

She shrugged and said, "He loves me, and wants me to be happy. So tell me, Mr. Delvecchio, why would he send you to follow me to find out something he already knows?"

"I think it's fairly obvious, Carla."

She thought it over a moment, and then said, "You mean he sent those two men to kill me?"

"No," I said, "he sent one to kill you, and one to kill me."

Now she was getting it.

"He was going to have me killed, and frame you for it?"

"He was probably going to make it look like we killed each other."

"That son of a bitch!"

"Good," I said. "I thought I was going to have to convince you."

"You don't have to convince me," she said, "but I'd like you to tell me what we can do about it. Killing two of his men isn't going to stop him."

"I'm sure they weren't his men," I said. "I'm sure Koenig hired these two guys free-lance."

"There is plenty of free-lance talent around," she said. She wasn't only beautiful, she was sharp. I liked her. She knew what was going on.

"I have a plan."

She smiled and said, "I hoped you would."

"Why don't you make us some coffee and I'll tell you about it."

7

We presented ourselves at the offices of Walter Koenig, Esq. at 10:00 A.M. the next morning—after a stop over at the seven-seven precinct.

After I had outlined my plan to her the night before she had smiled and said, "That's mean. Oh, that's delicious."

The word "delicious" sounded entirely natural coming out of her mouth.

"You don't have an appointment, this time," the secretary said as we entered.

"That's all right," I said, "just tell him I'm here, and then we won't need you. We can get our own coffee."

"I don't get cof—just a minute," she said, annoyed. "I'll announce you."

"Why don't you go out and get a donut or something, honey?" I picked up her purse and handed it to her. "We'll announce ourselves."

She looked at us, then took her bag and walked out the door.

"I'll wait here until you call me," Carla said.

I nodded and walked into Walter Koenig's office.

"What are you doing here?" he demanded. "Where's my secretary?" If he was surprised to see me alive, he hid it well.

"She said something about going out to get a donut."

He stood up and said, "I have a court date, Mr. Delvecchio. What do you want?"

"I want the rest of my fee," I said. "The job is done."

"What?"

"I know who's been porking Mrs. Cabretta."

"You know—" He stopped and frowned. "Who?"

I smiled at him and said, "You."

He looked stunned.

"That's ridiculous. I've never laid a hand on Carla. What are you trying to pull?"

"What do you think Frankie will say when I give him my report, Walter?"

"You wouldn't—he would never believe you."

"I have a witness."

"A . . . witness? How could you have a witness? I've never touched her, I tell you. I swear!"

Only someone who was telling the truth could be that indignant, but it didn't matter that he was telling the truth.

"An unimpeachable witness."

"That's not possible," he said. "Who could the witness be?"

I smiled, walked to the door, and opened it. Carla Cabretta walked in and smiled at Koenig. I left the door ajar.

"I'm sorry, darling," she said, "but he beat it out of me."

He gaped at her, then at me, and then understanding dawned in his eyes.

"You're framing me."

"Why not?" I asked. "You were ready not only to frame me for killing Mrs. Cabretta, but to kill me as well."

"You were never to be killed," Koenig said, "just framed."

"Well, that makes all the difference in the world, Walter," I said. "Turnabout is fair play. How do you like the frame?"

"I don't," he said. "If you tell Frank . . . he'll have me killed."

He looked at Carla for support and she said, "I'll shed a lover's tears at your funeral, darling."

"You can't—" he said to her, and then he looked at me and said, "You can't—"

"Don't worry, Walter," I said, "I'm a reasonable man. We can work something out."

He stared at us for a few moments, and then sighed and said, "What do you want me to do?"

"I'd like you to meet a friend of mine," I said. I went to the door and opened it all the way. Detective Weinstock walked in. After we stopped at the precinct to make our statements I had convinced him to come with us to Koenig's office.

"The detective will be happy to take your statement," I said to Koenig.

I took Carla's arm and led her out of the office.

Down on the street I said to Carla, "I don't think you'll have any trouble getting that divorce now. In fact, with the extra time this murder conspiracy will add to your husband's sentence, you might even be able to get the Catholic Church to grant you an annulment."

Carla Cabretta said, "I'm very impressed, Nick . . . and grateful. Perhaps you'll let me express my gratitude, over dinner?"

"You gonna chase me home, like you did last night?"

Her delicious mouth smiled and she said, "Why don't you take a chance and find out?"

What's in a name?

According to John Lutz and Margaret Maron, it's everything.

before
you leap

JOHN LUTZ

John Lutz has two very successful PI series. One features "Carver" and is set in Florida. The "Nudger" series, of which "Before You Leap" is a chapter, is set in St. Louis. Mr. Lutz is a past president of PWA, and the winner of Shamus Awards for Best Novel and Best Short Story. He is currently serving as president of the Mystery Writers of America. For a soft-spoken, low-profile kind of guy, he sure has spent a lot of time as president. I wonder if he gets to fly around in "MWA-1"? (He is the president who was flying around in "PWA-1" when Jerry Healy was vice-president. If you're confused, see the intro to the Healy story.)

"Before You Leap" is probably the perfect "Nudger" story. You'll see what I mean after you've read it.

Nudger was being attacked by snakes. The telephone jangled, halfway waking him. He groped for it, got the cord tangled around his wrist. Huh? *Help!*

He awoke all the way, trying to throttle the plastic receiver and keep it from sinking long fangs into him.

When he realized the snake was a phone and he'd been dreaming, he pressed the receiver to his ear, still not completely comfortable about doing that. He'd just finished investigating the theft of some endangered species from the zoo, some sort of cute little rodent, and a snake not so cute. The guy who'd stolen them had returned the snake, but couldn't say what had happened to the rodent.

"Nudge?" Hammersmith's voice. What was a police lieutenant doing calling him at—Nudger squinted at the luminous digital numbers of the clock—3:00 A.M.? Oh God, was it only 3:00 A.M.?

"Nudge?"

"You know what time it is?" Nudger mumbled thickly.

"Sure. Temperature, too. But that's not what I called about."

Hammersmith and his sadistic sense of humor. Still rising toward total wakefulness, Nudger realized he should maybe worry about the reason for this odd-hour call. "What *did* you call about?"

"You know a guy name of Ernest Gate?"

"Think not."

"Well, he knows you. He's asking for you."

A long pause. Hammersmith and his telephone games. "So put Ernest whatsisname on the line."

"Can't. He's perched on a ledge of the Merrimont Hotel, threatening to walk out into the night thirty stories high."

"Wait a minute. You got a jumper, and he's asking for me?"

"You and no one else, Nudge. Demands to talk to you, in fact, and human life being held to be of high value, he's in a position to make demands. So the department figured I'd be the guy to call you, see if you might wanna chat with this Gate character."

"Bates?"

"Gate."

"Well, I know nobody name of Gate. Bates, either."

"Maybe by some other name."

Nudger, his mind still clouded with night webs, couldn't deny it was possible. Three A.M. Whew!

"You coming downtown to try and talk this guy in off the ledge?" Hammersmith asked.

Nudger said, "That sounds like a scene from an old movie. There gonna be a priest there, and the demure Mrs. Gate, maybe?"

"Just you," Hammersmith said. "He wants you and you alone."

Nudger's nervous stomach kicked. He hated heights. But what was he supposed to do, let this Ernest Gate fly?

"Nudge?"

"The Merrimont you say?"

"Right. On Pine Street."

Nudger said he knew where it was, but Hammersmith had already hung up. Hammersmith had a thing about hanging up first.

Nudger struggled out of bed and got his legs working. He chewed two antacid tablets while he was getting dressed.

After parking the Granada behind a blue unmarked Chevy that screamed POLICE! Nudger walked through the sultry night toward the department barricades. Typical July weather in St. Louis; the temperature was still over eighty degrees and the humidity was almost high enough to float ships. It was possible that if this Ernest Gate did jump, he'd sink slow enough not to break when he hit.

The sweating and irritable uniform near the barricade must have been told Nudger was on his way. As soon as Nudger identified himself, he said, "See if you can make this guy go one way or the other, okay, Nudger?"

"That's not exactly the idea."

"It'd solve things short term for a lotta people," the uniform said.

Nudger thought that was an odd concept of civic duty, but he let the remark pass and the uniform let him pass.

The Merrimont was bathed in spotlights, and high above the sidewalk a figure was outlined pressed against the stonework at a point precisely between two windows. Windows on either side of the man were open, and people were leaning out looking at him, probably talking to keep his mind off death. Lit up like it was, Nudger couldn't help noticing how

beautiful it looked now that it had been bought and refur-
bished by one of the major chains. Downtown sure was coming back.

The uniform who accompanied him up on the elevator
was also appreciative. "They done a great job on this place,
huh?" He caressed the oak-paneled wall above the control
panel. "I tell you, some of the architecture in these old buildings—"

He shut up as the elevator doors opened onto the thirtieth floor and he saw Hammersmith waiting in the hall like an
impatient Buddha, puffing on one of his greenish and abomi-
nable cigars.

"Glad to shee you, Nudge," he said around the cigar.
"Maybe you can shave this guy an' we can all go home an'
get shome shleep."

"If you don't put out that cigar, I'm not gonna talk to
him," Nudger said. "Even if he jumps, you and everybody
near you might be dead before he is."

"Shorry," Hammersmith said. He buried the cigar's
glowing ember in the sand of a nearby pedestal ashtray. It
died hard, emitting a green mushroom cloud that looked like
a miniature nuclear mishap. "I forgot about your delicate
stomach."

"Fear bothers it, too," Nudger said.

Hammersmith said, "I know. That's why you quit the
department."

"And I guess that's why you called me to help cope with
this problem thirty stories high."

"No choice in the matter." Hammersmith actually
sounded apologetic. Graceful for such an obese man, he
seemed to glide over the red-and-blue carpet as he led
Nudger to a room near the end of the hall. The door was
open, and Nudger could see a uniform and several plainclothes types milling around inside. Everyone stopped talking and looked at Nudger and Hammersmith when they
stepped into the room. "You go in the bathroom, there's even
a complimentary shower ca—" a plainclothesman was saying
before he clamped his lips together. Even the guy leaning
halfway out the window turned and stared.

Hammersmith said, "Here he is at last."

"Great!" said the guy on the windowsill. He immediately
straightened up and moved back away from the window. Everyone looked relieved, as if Nudger had the strength of ten

men and could fly and would wrap this thing up in a few minutes.

Nudger said, "You got a net set up?"

"Sure," Hammersmith said, "but I don't know how much good it'll do thirty stories down even if he hits it like a dart nails a bull's-eye. We're trying to set up something to snag him on the twenty-fifth floor, but it's a slow process 'cause we don't want him to see what's going on and jump before the device gets strung below him. Also, it's a new contraption still in the testing stage. Anyway, see how this guy knows you and maybe you can convince him to come back in and end this thing without anybody getting hurt."

Nudger moved to the window and leaned outside, looked down, got dizzy. He clasped a hand on the window frame and swallowed a burned metal taste.

"'S matter, you don't like heights?" a voice asked from outside.

Nudger leaned out a little farther and peered over at Ernest Gate.

Gate was a small, moon-faced man about fifty. He had thinning hair combed straight back but mussed by the wind, a dark widow's peak, and old-fashioned-back-in-style round glasses. He was wearing baggy pants whose legs were whipping like sails in the high, warm breeze, a button-down white shirt with perspiration stains under the arms, a tightly knotted narrow red tie. He looked like an accountant gone mad, which for all Nudger knew he maybe was, because Nudger was sure he'd never seen Gate before.

"Do we know each other?" Nudger asked.

Gate laughed. Spat. They probably appreciated that down on twenty-five.

"I don't get the joke," Nudger said.

"You got your money, though, you bastard. And you caused what's about to happen here. So how's it feel?"

"Listen, there's been some mistake. For God's sake, come in and let's talk about it." Nudger couldn't bear to think about what this average and pleasant-featured little man would become down on the sidewalk if he stepped off the ledge. "Nothing's worth what you're considering doing."

"You figure I'll live to regret it?" Gate asked.

"Well," Nudger said, "not for long." His stomach seemed to zoom out beyond the Merrimont's stone facade and plunge through the floodlit night. "Just come back in, please, and we'll iron this thing out." *Iron. Flat. Oh Christ!*

"So you're begging me, huh?" Gate said, sneering. "You afraid of your conscience or something? I've gotta say I'm surprised. Pleased, though. This is better'n I hoped for. I knew you'd never agree to holding my hand when I stepped off."

"Why me?" Nudger asked. "Why did you ask to talk to me? I'd at least like to understand what this is all about."

"Why you, huh? It's because you're responsible for everything. You're the reason I'm standing here. The reason I'm gonna do what I'm gonna do, my friend." Gate's eyes were glowing feverishly behind the round lenses now; he seemed to be working up to something, all right.

"If you were to calm down and come in here," Nudger said, trying not to look down again, "I bet we could straighten out this misunderstanding in no time at all."

"Sure, I'll be right in," Gate said. "I'll take a shortcut, Nubber."

Nubber? "Hey, wait a minute!"

But Gate had casually stepped off into space.

He seemed to be suspended by wires there for just an instant, then he plunged into the haze of light.

Nudger groaned and leaned out, saw Gate change his mind and begin to flap his arms wildly, heard him scream as he passed twenty-five and the horrified faces of the uniforms setting up an awkward arrangement of metal arms and netting that didn't look as if it would stop a pillow.

Gate frantically beat his arms like wings all the way down. Nudger watched the rescue workers with the round net, far, far below, desperately maneuvering to meet him at street level.

They succeeded.

Gate rocketed through the net as if it were made of paper.

Ten minutes later, down on the sidewalk, Hammersmith said, "That's okay, Nudge, you tried. They go whacko, sometimes there's nothing anybody can do to stop them."

They were standing about twenty feet from where Gate's body lay covered with a dark blanket. Fluids were soaking through the blanket. After the first glance, Nudger couldn't look at it again.

"You wanna take another peek at what's left of his face?" Hammersmith asked. "Make sure beyond any doubt you don't know him?"

"I don't know him," Nudger said, gulping down bile. "And I don't think he knew me."

"Really? Why not?"

"He called me Nubber."

"Oh? You sure about that? It mighta been the wind distorting his words."

"I'm sure. Nubber."

"People mispronounce names under stress sometimes. Or hear them wrong."

"Nubber, Nubber, Nubber!"

"Okay, okay." Hammersmith raised a bloated hand in a halt signal. "The wallet we got from the body says he checked in under his real name, Ernest Gate. Address is out in Chesterfield. The doorman says he thinks he arrived in a cab, and there's no driver's license, only forty-two dollars in cash, a Visa card, and one of those ID forms that come with wallets. Looks like a fairly new wallet, though it's hard to say for sure 'cause it got a little messy."

Nudger's stomach took off again. He swallowed, willing his abdomen to stop twitching against his belt buckle. "Let me know what else you find out, all right?"

Hammersmith fondled an unlit cigar and looked puzzled. "Else? Find out?"

"When you investigate."

"Nothing to investigate," Hammersmith said. "The guy's dead 'cause you couldn't talk him in off the ledge. We notify the next of kin and it's case closed."

"But he obviously had me mixed up with somebody else."

"That was his problem, not ours. Hey, there's an all-out war on drugs! We only got time and manpower for so much other'n that, you know?"

Nudger knew.

Hammersmith laid sausagelike fingers gently on his shoulder. "Why don't you go back to your apartment and see if you can get some sleep. It's not even"—he rotated his thick wrist and glanced at his watch—"four o'clock."

Nudger nodded, then turned and walked away.

He drove home chomping antacid tablets and knowing his sleep was finished for the night. For the next several hours he'd slump on the sofa in front of the TV and watch gold chains being sold on the home shopping network. He was afraid even to doze off, not knowing what terrors his dreams might hold.

The next morning, Nudger sat in his office above Danny's Donuts, nibbling on a greasy and weighty Dunker Delite and sipping a foam cup of Danny's acidic coffee. A breakfast like that could hurt you, but it tended to keep you awake. "Nooooo," his stomach seemed to growl, so he shoved the Dunker Delite, lying like a lumpy corpse on its white paper napkin, off the side of the desk and listened to it *thunk!* into the metal wastebasket. A nutritionist would cheer.

After brushing sugar from his hands, he got the phone directory out of the desk's bottom drawer and turned to the back section where businesses were listed.

There it was, "A. Nubber, Private Investigations," right above Nudger's listing. A. Nubber had to be who Gate had mistaken Nudger for. Had to be.

Nudger copied Nubber's address, poured the rest of the coffee down the drain in the office's tiny washroom, then descended the creaking stairs to the street door. He pushed outside into the morning glare and heat, knocked on the donut shop's grease-coated window, and signaled to owner and manager Danny Evers that he was leaving for a while. Danny waved and nodded, then mopped his face with the gray towel he kept tucked in his belt. It was hot in the donut shop, with all that determined baking going on; each Dunker Delite was forged with great effort and sacrifice. It was a shame about the way they tasted.

A. Nubber's office was classier than Nudger's. It was in the Central West End, on the ground floor of a large Victorian house that had been converted to an office building. Nubber had his own private entrance, a colonial-blue door that bore his name on an antique brass plaque.

As Nudger reached for the doorknob the door swung open and a beautiful blond woman emerged. She was wearing a lightweight blue business suit, but had the jacket slung over her shoulder. Her silky sleeveless blouse revealed shapely tanned arms. She nodded to Nudger and smiled. His stomach and his knees felt it in a big way. Probably she was an A. Nubber client. People like this never came to see Nudger in his office above the donut shop. Where was justice?

Nubber had a classy waiting room. A classy receptionist, who took Nudger's name, spoke into an intercom, then ushered him into a large, high-ceilinged office with a mammoth antique desk beneath a slowly revolving paddle fan. This would impress clients, Nudger thought, and Nubber wouldn't smell like a Dunker Delite and scare them away by seeming low-class and high in cholesterol.

Nubber himself was seated behind the desk, wearing a black-and-white-checkered sport jacket and a yellow tie. He was a smiling, bland-faced man, but with glittering dark eyes that gave him the look of the tiger. He seemed the sort who should be hawking used cars or life insurance rather than working as a private detective. The tennis court–size desk made Nubber look smaller. When he stood up, Nudger saw that he was about his size—just under six feet tall—though a bit on the pudgy side. Well, Nudger was getting a little paunchy himself.

Nubber shook hands with Nudger and said, "What can I do for you, Mr. Nudger?"

"Fill me in on a few things," Nudger said. "I'm not a prospective client; you and I are in the same business, have similar names. I'm A. Nudger. You're"—he looked at the name plaque on the desk—"Abner Nubber."

"What's your 'A' stand for?" Nubber asked.

"Doesn't matter," Nudger said. "Thing is, you're listed above me in the phone directory, and it appears somebody got us mixed up."

"Mixed up?" The cheerful but feral dark eyes became wary but no less predatory. "Maybe you're mixed up, I'm sure I'm not."

"Mistook me for you." Nudger explained to Nubber what had happened last night at the Merrimont Hotel. While he talked Nubber sat swiveling this way and that in his padded desk chair, listening carefully and tapping a cheekbone with a gold pen.

"I read in the morning paper about that poor guy," he said, when Nudger was finished. "Gates, or Bates was his name. Went right through the net, hit the pavement—*splat!*" Nubber slapped the desk with his palm. Nudger winced. The stained, bunched blanket on the sidewalk in front of the Merrimont flashed on the screen of his mind. His stomach grumbled.

"Ernest Gate was his name," he said.

"Ah, yeah."

"So what's the connection?" Nudger asked.

"Connection? Why, there is none. I never heard of this guy Ernest Bate."

"Gate."

"Whatever."

Nudger was surprised. This had all seemed so logical. "You positive about that?"

"Sure am," Nubber said. He began to tap on the desk with the pen, holding it as if it were a drumstick and beating out a soft but insistent rhythm. "Never crossed paths with the unfortunate gentleman." His mouth was always smiling even if his eyes were fierce.

"Might you have known him under another name?"

"Nope. His photograph was in the paper. Guy looked like everybody's accountant, but I never met him."

There seemed nothing more to say. Nudger thanked Nubber, who stood up again behind the huge desk, becoming Nudger-size once more, and smilingly walked Nudger to the door.

"Sorry I couldn't help you, pal," Nubber said. "But we both know how it is. Coincidence is what keeps us working and what makes our jobs so hard."

Nudger hadn't thought of that and wasn't sure if it was true, but he nodded agreement, thanked Nubber again, and went out into the anteroom. A young and attractive couple was seated on the Early American sofa, waiting to see Nubber. The man looked away from Nudger. The woman was engrossed in a glossy fashion magazine. Nubber's redheaded receptionist smiled dazzlingly at Nudger and said, "Something sure smells good."

"Like a donut?"

Her smile widened. "That's it exactly. Wonder what it is."

Nudger told her he had no idea, then went out into the shade of the Victorian front porch. He left it grudgingly and walked across the street to where the Granada sat with its broken air conditioner. Sweat was already zigzagging down his ribs. This was going to be another day on the griddle.

He drove back to his office, checked with Danny, and

was told no one had been by. There were no messages on his answering machine. Business as usual. He got the rickety window air conditioner gurgling and humming away, and sat behind his desk, sipping a glass of water and feeling the cool push of air from the plastic grille caress his bare arm.

When the glass was empty and he was reasonably cool, he called Hammersmith at the third-district station.

"Ah," Hammersmith said, "I was gonna call you, Nudge." Nudger doubted it but said nothing.

"You remember that jumper last night, Ernest Gate?"

"I remember him," Nudger said.

"Well, that address out in Chesterfield is three years old. His last address was the state penitentiary in Jefferson City, where he did a stretch for embezzlement. He was released two days ago."

"What about the Visa card you found on him? The issuing bank got an address on Gate?"

"No, he was sent that card in prison, just before his release."

"You said his wallet was new and the address was written on its identification form. Why would he write an address three years old?"

"Only address he could think of, I guess. The guy didn't live in the Jeff City pen anymore. Or at the Merrimont Hotel. He was only there about an hour before somebody spotted him on the ledge."

"What about his family? Where do they live?"

"No known next of kin," Hammersmith said. "Gate was alone in the world."

And left it mad as hell at me, Nudger thought. He couldn't get that off his mind.

"He had a wife before he went into prison," Hammersmith said. "She divorced him just before he began his stretch, never visited him until about six months ago, and she apparently said something that got him in a crazy rage. The guards had to restrain him. Other than that, no visitors except for his lawyer in three years."

"Who was his lawyer?"

Hammersmith was quiet while he apparently studied the file on Ernest Gate. "Guy named Buddy Witherton. I know him; he's still practicing criminal law. Hasn't gotten it right yet."

Nudger said, "How can you not go to prison with a lawyer named Buddy?"

"Well," Hammersmith said, "Gate did go. Just like most of Witherton's clients. And I better go, myself—back to work."

"I'm gonna call this Witherton—"

But there was a click on the line and Hammersmith was gone, returned to the front in the War on Drugs.

After depressing the cradle button for a dial tone, Nudger phoned Buddy Witherton. He wasn't in his office, but his secretary took Nudger's number. Everybody had a secretary but Nudger.

Half an hour later, Witherton returned Nudger's call from his car phone. Sure, he remembered Ernest Gate. He was sorry to read about Gate's death last night. He'd done what he could in court, but frankly Gate had been guilty as Charles Manson. He'd embezzled twenty-thousand dollars from the catering firm he worked for and used it to finance an illicit romance, but his wife found out about the other woman and everything else, and revealed the embezzlement out of spite during the divorce proceedings. Witherton had represented Gate in the divorce, too. Gate had apparently been the kind of guy who stayed with a winner. Did Witherton remember the wife's name? "Let's see," he said, "Edna or Irma, it was. She lived out in Chesterfield."

Nudger phoned Hammersmith and got the Chesterfield address that was in Ernest Gate's wallet.

The name on the mailbox was Edna Vickers. Nudger figured Gate's wife had gone back to using her maiden name; stigma of prison and all that, and not wanting to be reminded of Ernest while he was rotting away in his cell. Her conscience must be eating her alive. Hell hath no fury, but after the fury died, maybe hell was all that remained for some scorned women.

The woman who came to the door was in her midforties, at least five feet ten inches tall even without her high heels, and wearing a red halter and blue shorts that displayed a fine figure, most of it legs. She was attractive in a gaunt sort of way, with a smooth complexion and large dark eyes. The eyes took a moment to focus on Nudger, and he realized something wasn't quite right about them.

He identified himself and said he'd like to talk to her about her former husband.

"*Late* former husband," she corrected, slurring the words and filling the air with eau de gin fumes. It was early to be so smashed, but then ex-hubby had died only the night before —this morning, really—and possibly had been extinguished before what was left of the flame of love. "He was a son of a bitch," she said, and Nudger forgot that flame-of-love idea.

"Kind of warm out here on the porch," he said, and she seemed to get flustered about forgetting her manners. She stepped back and invited him in.

The inside of the house was cool, dim, and furnished modern, with lots of angled smoked glass and stainless steel. The leather sling-sofa looked like a torture rack, and the matching chairs looked like futuristic birthing stools. Nudger couldn't imagine being comfortable there.

"Wanna siddown?" Edna Vickers slurred at him.

Well, maybe he should, if he wanted to gain her boozy confidence. He lowered himself into one of the chairs. The leather squeaked like a new pair of boots. Edna Vickers perched her trim little rear on the sofa and crossed her long, long legs. The house was so cool there were goose bumps on her thighs, even where her shorts had worked up to reveal the curve of her buttock. She didn't seem to notice. Nudger did.

"Is Vickers your maiden leg—er, name?" he asked.

"Yep. I ain't gonna call myself Gate, that's for sure. I really hate—or I guess hated—that son of a bitch. *Late* son of a bitch." She seemed openly pleased by Ernest's new prefix.

"He asked to talk to me before he jumped," Nudger said. "Do you have any idea why?"

"Nope. Ain't talked to the bastard in almost three years. Since right after I caught him going out on me, and he got caught embezzling money to support his other woman."

"I guess that's what caused the divorce, the other woman."

"You betcha. No man plays me for that kinda fool. I nailed him good. Hired a detective and caught him in the act. In flagrante delicto, it's called. I learned that from the legal proceedings, which didn't take long, because I had his hide nailed to the wall in court, what with photographs and everything. You shoulda seen what him and that woman were doing. He never showed that kinda imagination with me."

"Did Ernest write to you from prison?"

"Nope. I told you, we had no contact and I didn't want any. If he eventually realized the mistake he made dumping me, that's tough cheese, the way I figure."

"But prison records indicate you saw him about six months ago, and after your visit he was in an agitated state."

Her gin-blurred eyes suddenly became cunning. "Well, some mistake musta been made, there at the prison. Maybe it was that other woman who visited him. It's been years since I seen Ernest, and the fact he's passed on is no sorrow to me." She stood up, looking very tall and a bit wobbly on her high heels. Nudger wondered if she always wandered around the house in shorts and high heels, or if she'd peeked out the door and seen him and thought she might impress him. He could have that effect on some women.

Taking her rise from the sofa as his signal that the conversation was over, he stood up also. Gave her the old sweet smile, though he had to look up at her to do it.

"Whoa, I almost fell down," she mumbled. "Trying to break in these new shoes. Anyways, I said all that needs saying about the *late* Ernest R. Gate. I don't even wanna think about that scuzzball ever again, and I don't hafta."

"No, you don't," Nudger agreed. From where he stood he could see into the kitchen. An empty gin bottle and a glass sat on a counter near the sink, next to a Mr. Coffee. "Maybe you oughta make yourself some strong coffee, Mrs. Vickers," he suggested.

She looked perplexed. "Why? I ain't gonna drive."

She had him there. He thanked her for taking time to talk with him, then moved toward the door.

"And it's *Miss* Vickers," she said. "Far as I'm concerned, I never been married to any of the species of man, and I never even met the *late* and *un*lamented Ernest R. Gate. That's how I got my memory arranged, and that's how it's gonna stay."

"One thing," Nudger said, his hand on the doorknob. "You mentioned you hired a detective to get evidence against Ernest. Remember his name?"

"I just said it: Ernest R. Gate. The 'R' stands—stood—for Robert."

"I meant the detective's name."

"I'm not sure."

"Was it Abner Nubber?"

"Mighta been." She slumped back down on the creaky leather sofa, looking pale and ill. Her mouth went slack and she swallowed laboriously, her Adam's apple working beneath the smooth flesh of her long neck. "Yeah, Abner Nubber."

"Better think again about that coffee," Nudger told her, then went out into the July suburban heat.

Something was bothering Miss Edna Vickers. Maybe she still loved Ernest Gate more than she cared to admit to herself. Or maybe something else was causing her to drink and not drive.

Maybe it had something to do with Abner Nubber lying about not knowing her former husband.

Late former husband.

Since Nubber had lied, Nudger figured the next logical step in the investigation would be to watch and follow him. He parked the sweltering Granada in the shade half a block down from Nubber's office. He wasn't too worried about Nubber spotting him; detectives were geared to tail people, but not necessarily to spot a tail.

Nubber stayed in his office most of the day, leaving only for lunch at a restaurant a few blocks away. Only a few people came and went in the big Victorian house. Nudger couldn't be sure if they were there to see Nubber or visit the other tenants. The three women who'd come and gone were remarkably attractive, or maybe Nudger just thought so because he hadn't seen his lady love, Claudia Bettencourt, for almost a week. She'd been following her psychiatrist's advice for her self-actualization and seeing Biff Archway, the volleyball coach and sex-education teacher at the girls' high school where she taught English. Nudger didn't like to think about the two of them together, so maybe it was natural he'd see something special and immediate about these other women.

At five o'clock the classy redheaded receptionist left. Ten minutes later Abner Nubber, who must have had a parking space in back, roared around the corner in a red Corvette convertible. Nudger only got a glimpse of him, but he seemed to be smiling.

The Corvette had no luck with traffic signals, which allowed Nudger to keep the Granada close and watch Nubber pull into the underground parking garage of a modern condominium on Skinker Boulevard.

A little after six o'clock, the Corvette snarled back out of the shadowed mouth of the garage. Nudger gulped down the rest of the Big Mac he'd taken time to buy at a McDonald's drive-through, shoved the Granada into drive, and followed.

Nubber had changed into an expensive-looking cream-colored jacket, white shirt, and mauve tie. At an apartment building on Lindell he parked and went inside, and came out a few minutes later with an elegant dark-haired woman on his arm. Something about her reminded Nudger of Claudia.

Nubber and the woman drove downtown and entered Tony's on Broadway, probably the city's best restaurant. Nudger had never eaten there.

He finished his french fries and chocolate milkshake and waited, watching Tony's entrance.

Nubber and the woman came out at nine o'clock and drove back to her condo. Nudger caught a glimpse of her at one of the windows and got a fix on which unit was hers. The lights stayed low in the condo; maybe she and Nubber were watching television. The Cardinals' game with the Mets was televised tonight; Nudger ordinarily would be home watching it.

He listened to the game on his static-filled car radio, rooting for the Cards to hold on to their one-run lead.

They didn't. They lost three to two after committing an error in the ninth inning. Nudger often lost that way.

He kept an eye on the woman's windows until ten o'clock, when all of the lights went out.

Hating Abner Nubber, really hating him, he drove back to his apartment and tried to get some sleep.

The next morning Nudger missed Nubber at the woman's apartment but located his car parked behind the Victorian office building. At ten o'clock he followed Nubber to a house in St. Louis Hills, where a heavyset woman with dark bangs answered the door and invited him in.

Fifteen minutes later Nubber left the house and drove to the Branton Hotel downtown, where he met a blond woman in the cocktail lounge. This Nubber was something with women.

As he stood in the lobby pretending to talk on a pay

phone, watching Abner Nubber and the woman at a table near the bar, Nudger realized the woman was the striking blonde he'd seen leaving Nubber's office yesterday as he was entering.

He moved away from the phones and sat out of sight in the plush lobby, where he could watch the lounge entrance.

After about half an hour the blond woman left the lounge and walked to the elevators. She was the only one who got in the elevator when it arrived.

Nudger watched the floor indicator and saw that the elevator stopped on nine, then started back down.

Oh-oh, he'd almost missed Nubber coming out of the lounge. Nudger followed him outside and back to where the red Corvette was parked at the curb a block away.

Nubber lowered himself into the car, but he didn't drive away, merely sat chain-smoking cigarettes. Nudger found some shade and leaned against a building with his hands in his pockets, playing Mr. Casual, sweating profusely and keeping an eye on Nubber. After the third cigarette, Nubber started the Corvette's engine and Nudger thought he might have to sprint for where he'd parked the Granada. But Nubber only wanted the car running so he could switch on the air conditioner. Nudger stood back and watched, not liking this, thinking even his fingernails were sweating.

Two cigarettes later Abner Nubber climbed out of the Corvette, stretched languidly, then stooped to get something out of the car. Carrying a large leather overnight case and what looked like a folded black umbrella, he walked back to the Branton. Nudger followed, and wasn't surprised to see Nubber file into an elevator with half a dozen hotel guests. Nudger got in the next elevator that arrived at lobby level and pressed the "9" button.

When the elevator doors opened on nine, a family of a man, wife, and four boisterous preschool kids was waiting to pile in. They almost knocked Nudger over as he wedged out into the hall and looked both ways. Nubber was nowhere in sight. Other than a maid listlessly pushing a linen cart far down the hall, the ninth floor appeared deserted.

Some detective, Nudger thought, and rode the elevator back down to the lobby.

He sat in one of the lobby's soft armchairs, pretending to read a newspaper, like a character in late-night film noir, for almost two hours. Then he saw the blond woman leave, not with Nubber but with a husky, crew-cut man wearing a wrinkled blue business suit without a tie. Hmmm.

This was getting involved. Nudger didn't know who to follow.

He decided to wait for Nubber, who hadn't checked in and would surely be back downstairs soon.

Right. Nubber stepped out of an elevator fifteen minutes later, left the hotel, and drove back to his office.

More waiting, this time in the hot Granada, using a cleverly altered plastic water bottle to relieve himself while he watched Nubber's office. Nudger wiped his forehead with the back of his wrist, looked at Nubber's parked Corvette, looked at the plastic bottle, wondered if he might be in the wrong line of work. He could get a job selling appliances, probably make more money, meet his alimony payments easier. His former wife, Eileen, would like that. Maybe that was why he remained in his strange and sometimes ugly occupation.

Okay, here was Nubber roaring away in the Corvette at 4:30, probably heading for the apartment of the woman he'd stayed with last night. Nudger wondered what Claudia was doing tonight, and where was Biff Archway, as he gunned the old Granada and barely managed to keep the sleek red trunk of Nubber's car in sight.

That was when things began to shape up. Nubber drove back to St. Louis Hills and turned on the block where he'd visited the heavyset woman with the dark bangs. Only this time he didn't stop the car. The red Corvette slowed momentarily near the house, then its rear end dropped low and it accelerated down the street and around the corner.

A man was in the woman's front yard, cutting the lawn with a power mower. He was short, muscular, had a close haircut, and Nudger was sure he was the man who'd left the Branton Hotel with the blond woman.

Nudger drove around the corner but didn't bother trying to keep up with Nubber. Instead he pulled the Granada to the curb and sat for a while letting his brain idle with the engine.

After about five minutes, he said, "I'll be damned," and drove away. He wanted to talk one more time with Edna Vickers, be she drunk or sober.

•   •   •

She was home. At first she stood motionless in the door-way squinting at Nudger, as if he were some gift of the cat and she couldn't quite place what she was looking at. Then she recognized him. "You again." She sounded disappointed. Not as if she'd been expecting someone else, though, just disappointed. She seemed sober enough this time and was wearing form-hugging red slacks and a white blouse pulled tight at the waist. Still had on her high heels, which made her seem to loom over Nudger. "Didn't know you at first," she said.

Nudger shrugged. "I've got one of those faces."

"Wouldn't have remembered you at all except for that funny cologne."

"Cologne?"

"Smells like dough and sugar baking."

"Oh. Mind if I come in? I need to ask you a few more questions. Won't take long."

"About Ernest?"

He nodded.

"Then the answer's no." She started to close the door.

"It'll be me or the police," Nudger said.

"I got nothing to fear from the police."

"Maybe not, but it's a maybe. Nothing to lose by talking to me."

"You offering me some kinda deal?"

"Why? Do you need a deal?"

"Nope. I haven't done a thing illegal. I know because I checked with my attorney."

Nudger said, "Your attorney didn't steer you wrong. So why not talk to me? I'm definitely more pleasant than the cops."

She gnawed her lip, glaring down at him. She'd probably been stunningly attractive five years and a lot of bottles ago. "Oh, all right, but let's get it over with in a hurry. I got someplace to go."

He followed her inside and sat down on the creaking leather sofa. She remained standing, towering as a pro basketball player, ready to block his best shots.

"I've got it figured out," he said, driving toward the basket.

"What? Today's crossword puzzle?" She fancied herself cute when she was sober.

"The puzzle about how you got the evidence on your

husband that enabled you to divorce him on your terms. Ernest had an affair, Abner Nubber provided you with proof —probably videotapes—and also told you about your husband's embezzlement from his employer."

"Nothing illegal there on my part. And it was photographs, not videotape."

"Except that you paid Nubber to *arrange* the affair so you could get the evidence. That's what Nubber does, has charismatic employees who seduce the spouses of his clients and set up the right odds in divorce cases. Very ingenious."

"And provides him a good living, I'm sure, considering the rates he charges. But I guess business is business."

"Some kinda business he's in."

"It fills a need."

"For a lotta people," Nudger had to agree.

She paced, then wheeled and stared down with open distaste at him. "The thing is, nobody forced Ernest to go to bed with that woman!"

"But he got a lot of expert coaxing. You probably even provided Nubber with information to make it easier for his female employee to seduce poor Ernest. What about the woman? Who was she?"

"Some blond pro. What's the difference who she was? It was part of the deal that she disappear after the photos were taken. Nobody, not even Ernest's lawyers, were ever able to find her, but the photographs were proof enough Ernest had been unfaithful. Even kinky unfaithful. The fact he didn't so much as know the woman's real name or address just made it look all the worse for him. I could never catch the little weasel cheating on me any other way, so I did it this way. Fair's fair, I say."

Nudger said, "I'd call it entrapment."

"Call it what you will. I didn't intend to send the poor schmuck to prison, but there was no way to clue the law in on the affair with the blond without revealing the embezzlement to the police—so tough cheese."

Nudger stood up. "You're a hard woman."

She smiled. "Better believe it. And a smart one. I wouldn't be telling you any of this if the law could touch me."

"Your lawyer must have mentioned that the law can touch Abner Nubber."

"Tough cheese there, too. Nubber can just figure that as

part of the cost of doing business. He supplies male and female heartbreakers to seduce unfaithful spouses, then he provides proof and favorable conditions for divorce, he has to know he's running a risk. That's why he gets paid so much and has a swank office and drives around in a nifty car. You're a private investigator, you got an office and car like that?"

Nudger had to get out of there. He'd had enough of Edna Vickers. Ernest Gate might be better off.

He told her he didn't have an office or car like Abner Nubber's. Pointed out that he didn't have a future like Nubber's, either. Then he told her good-bye and went to the door. She didn't move except to prop her fists on her hips and stand there like a female colossus.

"You gonna tell the cops about this?" she asked.

"Sure."

"Make it a point to also tell them Ernest was a son of a bitch."

"*Late* son of a bitch," Nudger said, and went out the door. He could sense her edging toward the phone behind him.

Abner Nubber's redheaded receptionist said Nubber had left the city on urgent business. But when Hammersmith and a couple of uniforms arrived, she soon buckled and revealed the name of the hotel he'd fled to where he could hole up after Edna Vickers had called him. It was the Emporium, a sleazy near flophouse down by the river. Nubber was seeking his level.

Hammersmith was a homicide cop and was there only because of his previous involvement and his friendship with Nudger, so they waited for a lieutenant named Giardello from the bunko squad to arrive at the hotel before going inside.

A one-eyed desk clerk stared wildly at Hammersmith's badge and said there was no one named Nubber registered but that someone who looked like the man Nudger described had checked in a little over an hour ago and was in Room 815. Uniforms were posted in the lobby and at the base of the fire stairs, and Lieutenant Giardello led the way into the clanking and thrumming elevator that carried them to the eighth floor.

The knock on the door of 815 wasn't answered, but the

faintest of sounds came from inside the room. A slight scraping of wood on wood.

Hammersmith knew what it was an instant before anyone else, and he raised a tree-trunk leg and smashed his foot into the door with all his weight behind it.

The doorjamb splintered and the door crashed and caromed off the wall so hard it nearly closed again. But Hammersmith and Giardello almost made the doorway wider rushing inside. Nudger and the uniform they'd brought with them followed.

Almost in time.

Nubber's pants leg and shoe disappeared outside as he scampered out the window he'd just forced wide open.

At first Nudger thought he was trying to get down the fire escape, but there was no outside fire escape.

Nudger was ahead of everyone else getting to the window, and when he looked outside, there was Nubber poised on the ledge exactly the way Ernest Gate had been three days ago. The same desperate backward lean against the safe solidity of the wall, and the same something dreadful and magnetic that seemed to contaminate reason and pull toward space and death.

Nubber was staring at Nudger as if now they belonged to two different worlds, and maybe they really were close to that status. The breeze was playing over Nubber, plucking at his clothes as if trying to coax him off the ledge; come out and play, flying's so much fun.

"It's over," Nudger said. "Don't make things worse for yourself. Get in here. Please!" he added. God, he didn't want to see it again, Ernest Gate making like a featherless bird too soon out of the nest. Ernest Gate plummeting like a stone to challenge the pavement with soft flesh and brittle bone. Nudger looked down. The foreshortened people that had gathered and were staring up, the downscaled cars, the tops of streetlights, all of it started to spin and he leaned forward, forward . . .

A hand clutched his belt and yanked him safely back into the room.

Hammersmith.

"Lemme talk to the asshole, Nudge."

He leaned his great bulk out the window and stared angrily over at Nubber. "You ain't gonna jump, 'cause you're too smart. Think this situation through. You get a good lawyer, you might walk away acquitted of a fraud charge. You get a bad lawyer, you'll probably do at most two years of a five-year stretch. Not nearly as long a time as what you're thinking about. So walk yourself back in here, Nubber, or else step off, but don't waste our time. You ain't worth it."

Hammersmith moved back away from the window and exchanged glances with Giardello.

They waited.

After about a minute a gray cuff and a black shoe appeared on the ledge, and Nubber clumsily backed himself into the room, falling onto the threadbare carpet and scrambling to his feet. The uniform had him immediately and cuffed his hands behind his back. Giardello read him his rights.

"That the truth?" Nudger asked Hammersmith. "About him only doing a few years at most?"

Hammersmith looked grim. " 'Fraid so, Nudge. He's a businessman who went too far, that's all. These days, even the federal government does the kinda thing Nubber'll plead guilty to."

Where was justice? Nudger wondered, watching Abner Nubber being led away. Thinking about Ernest Gate and the man mowing the lawn in St. Louis Hills. About the many other men and women who might not have dreamed of being unfaithful to their spouses, except for the amorality and entrepreneurship of Abner Nubber, and temptation too professional and potent to be resisted. Where was justice? And where would it be when Nubber was set free?

As they wrestled Nubber out the door he glanced back at Nudger.

He was smiling, his eyes fierce as a tiger's.

hangnail

MARGARET MARON

Margaret Maron lives on her family farm in central North Carolina. An amateur naturalist who photographs spiders and butterflies, she was the 1989–90 president of Sisters in Crime. Her Lieutenant Sigrid Harald of the NYPD has been featured in eight books, including Corpus Christmas, *which was nominated for an Agatha, an Anthony, and the American Mystery Award as Best Novel of the Year. In each, the no-nonsense Sigrid Harald deals not only with crime but also with her own physical and emotional quirks, a theme explored bravely and with good humor. A new series featuring Judge Deborah Knott of Colleton County, N.C., was introduced in* Bootlegger's Daughter.

Annoying, nagging, bothersome: a "hangnail" of a clue insinuates itself into another baffling Colleton County case until the right person picks it apart.

The first call for police help came approximately four and a half minutes after Toni and Pete Bledsoe arrived for breakfast at their nearly finished house out at Tinker's Landing, one of Colleton County's newest residential developments.

The house was supposed to have been ready in time for them to move in as soon as they came back from their honeymoon in Hawaii; but what with rain delays, mix-ups in materials orders, and an unreliable sheetrock crew, it was now seven weeks past the wedding and looked to be at least another week more before the painters and electricians would be through and they could install the wedding presents, which were currently taking up one whole room at Toni's mother's house.

At least the cedar deck was finished, and they had been out the night before to take delivery on the white wrought-iron patio table with its glass top and four matching chairs that Pete's aunt from Georgia had sent them.

Everything was fine then, they told the deputy.

That morning, they'd driven over shortly after sunrise with a thermos of coffee and a takeout order of sausage and biscuits from Hardee's, intending to enjoy a romantic breakfast on their brand-new deck at their brand-new table before heading off to their jobs in the Research Triangle.

Now that I-40 had put Dobbs within easier commuting distance from Raleigh, the whole western part of Colleton County was growing. Tinker's Landing lay three miles west of the little county seat, but it had adopted big-town upscale zoning regulations. The smaller lots began at two acres and each custom-built house had to contain at least twenty-five hundred square feet, set back no less than seventy-five feet from the road.

Unlike the new trailer parks and budget developments creeping like kudzu vines across one-time tobacco fields, treeless and bare of all vegetation except wiregrass and cockleburs, Tinker's Landing lay along the river in a lush stand of second-growth hardwoods. The doctors, lawyers, or young professionals who bought lots here were, like the Bledsoes, affluent enough to bring in clever architects and landscapers who would incorporate the natural into their designs and cut no more trees than were absolutely necessary.

Poplars, oaks, and black gums flamed with September's

gold and scarlet, but few leaves had actually fallen. Red-berried hollies, ironwoods, and huckleberries formed bushy barriers; honeysuckle, Virginia creeper, and poison ivy added their thick curtains; and bracken filled in the few bare patches that sloped down to the river.

A twisty road ambled artfully from the four-lane highway down to the old ferry landing that gave the development its name. Trees overhung ditch banks thick with Queen Anne's lace, purple-stemmed pokeberries, bright yellow coreopsis, and pink-flowered beggar's-lice. There were no streetlights to compete with the stars at night, and utility lines had been buried so that nothing spoiled the daytime illusion.

If not for the anachronistic sound of power saws and electric hammers that were due to shatter the morning stillness as soon as various building crews began work in another hour, this could be the archetypal backcountry road. Any minute now Andy and Opie might come strolling around the next curve with their cane poles, heading for the old fishing hole.

At 6:30, though, Pete and Toni Bledsoe had found the morning every bit as quiet and beautiful as they'd expected. A light haze hung over the river like a gauzy bridal veil, birds twittered in the tulip poplars, and as the newlyweds walked around to the side steps with their picnic basket, a young rabbit reared up on its haunches and watched until they were almost near enough to touch before scampering off in the tall grass.

"I'll get the cushions," Toni said as Pete poured steaming coffee into new hand-thrown pottery mugs and unwrapped the savory sausage biscuits.

She'd left the mauve chair cushions on top of their new shiny black washing machine the night before, but when she unlocked the French doors and entered the hi-tech utility room off the kitchen, she was at first puzzled to see the cushions tumbled on the marble tiles. It took a minute to register that the reason they were lying on the floor was because the washer was no longer there.

Nor was its matching dryer.

Upon hearing her startled yelp, Pete rushed inside and immediately realized that not only were washer and dryer gone, so was their oversized upright freezer. A hasty check of the house revealed a forced lock on the basement door. Also missing were an electric stove and refrigerator that had been delivered two days earlier and hadn't even been uncrated yet.

"Mama's gonna have a hissy," moaned Toni. The missing kitchen equipment had been a wedding present from her mother. "We like to've *never* found a black freezer."

"Don't touch anything," Pete cautioned his bride.

He spoke to an empty room. Toni was already storming for the front door and the cellular phone in their BMW.

Less than ten minutes later, a deputy from the Colleton County Sheriff's Department pulled into their new drive.

Carefully, he listened to their account of how the theft had been discovered. He followed them into the house, took a close-up picture of the tool marks on the forced door, and dutifully looked at the empty utility room where expensive major appliances were no longer sitting. He shook his head over the empty doorway between the formal dining room and butler's pantry where the thieves had carefully removed a custom-made stained glass door from its hinges. Then the three of them sat down at the new wrought-iron table out on the deck and the deputy accepted the offer of a cup of coffee as he filled out his report, because by that time they'd discovered that Toni's older brother and Deputy Raeford McLamb had played on the same high school baseball team the year they made the state playoffs.

"I'll be honest with you," McLamb told them. "I can send for our crime scene unit if you want me to, and they'll smear fingerprint powder all around, but as many people as go in and out of a new house, I doubt we'll get anything helpful."

He described the difficulties of removing grimy graphite from fresh white enamel or gleaming marble tiles, and both Bledsoes told him not to bother.

The deputy had barely finished both his coffee and his report when the two-way radio clipped to his belt crackled with an order to check out a second house three lots away. More new appliances had disappeared.

"Looks like you folks aren't the only ones got hit," said McLamb as he left the Bledsoes after telling them to tell Toni's brother that he said hey. Before he reached the second house, his radio squawked again with reports of a third.

And then a carpenter on the Hardin job called in and all hell broke loose.

• • •

Lieutenant Dwight Bryant, Detective Chief of the Colleton County Sheriff's Department, read again from the form in his hand: *Jennifer Paula Hardin (Mrs. K.C.), née Brantley, Cauc. fem., 26, blk hair, brn eyes.*

That's how Deputy Raeford McLamb, first deputy on the scene nearly two hours ago, had listed her on the new check-off form recently approved by Sheriff Bowman Poole.

Chapel Hill would eventually submit a fuller report, thought Dwight as he surveyed the unfinished sun-filled room where she'd been murdered. The state's medical examiner would give them her height and weight, a description of her multiple injuries, an itemized analysis of her internal organs, and the results of a dozen laboratory tests; and all would do their bit to describe Jenny Paul Hardin's physical makeup at the time of her death. Yet nowhere on any of their report forms were there spaces to mention pixie features, the swing of her dark hair, the tilt of her head when she listened, or the infectious laugh, which, according to Curtis Weill, got more work out of the men than two hard-nosed foremen or double wages ever could.

"She was a real lady," Weill said sadly. The head carpenter on the Hardins' nearly completed house was a lankily muscular man in his mid-forties. The gnawed stub of a toothpick perpetually resided in the corner of his mouth. It was he who'd found the body and sent one of his men out to the highway to phone the sheriff's department. "Gutsy, too," he added.

Dwight Bryant didn't need his years of homicide experience to read the trail of blood across the new living room's wide-planked floor. Jenny Paul Hardin had been setting nails in the baseboard when she was attacked last night. J. V. Pruitt, the local undertaker who acted as Colleton County's coroner, hated to be pinned down to specifics, but before he took away her slender body, he'd made an educated guess that death occurred sometime between seven and midnight.

Blood had splattered against the unpainted sheetrocked walls and pooled on the floor. The young woman's steel nail setter still shared that crimson puddle with an open tube of wood putty; but her hammer was on its way to the lab, its bright head caked with blood and hair after her killer had left her for dead.

Except that she hadn't died.

Not immediately anyhow.

Gutsy wasn't a strong enough word for her, Dwight thought. Her right hand smashed when she tried to ward off the blows, her head a pulpy mass, where on God's green earth had she found the strength of will to crawl more than twenty feet across the unfinished floor?

And what muddled logic had flickered through her dying brain and propelled her to the raised hearth now jumbled with new nails of all sizes? Surely so much determination signaled an intelligent reason. Several of the heavy brown paper sacks that stored the nails bore bright red stains, and three of the bloodiest were upended altogether.

"She spent a lot of time keeping them nails sorted," said Weill, whose eyes had also followed the ghastly trail to the hearth. "Made it one of her special jobs."

"You knew Mrs. Hardin pretty good?" asked Dwight.

Since returning to Colleton County after resigning from D.C.'s Capitol City Police Department two years ago, he'd occasionally seen her picture in the Dobbs *Ledger*. She had chaired United Appeals, presented awards at high school graduations, given blood when the hospital's bloodmobile visited her neighborhood, and appeared alongside other socially prominent women as they went through the socially aware motions Dobbs expected of its socially prominent families. (Dwight's ex-wife came from such a family in a small Virginia town and he regarded the species with sour wariness these days.)

In those grainy black-and-white photographs, however, there'd been something about Mrs. Kevin Charles Hardin that set her off from the other women. Jenny Paul Hardin had lacked the glossy surface sheen and easy complacency of the town's more fashionable Merediths and Dardens and Glenns. Her backbone was always a little too straight, her smile a shade anxious, as if she were uncomfortable in the Junior Women's Club role thrust upon her simply because her jack-of-all-trades father had left her a fortune larger than most in Dobbs.

"She took a couple of shop courses I once taught at the high school," said Weill, confirming Dwight's impression that she'd found blue jeans more comfortable than silk dresses. "Guess she was her daddy's daughter, all right. They say Paul Brantley could've built a tree if he'd a mind to, and Jenny

Paul was real good with her hands, too. She didn't just work hard, she worked smart. I used to tell her if she ever needed a job, I'd take her on as a journeyman. Wasn't fooling, neither. All that money, yet if you didn't know, you'd never think it. Not like that banty-cock husband of hers, *Doctor* K. C. Nit-picking Hardin. Good thing State College keeps him busy or he might've accidentally got himself beaned with a two-by-four."

"He get in y'all's hair a lot?" asked Jack Jamison. He was young, new to the force, and didn't talk much, but Dwight suspected he was going to shape into a shrewd detective.

Weill gave a noncommittal shrug and Dwight filed the animosity for later examination. "But you didn't mind Mrs. Hardin being underfoot?" he asked.

"She wasn't," Weill said flatly. "She'd show up with a cold six-pack for our lunch and then pitch right in wherever she could help—not just me, but Vic or Neal or Billy, too—asking a million questions and listening to the answers. She wanted to learn it all and she wasn't afraid to get her hands dirty either. Why would a bunch of sneak thieves hurt a lady like that?" he asked angrily. "You reckon they walked in on her, not knowing she was here, and she recognized one of 'em?"

Dwight sighed and wished the room could speak.

The body was gone now, but a chalk outline remained near the hearth where Jenny Paul Hardin had finally died. Fingerprint powder lay like gray dust on every surface his crime scene unit had tested after they'd collected the usual fiber samples and other bits and scraps. Theoretically the detritus they collected would link a killer to this particular scene; in reality, as many different workmen who'd swarmed over this place the last month, it was probably a useless exercise.

Dwight eyed the jumbled nails. "What'd you mean when you said she made them her special job?"

Weill spat out the toothpick he'd chewed down to a nub and pulled a fresh one from the bib pocket of his denim overalls. "See, during the day your nail apron fills up with different types. Most jobs, you just dump 'em all in a box. By the time a house is finished, you could have forty or fifty pounds of nails mixed up. It's wasteful, but you can't pay a man carpenter's wages to sort nails; so every evening, Jenny Paul'd put 'em back in the right sacks. She kept 'em lined up from threepenny finishing nails"—he gestured with his toothpick to the left of the long hearth where several sacks stood undisturbed—"up to twentypenny stud-setters."

On the right, more sacks remained standing. Between the untouched sacks were those that were bloodstained or had been overturned.

Dwight had grown up out in the country where every farmer kept a supply of big nails on hand, but he'd never given much thought to the different types. "And each nail has its own specific job?"

"Sure. See this?" Curtis Weill parked the toothpick in the corner of his mouth and held up two slender headless nails, identical in size and length except one was brighter. "Both are eightpenny finishing nails, but the shiny one's galvanized so it won't rust. It's for outside trim. The other's for inside, where you don't have to worry about rain."

Weill handed Dwight another nail of similar length and girth except that it had a duller finish and a large flat head. "That's an eightpenny, too; easier to hammer, but you have to use it in the underwork where it won't show. There's nails for wood, masonry, grooved ones for sheetrock, roofing tacks—"

His callused hands reached in and out of the bags as he explained the differences.

"And Mrs. Hardin knew all the names and uses?" asked Jamison.

"I said she listened, didn't I?" he growled.

From the pocket of his gray corduroy sports jacket, Dwight drew out an envelope that held a single nail and handed it to Weill. "What would a nail like this have meant to her?"

Three inches long and a quarter-inch wide at the head, the nail was flat and it tapered very slightly to a squared point, rather like an extremely skinny wedge of chess pie with the point nipped off.

Weill held it delicately in his rough fingers. "This what was clenched up in her hand so tight?"

Dwight nodded. The bloodiest sack still crumpled on the hearth had held others of this type.

"Well, it's a sixpenny cut nail," Curtis Weill said, choosing his words with obvious care. "It's made flat so it won't twist and split the wood when you nail it. This type gets put through a special heat treatment at the factory so's to harden the outer casing for extra strength. They'll go through concrete, but we used 'em for the flooring here. It's hundred-year-old heart pine we salvaged from an old house over in Raleigh, back of the governor's mansion. Hard as a rock."

The two detectives looked down at the mellow brick-toned floor, but could see no nails in the wide planks.

"Tongue-and-groove," Weill explained. "Each row's nailed on the tongue and the groove of the next board hides it."

Even though the floor still needed to be sanded and sealed with varnish, it was a beautiful piece of work, and Curtis Weill gave it a professional's accolade: "Best job Billy ever did. Old flooring's like doing a jigsaw puzzle the way you have to piece and fit, but he didn't face-nail one single plank."

"Billy Partin do the whole floor by himself?" Dwight asked.

Weill's eyes flicked over the deputy's face and looked away. "We all gave him a hand when he needed it—Vic, Neal, even Jenny Paul."

"But here in this house, on this job, this particular nail means flooring and flooring means Billy Partin, right?"

Curtis Weill nodded reluctantly.

Dwight slipped the nail back in the envelope and tucked it in his jacket pocket. "Did she always work here alone at night?"

"Sometimes. She said it was relaxing. Gave her a chance to think."

"About what?"

Weill shrugged. "Couldn't say. But her husband was away this week, down at the coast—Wilmington, I believe—at some sort of conference for college professors, so she'd been staying late. Sometimes till ten or eleven."

"Who knew that?"

"Hell, all of us did. Wasn't no secret."

"She wasn't worried about being out here alone?" asked Dwight.

He knew every construction site was subject to minor pilfering, but up until last night, nothing very major had gone missing from Tinker's Landing. They should have realized it was just a matter of time, he thought. Last night's haul had been the biggest and most methodical yet—in all, four houses had suffered an estimated combined loss of nearly thirty thousand dollars—but all across the county there had been sporadic instances in which expensive plumbing fittings and newly installed appliances suddenly sprouted legs and walked off.

Until last night, though, there'd been no incidents of physical violence.

"No, being alone never seemed to bother her," Weill told them. "And we rigged her up a light she could move around easy." He gestured toward the rough tripod of slender one-by-twos that supported a drop cord and a bare light bulb.

The room was flooded with bright September sunshine, but the bulb was still lit, just as Weill's crew had discovered it when they arrived at 7:15. There had been no sign of forced entry, but the front door was unlocked.

Dwight Bryant could understand the appeal of virgin landscape; unfortunately, all that natural foliage had allowed the thieves—Jenny Paul's killers?—to slip in and out of the houses unseen. With sight lines almost nonexistent, a dozen vehicles could have come and gone unnoticed. Nevertheless, two deputies had patiently begun to canvass the other building sites scattered through Tinker's Landing.

Now he sent Jamison to question the Hardins' housekeeper and to radio back when Dr. Hardin returned. It had been nearly ten o'clock before the murdered woman's husband had been located at a large educational conference down at Wilmington, so they couldn't expect him much before noon or 1:00 P.M.

While he waited for that call to come, Dwight turned his attention to Billy Partin, Vic Lincoln, and Neal Cutler, the other three carpenters. If there had been any friction between Jenny Paul Hardin and the men, it wasn't immediately apparent.

Billy Partin seemed bewildered that anyone could have hurt such a nice lady, and even after Dwight rephrased his questions in simpler language, the forty-year-old laborer appeared not to understand that every workman in the development was a potential suspect.

Vic Lincoln, an easygoing, husky blond with muscular forearms, admitted he'd once made a pass at her, but claimed that she'd handled it as a flattering joke and that they'd become friends.

Neal Cutler, dark and close-faced, chain-smoked through the whole interview and denied any knowledge of anything.

A disconsolate Curtis Weill reduced half a dozen toothpicks to splinters with his callused fingers as he listened to his crew answer questions about his young client's death. When Dwight was finished, Weill had the men gather up their tools. There'd be no more work on this house probably until after the funeral.

If then.

Dwight left a patrol officer posted at the house and drove back to his office in the basement of the new courthouse. As he passed between the stone pillars at the entrance of Tinker's Landing, he saw several cars and trucks backed up in front of the roadblock they'd established earlier to screen out the curious. There were work crews in dusty pickups coming back from early lunches; architects in shiny imported sports cars; a huge yellow backhoe; a delivery truck from Pennywise Discount Appliances in town; another delivery truck from Heigh's Building Supplies out on Highway 70; a green-and-beige furniture van from The Gallery, a high-priced decorator over in Raleigh; and a nursery truck with a large flatbed that held an expensive array of half-grown rhododendrons, azaleas, and other flowering shrubs that were going to give some new home owner an instant splash of color next spring.

"You can pack it in," Dwight told the two uniformed officers who were manning the checkpoint. Within minutes, the intersection was deserted as the vehicles rumbled through the gates unrestrained and disappeared around tree-lined curves. For a moment, Dwight stared after the green-and-beige van, trying to recall where he'd last seen the driver's face. And now that he thought about it, wasn't Tinker's Landing a little more upscale than Pennywise Discount Appliances' usual clientele?

Something else to file for future reference, he thought, and headed back to town.

Word had spread through Dobbs and already the Hardin house was beginning to fill as shocked friends and neighbors came with hushed voices and platters of food. Dr. K. C.

Hardin might not be Curtis Weill's favorite client, but he was a respected member of the town's intellectual community, and Jenny Paul's Brantley roots went back to the earliest settlers in the county, so there were many to mourn her death.

Dwight arrived at the house shortly before one P.M. and was met by young Deputy Jamison, who'd spent the last hour with Miss Lily Freeman, the Hardins' grief-stricken housekeeper. The two men walked out onto a deserted side porch to confer. Hardin had called from Clinton and was due to return in less than twenty minutes.

"You learn much?" asked Dwight.

Jack Jamison gave a noncommittal shrug.

He was a tubby youngster with a quiet, good-natured demeanor that put most people instantly at ease, which was why Dwight had started sending him first to a victim's bereaved family. As usual, Jamison's sympathetic murmurs at the right places had elicited from the housekeeper more background information on the murdered woman.

Her father, Paul Brantley, had possessed a wide-ranging curiosity about the way things worked in the building industry, and among his innovations to streamline production, he'd patented a cheaper method of making concrete blocks. Jenny Paul was his only child and he'd left her a fortune. She planned to build an industrial arts center in his memory to train high school dropouts, "but Dr. Hardin wanted her to endow a Chair of Education at his college with guess who as the first holder?"

The housekeeper wasn't just a hired woman, but also a distant cousin who had raised Jenny Paul in this very house after her mother died in childbirth, and she was clearly jealous of the man her charge had married.

"And what was so wrong with this house?" she'd asked Jamison tearfully. "If he hadn't of had to have a big fancy house to impress his friends from Raleigh, Jenny Paul would've been safe at home here last night."

Dwight glanced about them. The house was typical of this section of Dobbs. Built in the early twenties, in a neighborhood then peopled by skilled workmen and white-collar clerks, the comfortable unpretentious bungalow had large rooms and was wrapped in broad porches. Now that the tall Victorian houses a few blocks over were in short supply, tradition-minded Yuppies had begun to snap up these solidly built houses and to restore them with loving care. Even so, the contrast between this shabby old house and the luxurious new one out at Tinker's Landing was striking.

"Mrs. Hardin didn't want a new house?" asked Dwight.

"Not necessarily," Jamison said. "Miss Lily says she didn't, but she also let on that Mrs. Hardin kept talking about how nice it'd be for Miss Lily to have more privacy. I get the feeling it wasn't just Miss Lily's privacy she was interested in."

"Any hanky-panky on either side?"

"Not on Mrs. Hardin's part," said Jamison. "Leastways, not according to Miss Lily. And as much as she doesn't like him, I bet she'd be the first to tell it if Dr. Hardin was catting around. She says his idea of a big time's to have a bunch of guys from the college over for dinner to talk about how the country's educational system's going down the slop chute."

His tone was regretful. Both men knew that more murders were committed by friends and relatives than by total strangers, but except for Hardin and Miss Freeman, Jenny Paul had had no close family.

"I talked to the deputy who went over to Hardin's motel to break the news this morning," said Dwight. "She sounds pretty sharp. Says the night clerk's positive that Hardin's Volvo didn't leave the parking lot last night after nine o'clock and that a Professor B. L. Arnault had dinner with him from eight to ten."

Even with I-40 now open all the way, it still took more than two hours to drive to Wilmington.

"Say two hours here, two hours back, and a half hour to do it," mused Dwight. "Even if he left there at ten on the dot, it'd be midnight before he got here."

"And the coroner said she died between seven and midnight." Jamison reluctantly relinquished Hardin as a suspect. "What about the carpenters?"

"No simple solutions there, either," Dwight said. "Weill was at church and the other three were in a bowling-league playoff till after ten last night, and then they all say they went home alone, so where do we start?"

"With the nail?" Jamison suggested. "Miss Lily says she really loved word games. Scrabble. Balderdash. And you should see the puzzle magazines in her bedroom—codes, puns, anagrams, you name it."

"So it really does mean something?" The big-framed

detective leaned against a porch post and studied the slender flat nail with bemusement. "Twelve years a policeman and this is my first honest-to-goddamn dying clue. I thought they only happened in those old Ellery Queen stories."

A stir from the front of the house drew their attention, and when they walked around the corner, they saw Dr. Hardin step out of his Volvo to be enfolded by several women from the church he and Jenny Paul had attended.

From the way he was dressed, Kevin Hardin could have gone straight to the church for the funeral, thought Dwight. His three-piece suit was dark and conservatively cut, his tie was subdued, every hair was smooth. But his handsome face seemed to have aged; his eyes were red-rimmed and bloodshot, and his voice broke when he first tried to speak to his friends.

The two deputies waited till after the first crush of condolences and then kept their interview short.

"A sixpenny cut nail?" asked Hardin when they were alone.

They had diplomatically elicited the address and phone number of the colleague with whom Hardin had dined the night before, and now that formalities were out of the way, they invited him to speculate on what that nail could have meant to his wife.

" 'For want of a nail, a battle was lost'?" Hardin shook his head and seemed genuinely puzzled. "My wife wasn't a great intellectual, but she did have a quick flair for puns and wordplay. If this is one of them . . ." His voice trailed off as he turned the nail in his smooth hands. "All I can think of is that old marriage rhyme: 'Something old, something new; something borrowed, something blue; and a sixpence for her shoe.' "

The rhyme echoed in Dwight's head all the way back to the courthouse.

. . . and a sixpence for her shoe.

For her shoe?

For Hersh Shue!

Jack Jamison pulled into the next parking space and glanced over with curiosity.

"Hershell Shue," Dwight told him. "He's a driver for

Pennywise Discount Appliances. I thought it was odd to see their truck in a place like Tinker's Landing."

Jamison caught the implication instantly. "A delivery van sure makes a good cover for unscheduled pickups. Want me to ask him to stop by?"

It was easier said than done.

According to Pennywise's dispatcher, Hersh Shue had gone to pick up a special order at their warehouse in Sanford and wasn't expected back till after their shift was over.

"And his delivery to Tinker's Landing this morning was legit," Jamison reported.

"Guess that's what I get for jumping to conclusions," said Dwight. "Just the same, though, let's put out the word to all patrol units: they're to keep an eye on any furniture vans roaming around after normal business hours. Especially anywhere near half-finished construction sites."

Routine procedure filled the rest of the afternoon. Jamison called the bowling alley to see exactly when the three carpenters had left, and he checked with someone from Weill's church to learn when prayer meeting had ended.

Dwight called around town and discreetly shook the grapevine of mutual acquaintances. No ripe juicy grapes of scandal fell into his lap.

"They were already into separate bedrooms, but that's life, Dwight," said a young woman who'd known Jenny Paul fairly well. "People like them don't get divorced, they get hobbies. Hers were word puzzles and working with her hands."

"What was his?"

"Work?" she hazarded.

"Sounds dreary," he said.

"Tell me, sugar," she needled. "Is divorce any better?"

"Touché," he said, only he slipped back into their childhood banter and pronounced it "touchy."

Nevertheless, even after he'd hung up, he continued to toy with the possibility that B. L. Arnault, Hardin's main alibi and the colleague with whom he'd dined the night before, might be a sex-starved little blondie named Betty Lou. Neither the Wilmington deputy nor Hardin had referred to Arnault by pronoun.

He pulled the phone over and punched in the Raleigh

number Hardin had given them. A breathy female voice answered on the third ring. "Arnault residence."

Bingo! thought Dwight. "Professor Arnault?" he asked. "B. L. Arnault?"

"I'm sorry. He's not here at the moment. Take a message?"

Dwight explained that he was a sheriff's deputy from the next county. "Is this Mrs. Arnault?"

"Good Lord, no!" The voice was amused. "I live next door and feed his cats when he has to be out of town. That's where he is now. In Wilmington. I have the number if you need it."

Disappointed, Dwight wrote it down. He heard a cat's mew in the background. "How many cats does Professor Arnault have?"

"Four young toms," she answered, and laughter bubbled just beneath her words.

Over the telephone, Arnault sounded rather young himself when Dwight ran him to earth at the conference on higher education. He answered questions hesitantly, with an upward inflection at the end of each sentence, even though his choice of words was that of a pedant-in-training. Nevertheless, he did confirm that he and Dr. Hardin had discovered a mutual appetite for she-crab soup and had availed themselves of a restaurant that served it down on Wilmington's restored waterfront.

"We drove back to the motel in my car shortly after ten and I then retired for the night," he said, his words as precise as if he were reading from a tome of lecture notes.

Jamison got no further with the carpenters. All could be accounted for by independent witnesses until ten o'clock. After that, it was either a wife (Curtis Weill and Neal Cutler) or elderly mother (Billy Partin).

Vic Lincoln didn't even have that much.

A clerk stuck her head into the room. "You know those names you gave me, Lieutenant? I got a hit on two of 'em."

She laid the printouts on Dwight's desk and he scanned them quickly. Eight years earlier, Billy Partin had served a sixty-day sentence for breaking and entering and stealing a color television.

That would have been interesting enough in view of the

stolen appliances, but it was outweighed by the second report.

Fifteen months ago, Neal Cutler had been arrested for beating up his wife. According to the complaint she'd signed at the emergency room, he'd broken two ribs and her nose, but when the case came to trial, she refused to testify and so was charged with malicious prosecution and fined for costs.

Three months ago, he'd blackened both her eyes. Again she refused to press charges when court convened.

"A habitual wife-beater doesn't have much respect for *any* woman," Dwight said grimly.

"Neal Cutler," Jack Jamison mused. "Cut nail?"

Dwight found a clean legal pad and listed in block letters and alphabetical order the name of every man they'd yet encountered in the case: Neal Cutler, Dr. K. C. (Kevin Charles) Hardin, Vic (Victor) Lincoln, Billy (William) Partin, Hersh (Hershell) Shue of Pennywise Discount Appliances, and Curtis Weill.

He tried to think himself into the mind of a woman he'd never known. A down-to-earth young woman who'd delighted in puns. Would she have chosen something too arcane to decipher?

"She was dying, Jack. Yet she crawled across that floor on her hands and knees to get one particular nail. She thought it would be as obvious as writing us a name. Yet what've we got? Her shoe and cut nail."

Suddenly something caught his eye. "Hey, wait a minute! When you think of a penny, you think of Lincoln's head, right? And the first two letters of Vic make the Roman numeral six. *VI Lincoln—sixpenny!*"

"But why *this* sixpenny nail?" argued Jack Jamison. "There were at least four more types—with heads, without. Remember the bloodstains. She even had her hands on some of the others, so why this one if she didn't mean Billy Partin or Neal Cutler?"

They worried with Jenny Paul's riddle another twenty minutes and then called it a day.

Next morning, when Dwight arrived at his office in the basement of the courthouse, Curtis Weill was waiting for him. Dwight almost didn't recognize him. Weill was dressed in a suit and tie and without his coveralls. The grim tiredness on the man's face didn't fit either. Only the toothpick in the corner of his mouth was familiar.

"I don't care how it looks," Weill said, "he didn't kill Jenny Paul."

"Huh?"

"Vic Lincoln," Weill said impatiently.

Dwight was puzzled. "You want to back up and tell me what you're talking about?"

Jack Jamison entered the office. He stood silently but Dwight sensed a suppressed excitement.

"What?" he asked.

"McLamb arrested Vic Lincoln and his brother Danny about six this morning," Jack said. "You know that fancy decorating place over in Raleigh? Danny Lincoln's a deliveryman for The Gallery. Only, he and Vic make pickups from some of the same houses. They've been stashing the stuff at a potato house over in Little Creek Township and then selling it at a flea market down in Georgia."

"You knew about this?" Dwight asked Weill.

The carpenter shook his head, but his eyes shied away from Dwight's as he dropped the gnawed toothpick in the wastebasket and pulled a fresh one from his pocket. "I didn't *know*," he said, "but, yeah, I guess I was starting to wonder. Every place we worked, it'd either be the house we were working on or someplace nearby. Soon as new appliances got delivered, they'd get ripped off. First two or three times I thought it was a coincidence. But Vic was always wandering off to check things out during lunchtime—he was friendly with everybody."

He took a deep breath. "He called me this morning to see if I'd help with his bail. And he's scared y'all are going to say he killed Jenny Paul. He might could steal, but I promise you he couldn't kill."

"No?" Dwight said sardonically. "What about this?"

He showed Curtis Weill the list of names he'd doodled with the afternoon before, including what they'd worked out for Vic Lincoln.

Weill's eyes leaped from Vic's name to his own. "You really believe one of us did it?"

"I really believe that nail means something. Don't you?"

"Well . . . yeah, I guess I do," Weill said slowly. "That's the way Jenny Paul's mind worked, all right. Lucky for me she stayed away from the little ones."

"Why do you say that?"

Curtis Weill pulled out a small gold brad. "When we started the house, she gave me this for good luck. Seems some guy with my name wrote a play called *The Threepenny Opera*."

"Kurt Weill!" Chagrined that he'd missed that coincidence, Dwight pointed to the rest of the list. "We can make Vic Lincoln and Neal Cutler fit if we have to, and there's always Billy Partin. He's the main one who used those heat-treated cut nails and—"

"Not 'heat-treated' cut nails," the carpenter corrected with a faint smile for their laymen's ignorance. "They're 'case-hardened' nails."

His flat country drawl drew out the "case" and clipped off the "hardened."

The three men stared at each other and Weill's jaw tightened angrily as he suddenly realized what the young murdered woman had tried to tell them.

Dwight Bryant cupped the nail in his hand, the only case-hardened type in Jenny Paul Hardin's new house. Now that its message was finally clear, it shouldn't be too hard to break down the colleague who'd alibied Dr. K. C. Hardin. Maybe B. L. Arnault was going to turn out to be Hardin's little sex-starved blondie after all.

"I hope you hang his hide on the jailhouse wall," Weill growled.

"Don't worry," said Dwight. "She's already nailed him herself."

Julie Smith and Loren D. Estleman use two very different styles of writing and storytelling to illustrate that the most difficult task may be dealing with your feelings—that is, unless you don't happen to have any.

———————————

silk strands

JULIE SMITH

Julie Smith, former reporter for the New Orleans Times-Picayune and the San Francisco Chronicle, has a keen eye for the landmarks, the language, and the unspoken rules, values, and customs that shape a place. Her Rebecca Schwartz mysteries (most recently Tourist Trap *and* Dead in the Water*) and the Paul McDonald books (*True-Life Adventure, Huckleberry Fiend*) are clever, entertaining, and fast-paced. With the introduction in the Edgar Award–winning* New Orleans Mourning *of Skip Langdon, New Orleans Police Department rookie, Julie gives readers a complex character whose often unsettling and sometimes even painful self-awareness is intriguing. Skip returns in* The Axeman's Jazz.*

In "Silk Strands," a woman finds that the events of her life are delicately but firmly tied to the images in the poetry she writes, when a former lover is murdered.

She looked at the clock. Eight-ten. Two hours before anyone who knew her habits ever called, much less rang her door-bell. What was going on? Even the UPS man never showed up till 9:30.

She sat up suddenly, remembering the events of the last couple of days. Dennis! He must have gotten so mad he'd come over to rant. She had a moment of doubt, a flash of fear, but that was all.

Pulling on a pair of sweats, she smiled. Good. She wanted to see him rant, yell, really get down for once. She wanted to see his famous lack of affect replaced with purple rage. She wanted to see any emotion at all, even blind fury flow out of him, knowing it would make her feel less sad, less discon-nected, less as if she'd just spent the winter at the North Pole.

A man and a woman stood on the threshold, the man holding up a badge. "Police. Are you Morgan Ellender?"

"Yes."

"You know a man named Dennis Hargett?"

God! She hadn't done anything illegal. How had he got-ten them to do this? Harassment—that would be what he'd claimed. He'd probably actually gone to the police station and reported her. But they wouldn't be here if it weren't for the damned TV station. They'd undoubtedly come as a favor to him. She declined to be intimidated.

"I really don't have time to talk to you now." She looked at her wrist as if she were wearing a watch. "I have to be somewhere at nine."

"I'm afraid we have bad news for you, Miss Ellender. Mr. Hargett was shot last night."

The woman spoke: "I'm sorry, Miss Ellender. I'm afraid he's dead. We understand you were involved with him."

Oh, dear God! Dead was the last thing she wished him. She'd spent weeks trying to ferret out incipient signs of life, nourish them, fan them till they burst into flame, hoping to warm them once they'd become stranded together, two ur-ban souls lost in a bewildering fog of hormones. And all he had done was freeze her with his already half-deadness. It wasn't she who had finished the job, but she knew why the cops were here.

She let them in, offered tea, and let them show her the pink message slip.

•   •   •

She had met him at a party given by a friend of a friend. She hadn't known many people there and had been surprised when the nice-looking man in glasses, the only man there wearing a tie, had spoken to her.

"Aren't you Morgan Ellender? I've heard you read."

That one was always a difficult beginning. Was she simply to smile expectantly, hoping for the crumb of praise that was often a poet's only pay?

"I hope you enjoyed it," she said.

He said, "I'm Dennis Hargett," and as they shook hands she felt a surge of energy between them. He was a big man, very preppy, not her usual type, but blond, and she had a weakness for blonds. Her last husband had been one.

"You look like Joan Baez," he said. "But everyone tells you that."

In fact, no one had in a long time. She had worn her hair short for years, and then had lost most of it. In reaction, she had grown it long again, like the young Baez, and realized with pleasure that it was making the statement she wanted. Gradually, she had felt herself coming back, coming out of her shock and sadness, her vulnerability, and she wanted long, free-swinging hair as a symbol of her return to life.

Her husband had left—the third one, Gordon, the one whose bronze skin and gold hair had inspired fifty poems about precious metals, most of them unpublishable. She had fallen into what they had called a swoon in earlier centuries —a wounded withdrawal from life, an overweening sadness, a melancholic lassitude. And then she had spotted the first blood. After that it was a battery of ever more morbid tests, preceded by hideous fasts that left her feeling as if she were half-gone already.

And after that, it was fighting. They said from the first that she would live, that the chemo would work if the surgery didn't, that she was very lucky indeed.

As soon as she was out of the hospital, she went to the best, the most expensive restaurants, ate course after course, ate garlic and basil and drank red wine. She had bought her house, a cottage really, during the chemo, decorated it, begun putting in the garden as soon as they said she could exercise.

The world (or that tiny part of it that had heard of her)

knew nothing of this. It wasn't who she was. She was neither ill nor mournful. She was Morgan Ellender the Earth Poet. That was the way she'd been described when her second volume, *Songs of Earth*, had been published—her favorite way.

The "Songs" part was an obvious homage to earlier poets, the earth part not really her idea. She had wanted to call it *Songs of Dirt*, to show that all of life, all on earth should be sung, that she embraced even the grit, even the dirt, and invited her readers to do so with her. But her friend Harmony had said there was something housewifey about it, something that suggested jingles for detergent commercials, and her publisher had agreed.

Morgan had a good publisher and good sales, for a poet. She was no Rod McKuen, indeed considered herself literary and was so considered by the literary world, but she had achieved a readership rare among her fellows. She thought it was because she had something to say, something people needed in these sterile times. One interview had been head-lined, ELLENDER SAYS 'YES!' TO LIFE, and that pleased her.

Her poems were sensual, often erotic, heavily mythological, celebrating universal rhythms, yet frequently gritty, also celebrating the "dirt," if people wanted to call it that. She had written often of menstruation, depression, the fluids of sex, the literal dirt of the garden, the insects it harbored. And then she had rejected it all.

In those months after her marriage broke up, when she had had to leave her stepchildren as well as their father, she had wrapped herself in blankets, both literal and figurative, missing the warmth, able to do nothing but mourn. But now her hair was long, her house full of bright chintzes, and she was starting to write again, stronger poems than ever. Sexual energy flowed within her.

And this handsome stranger, Dennis Hargett, was sending out strong signals. Her last husband was a carpenter, a literate one, but a man of the earth who worked with his hands; the one before him had been a performance artist. She couldn't remember the last time she'd been out with a man in a suit. Dennis worked in television, a special-projects producer. To her surprise, she liked that, she welcomed his solidity.

Harmony dragged her off to meet someone else, and that

would have been the end of it if they hadn't run into each other at another party.

But she started a new poem that night, the night she met him. Images of moths came to her, moths lighting on magnolias, camellias, lilies—oddly formal flowers, all white, that seemed to need the moths, that needed their animal warmth. She had caught moths as a child and she knew they were warm in one's hand, that even these feathery, delicate things throbbed with life. She called the poem "Transfer," though she had no idea what it meant. The moths, of course, had come to the flowers; perhaps each needed something from the other. Perhaps that was the meaning. It would unfold, like wings, like petals; that was the nature of a poem.

When they met again, it was only a week later and he was fresh in her mind. She had thought of him several times, had an idea well up in her, would have phoned if she'd known where he worked. (He had told her, she thought, but she was no good with number names—Channel 4, Channel 7, what was the difference?)

Seeing him again, she told him her idea, which she called Underground Aesthetics, a series on the new crop of performance artists, poets, musicians, painters who hadn't yet been noticed, but who formed a very real movement in San Francisco's cultural life. She felt a strong kinship with them, was a part of the movement herself, but she was more successful than most and slightly guilty about it.

He seemed intrigued. He said he'd phone.

When he did, she hated his voice. She hadn't realized it was so flat, so distant, so distancing, had a slightly hostile edge. It must happen when he's nervous, she thought.

They had dinner "to talk about the project," she invited him in afterward. He took her wineglass from her hand and kissed her in earnest midsentence, nearly making her giggle at what she and her friends called White Man's Syndrome. (Her black friend Danielle had once lamented to a group of white women that white men obviously didn't respect her, the way they suddenly jumped her out of the clear blue. It was ten minutes before Morgan, Harmony, and company could stop laughing long enough to reassure her the behavior might be deplorable but at least it wasn't selective.)

Dennis, a big man, had been almost too insistent for comfort, but eventually Morgan had hustled him out.

It was an odd encounter, surprising, curiously . . . what? Flat? Passionless? On his part or hers? She searched for words, wanted them desperately, got out her notebook. She found her notes for "Transfer" and for the first time that evening felt comfortable. It wasn't words she needed, it was images. Why could she not remember that?

The flowers were rocks now, or salt flats, white and desolate. Tiny animals scurried there, rodents perhaps . . . prairie dogs? Prairie dogs were cheerful beasts, canine-seeming rodents, as eager to please as cocker spaniels. She fell asleep feeling better.

They had dinner again, and he told her about his current project, *Rumors and Gossip,* a local game show he was developing. It was their second date—low-key, yet with undertones, memories of earlier kisses, a new one at the end. And in her dreams, the poem: ants walking on crystals, quartz crystals, hard, mystical, the ants carrying things—bits of smaller insects.

After that, Morgan had gone away for a week, saying she'd phone when she returned. "Not at the office," he said, and gave her his home number.

When she returned, he had Underground Aesthetics under way and they celebrated by making love. He had specifically invited her to his condo, and she knew that was what he intended, but it almost didn't come off.

It was still daylight when they arrived, but dark in the tiny condo. It was dusty there, furnished with utilitarian simplicity. Not a picture on the walls. As she walked in, as the dark hit her, a wave of depression engulfed her. *Does he really live here?* And then: *Do I want to get involved with the person who does?* It got worse when he couldn't, in his little-used kitchen, find glasses for the margaritas he was making, and then when he did, they looked as if they hadn't been washed in a year.

But she knew something by now—she was violently attracted to him, felt irretrievably enmeshed in some unlikely but inevitable joining.

He said he, too, was divorced, hadn't dated in a year and a half.

"Why?" she asked.

"My standards are high."

The answer was meant to flatter, but there was something joyless in it.

"You're so alive, Morgan. I'm so attracted to you I don't know what to make of it. What do you think it's about?"

She thought she knew, and her heart sank. But the worst of it was, she felt the same. She should wait, she should get to know him better, this was dangerous. . . .

The phone rang at a crucial point. The machine answered, a woman's voice said, "Dennis, this is Cathy Eicholz. We've got to talk about *Rumors and Gossip;* this is grossly unfair to me. I worked on that project for two years and you're not going to get away with this. . . ."

Bitch! How dare she interrupt their lovemaking? What a nasty, nasal, raspy voice she had! How furious she sounded. How did Dennis come to know such a person?

He kicked the phone off the hook.

But it was a harbinger; theirs was always a bumpy acquaintanceship. Sex was fantastic. Everything else was a little off.

A week or so into it, he called and asked if she'd like to "get together for coffee or something."

Why doesn't he just do it over the phone? she thought, sure he intended to dump her, knowing coffee was either a first date or a last. She was speechless, not wanting to go through the bother of breaking up with someone she hardly knew, but he said, "Or we could have dinner."

She had a small emergency, couldn't avoid being late, and knowing he'd come straight from work, cursed his prohibition on calling him there, a hard-and-fast rule he'd reiterated since the first time.

"Why?" she'd asked.

"I don't take personal calls at the office. Never. I just don't do it."

He was almost ebullient at dinner, as if he'd tapped into some new energy source, some secret stash.

He toasted her. "To Morgan Ellender, the world's sexiest poet." And then he said, "I have to apologize for something —when we do the series, I can't use you in the poetry section. I'm afraid it might tip our hand, as it were."

"You mean somebody might think we're dating?"

"You have to understand, I'm a very private person. I feel

bad about the series, though, because that was why I sought you out; ever since I got the idea, I'd intended to use you." He shrugged. "I'm sorry it worked out this way."

"Listen, it's no problem. I wasn't looking for publicity when I suggested it—I just thought there were some really fine artists who weren't being recognized."

"What do you mean when you suggested it?"

"When I gave you the idea."

"You didn't give me the idea. You sound like this other woman who claims she thought of *Rumors and Gossip*."

"Don't you remember the second time we met—at Deborah Percy's party? I told you about the movement and gave you all the artists' names."

"Did you?"

They drank too much and he confessed he hated his job, had wanted something wildly different. He had wanted to be a journalist and had failed.

It was an odd confession, she thought. How many failed journalists could there be in the world? When she thought of all the unpublished poets, unnoticed painters, unloved musicians, journalism seemed a peculiar art to pine for. But she understood that this was his love, as poetry was hers, and it had been taken away; he had chosen to barter himself to a corporation, to spend his days making money, just getting through. "Sometimes I say to myself, you can do it, Dennis. Just put one foot after another. Just go in there and stay all day. And I do and next thing you know it's five o'clock."

"And then what do you do?"

"I'm with you right now."

"Yes, but when I'm not with you, I write poetry. I visit friends. I take my stepchildren to the movies. What do you do? You don't cook at home, I've seen your kitchen. Do you eat at all? Do you watch prime-time TV in a mindless stupor?"

He stared at his plate. "I don't know. How's the fish?"

Taking the hint, she changed the subject, asked about the project. He shrugged. "It's okay. It's fine. Except that most of this avant-garde stuff's pretty pathetic."

"You're not enjoying it?"

"Let's put it this way. It's not the best stuff being done."

"What isn't—the music or the painting? What *do* you like?"

"I don't know."

She learned to avoid two subjects—who Dennis Hargett might be and whether there was anything in the world he approved of or liked. Thus freed, Dennis could be witty and charming, excellent company. Their dates formed a pattern: when she was with him, she felt excited, as if they danced on a precipice, and the next day she felt empty.

The first weekend he already had plans, the second he said his parents were in town, and the third it was something else. They had been "dating," if you could call it that, for nearly a month, had had sex a lot, when she mentioned to Harmony that she'd never seen him on a weekend. "Another woman," said Harmony, and she remembered his adamant order not to phone him at the office.

"I'm a very private person," he had said repeatedly now, and she could see that it was true. He never mentioned friends, much less introduced her to any. There were no photographs in his apartment, either framed or lying in casual stacks. She never saw letters there, waiting to be opened or mailed. It was the perfect setup for a workaholic, except for one thing—he hated his work.

He was calling her less and less, exactly as someone would who was trying to stabilize an illicit affair. But somehow she didn't think it was that. What she thought was, a cold wind was blowing and she had to get out of the draft.

She phoned, her speech all planned: "Listen, I can take a hint. Really. No problem. 'Bye now."

But he was delighted to hear from her, chattered brightly for twenty minutes or so, and asked her to a movie that week.

Had she misread the thing? Was he just out of it? She still didn't know why he'd asked her to coffee that time—didn't he know the simplest social rituals?

"That would be nice," she said, "but you know, I feel really bad that I never get to see you on weekends. And it seems so odd I can't call you at work. . . ."

His voice turned hard and flat. "Well, I'm going to retain my preference on that. But you can see me on the weekend."

"Retain your preference, will you? You sound like a legal document."

"Sorry." And he truly sounded sorry, as if he'd just gotten carried away.

"What weekend?"

"This one. Saturday."

Saturday morning the sun streamed into her cottage, revealing the dust on her coffee table, but also catching a plain glass vase full of irises and turning it into a crystal prism. Morgan took her tea into her tiny city backyard and walked around it, feeling herself its queen, examining each new flower and each bud. There were new bugs, too, and she welcomed them as well.

But for the first time in her garden, she felt uneasy. She found herself wanting to stay in that night, to cook, to warm herself up. She looked through cookbooks, planned a menu, went shopping. She bought Dennis a small gift, a book she knew he wanted. By mid-afternoon she had shaken the odd melancholy and settled into a contented lassitude. She talked on the phone to Harmony, washed her hair, selected music for the evening, listened to some. It wasn't a day to write, it was a day to live.

When Dennis phoned, she was bubbling. "I thought it might be nice to stay in tonight if you don't mind. I have this terrific recipe. . . ."

"I had a really late lunch. I'm going to pass on that."

She felt the chill again, a cloud passing over the sun. He didn't seem to notice she hadn't spoken. "Look, I feel sort of —I don't want to say tired—well, yes, why don't we call it tired. I'd rather not do anything, if that wouldn't anger you unduly."

She saw her hands turn blue, felt her teeth start to chatter. No such thing was happening, but the image was so strong that for a moment she was convinced of it, thrown off her stride, able to answer not as herself, Morgan, a grown woman, but only politely, like some teenage patsy.

Harmony was a psychotherapist by trade, but declined to ply such trade unless she was getting paid for it. On this one, she laughed her head off: "This is no simple wife or neurosis problem, baby. A couple of weeks ago I thought probably mob, but now I can see it's a lot worse than that. A *lot* worse. There are organizations in this country that some men aren't free to talk about, you know what I mean? When our national security is at stake, it behooves us all not to ask too many questions and I know you'll want to do your part and bite that little old bullet like a good American."

Shamed, Morgan had called him back. Afterward, she never knew how she had persuaded him to come over, but thought it must have been not with words, but the icy fury in her voice. He arrived fresh-shaven, wearing knife-creased slacks and perfectly pressed button-down collar. She realized with a pang that she'd never seen him in jeans and T-shirt.

He was chattering, trying for casualness. "Should I have brought my boxing gloves?"

She handed him some wine. "This isn't about fighting."

"But you're mad."

"Mad about your breaking the date. The other stuff is more . . . well, I have my feelings hurt, that's all. The stuff like never seeing you on weekends, I mean, never being introduced to your friends . . ." She outlined it for him, the way he'd been treating the thing like a back-street liaison. "I thought when you broke the date tonight, 'Oh, great, the girlfriend found out and that was that.'" But it was bait, she didn't really believe it.

He said: "There is no girlfriend." *Certainly not you* was as clear as if he'd said the words.

"You know we've never even rented a movie and sent out for a pizza?"

He didn't answer.

"What I'm trying to say is that the friendship element never kicked in . . . this thing has just never developed into a normal dating relationship."

He sat up straight, going off the defensive, suddenly sure of his ground. "I don't do relationships."

Had he really said that? She repeated it: "You don't do relationships."

"I told you that."

She could see her breath. "No. You didn't."

"I told you I hadn't had a date in a year and a half."

"Dennis, I work with words. That's very different from 'don't do relationships.'"

"This is what happens when you try to do somebody a favor. I wish I'd never thought of that damned *Underground Aesthetics*. Nothing but a bunch of no-talent losers and look where it got me!"

Shocked that he'd now twice claimed her idea as his own (never mind that he was being such a baby), she couldn't let it go by: "You didn't think of it. I did."

He looked surprised. "You did?" He let a beat pass. "You know why I don't do relationships? So I won't have to have conversations like this."

"What's so bad about this?" *Compared to being treated like a cheap lay, for instance?*

"I could have just stiffed you completely. I didn't have to come over here today."

"Well, thank you. Thank you very much for all the truly terrible things you could have done and didn't. I'm just beginning to see how grateful I ought to be."

"I didn't know anything was wrong."

"Well, no. The only way to find out would have been to have a conversation like this. And you don't have those because you don't do relationships. So you won't have to have conversations like this. So how could you know anything was wrong? But guess what? We're having one now. Read my lips: something's wrong."

"You know, you really should get to know people better before you sleep with them."

"Oh, great. If you were a rapist, you'd probably say the woman asked for it."

Red spots appeared on his cheeks. "I didn't rape you."

"Take it easy. I didn't say you did."

"I had a good time with you. . . ."

"Why not? You had everything your way."

"That's another reason I don't do relationships. Everything is always on someone else's terms."

Why don't they do something about the immigration laws? Every day you see more and more of them—Martians, trying to pass.

But she knew that was a defense. As she had earlier seen her hands blue on the phone, now she saw him backed up against a wall, hanging on to the rough plaster with his fingernails, a shadow, a hundred pounds thinner, a wreck.

She felt horribly sad for him, but frightened—*if you touch a corpse, its skin will rub off, it will come off on your fingers.*

Could she tell him about the chill without hurting him? No, of course not. He had treated her like a sweetie-on-the-side and she had hurt him just by calling his game. She had hurt him by asking to see him tonight, would have hurt him by presenting the paperback she'd bought him, and was now hurting him with every word she said. For him, everything hurt. Giving hurt, receiving hurt. Any time a feeling got activated, it hurt.

The words "pleasure anorexic" came to Morgan and with them a plan for a cycle of poems, a very sad cycle, the other side of her celebration of life. Like *Songs of Innocence, Songs of Experience*, she thought. *Songs of Earth, Songs of . . .* what? Hell? Hell was too exciting. Limbo, maybe. It would be about living life on hold. Not even living; existing in a void.

A serene look settled over his features, as it had when he'd announced that he didn't do relationships. He was once more in command. "Well, look. We were going to have to talk eventually. . . ."

So it's okay to talk if you initiate it. And suddenly she saw why he hated "conversations like this"—because for once he wasn't in control. It frightened her to realize how completely she'd let him dominate.

"Now's the time, I think, to change things around a little. Why don't we just move into a friendship?"

"Dennis, you've never even mentioned friends. Do you really have any?"

"I know people. I don't know what you mean by friendship."

"Well. I don't think we can have one then."

"I thought we had a lot in common."

Did you, you superior shit who's never read a single one of my poems and never written a fucking word of your own and has the gall to call my friends no-talent losers? Is that so, you Benedict Arnold who's just committed high treason on my person? How dare you, you Martian who wouldn't know a human feeling if it jumped out of your chest and rammed itself down your supercilious throat?

"Sex just muddies the waters," he said.

She breathed deeply, trying to calm herself. "Mud. That's dirt. That's earth. I could use that. I could write about that."

"You don't want to be friends?"

If he said it again, he was dead meat. She tried to summon a facsimile of his telephone voice, the one she hated so much. "I want you to go."

"Oh. Well, look,"—his tone was placating—"I really have to thank you for getting me out of my isolation. . . ."

"Which made it possible for you to sexually exploit me. Excuse me if I don't say you're welcome."

"I guess I'd better go."

"I guess so."

•   •   •

She and Harmony got two movies, two pizzas, and lots of red wine. For a while Harmony's husband Doug joined them, and Danielle, but finally it was just Morgan and Harmony and Dennis Quaid, to whom Harmony kept referring as "the good Dennis."

Enjoying the warmth and energy of her friends, seeing their horror as she told her story, Morgan felt the anger that had begun with Dennis's empty offer of "friendship" come to flower. It was a foul-smelling, malevolent blossom, like that of the vegetable carnivores that grow in deep, loamy woods —ugly, but it would wither and die in a day or two, and it was better than the cold, the ice he left in her vitals.

She and Harmony got silly, plotting revenge.

"Call him at the office," said Harmony, and suddenly the pitcher plant was gone, replaced by an imp.

"Yeah." Morgan was delighted. "I could wait till lunchtime, when his secretary's bound to answer the phone."

She had a great idea for a message, but Harmony said no. "Make it something intimate. Bet he hates the 'i' word. How about this: 'Tell him we got our favorite cottage at the Elk Cove Inn. I can't wait till Friday.'"

"His secretary'd probably be so thrilled for him she'd read it aloud instead of leaving it on his desk."

"He'd die."

He had died. And Morgan *had* left a message—not the one Harmony suggested, but the one she had first thought of. Harmony said it was no good because no one who meant it would really leave one like that, but Morgan felt the point was not belief, but a public thumbing of her nose.

The message was silly. What counted was her art. Once again she pulled out her notes for "Transfer," hoping to weave the images together but the word "weave" made her scalp prickle, turned her mind toward the web in which she'd been caught.

This time the image was sharp as a sting, and she drew in her breath, seeing it so stark, so vivid—the thing she hated most, feared most, the thing that had haunted her dreams when she was ill. The flowers of the first effort, of that innocent other time, were now an ice floe, a white expanse the size of a continent, and on it crawled a spider. No small spider, but a spider like a teacup, big enough to show in perfect detail against the ice. A black one; a hairy one. A long, nasty, fat-bellied one, full of things it had killed.

Morgan wrote of snakes, she wrote of beetles, she nattered on about rotting wood and lichens. But deep in her heart she knew that she did not embrace everything the earth had to offer. She did not and would not write of anything with eight legs and mandibles. She'd been told as a child that they'd kill you—not could but would—the tiniest nip and it was curtains. She'd been in a basement at the time; they were everywhere.

She wouldn't write the poem. Couldn't describe the thing, had to get it out of her head.

The nice officers said they were Jane Patterson and Ward Donaldson. Patterson said, "You didn't leave your last name, is that correct? The secretary said you said he'd know. What did you say exactly?"

"Obviously you know. You have the message slip."

"We'd like to hear it from you."

What had seemed so childishly amusing, so deliciously silly only a few hours ago, looked suddenly psychotic. Or was Harmony right? Was it really something you couldn't take seriously?

Morgan sighed. "I guess I'd better call my lawyer." Harmony's husband, Doug. Doug was a criminal lawyer, someone used to drug dealers and white-collar sleazebags. If she'd expected him to laugh, she was mistaken.

"I'll be right over," he said. "Don't say a word."

The message she'd left for Dennis was this: "The herpes test was positive. You'll be hearing from my lawyer."

At the time, she hadn't thought of Doug as her lawyer, hadn't ever thought she'd need him.

As soon as she got back from the phone, mentioning Doug's name (which they obviously recognized) and saying he was on his way, Patterson and Donaldson started backpedaling.

"Miss Ellender, I've been a fan of yours for years," Patterson said. "You're not a suspect in this. You're not even the only one who ever left Hargett a message like that, although the last one was years ago, his secretary says. If he really didn't want women to call him at the office, he probably shouldn't have told them that. It's like when somebody says,

'Whatever you do, don't open that door.' Of course that's the door you're going to open."

She spread her hands, palms up. "We just came to you because we're trying to get some insight into this man. We've been through his calendar, his address book, his phone tape, and his private correspondence, if you want to call it that. His mother sent him cards on holidays, that's about it. Frankly, the guy just doesn't seem to know anybody."

"But he's a producer."

"He has a ton of professional acquaintances, but nobody who says they knew him well." Patterson flicked something from her skirt. "Did you?"

"Know him well?"

"Yes."

"Doug said I really shouldn't talk to you."

Donaldson made a sound somewhere between a sigh and a snort. "You know there's one guy says he worked with the man for seven years, doesn't even know whether he was gay or straight."

"You dated him, that's obvious," Patterson said. "Don't you care that he's dead?"

"Of course."

But something tugged at her, a conscience-like something, telling her to level with herself, if not with these two. And looking into herself, she really couldn't summon any deep reserves of sorrow, had felt more when she had heard Elvis was dead, or Sammy Davis, Jr.—men who exuded life energy. Dennis dead didn't seem that different from Dennis alive.

"Isn't there anything you can add that might help us? He just doesn't seem the sort of man anyone would bother to kill." Patterson paused, taking a breath. "I mean he didn't arouse that much emotion in people—a phone message to get his goat, that was about it."

"I found him very distant," said Morgan primly.

Doug arrived then, and the officers said they were just leaving. Nonetheless he huffed and puffed at them, and then, when they were gone, huffed at Morgan as well (about the phone message). Then he asked if she were really all right, offered to send Harmony over, kissed her, and went off to save a drug dealer.

Teapot in hand, Morgan went outside to sit in her garden. Her trumpet vine was in full flower and a joy to contemplate.

But her mood was far from contemplative. Her pulse raced with the excitement of the new experience she was having—that of defying authority, of keeping a secret. She had never had secret knowledge before, and it occurred to her that Dennis Hargett had lived his life as if *it* were secret knowledge. The random facts of trivia and mundaneness for which other people cared so little they broadcast, Dennis had hoarded as if they were Kruggerrands.

It would be something of an homage to him to hoard her own secret knowledge, something he would almost certainly have done if she were the one who was dead.

Morgan had a pretty good idea who had killed him and why.

The police would have known, too, if Dennis hadn't been so damn secretive—he had certainly erased the telltale phone message or Patterson and Donaldson wouldn't have bothered with so small a fish as Morgan.

She put herself in Cathy Eicholz's position. If she'd really cared about her show idea, if she'd worked on the idea for years as Cathy claimed she had, if perhaps she'd hoped for a job working on the show, she would have been furious, felt horribly betrayed and cheated to see Dennis claim it as his own. He didn't, Morgan supposed, "mean any harm," as people said, he was simply turned too far inward to notice other people; they existed so dimly for him it was probably hard to imagine they could have ideas, which *were* real to him.

It was Patterson's remark about Dennis's failure to arouse emotion that had tipped Morgan off. She'd remembered Cathy's message then. It was full of emotion: red rage. Murderous rage, perhaps.

Morgan herself had never in her life done anything so stupid as leaving the phone message for Dennis. But it had seemed important. She'd felt so discounted she just wanted him to notice that she, Morgan, could have an impact on his life. What if you multiplied that feeling by a thousand or so?

Morgan watched a butterfly, sorry its life would be so short, glad hers had been given back to her. She decided definitely not to mention Cathy to Patterson and Donaldson. After all, she was a poet. While she felt she would like to steer clear of the obvious phrase regarding justice, she did see a nice irony in the situation.

Besides, Cathy was probably a person with a family and

friends, people who cared about her. No one had cared about Dennis.

She took a sip of tea and leaned back, at peace. But out of the corner of her eye she caught movement. The wind was blowing white cosmos. Was it that? No, something else, something inside a flower: a spider with a moth, a moth it had caught and was wrapping somehow with strands of silk. She watched unflinching, fascinated, not even surprised she was doing so. The first line of the poem formed in her head.

safe house

LOREN D. ESTLEMAN

Not yet forty years of age, Loren D. Estleman has secured for himself a place in private-eye fiction and western fiction by winning three Shamus Awards and two Western Writers of America Spur Awards. His novel Whiskey River *is an in-depth look at Detroit during Prohibition, the first of a trilogy tracing the rise and fall of crime in Detroit. Mr. Estleman's greatest claim to fame, however, is the creation of PI Amos Walker. Critics and readers hail Walker as the heir apparent to Philip Marlowe. We prefer to point out that Walker is Walker, and is very much his own man. To describe him as anything else is to do him a disservice. Judge for yourself. "Safe House" is pure Walker, at his best.*

———

Our host was a county deputy who wore a lumberman's checked jacket over his uniform blouse and nonissue wool pants. His name was Jerry and he had a long slab of blue chin and a .38 Chief's Special in a holster behind his right hipbone. I wanted to ask how the hunting was in that country, but I'd been told not to speak to anyone except the two detectives who were guarding me. Jerry no longer looked at me, having filed me with the antlers over the door and the ulcerated leather sofa he said his father had died in with a .30-30 round in his chest during the 1966 deer season.

"Boys need anything?" he asked at the door. "How you fixed for eggs and shit?"

"Eggs we can use. Walker here gives us all the shit we need." Sergeant Coyne, seated as close to the oilcloth-covered table as his hard thick belly would let him, booted two cards out of his hand and accepted fresh recruits without looking up.

Jerry left. Outside, his Jeep Cherokee started up and clattered away. Officer Blevins, a long sinewy strip of busted University of Detroit basketball scholarship in an unbuttoned vest, as black as Coyne was pale, bumped the pot up six bits and the sergeant threw in his hand with an oath.

"Two players sucks. Just pushing the same three-sixty-seven back and forth. Sure you won't sit in?" Coyne looked at me.

"How long have you two partnered?" I asked.

He frowned at Blevins. "Six years?"

"Eight." The black detective raked in the pot and shuffled the deck.

I said, "I'll pass. I got cleaned out once playing checkers in Huron Metropark with this old wheeze who spent his retirement playing with his friend. Either one of them could tell you in three moves where the game was going from there."

"Hear that, Marcus?" Coyne said. "You and me are too good for the private flash." Blevins grunted and dealt.

Actually the sergeant was the worst poker player I'd seen in a long time. His face mirrored every card he drew and he fell like a piano for the most transparent bluffs; but I needed his good opinion. They'd been shoving three bucks and change around the table for eight days, ever since I'd been tagged to testify before a grand jury investigating the death of a hood named Frank Acardo in front of my building. I'd missed the shoot, but I'd seen the Colombian hitters waiting for him earlier, and so far I was the only witness who could place them at the scene. Rumor said the Colombians were laying out ten grand for me dead, which was a good deal more than I was worth alive. I hadn't had a client in weeks.

"Spicks got all the hotels staked out," Coyne had said when we'd arrived at the safe house, a hunting cabin in Oakland County arranged by a friend of the deputy's in the Detroit Police Department. "Sorry we got no mints to put on your pillow."

I didn't mind. There was nothing waiting for me at the office and the smell of knotty pine reminded me of hunting trips north, a long time ago. I ate Blevins's greasy cooking and read old paperback westerns and watched Coyne get himself bluffed out of everything but his shoulder rig.

He tossed in his cards again and leaned back, shoving his hands in his pockets. "Ten Gs, that's a year's pay after taxes for me. How's come the Spicks got more to spend than the city?"

"Less overhead." Blevins reshuffled. "Spit-in-the-Ocean?"

"I ain't got spit. You cleaned me out." He rose to answer the telephone. "Coyne. Sure, he's still breathing. What time? 'Kay." He hung up. "Pack your panties, Sherlock. You go on at three."

I got up from the sofa. "I'll miss this place."

"You and Grizzly Adams," he said, shrugging into his sportcoat.

It was a forty-five-minute drive to Detroit and the City-County Building, where a soporific clerk directed us to a row of seats outside the jury room. The seats across from us were occupied by the man I was there to give evidence against and his entourage. This included his lawyer, young and black in a gray sharkskin suit and one of those bottle-top haircuts they go in for now and a pair of dark-skinned, long-haired bodyguards that would dress out to five hundred pounds and look at home in Aztec ceremonial kit.

The man seated between the two hulks belonged to another species. Hector Matador was narrow enough in face and body to vanish when he turned your way, which may have been why he always presented a three-quarter profile, looking at you out of one eye. He had small hands and feet, big eyes, a hawk nose, and wore his black hair in bangs like Al Pacino in *Scarface*. Dressed like him, too, in fawn-colored suits with peaked lapels, pink silk neckties, and a camel's-hair overcoat flung across his shoulders cape fashion. He glanced at me with one mahogany-colored eye that had no bottom, then looked away. He recognized me, all right. The last time I'd seen him he was seated beside the driver of the car that sped away from the scene of Frank Acardo's murder.

After a brief whispered consultation with the assistant city prosecutor, a big man named Fallon with red hair and the broken-knuckled hands of an Irish bricklayer, I went in to answer questions. Thirty minutes later I paused at the top of the outside steps to shake Fallon's hand.

"We'll get an indictment," he said. "I'll call you when we have a trial date. I wish you'd reconsider and remain in custody."

"Being a witness doesn't pay enough. I'll watch my back." I'd said good-bye to Coyne and Blevins outside the jury room.

"Watch your front, too. These Colombians don't care what direction they come at you from."

I took a cab to the office, circular-filed most of the mail I found waiting for me under the slot, paid some bills, and ran a duster over the desk. My answering service had no messages for me; just to make sure they asked me to repeat my name. The investigation business has more slumps than the Tigers. I was thinking of signing up for a course in word processing when the telephone rang.

"Walker's School of Dance. Fox-trots our specialty."

Pause. "Is this Amos Walker?" Female, middle register, thirty to thirty-five. I took my foot off the file drawer and said it was. "My husband has been missing for a week."

"Do you want him back?"

"I wouldn't be calling you if I didn't. Do you know the Blue Heron?"

"It takes a month to get a reservation there," I said.

"I'll meet you there at six. Ask for Glasscock." She hung up.

The restaurant was tucked back from four lanes of solid traffic in West Bloomfield, identified only by a blue long-legged bird taking off from a sign with no lettering. A rangy hostess in a white silk blouse and long black skirt came out from behind a trellis and towed me to a corner table looking out on the garden.

"I'm Natalie Glasscock. Thanks for coming."

I took a slim hand with a ruby the size of a typewriter attached and gave it back to the woman seated at the table. I'd guessed her age right over the telephone. She had a lot of black hair brushed back without ceremony and a little makeup on the kind of face that writers call handsome to keep from slobbering all over the keyboard. She wore a grayish-pink suit with no blouse that was plain enough to have cost plenty. The ring was her only jewelry. It would have been enough for Imelda Marcos.

I sat down. "Glasscock Bodies?"

"Now it's GlasCo, and we make everything from surgical lasers to those easy-exercise gadgets that get a ten-day workout and then wind up in the attic. Cars don't have bodies anymore. Drink?"

She had a full martini glass in front of her. I got rye from the waitress who'd materialized when she made the offer. The help faded. "Your husband is a Glasscock?"

"My husband is an Emmett Firman. My great-grandfather founded the company. He's hypertensive."

"Your great-grandfather?"

"He died in 1930. Emmett's the hypertensive one. I thought it might help you locate him."

"You mean by making faces at strangers until one turns red and keels over?"

"I mean by canvassing drugstores. He needs medication. I brought his prescription." She took an empty plastic vial out of a purse with a clasp that looked like a Krugerrand and gave it to me.

I glanced at the typewritten label and pocketed it. "This is Detroit. People with high blood pressure outnumber the muggers. I could peddle Emmett's picture around drugstores every day for a month and not cover them all. That's a manpower job. Any reason you haven't called the police?"

"Just one. The same reason I haven't called the *Six O'Clock News*. Except for the occasional wedding and death, the name Glasscock has never wandered beyond the newspaper business page. As the last one to bear the name, I'd rather keep it that way."

"When'd he leave?"

"Last Monday morning about eight o'clock. He has an office in the GlasCo Building on Grand. He never arrived."

"Did you have a fight?"

"Emmett and I never fought. He's entirely without passion. Frankly I was surprised when his doctors diagnosed hypertension. It was the first I knew he had any blood pressure at all."

"I guess that rules out a mistress."

Something stirred behind her face. She opened the purse again and handed me a matchbook. "I found that in the pocket of one of his jackets. He didn't take any of his clothes with him."

It had an advertising cover, "The Delphi" in blue on marble gray, with a telephone number and an address on Watson. I gave it back. "The Delphi's a gay bar," I said. "Is your husband a homosexual?"

"I can't believe he practices. He lacks passion, as I said. But it wouldn't shock me to learn he leaned that way. We haven't had relations since our honeymoon, and *that* was a disaster."

Our waitress was back. Her flush said she'd heard more than she'd cared to. We read our menus and ordered appetizers. I waited until we were alone again. "Personal question."

"I married Emmett because my father's will stipulated I had to have a husband in order to collect my inheritance. A wedding was cheaper and less involved than an attempt to break the will. I don't think I have to tell you why he married me."

"Are you sure you want him back?"

"I'm used to him."

I asked her a few more questions and then the food came. "Another drink?" Natalie Glasscock asked.

"Not if I'm going to a bar later."

The waitress left. "Is that an acceptance?"

"Seven-fifty will do for a retainer."

When you visit a gay hangout, and you're not trolling for truckers, it pays to bring reading material; it turns away all but the most rabid pickup artists while you check the place out. I drank a beer at the bar and read a veiled piece in the *News* about my testimony in the Matador case. There was a sidebar listing Hector's various money-laundering operations under the umbrella of his dummy company, Corrida Ltd. I guess I was out of town the day the hoods moved from the police blotter to the financial pages.

Except for the lack of women, the Delphi didn't look all that different from a straight bar. These days they all have ferns and the Best of Broadway in the juke. The bartender was a cruelly handsome brute of twenty-two with short-cropped blond hair and a curl on his lip. I ordered another beer and laid a twenty on the bar. When he picked it up, I told him I didn't want change.

He gave me change. "There's a rule against dating customers," he said, "and if there weren't a rule against it, I'd have one of my own, and if I didn't have one of my own, I still wouldn't do it because I'm not gay."

"I like brunettes with big lungs myself. What I want is information." I dealt him a picture Natalie Glasscock had given me of her and Emmett Firman taken in a studio. He had one of those faces that made you think the photograph was fading in front of your eyes. "He been in lately?"

He handed it back, shaking his head.

"I'm not a cop, if that's what's bothering you."

"I knew that when you gave me the twenty. This guy could be sitting where you are and I'd forget what he looked like by the time I looked up from the picture."

"Got any regulars?"

"They're *all* regulars." He stroked the bills on the bar. I nodded. He folded them into the pocket of his green vest. "Try Rodney there in the booth. They built the place around him."

When I slid in, I thought the man sitting opposite holding a stemmed glass was another youthful towhead, but as my eyes adjusted to the candlelight his face took on a burnished sheen and I saw the creases by his ears where the surgeon had folded back the skin. His hair was snow white under a blue rinse and curled over the collar of his tailored jacket. When he lifted his black, plucked eyebrows, I held up another twenty. "Five minutes."

He smiled carefully, lest his face split. "I used to make twice that for five minutes."

I didn't withdraw the bill. "Everybody's into youth now."

He sighed and took it. I showed him the picture. "His wife wants him back."

"One wonders why."

"Do you know him?"

"Just to do business with." A wry look pushed at the taut skin.

"When?"

"The first time, about six months ago. It's been almost two weeks since the last time."

"Most people would have to think a little before being that specific," I said.

"Specificity's a tough habit to break. I was with the mayor's press corps for four years."

"What happened?"

He sipped wine. "Let's just say I prefer the people I'm working with now."

"Do you have a place near here?"

"Ernest did. That's where we always went."

"Ernest?"

"I never did believe it was his name."

"I take it he didn't confide."

"It was business, as I said."

"Where was his place?"

"The Czarina, Room two-oh-one. Around the corner on John R."

"Thanks." I slid out of the booth. His eyes followed me up.

"Aren't you going to ask who did it to whom?"

"I'm a detective. Not Geraldo." I hung back. "I guess I wouldn't be the first to tell you to be careful."

He smiled a tragic smile and saluted me with his glass. "I'm an invert," he said. "Not an imbecile."

Gay, they're called.

The Czarina had been an elegant hotel when Detroit was the stove-making capital of the world, before Henry Ford and the carburetor. Since then some aesthete had dropped a Styrofoam ceiling under the vault in the lobby, plastered over the marble, and laid linoleum on the parquet. You had to look twice to see where the dusty counter left off and the faded black clerk who was leaning on it began. "Two-oh-one," I told him.

Instead of ringing the room, he reached behind the counter without taking his other hand off it and gave me a key. I was still dizzy over the security of the place when the little coffin of an elevator deposited me on the second floor.

I knocked first, for delicacy, then used the key. Like the lobby, the room had been plastered and paneled into the twentieth century and truncated by a cheesy partition into something less spacious. The bed was unmade, the tub in the bathroom needed scrubbing, and there was a litter of change and pocket fallout on the glass-topped dresser. The drawers were empty, vacant hangers sagged in the closet. The scraps of paper on the dresser included a few odd cash-register receipts and a credit-card statement in an open envelope. There was a charge from American Airlines for a one-way flight to Muskegon on the tenth. According to his wife, Emmett Firman had disappeared on the ninth.

I'd seen everything there was to see. There was no telephone in the room, so I added twenty cents to the expense account to call Natalie Glasscock from the lobby.

"Muskegon," she repeated, after we were through greeting each other. "Dear God, I forgot about the cottage."

"Now's a good time to start remembering." I didn't try to strangle the telephone cord. The desk clerk was watching.

"My father had a house in Muskegon. He called it his fishing cottage, but he never went there to fish. It was just a hideaway. I haven't seen it since he died. Do you think Emmett's there?"

I looked at my watch. "I'll know tomorrow. The airport will be closed by now. Have you got a key to the place?"

"I'll have it dug out by the time you get here."

I said tomorrow morning would be fine and told her good night. Hanging up, I waited for the rush that comes when the thing you've been hunting wanders into your sights.

It didn't come. This one hadn't wandered in at all; it had done a big fat brodie and landed on its face wearing a neon suit.

That night I slept in my own bed for the first time in more than a week. I dreamed of hunting cabins and fishing cottages: safe houses. When the alarm rang, I called Fallon's office in the City-County Building. He was there early, shuffling papers in the Matador case. When I told him what I wanted, he got one of his aides on the intercom and sent him after it. While we were waiting I asked Fallon how the hearing was going.

"We got an indictment last night."

"Congratulations."

"Save that for when we get a conviction. You still have

to—just a second." The aide had returned. Fallon gave me what he'd brought. "That what you needed?"

"More or less."

"I won't ask why." He left a pause, which I didn't fill, and cleared his throat. "We need to go over your testimony before the trial. Where are you going to be?"

"Fishing."

I swung through Grosse Pointe, where the maid who answered Natalie Glasscock's doorbell said her mistress was out and gave me the keys and the address of the house in Muskegon. I drove to city airport from there.

What the Glasscocks called a cottage would have housed Detroit's homeless with room left over for all the crooks on the mayor's staff. Sprawling over two acres of prime Lake Michigan shorefront, it was all glass and timber and stank architect. I parked my rental down the street and approached from the side.

I looked in on three empty rooms, then risked a peek through the big window from the deck overlooking the lake. If he hadn't worn a bright red sport shirt, I might have missed him. Seated in a scoop chair reading a magazine, Emmett Firman looked even more faded than he did in his picture; and he wasn't alone. A burgundy loafer on a foot attached to a crossed leg in tan slacks showed in a corner of the window. Whoever was attached to the leg was sitting behind the wall.

I rang the bell on the street side. When Emmett opened the door, I showed him my ID. "Natalie's worried," I said.

His face faded another tint. "Come inside."

I followed him through two of the rooms I had looked in on into the big sunny room on the lake. Out on the water a number of sailboats were flitting around like bright moths. Hector Matador, having risen from his chair to stand at the window, was watching them. He had on a fawn double-breasted with the collar of his open shirt rolled over the lapels. His hands were in his pockets.

"Are you a sailing man, Señor Walker?" He didn't turn from the window.

"If God had meant us to sail, he wouldn't have given us gasoline."

"Is too bad." His head slid my way. "By now I guess you have figured out that Señor Firman was never missing."

I said, "Thanks. Up until you said that I wasn't sure his wife was in on it."

"He came here to lead you away from your official friends in Detroit. We could not stop you from talking to the grand jury, but there is no reason you should be made to repeat yourself at the trial."

"You must have driven all night to get here ahead of me. How'd you make bail so fast?"

"I have official friends as well."

"Where's the Aztec backfield?"

"If you mean Luis and Francisco, they are making my house look lived-in for the police who think they are watching me." He shrugged. "I am among friends, no? So who needs bodyguards?"

Emmett said, "May I go now?"

"What I can't figure is why you ran me through the Delphi," I said. "Natalie Glasscock could have told me about the cottage."

"Then you would have asked why she didn't check on it herself. It was more convincing to say she forgot. We knew you'd find the room at the Czarina and the airfare bill to Muskegon sooner or later. Almost *too* soon, as it turned out." He grinned.

I took the Smith & Wesson out of my coat pocket. "Get your hands out where I can see them."

Still grinning, he turned from the window and drew them out of his pockets, empty. "Señora Matador's eldest son is too smart to drive two hundred miles carrying a firearm while he is out on bail," he said.

But Sergeant Coyne wasn't. He came out of a side door behind his department-issue automatic, pale and thick-bellied as ever in the same rumpled suit he'd worn for eight days at the safe house in Oakland County. "Ditch the piece, private flash."

I hung on to it. "When'd you go over?"

"Always was. Couldn't cap you while you was in custody, now, could I? Not with Straight-Ass Marcus Blevins giving me the fish-eye the whole time. Ditch it, I said."

Emmett said, "I'm going."

Matador said, "You stay."

"I don't want to be part of this."

"You already are. You stay through or you go sailing tonight with Señor Walker. Either way you don't talk, *comprende*?"

Emmett opened his mouth, closed it, fumbled in a pocket, and took a pill from a vial like the one his wife had given me.

"I won't tell you again." Coyne gestured toward my Smith & Wesson with the automatic.

I said, "You still made it too easy, Matador. That's why I called Fallon this morning and had him give me a rundown of all the companies your Corrida, Limited uses to launder money. When GlasCo came up, I knew Natalie Glasscock had called you last night to tell you I was coming today. She and Emmett owe you too much to refuse when you tell them to set somebody up. Did you think that after all that I'd come here without the cops to back me? There are fifteen of them surrounding this place right now."

Nobody said anything.

I don't know how I was doing with Matador. I was watching Coyne. Uncertainty flickered on the sergeant's face and I shot him in the stomach before he could activate his gun hand. By the time he thought of it he was firing at the floor.

He was still falling when Matador lunged for the automatic. I took two quick steps, kicked the Colombian's legs out from under him, and booted the automatic out of Coyne's weak grip. I needn't have bothered; Emmett Firman was busy chewing his own hand in a corner.

I used the telephone in the room to call the law and an ambulance. I would have hollered cop earlier, but GlasCo hadn't been on Fallon's list and I thought I'd guessed wrong. But Coyne didn't know that. As I said, he was easy to bluff.

Lies, long buried in the past, have a way of forcing their way through layers of time to make their presence felt at some unpredictable—and often inconvenient—moment. And when the lies are connected to murder, the persistence of memory leads to consequences that are especially dangerous, as Rob Kantner's "Unfinished Business" and Marilyn Wallace's "Reunion" demonstrate.

———————

unfinished
business

ROB KANTNER

*Rob Kantner is very nearly a natural—or unnatural
—phenomenon. He has won three Shamus Awards
for Best Paperback Novel, and one Shamus for Best
Short Story. With his friend, Loren Estleman, he
forms a formidable Detroit one-two PI punch.*

*In "Unfinished Business," Ben Perkins learns the
dangers of having a friendly beer in your neighborhood tavern. You're minding your own business, and
suddenly you're up to your ears in someone else's.*

The day I met Holly Norwood, I arrived at Under New Management around five, as usual. Took the third stool on the
left, as usual. Eddie Cabla, the owner, was working the stick;
Jimmy Joe Putnam, professional Vietnam veteran, was talk-

ing Detroit Tigers; Bob Stella, retired foreman out of Michigan Truck, was arguing with him.

All as usual.

I ordered a Stroh's beer and lighted a cigar. As usual, Jimmy Joe demanded my "expert" assessment, as a high-school vintage third baseman, of the Tigers' trade of Tommy Brookens to the despised Yankees. I was, as usual, about to trot out my Sparky Anderson imitation ("It don't matter none nohow"), when the door opened and a woman walked into the bar.

Unfamiliar, alone, and attractive.

*Un*usual.

"Help you, miss?" Eddie asked. His courteous tone turned heads, but then Eddie likes them low to the ground and soft and round, which this one definitely was.

She looked around the bar room, giving it more attention than it deserved. "Wasn't this Chip's Market once?"

Eddie's eyes widened. "Yeah, way back in the sixties, before I bought the place."

"And made it legit," Jimmy Joe added.

"Dressed up the neighborhood," Bob said.

"Historical plaque's going up next week," I put in.

"Shaddap!" Eddie snarled. He snapped his cloth open and began to buff the bar top. "You don't look old enough to remember that far back," he said to the woman.

Flattered by the fiction—for that's what it was; her forti-eth summer was imminent—she drifted closer to the bar. She was five one or so, and heavier than she probably liked. She wore a sleeveless blue-checked top and sky-blue slacks over white sneakers. Her deep red hair waved thickly down to her shoulders, and her dark eyes sparkled as bright as her even white teeth. "Why, thank you," she said. "So gallant."

The other men chuckled. We all knew that Eddie's gallantry was aimed at an early round of what Bob Seger calls the horizontal bop. "How about a drink?" Eddie asked. "On the house, how about that?"

"Lovely. White wine?"

"Coming right up. My name's Eddie, but you can call me Ed."

"Leah," she said. She pronounced it Lee, and I didn't know about the "H" till it appeared in the papers. "Leah Norwood."

Eddie nodded, then scooted into the back as she took the stool at opposite end of the bar from me, equidistant from Jimmy Joe to her left and Bob Stella to her right.

Bob's good-natured potato face split into a grin. "You're from around here, huh?" he asked hoarsely.

"That's right," she said. "Haggerty at Begley. My mother used to send me up here for bread and milk. When this was Chip's Market."

"Back for a little sentimental visit?" Jimmy Joe asked.

Her expression was dreamy. "More than that. I'm here to stay. I just bought our old house back. Moved in today."

Eddie delivered the wine with such flair, you'd never have suspected it was no-name jug white in that jelly glass. Leah toasted the bar at large, took a sip, and seemed to find it tasty.

Bob Stella drummed his empty beer mug on the bar and, as Eddie took it, said, "Haggerty at Begley. That old tri-level?"

"No, no," the woman said. "Kitty-corner from there, the big three-story fieldstone."

Bob's bushy eyebrows arched. "That's old Duke Werden's place. I didn't know he sold out. Where'd he go?"

"Florida." Leah pegged back the rest of her wine. "And here I am, back home again. Except this isn't Chip's anymore. Now it's—what *is* this place called, anyway?"

"Under New Management," Jimmy Joe said.

"The fastest saloon in the west," Bob Stella said, laughing.

"Western Wayne County, that is," I added.

She was shaking her head, half smiling, looking misty. "Things change so much," she said. "I've been away for so long, and—you know what? There's one person I'd really, *really* like to see again."

Eddie propped an elbow on the bar and leaned toward her. "Now who'd that be, honey?" he asked, all velvety.

"My first-grade teacher from Belsen School. Mrs. Anderson. Edna Anderson." She glanced around at us. "Any of you men know her?"

"Belsen's still there," Jimmy Joe said. "Never heard of no Edna Anderson, though."

"Twenty-five years," Eddie said doubtfully. "I'll put this gentle as I can, sweetie. The old broad could be croaked."

"But who could find out for ya, toot sweet," Bob said, "is old Benjy down there. He's a private detective. The best in Michigan."

"Metro Detroit," Jimmy Joe said.

"Wayne County. Maybe," Eddie said.

"Ben's definitely the best in this corner of the county," Bob insisted.

"Whenever Norris Johnston is away," Jimmy Joe amended.

Pals.

The woman's eyes were on me hopefully. "Can you help me?"

For once I wasn't terribly broke. And I had no special desire to take on a humdrum locate job. But my friend Carole had a week off coming, and I planned to take her and her son out to the Lake Erie islands before she was, as she put it, "too gross" to be seen in a swimsuit. Trip like that costs money if you want to do it right. "You want somebody found," I answered, "consider her found."

The woman slid off the stool and walked over to me, smiling. She put out her hand and shook mine with a surprisingly strong grip. "Benjy?" she inquired.

"Ben Perkins," I answered. "Give you a ride home, and we'll talk about it."

She smiled graciously. "I accept! What a gentleman!"

We started for the door. "Me? Oh, I'm no gentleman."

"Good," she answered, and took my arm.

Her house was one of those well-maintained gems they put up a hundred years ago: gray fieldstone and brown beams rising three stories, held down by an ornate red slate roof. It sat on a couple of heavily wooded acres just west of Haggerty Road about a mile from the bar. I wheeled my '71 Mustang into the gravel driveway and parked next to a copper Honda Accord with Illinois plates. "From Chicago, are you?"

"Lived there a few years," she replied, unsnapping the seat belt. "But I'm a Michigan girl, through and through."

I shut off the rumbling motor. "Nice wheels."

"You should see me in a skirt."

"I meant your car."

"Oh. Well, I liked it fine, till it died on me. Rent-a-Jalopy's ferrying a rental up to me tonight to tide me over." She climbed agilely out of the Mustang and I followed suit. The massive trees around the big house whispered softly, and Leah spread her arms in an all-embracing gesture, looked at the house and then at me with a rapturous smile. "Oh, it's so good to be back here! I spent the best years of my life in this house."

"Gorgeous old place." I rescued a short cork-tipped cigar from my shirt pocket and lighted up. "Your family been back to see it?"

She laughed. "Oh, there's really no family left. Come on inside, we'll talk business." I followed her up the meandering brick walk toward the front stoop. "My parents are both dead and my sister is in an institution. That's all there was, just the four of us."

"Sorry to hear that." We went through the screen door and into the foyer, which yawned up two full stone-and-wood stories. A massive oak staircase rose to the right, curving majestically to create a balcony on the second floor. I didn't have time to gape, because Leah guided me through an archway into a big, sunny country kitchen, all bright yellow and brown. "Married or anything?" I asked.

She threw me an intent look. "Not married," she said, smiling slyly, "or anything. I suppose you're single. Not that it matters," she said, laughing. While I tried to sort that one out she went to the refrigerator. "How about a drink, Ben?"

"Beer, please, if you've got it."

She peered inside. "Beer . . . let me see . . . right. Here." She came out with the bottle and saw me looking at a big scattered pile of mail lying on the table. "That's all for the previous owner," she said. "Stupid post office messed up his forwarding order, I guess. Here you go." She opened a pair of Stroh's, handed me one, and clinked her own against it. "Cheers!"

I took a schlook and set the bottle down. Leah put away half of hers and licked her lips. "Well now, Ben! What'll it cost me to find my old teacher?"

"Depends on how much time I use. I get two-fifty a day

plus expenses. I like to get an advance. I figure two or three days, tops—"

She was nodding her head vigorously. "That's fine, that's fine. I've got loads of money. I'm a clinical psychologist, I'll be signing on with the Reuther Center or Ypsi State in a few days. Wait here, I'll be right back."

She disappeared through the archway into the foyer. I smoked my cigar, paced the kitchen slowly, then pressed the smoke dead in an ashtray on the table amid the scattered envelopes. Being nosy, I couldn't help reading over the return addresses. Something felt vaguely wrong, but then I'm a private detective. To me, most everything feels vaguely wrong.

Leah bustled back into the kitchen and handed me a thick wad of currency: twenties and fifties, old bills, a half a grand worth. "Any objection to cash?" she asked coyly, leaning her plentiful rump against the edge of the table.

"God, no." Questions, yes; objections, no. I put the money away; Lake Erie islands, here we come. "You get half back if I only use one day. No refunds if the lady's dead."

I meant that mostly in jest. But Leah's eyes narrowed. "She can't be dead," she said.

"Hey, lighten up. If she's alive, I'll find out where she's at. If she's dead, I'll find out where they planted her. Fair enough?"

Leah's expression went suddenly sunny. "Oh sure, that's fine. Fast as you can, okay?" She rattled off a phone number.

I wrote it in my pad. "I'll get back to you," I said. I started for the foyer, and stopped at her touch. As I turned she came to me in a smothering rush, engulfed me with her arms, and teetering on tiptoe, kissed me hard on the mouth.

Her body was warm and vivid, her ardor evident in her heartbeat. And she was stronger than she looked. It took me a moment to ease myself loose. She stepped back, eyes alight, hands on my hips. "Come on, Ben," she said, half-breathless, "stick around awhile."

"Sorry, kid," I managed, "I got things to attend to."

"Oh," she said. For an instant she looked cross, then she beamed. "Okay. Some other time?"

"Sure." I made some kind of parting gesture—a nod or a wave, I don't remember which—and left.

Strange, I thought as I drove, that she hit on me so early, so forcefully. Stranger still that I turned her down. But the strangest thing of all was that I had felt no desire for her, not even the slightest bit.

Getting older, I guessed.

Scary.

The G. Mennen Williams Residence is a retirement facility in Westland, that capital of the aged a couple of suburbs north of me. It's a single-story building shaped like an octopus, surrounded by lush lawns and groves of trees. A far cry from the typical nursing home, and a very clear sign that Edna Anderson had made like the frugal little squirrel, storing away nuts against the coming of winter.

I arrived there after lunchtime the next day. The polite desk clerk found my name on the appointments list and had me escorted to a small flagstone courtyard at the back of the complex. The lady who rose to greet me there was in her mideighties and certainly a shadow of her former self: translucent wrinkled skin clinging to fine bones, stooped and trembling, her bluish-white hair so fine and thin you could see her scalp beneath. But she was well dressed in tan slacks and blouse. Her grip was firm and sure as she shook hands with me. Her gray eyes, behind heavy glasses, were defiantly youthful.

"Thanks for seeing me, Ms. Anderson," I said.

"*Mrs.* Anderson," she said, smiling. "And it's I who must thank you. It's not every day I get a handsome young visitor." She winked. "What I wouldn't give to be thirty again, just for this afternoon!"

"Hey, me too." I grinned. She sat down slowly in her lawn chair and I took one facing her. "I was hired by one of your former students to find you, ma'am."

"And you succeeded." She nodded. "Very resourceful. How did you manage it?"

"Well, Belsen School's long closed. So I called the school district, and they shuffled me to the teachers' union. They refused to give out the information. So I called back and said I was Inspector O'Gannon from the Social Security Administration and had to verify your current address. Otherwise, you wouldn't get your check, probably go on dog food or starve or whatever. That turned the trick."

She nodded, an admiring glint in her old eyes. "And why, may I ask, are you here? Why didn't you simply give my address to your, um, client?"

I shrugged. "I'm funny about that. I don't think everyone has the automatic right to find anyone else. I mean, God knows there are a few people around I'd rather never found *me*. So, in locate jobs, usually I let the findee have a say in whether he or she gets found."

"I see," she said. When I didn't go on, she said, "Now for the sixty-four dollar question. Which ex-brat is it?"

Her harshness startled me. "Brat?"

She waved a hand, a hard edge to her mouth. "Oh, most of them *were* little brats. Demanding, obnoxious offspring of demanding, obnoxious parents. I'm eighty-six and long retired; I no longer have to maintain the pretense." I had no answer to that. "Don't keep me in suspense," she said sharply. "Give me the name."

"Leah Norwood." The old lady's expression did not change. "First grade at Belsen School, nineteen—"

"I remember," she interrupted. Her expression softened and her eyes went very far away. "Little Leah," she murmured. She looked at me and her smile was self-conscious. "One of the good ones. Such a sad little girl. How is she?"

"Seemed just fine to me. I gather she was living out of state for a while, but she just moved back into the area. Bought the old family home, matter of fact."

"That surprises me."

"Why is that, ma'am?"

"I would think that house had such awful memories for her, she'd never go near it again. Let alone live there." The old woman's voice dropped to a confidential pitch. "Her mother committed suicide there, you know."

"Oh, really?" I asked. Priming the pump, we call that.

"Jumped twenty feet to the foyer floor, right in front of the daughters. Officially it was called an accident, of course, so she could be put in consecrated ground. But everyone knew it was suicide."

I remembered the foyer and the majestic staircase that rose up to a long balcony, twenty feet above solid slate. The vision made me uneasy.

She sat back in her chair and gripped its arm with whitening knuckles. "The father died drunk in a car crash a while later," she said, almost in monotone. "No loss, frankly. Looking back on it, I think he abused his daughters—Holly for sure, and maybe even Leah. Why didn't we notice such things in those days?"

"Maybe it wasn't as common then?" I ventured.

"No," she said softly. "Everyone looked the other way." The old lady was silent for a moment, clenching and unclenching one hand. "After he died, Holly and Leah were split up and sent away. I never knew what became of them. I'd had Holly two years before Leah. An intense child. Very difficult. But Leah . . . a sweetheart. And such a sad little girl. I did my best for her. Down through the years I've wondered what became of her. I've thought of her as unfinished business."

"She seems okay now," I observed. "And you can see for yourself, if you want to."

"That's true," she said, brightening. Her smile had the glint of gold in it and her eyes, back in the present, shone behind her glasses. "Please, Mr. Perkins, give Leah my number and address and tell her I'd very much welcome a visit. What an occasion it will be!"

I got hold of Leah that night and gave her the information. She seemed thrilled, gushed her thanks, and invited me by for a beer. I begged off politely and didn't give her a second thought, then.

Late that night, Bob Stella's wife called my apartment, upset and anxious. Bob never came home the night before, no one had seen him all day, and he hadn't called. That was definitely unlike him. I promised to keep an eye out.

By two the next afternoon I had wrapped up the maintenance chores around Norwegian Wood, the apartment complex where I live and—sometimes—work. I sat at my desk, alone in the office, flipped paper clips at the wastebasket, and thought about Bob, about Leah, about Mrs. Anderson, and about how uneasy I felt.

Lived in. That was the problem; Leah's house looked too lived in. Though she'd just moved in, her kitchen was neat, orderly, *lived in* already. I'm not personally neat and orderly, but I've been an apartment maintenance manager for a lot of years; I know lived in when I see it.

What all this meant I did not know, but no way could I let it go. When in doubt, check it out.

I called directory assistance and learned that there was no listing for Leah Norwood in Van Buren Township, Belleville, or anyplace else in metropolitan Detroit.

From the edge of oblivion I snatched back the name that Bob Stella had mentioned. Called directory assistance again and asked for the listing for Duke Werden. The robot recited the number that Leah Norwood had given me as her own.

I sighed, lighted a cigar, and began twisting a paper clip, working it till it gave up the fight and broke. Then I picked up the phone again and called Jon Paluzzi at the Belleville Post Office. He fussed and grumbled, as usual, but could find no forwarding order for Duke Werden to anywhere, let alone Florida.

This was starting to bug me a lot. I pawed through my desk drawer, rescued a tattered business card, and dialed Owney Busbee at Bullet Realty in Wayne. Owney, who keeps an up-to-the-minute multiple listing between his ears alongside a history of real-estate transactions going back to antediluvian times, told me that the Werden house had not changed hands the previous week, the previous month, or at any time in the past twenty years.

The big fieldstone house sat silent beneath its tall trees, unattended except for the crippled Honda sedan. I parked the Mustang facing the road, got out, and walked with deliberate caution onto the stoop to the front door. A brisk knock netted only sore knuckles, so I tried the knob. The door opened easily and I went inside.

The enormous foyer was empty of everything but long slender fingers of sunlight that glowed the airborne dust and splashed yellow on the gray slate floor. Before starting my search, I looked at the second-story balcony, and then straight down to where Leah's mother collided with the floor a quarter century before. The suicide explanation troubled me; most people jump from much higher places.

One investigation at a time, I told myself. With a profound sense of unease, I went to work.

And came up empty. I toured the house, top to bottom, and found no Leah, no Duke Werden, no anybody. One thing was obvious. The house's otherwise uninteresting contents had clearly been in place longer than two days. More like twenty or thirty years.

Evidently, Duke Werden had had no further use for them, when he left.

I went out back. A broad lush lawn, shaded to near darkness by gigantic pecan trees, ran back to virgin woods. To the left was a stumpy, squarish wood building, painted bright white, that was probably older than the house itself. I walked over, disengaged the simple metal hasp, and pushed the wood door open.

The interior walls were made of heavy wood beams caulked with mortar, suggesting that this building had once been a smokehouse, and a very well made one indeed, judging from the way it had bottled up the smell of the two corpses lying on the concrete floor. Bob Stella lay in a lake of his own making, throatless. The other man, whom I guessed was Duke Werden, had lost a hand warding off the swing of a sharp instrument, most likely the machete lying in a pool of congealed blood on the floor. From the looks of things, his attacker had then stood over him and whacked at him as if his face were a tree stump.

Taking very controlled breaths through my mouth, I forced another look at Bob's corpse. Nosy old fart, poor sad sorry bastard. All he ever wanted out of life was his beer, his Detroit Tigers, his *America's Funniest Home Videos* on Sunday nights, and his friends. That's why he'd come looking, because Duke Werden was his friend, and had up and left, and that made no sense to Bob. So he'd come over and walked right into it.

I stepped back from the door and started to turn blindly, but changed my mind when a woman's sharp voice barked, "*Freeze*, asshole! Police officer!"

I raised my hands. "Okay," I said finally, "what now?"

"Back up, belly down, eat lawn *now*."

I complied. Suppressed a gasp when she stepped on my left ankle—no doubt to give me something to think about while she frisked me. After a moment the pressure on my ankle ceased. "On your feet. Turn around."

I complied. The plainclothes cop was maybe thirty-five, on the tall side and thin in the manner of a pro athlete. Her hair was brown and close-cropped around a freckled face that was pretty but all business. She wore jeans, an open-necked white-on-white shirt, two gold chains, and a cast on her left arm from armpit to wrist. All in all, the only danger-ous thing about her was the Colt Mustang she aimed at my chest.

"Don't fuck with me," she said.

"I wouldn't dream of it."

"I want to know who you are and what you're doing here. Right now."

The shock of the corpses had worn off. The relays were clicking and things were falling into place. Certain things about this woman—the tilt of an eyebrow, the way she pro-nounced her Rs, stuff like that—set off faint echoes. I said, "My name's Ben Perkins. And I have a feeling—just a wild guess, now—that your name is Leah Norwood."

She nodded abruptly. "So?"

"Which means the woman who's been running around here, claiming to be you, is—"

"Holly," she said, unsurprised.

"Your older sister."

"That's right. Where is she?"

"Don't know. I can tell you where she's been, though," I said, gesturing toward the smokehouse door.

Eyeing me warily, Leah Norwood—the real one, this time—stepped to the smokehouse door and peered in. After a long moment she turned back to me, sickened and trying not to show it. "We've got to find her," she said grimly.

"And when we do," I said, lowering my hands, "I have a feeling we're also going to find a retired schoolteacher in a hell of a lot of trouble."

As I fought the miserable late-afternoon traffic up Wayne Road toward Westland, I asked, "What department you with?"

"Matteson, Illinois. Fifteen-year veteran." She stirred un-comfortably on the bucket seat of my Mustang. "That's why what she did to me is so fuckin' embarrassing. I didn't even know she'd escaped from the institution. First I knew of it was when she ambushed me inside my apartment door and knocked me down the stairs and broke my arm. Guys on the shift laughed their asses off."

"Surprised she didn't whack you. Seems violent enough."

"I think she wanted to, but she'd made too much noise, she had to get away. She stole my car and took off."

"In the Honda."

She nodded. "I knew she'd head here. She always had a thing about settling accounts, paying people back, and so forth. When I saw my car in front of our old house, I knew I was getting warm. So I was extra careful, and got the drop on you." She laughed without mirth. "I thought private eyes were supposed to be clever, Perkins."

I felt it would be tasteless and insensitive to remind her which one of us wore a cast. "Holly always been violent?"

She snorted. "Look at this, and tell me what *you* think." She handed me an old, faded black-and-white snapshot. It showed two pretty girls in bobbed hair and jumpers. The eyes had been poked out of each one. "Holly did that to all our pictures."

I gunned around a bevy of slowpokes and crossed into Westland. Five minutes away now. "Likes to cut things, huh?"

"Including herself. After her third suicide attempt I finally had her declared incompetent," she said in cop monotone. "I got custody and put her in the institution in Chicago. They told me she was getting better. They told me not to worry. They *didn't* tell me she'd get loose and go on a killing spree and I'd have to track her down."

"Damned inconsiderate, I'd say."

She ignored me. "Hell, I'm using *sick days* for this."

"Life's a bitch," I observed.

"The things we do for family," she grunted.

I glanced at her as we swung into the driveway of the G. Mennen Williams Residence. "Yeah," I murmured. "The things we do."

"I'm sorry, Mr. Perkins," the receptionist said. "Mrs. Anderson has gone out for the day."

"Where to?"

Leah, face intent, silently flashed the tin. The receptionist looked startled. "One of her former students came by and took Mrs. Anderson for an outing. I don't know where. Is there some sort of trouble, officer?"

Leah ignored her. She locked stares with me. "Belsen," we said in unison, and bolted for the door.

I two-wheeled the Mustang around the corner from Polk Road onto Belsen Road and punched the gas. Belsen is little more than a strip of heaved tarry asphalt, pocked with chuckholes; a real spine-mangler for a stiffly suspended car like the Mustang. The noise was such that I barely heard Leah's voice as she said, "I'm going to shoot her."

I looked at her pale, resolute face. "We can always whistle up the cops, let them handle it."

She glared at me. "No. She's my sister, my problem, and I'm going to handle it. I'll do what I have to do and I don't need the local yokels to take her. I thought we agreed on that."

We did. Holly Norwood had flimflammed me and killed one of my friends and I wanted to pay her back myself. If that meant standing by and watching her cop sister put a warning shot in her shoulder, that was just peachy.

Only three things bothered me. One, I was unarmed. Two, I was worried that we'd guessed wrong. Third, even if we'd guessed right, I was afraid we'd be too late.

Belsen School appeared on the left as we barreled up a slight rise. It's a single-story orange brick building, plunked down in a large, treeless, and very cheerless plain. A quarter mile away, beyond the school property, was a heavily wooded neighborhood of older clapboard homes, but there were no people about and no signs of life at all.

"I don't see a car there or anything," Leah said as we approached the school.

"Hang tight." I slowed and swerved left into the school's driveway. Now, down toward the end where the weedy, disused playground began, we saw a car, a white Chevy Monte SS. It was parked slantways to the curb, casually and as an afterthought, as if it had served its purpose. Which, I saw on further examination, it had; someone, presumably Holly, had used the car to bash open the two steel double doors, which had been secured with heavy chains.

I shut off the Mustang engine and let the car roll to a stop, about twenty feet from the door. Leah and I got out of the car with a minimum of noise, not even allowing the doors to shut, and walked quietly along the sidewalk and through the ruined doors, crunching over broken glass into the hallway of the abandoned school.

In the echoing distance we heard an echoing female voice: "All those days when I'd sit here and watch you. Watch you lecturing us, and what I've always remembered and never forgotten is your silly little face. All those games you'd play, and those stupid parties. You'd put on dumb hats, and . . ."

We walked down the hall, practically on tiptoe. Leah held her Colt in her good hand, pointed down, ready for action; her face was tight, eyes narrow.

". . . tried to tell you what Daddy was doing. But did you listen? No. All you gave me was that silly little face. Remember the time with the shoes? When you made me walk around the room barefoot? I kept looking at you, and there it was, your *silly little face*. I wanted to . . . all I could think about was . . . I had to *do* something about that *silly little face*—"

The double doors of the classroom at the end stood open. We walked in. The large classroom was bathed in gray light from the dirty, blindless windows. Some evidence of the room's former purpose remained. ABCs in capitals and small letters were stenciled on the wall above the blackboard. A mobile of Winnie the Pooh characters hung limp in the ceiling in one corner. An old upright piano stood in the other corner, and some poignantly small kids' chairs were scattered around. At the far end of the room were Holly Norwood and Edna Anderson.

The retired teacher was crammed viciously into one of the tiny pupil's chairs. She was pale, limp, shoeless, legs twisted, eyes dead, and the rest of her nearly. Her spidery wrists were bound to the chair leg with tightly knotted clothesline—a wholly unnecessary cruelty, considering what was happening to her.

Holly Norwood stood just behind her former teacher. Her left hand had hold of a twisted fistful of the old woman's fine, bluish-white hair. Her right hand held a long, chrome letter opener. Its shaft rested on Mrs. Anderson's right cheekbone and its point shone between her glasses and her eyelid. I remembered the picture Leah had shown me, and I felt fear and fury all at once.

We all stared at each other for one long silent moment. Then Holly let the teacher go and stepped away from her, allowing her to sag in a dead faint in the chair, out of the equation. Holly's smile was a skeptical smirk below her dark dancing eyes. "Well, well," she said as she faced us and tapped the business end of the letter opener in her palm.

Which was *all* she'd have said, had I been the armed one. You don't play patty-cake with an armed nut case. First splat, then chat. "Well," I said to Leah, "you said you wanted to shoot her. There she is. Shoot her."

"Yes, little sister," Holly said, beckoning with the letter opener. "Come on. Shoot me."

Leah held her pistol with her right hand. Her other hand peered uselessly out of the sling-borne cast. The little automatic was easy to aim one-handed; at this range it would take no marksman to knock the other woman down.

But Leah did nothing except stare glassily at her sister.

Holly's grin widened. She stepped forward, bent, put the letter opener on the floor and stood up again. "That better? I thought so. Go ahead, little sister. Shoot me."

"Take her out," I said roughly.

Leah stood motionless, as if engraved there.

"Can't do it, huh?" Holly said sympathetically.

"Well, I can." I took the pistol from the unresisting cop, turned on Holly, and drew down on her two-handed. Pick a knee, any knee.

"You wouldn't shoot an unarmed—"

CLICK

"—defenseless—"

CLICK

"—woman, would you?" she asked.

CLICK CLICK CLICK

"Jesus Christ!" I bellowed. Holly began to laugh. I popped the clip release of the weapon. Nothing came out. "The hell's wrong with you?" I shouted at Leah, whose face was vacant, uncomprehending.

Her sister was still laughing. "That's just like you, baby sister," she said. "Big tough cop. Gonna track me down and arrest me. But you conveniently forgot to load your gun. You know what they call that at the drool school, my dear. Significant, is what they call it. You show definite signs of ambivalence, along with a big dose of denial. But denial is your middle name. It goes way back—back to when I killed Mother."

At first the words did not register on me. But they did on

Leah. Her eyes were big and owlish, her mouth a hard pout. "You did *not* kill Mother!" she cried in a high, whiny voice, gesturing with a fist. "Don't say that! It was an accident!"

Holly rolled her eyes. "It was not," she said wearily. "She was standing on the balcony railing hanging balloons for your birthday party. I pushed her and she fell. You were there, you watched me do it, but you always denied what happened. Denied that Mother's death was anything but an accident. Why? You felt guilty. Because you hated Mother, too."

"I did not," Leah wailed.

"You wanted her dead as much as I did," Holly said lazily.

Leah turned and ran blindly from the room. "Call the cops!" I hollered after her echoing footsteps. No reply. I turned back to the sister, who had not moved from her position six feet away from the unconscious teacher. "Just you and me, babe," I said, tossing the useless pistol aside.

"Yep. Uh-huh," she answered jauntily, bouncing on the balls of her sneakers. "It's only fair to warn you that I learned judo and karate in the giggle house. I'm very very good. Very very strong. And fast. I'll snap your neck," she said, snapping her fingers, "given half a chance." She beckoned. "Come on!"

I walked toward her, kicked the letter opener away into a far corner, then squared off, eyes locked with hers. Holly's face was knotted with concentration; beads of sweat stood out on her forehead, and I could hear her breathe. One hand was out, as if for balance; the other was down behind her leg. I decided to make quick work of her. I feinted right and charged, planning to take her down with a full body tackle. She dodged nimbly and, as I charged past, slashed at my face with her hidden hand, drawing a blazing line of pain across my eyebrows. Sliding to a stop, I gasped from the pain and felt with a hand that came down bloody. She'd cut me.

"Surpriiiise," she sang, now standing where I'd been, still bouncing on the balls of her feet. Proudly she waved a tiny little silver knife, no longer than my pinky. "Nice and sharp," she said. "I like sharp things, don't you?"

I mopped blood again. I didn't bother to tell her that I *hate* sharp things. I favor blunt things, like a ball bat or a piece of pipe. I'm also partial to implements that blow large holes in people. But I had neither. Time for some creativity. Watching Holly carefully, braced to counter any move, I unbuckled my belt, slid it out of its loops and wrapped it twice around my fist, leaving thirty inches of buckle-tipped leather dangling toward the floor. "Oh, interesting," she said. "Ready?"

She feinted, jinked, faked a jab. I was swinging the belt over my head, timing my move, and when she made hers I was ready. As she lunged and slashed at me I swung for real, whistling the air, and the buckle smashed Holly's hand squarely and sailed her knife across the classroom to clatter uselessly into a pile of old student chairs.

Holly bent, nestled her hurt hand between her ample thighs, and began to wail. "Oh God, oh Christ, that hurts," she gasped.

I mopped blood again, wondering what other tricks she had in store, like the ones she'd used on Bob Stella, Duke Werden, her mother, sister, and God knew who else. But there was no question about my next move.

If I were a gentleman, I'd have left her be, or perhaps tied her up with all decorum to wait for the cops. But, as I'd told her the day we met, I'm not a gentleman. What I am is a feminist. The best kind, the kind that treats men and women the same. I stepped in, hauled off, and coldcocked her.

I hugged Bob Stella's widow, murmured some comforting words, and walked slowly away from the grave. Others did likewise in the brilliant sunshine, streaming across the lush lawn of Michigan Memorial toward cars stripped of their purple funeral flags. Bob, I thought, would have appreciated the turnout. The whole Under New Management crowd was there; even Jimmy Joe Putnam had forsaken his army field jacket and donned a blazer for the occasion.

Carole Somers, who'd preceded me through the receiving line, fell in beside me. She was tall-blond-stylish as ever, dressed for court in a blue business suit modified to allow for the extra, temporary girth in front. "You all right?" she asked. "You look sort of peaked."

"I'm okay. 'Preciate your coming along, kid."

"*De nada.*" She sighed. "I need to get off my feet, though. Soon."

"Well, how's about a big steak over at—"

"Hey, Perkins. Wait up."

I turned to see Leah Norwood advancing on me purposefully. It felt odd, seeing the murderer's sister at the victim's funeral. But what happened wasn't her fault, I told myself. Any more than it was big, amiable Bob's fault. You make the wrong move, you get dead sometimes.

"I wanted to thank you," Leah said when she reached us, "for helping out and everything."

"No problem," I said. "Leah Norwood, Carole Somers." The women smiled coolly at each other and nodded. "How's Mrs. Anderson?"

Leah brushed hair from her forehead. "I stopped by to see her this morning. She's being released tomorrow. She's okay. Shaken up, but . . . well, they built women of iron in those days, and—"

"Still do, kiddo," Carole said.

Leah laughed. "Damn straight."

"Headed home soon?" I asked.

"Tonight." Leah turned and looked back at the expanse of cemetery with its flat brass markers. "I've taken care of my unfinished business. Time to go home. Looks like that silly bitch sister of mine will be staying here for a while, though."

"Oh yeah," I said. "You won't be seeing her out Chicago way anytime soon."

Carole gave me a reproving look, but Leah ignored my tone. "I'm really glad I got to visit Mrs. Anderson." She squinted. "She kept saying I was such a sad little girl. Isn't it funny what people perceive? I've never been sad a day in my life. Bad things happen, but you go on, is what you do. You don't mope around."

"Sure," I said.

"You just take it easy," Carole said.

Leah smiled. "You don't have to worry about me," she said with just the slightest edge, then took my hand in a grip that was nothing like her sister's. " 'Bye, Perkins. Look me up if you're ever in Chicagoland." She turned and walked quickly toward the lot.

Carole and I trailed along after her at a significantly slower pace. I found myself thinking about unfinished business, about Leah's offhand statement that she'd finished hers.

Brave talk, but unrealistic. I stopped, turned, looked over the expansive graveyard one more time. Business, even old business, is never finished till you take up residence in a place like this. . . .

"You going to spend the night here," Carole broke in, "or are you going to waddle me out to dinner?"

I turned to her and returned her smile. "Dinner," I answered, and we started for the car.

reunion

MARILYN WALLACE

Marilyn Wallace, editor of the five-volume Sisters in Crime *anthology series, has written three novels featuring Oakland, CA, homicide detectives Jay Goldstein and Carlos Cruz. Each novel also focuses on a female "guest protagonist," among them the first woman to run for president of the United States. The Goldstein and Cruz series includes* A Case of Loyalties *(a Macavity Award winner), Anthony nominee* Primary Target, *and* A Single Stone. *Her novel of suspense,* So Shall You Reap, *explores the menace that lies buried beneath the bucolic surface of a rural community in upstate New York.*

"Reunion" brings together high school friends who have kept a deadly secret—and haven't seen each other for ten years.

———————

The moment I opened the invitation to my tenth high school reunion I knew, without having to consider it, that I would go. Donna and I had never meant to wait this long after the events at Talley's barn to tell Randy the truth. It had been, after all, a necessary lie and it had saved a life, but we should have told him at once, instead of trying to let guilt teach him a lesson.

The envelope with the "Class of 1982" return address rattled noisily in my hands. My throat swelled and my breathing quickened.

If a client in my therapy practice reports such visceral reactions, I interpret them as warnings, portents of subsurface tensions breaking through, and all my antennae begin quivering for the next signal. It didn't take a psychology textbook to see that I was disturbed by the prospect of attending the tenth reunion of Taconic Hills High School Class of 1982.

I tossed the announcement on the hall table and poured what was left of a container of orange juice into a glass, then plopped into a ladderback chair, slumping down to try to get comfortable. The Shakers must have loved these things for the way they kept the spine straight—no slouching, no relaxing, no letting go. I hate them. They're out of place in my airy, light-dappled nest in the Berkeley Hills but the damned things are indestructible and it feels like self-indulgence to buy new chairs to replace ones that are perfectly sound.

The notion of going back to the familiar lushness of Columbia County, which would be transformed by the fevered exuberance of October, filled me with cold dread. But I soon convinced myself that attending the reunion was an opportunity for closure. By telling the truth, I'd free myself from the burden of a ten-year-old lie and give Randy the chance to destroy some of his old tapes, as my Transactional friends would say, about having contributed to someone's death.

A sudden rush of images spun out before me. Randy, tie undone, his smile flashing above his by-then rumpled white shirt. The splintery rungs of the ladder to the hayloft of Talley's barn. The bottoms of Randy's feet, pieces of dry timothy stuck to his black dress socks. Then, the two of us dancing faster and faster, teetering above the gaping ladder hole.

I forced the pictures away, unwilling to look at the next sequence. Of course, I shouldn't blame myself—what happened had been a horrible aftermath of the combination of celebration and ceremony, of alcohol and adrenaline, Randy had assured me the next morning as watery gray light streaked the sky. Pale and disheveled, he stood in the tender grass and, as a measure of his regret, offered finally and sincerely never to drink again.

We went our separate ways after swearing to tell no one about that night. For ten years, I had kept silence, angry at Randy. I *would* go to the reunion—and I would, finally, insist that Randy acknowledge his part in what had happened.

Would it be dangerous to undo the cloak of denial under which he had lived all these years? I thought not; I thought it necessary.

The hamlet of Taconic Hills, one hundred and twenty miles north of New York City, is really a crossroads that separates a patchwork of dairy farms. It boasts a general store, an antique store, a post office, and a rigid but invisible social structure that keeps it poised somewhere between the fifties and the eighties. Somehow, it hadn't yet made it into the nineties, and I was sure most folks meant for it to be that way.

When my parents moved to Sarasota the year I finished college, I lost touch with the area, so my visit presented the minor problem of finding a place to stay. The village itself is too small and out-of-the-way to support a motel. If I stayed at the guest house in Copake, ten miles up the road, I'd have to drive past the stately white building that used to house my father's law offices. A video rental store and a wine-and-cheese shop now share the space, and I was just as happy to avoid that particular evidence of progress. So I found a motel near Hillsdale, one that caters to the ski crowd in season; the owner apparently saw no need to entice customers with amenities. At least it boasted a full-length mirror inside the closet door.

I gave myself a final once-over. My clothes were understated: the short black skirt showed off my legs, the brilliant purple tunic skimmed my body and clung in the right places. But my face reflected my emotional state, always had. The circles of fatigue under my eyes and the lines of tension around my mouth couldn't be hidden with makeup.

I had, at least, anticipated feeling this way, having had time on the endless plane ride from Oakland to La Guardia and then the three-hour drive north to think about what I could expect from the weekend. I like knowing the landscape so that potential disruptions can be sidestepped. That was one lesson I had learned before I left home; dysfunctional families create a need for predictability.

Not that much about my life in Taconic Hills had been remarkable until that night. I had been a Brownie scout, gone trick-or-treating, learned how to ice-skate on Miller's pond, made increasingly confident sketches of every tree within a mile of my parents' house, and meandered the streets and fields of Columbia County gathering proof that the world was a pretty unknowable place.

High school and hormones verified that. As a freshman, I was the designated class artist and therefore considered just a little flaky. Everyone assumed that because I was flat-chested and had no hint of a waist I didn't feel all the same stirrings as the cheerleaders. I did, of course, and they were all directed toward Randy Darlick. The boys had taken to calling him Hard Dick long before I understood what that meant, but when I found out, that only added to his appeal.

All earnest sweat, glittering smiles, and deft footwork on the soccer field, Randy was perfect, and if our first contact wasn't romantic—he spilled chocolate milk on my new white sweater—at least it was contact. Jackie Lambert's sneakers were sticking way out into the aisle; if Jackie hadn't left them there, Randy said, he never would have tripped and the chocolate milk would have stayed in its container. He was so sincere when he explained that it was Jackie's fault, so disconcerted by his automatic impulse to help me blot the brown stain spreading across the front of my sweater. I blushed; he managed an audible apology, wadded the damp napkins into a tight ball, and fled.

Already extravagant physically, Randy grew four inches between the close of football season and the spring picnic that first year. With those inches, he became the owner of broad shoulders and firm thighs. God, those thighs. Even now, my face gets hot at the pictures my lewd little fourteen-year-old mind couldn't help but paint.

I was a late bloomer, which meant that I didn't sprout breasts until the start of sophomore year, when I also became president of the Photography Club. Ellen Santopolo, my best friend and the class brain, was a member for a while, and when Randy slouched his way into the photography room during the first club period after the Christmas holiday, the room fell silent. His father, he grumbled, insisted that he have an extracurricular activity besides sports, for his college applications. I put Randy and his new Nikon to work on candids for the yearbook and we spent hours shoulder to shoulder, poring over contact sheets, checking the darkroom progress of pictures of Mr. Davolio with his hand creeping toward Mary Haver's butt. Randy's sense of framing needed tutoring; he didn't produce a single usable shot. The only one that came close was a scene from the drama club's production of *The Effects of Gamma Rays on Man in the Moon Marigolds,* but he wouldn't let me use it.

"That's terrible, I mean, pure garbage! Their feet are cut off. Torelli bumped my elbow and the camera moved," he huffed, and crossed his arms over his pecs and pouted.

Except in the darkroom, our paths rarely crossed. Randy moved among the muscled, raucous jocks while Ellen and I sought peer constituency in our own little cadre of the creative elite: some drama students, a writer or two, several painters, the one and only chess whiz in the school. When the weather was warm enough, we hung out in the field behind Talley's barn. Given an empty house—parents out for the evening or away for vacation—the jungle drums let everyone know and we partied often and with conviction. We drank gallons of White Russians, smoked some homegrown, and engaged in a bit of tentative groping.

Then Randy lost all the yearbook page proofs the day before I had to mail them to the printer. "Shit, I didn't *mean* to do it. I just put them down for a minute at Cindy's party and then they were gone," he said. "You're right, I was drinking, but someone must have walked off with them. Torelli, I bet, or Jenkins. It's not my fault."

We had a big fight over the lost pages. It was a doozy of a shouting match that ended with my stomping out of the photography room. In retrospect, I realize that I was angry more because I had to acknowledge his imperfection to myself than because of the actual loss of the pictures.

The next day someone turned the proofs in to the principal's office and I forgave all. Elated, I grabbed Randy and hugged him. When I tried to back away, he pressed me to him and bent to kiss me, his cool hand already moving beneath my sweater, setting small fires in places in my body he hadn't yet touched. Only dimly aware of the danger, we made sweet but hurried love on the floor of Mr. Behr's photography room while everyone else was at a basketball game, down the hall in the gym.

After that, we were a major item, practically inseparable and in some danger of losing touch with our respective friends because our time—and more important, our attention—was only for each other. Amazed at first, I soon concluded that Randy was smarter than people thought. He had, after all, recognized the lustful, tireless woman who lived beneath my essentially reserved exterior.

It took until April of our senior year for us to admit that we would be going our separate ways come September. I had gotten a scholarship to study psychology at NYU. Randy, helpless in the face of the mediocre grades he'd earned because of the pressures of the soccer, basketball, and softball practice schedules, was going to some obscure school in North Carolina where he'd been offered a softball scholarship.

Having reluctantly agreed to these plans, we were consumed with a desire to mark our ascension to adulthood, something that would at the same time acknowledge our connection. In the throes of those feverish days and nights, we had discovered the ancient need for a rite of passage, and then we invented one.

Randy and I talked for hours, planning our ceremony. My first thought was to have a party. "Not significant," Randy had scoffed. I suggested that we take mementos of our childhoods and seal them in a time capsule. "I don't have any cherished mementos, remember?" Randy had countered. "My parents never kept a thing of mine, like they didn't want to admit I was their kid or something because I wasn't perfect enough." Whenever he said things like that, I grabbed his hand and held it until my own pain at hearing about such coldness passed.

Then, while we finished our beer in dispirited silence and I sat swinging my leg back and forth, back and forth, Randy jumped up in triumph. "I've got it! It's perfect!"

At the time, I puzzled over the expression on his face, unable to understand why his idea to go out to Talley's barn and perform a little ceremony had so excited him.

You've come a longish way, baby, I reflected as I slipped on my gold earrings and looked again at the image in the mirror. I was no longer the girl who had participated in that ritual. That naive child was long gone. I entertained the fleeting wish that I'd done something truly glamorous—found a cure for AIDS, starred in a movie that I also wrote and directed, been elected the first female mayor of New York. I was a therapist, dime-a-dozen in Berkeley, downright suspect in Taconic Hills.

I snatched the keys of the rented Toyota from the motel dresser and stepped into the crisp evening air.

Streamers, orange and white and twisted, adorned the gym ceiling and walls and a giant CLASS OF 1982 banner hung from a basketball hoop. The lingering sharpness of sweat and sneakers and wax mingled with the grown-up scents of Poison and Obsession and Brut. Below the banner, a long white table held a plastic punch bowl and uniformly-cut finger food, drawing to it crowds of laughing, noisy people trying to talk above the familiar rhythms of Pink Floyd. Across the room, three short lines formed behind another table that served as the registration center.

Someone brushed against me and I looked up into the chipmunk jowls of Mel Marks, the star forward of the '81 district championship basketball team. He squinted down at me, mumbled hello, and heaved his premature paunch in another direction.

I joined the R-Z line, staring discreetly into the crowd until I realized that discretion had no place at a tenth high-school reunion. Perhaps at our thirtieth we'd have things to hide, failures of our dreams and our diets. We weren't yet thirty ourselves—the possibilities were still humid and alive.

I wouldn't have to work too hard to identify most of my former classmates, I was sure. People don't change much in ten years and I was sure I'd recognize nearly everyone. Even Randy. Even sober, though for most of our senior year and especially after dark, sobriety had been a state less and less familiar to him.

Andrew McIntyre, former chemistry genius and chess whiz, sat behind the white cloth of the registration table. He had been transformed into a dark-haired, dimpled knockout, self-assured amusement lighting his placid eyes. I smiled down at him and decided not to embarrass both of us.

"Beth Silver," I said clearly.

Heads on all three lines turned and necks craned. I was being supremely self-conscious. People *did* look, but when Jeff Klein announced his name, they looked, too.

"Here's your packet," Andrew said, grinning back at me. "Save me a dance, okay?"

I winked at him, the conspiracy of the formerly insecure and forcefully self-made joined.

Who had come tonight? I scanned the list in the pamphlet cleverly disguised as a black-and-white composition book, found Randy's name, wondered if he would actually show up. I had gotten his address from the reunion committee list and had struggled with the wording of a letter. Finally, I decided to go with the simple, albeit incomplete, truth: "Please come," I had said. "I have something important to tell you."

I scanned the list and smiled as names brought back memories. Inevitably, some were missing. Donna Porter wouldn't come to the reunion, of course. She'd dropped out in April of senior year after wearing the same shapeless sweater for weeks and weeks, fueling the talk that she'd quit school because she'd waited too long to do anything about her pregnancy. That was plausible, given that Donna was the one whose homework was always days late, the one who showed up at noon for an SAT test that began at eight in the morning. But it wasn't mere procrastination: I found out later that the father of her child told her he was going to marry her. The waiting made sense for a while and then she was too embarrassed and too large to ignore reality, so she stopped coming to school. And Lance Livingston wouldn't be here— he'd become a statistic two weeks after graduation when, after downing too many Buds in too short a time, he failed to negotiate the curve on Route 22 just outside of Millerton and slammed into the checkerboard wall.

"Beth!" The squeal behind me could only be Ellen. I turned around and there she was, flying toward me, arms outstretched. In the half second before she grabbed me, I saw that she was very nearly unchanged. Her thick glasses were gone, but the masses of dark curly hair, the tiny waist, and her perfect, perfect skin were unchanged. She even smelled the same, vaguely spicy and warm. When she released me, we grinned at each other wordlessly. I had missed her.

"You see Randy yet?" I asked as casually as I could.

"Not yet." She stepped back and appraised me. "You look mahvelous, dahling!" She grinned a Billy Crystal grin and then took my hand. "I mean it."

"Thanks, you too. *You* look like you just stepped out of the yearbook, kiddo. Tell me about your life."

As we wandered toward the punchbowl, she told me about her three-year-old son, her computer *wunderkind* husband, and her doctoral-thesis-in-progress on, of all things, Third World cinema. I told her my story, complete with self-mocking anecdotes about Berkeley colleagues who practiced past-life therapy, birth-trauma therapy, shamanistic therapy, birth-order therapy, hypnosis, herbal healing.

The crowd was thicker now, and every once in a while someone who recognized one of us would march across the room and shriek and we'd say the necessary things. The pattern soon became clear. Most of the people who had moved away from Taconic Hills still looked hopeful and young; many of those who had stayed to struggle with family farms and businesses looked worn down. As I always had, I felt on the periphery, outside the too-cozy knots, the circles of forced familiarity. Tonight, even more than in the past, I was happy with my position.

Then the door flew open, and as though he were caught in the beam of the biggest, yellowest spotlight, Randy entered. He was taller than most of the men, and adulthood had carved his features to a new strength. In his obviously expensive suit, he seemed the image of the successful stockbroker, which was what the pamphlet said he was. His body was lean, shoulders still prominent, and the early streak of gray at his widow's peak only accentuated his aura of authority. Looking at him brought a flood of vivid memories to which my body responded with an unanticipated buzz of pleasure.

He started toward the tables, his carriage so erect that it looked almost painful. As soon as he noticed Ellen and then me standing directly in his line of progress, he veered to the right and was surrounded by several members of the softball team.

"Old Randy's not ready for you, you think? At least he showed up. He looks good—like he works out or something. Sexy, too. So, it's like riding a bicycle, isn't it? You never really forget those feelings, right," Ellen said, peering at me to see if Randy's entrance had had any visible effect.

"At least he doesn't have that pink-tinged look of the chronic alcoholic, no bloat, no broken capillaries on his face like Craig Torelli. God, *he* looks forty. I just don't like that Randy's ignoring me," I said, knowing that she wasn't aware of the letter I wrote to Randy or why he might be avoiding me. Still, it was beginning to feel homey, comfortable, this connection with Ellen, this separation from the others.

"He probably doesn't trust himself to be too near you, that's all." She clutched my arm and giggled. Her smile was dazzling. "Let's get something to eat, watch the action. Give him a chance to look for you."

She sailed toward the table, her pink skirt swirling as she maneuvered through the crowd. I followed several steps behind her.

"Returned to the scene of the crime, eh?"

The words cut through me and I whirled around to find myself looking into the round face of Dan Jenkins. He was sturdy and shining, and the State Trooper pin in his lapel and his figure of speech didn't surprise me at all. Dan had always loved *Hill Street Blues*. He had been a significant part of my growing up, the "You show me yours, I'll show you mine" episode of prepuberty that remains forever mysterious, no matter how sophisticated you become. It was even a little laughable, occurring as it had in classic furtiveness behind some trees that marked the edge of old man Talley's cornfield.

"Guilty. Hello, Dan." I swallowed hard.

"I didn't expect you'd come, all the way from California. Why bother with these clowns, Beth? Unless you want to show off." His grin and his gaze said that I had something to show off, too, and he took my arm and steered me to the dance floor. He smelled nice, he felt nice, but I kept looking for Randy, and Dan bowed when the dance was over and said he'd catch up with me in a few minutes.

I tried to maneuver toward the door but didn't get too far before David Peersall appeared, his handsome face lit by a wide grin. He put his hands on my shoulders and kissed my cheek. "Beth—where have you been? I want you to meet someone. I've been looking for you since I got here." Flushed and nervous, David, who had practiced Hamlet's soliloquy on the school bus through the hooting and jeering of the others, steered me away from the corner where I'd last seen Randy.

"Over here, Kevin." A compact blond man approached us, his brown eyes twinkling with happy mischief. "Kevin, this is Beth Silver. Beth, my good friend, Kevin. You two have a lot in common."

I shook Kevin's hand and smiled, happy that David had a strong enough sense of himself to bring this pleasant man. Then my mind began to race. What did he mean? What image had David Peersall carried all these years? It was terribly mystifying and a bit intoxicating. I turned to him.

"That sounds like flattery to me. Just what do Kevin and I have in common?"

David grinned. "You both have a thing about dolls."

I felt the blood drain from my face. He hadn't been there —how could he possibly know? I hadn't seen David Peersall since graduation, hours before Randy and I went to the barn.

"What's the matter, Beth? You okay? You want a drink or something?" The concern in his voice was palpable, the earnest tone of the practiced rescuer.

"What do you mean, a thing about dolls?"

"Wasn't it you who brought in all those dolls from foreign countries for the sixth-grade hobby fair?"

My relief was enormous. David had made a mistake. "Nope. Must have been someone else. Does this mean that Kevin and I no longer have anything in common?" I had regained my equilibrium and adrenaline surged through me, making me feel powerful and fleet of mind.

David, to his credit, recovered nimbly. I made quick small talk with Kevin, who turned out to be a social worker in the county mental health department in Hudson, and then went off in search of Ellen.

Just as someone dimmed the light and announced a circle dance, I felt a hand on my elbow and I knew it was Randy. I leaned toward him, drawn closer by the familiar smell of his hair. Trembling suddenly with the danger of what was about to happen, I lifted my fingers from his arm. "I'm glad you came," I said.

Randy's warm lips grazed my cheek and he brushed my hair away from my face in a gesture of easy intimacy. "Your wish," he said softly. "You said you had something to tell me."

"We have to go back there," I whispered through clenched jaws as I directed him toward the door. "We have to free ourselves of the memories of that night."

He grasped my shoulders with clawlike fingers. "No! It was an accident. You have to stop blaming yourself. Let's just leave it alone. Forever, Beth." He released me but his eyes held mine in urgent entreaty.

"Randy! You look great!" Craig Torelli's deep voice boomed through the milling crowd. At that moment, our section of the gym was plunged into darkness again as the band began a slow ballad, and I could no longer see Randy's face. As I walked away, Craig grabbed Randy's elbow and slapped his back. "Still the ladykiller of the class of eighty-two, m'man. God, you were awesome. Ann Simmons, Betsy McCorkle, Beth Silver. And that girl who dropped out, Donna something. Pair o' jugs on her, boy! Heard she still lives around here, Craryville or something. Hey, Rand-o, come say hello to the rest of the guys."

Craig never did realize how far his voice carried. My little thrill of righteous indignation died quickly as I tried to assimilate this new information. When had Randy been hooked up with Betsy McCorkle? He'd never told me about that.

I wandered through the crowd exchanging banalities with people I had barely spoken to during our time in Taconic Hills High School, until the lights went up and the bandleader announced that they'd be taking a twenty-minute break. I spotted Randy and Ellen at the far end of the room.

I threaded my way past the football team and the Future Farmers, most of whom looked from their pale skin as though they'd had to take town jobs.

"I'm not going to let you go back there." Randy planted his feet wide apart and crossed his arms over his chest, peering at me with his smoky eyes. "I thought therapists knew how to deal with guilt."

"This *is* my way. I have to go and you have to come with me. It will be a laying-to-rest but we both have to be there. It's not just me. *We* need to do this. And I do have something important to tell you. But I have to do it there."

Randy shook his head and smiled, as though indulging this petulant girl was his obligation as a man, even though it was clearly a silly idea. I almost walked away alone into the darkness, but when I saw that sly smile I resolved that I wasn't going to give in to his version of the truth tonight, as I had ten years before.

We formed a short and somber caravan, me leading in my rented Toyota, Randy following in his blue Chrysler. We parked at the south end of the field, near a footpath that led to Talley's barn, our cars making an orderly little border along the thistle-edged road. The field in front of us was dotted with boulders, craggy eruptions that glinted icily in the night. Another dirt road marked the far edge of the field, about three hundred feet to the north. When we cut our headlights, the thick beauty of the place overwhelmed me.

The barn looked silvery in the moonlight, a velvet apparition rising from the mists that hung low over Talley's field. Clear-eyed and mantled with the chill of the October night, I stepped out of the car and listened to the sounds that live beneath the night silence in the country. Small rustlings. The wind pressing one branch against another. No crickets to mask the rush of the stream, half a hundred feet behind the barn, its icy water tumbling over the rocks before it spilled into a deep pool.

After we'd gone a few steps, Randy stopped. "What's that?" he whispered.

The moonlight outlined a low, curved shape across the field, on the other dirt road. I stared at it until I realized what it was.

"Just a car. Fishermen, probably, camping out near the stream." I held a finger to my lips and kept going toward the barn. My black pumps weren't really suited to walking through the wet, high grass. Stones, stands of heavy goldenrod, old crushed beer cans lay in wait. The cold dew soaked through my stockings. I was going to have to lead and not look back and trust that Randy would follow.

"Wait, Beth. I changed my mind. I can't. . . ." Randy's whisper hung heavily in the night air.

I kept walking, kicking away a fallen branch that lay in my path.

He started forward again, his steps making squishy sounds as his wing tips slipped on the wet grass.

I closed my eyes with gratitude, looked at the fat, leering moon, and said a prayer of thanks. With a sharp intake of breath hissing between his teeth, Randy stumbled over something and then moved on. I was now only twenty feet from the barn.

It loomed, large and sagging, tilting with tired abandon away from the road, as though it had seen too much and could no longer bear the weight of its load. A board was missing from the door; the one above the empty slot slanted down so that a triangular crack formed about at eye level.

My skin tightened on my arms and my breath caught in my chest.

"Come on, Beth." Randy now stood beside me, his face a round, white echo of the moon.

I shuddered and stepped back to avoid his touch. "I'll be right there," I said. "You go on."

He moved ahead, silent and dark.

I knelt in the wet, flattened weeds, my palms pressed against the sharp blades of grass. The cold seeped through my skin, traveled the length of my arms. I touched a stick, its bark knotted and rough like an arthritic finger, and then closed my fist around it.

I would keep it to remind myself that I had come here to tell Randy the truth, even if he reacted with rage at the ten-year-old deception.

"Beth!" Randy's husky whisper roused me. A black shape huddled against the wall of the barn, he looked like a limbless, leafless tree. "Let's get this over with."

I nodded, barely able to stop my head from moving. It was as though it would keep shaking of its own accord, from the fear and the momentum that had carried us here. This was a terrible idea. Hadn't I believed it when I read about people scaring themselves to death? Hadn't I truly understood that when the human mind participates in a reality too terrible, the only protection is to irrevocably disconnect?

"Come on, Beth. I can't hold this board all day." Randy stood to one side of the barn, ready to slip inside.

He has to be told the truth, I assured myself as I stepped over the concrete threshold into the cavernous dark of the barn. At once, the old smells embraced me. Rotted hay had been used as nesting material for small creatures who then dotted the concrete floor with their droppings and stained the wooden beams with their urine. Spiderwebs festooned every right angle, wherever beams met walls and posts joined floors. We held our breath, Randy and I, while a family of bats in the far corner peeked out from under their wings.

Or that was what I saw. Randy said they were barn swallows.

Finally, hands linked, we snaked toward the center of the barn. I said, "We're going to do what we did that night, reenact it so we can remember exactly. Everything the same.

Except tonight no one's had anything to drink, right? First, we have to climb the ladder and we have to sing and dance."

As I spoke, sweat sprang to Randy's palms. I squeezed his hand. We both needed strength to complete this ceremony.

I could barely make out his features; I certainly couldn't see his expression. We moved closer to the center and stood below a small, high window. Rays of moonlight fell onto our faces; we looked as though we'd applied shimmering paint to the prominences of nose, forehead, cheeks.

"Come on, Randy. We've come this far. Let's just finish it and get out of here." If I waited much longer, I'd lose my courage and I'd be sabotaging the purpose for which we'd come tonight.

Randy sounded as though he were choking, unable to breathe. I couldn't tell whether it was a trick of the light or whether all the color really did drain from his face as we approached the ladder to the hayloft. He worked his lips but no sound came out. I put one hand on the ladder, pulled one foot up to the first rung, and heard creaking and rustling behind me as Randy followed me up.

"We were standing right here." Hoarse and barely audible, Randy's voice struck new fear in me. I was about to undo his reality. By what right could I justify that? Human beings were such exquisitely self-protective creatures, functioning in wonderfully efficient ways to make bearable that which should never be borne.

"Let's get this over with." Randy sounded more impatient than anxious. "Okay, we were dancing around the loft ladder. It was cold and you had my jacket around your shoulders."

I stood without moving while he shrugged out of his jacket and put it on me. His scent clung to the fabric and I felt for a moment as though I would drown in it. But I squeezed the stick against my palm and moved away from him.

"I was leading," he said as he stepped in front of me and took my other hand.

As soon as he did, the scene took shape from a memory embedded not in my mind but deep in my body.

"And then we said those silly words about the end of childhood." Randy's voice was stronger now, more certain of the way things went. His words tumbled out and I was caught in the flood. "And we took turns naming something we would never do again, never want again, never say again. We told what we'd never be afraid of again. And then we said some stuff about the nature of existence.

"You said it was important to think of death as making way for the next cycle and that the death of our childhood was necessary to allow for the birth of adulthood. We nodded our heads to the heavens and to the earth, to the four directions, and we held hands and danced a circle around the moonlight."

We were moving around the moonlight now, drawn by a force neither of us could control.

"We started going faster and faster, pretending to be possessed and carrying on about it. Such an energetic dance, stomping and high kicks. As we danced, we got nearer and nearer to that ladder hole. The booze and the dancing and the, I don't know, the gravity of the whole goddamn thing made us dizzy. And then . . ."

The barn was spinning now. I heard wisps of our thin voices, caught in the memory of that night so long ago. I felt the horror of what I knew was coming. I wanted to be sick, to cleanse that awful, rotten burning in my gut, but I clung to Randy.

"And then as we danced closer to the edge, you kicked that bundle, Beth, the one that we didn't see until it was too late, and it went flying over the edge and landed on the concrete."

He had said it, the lie that he allowed me to carry all these years. I had really expected nothing else.

"But I didn't, Randy." My voice was remarkably even. "I knew it was there and I danced around it, waiting to see what you'd do. It was *you*. *You* kicked it over the edge and we heard it hit, thud, a sickening sound. You asked me what I tripped over. You tried to make me *think* I kicked it but I didn't." I was breathing hard now, panting, glad that I finally said it.

Randy still clutched my hand. He looked as though he hadn't heard a thing I'd said. "We climbed down the ladder and you got there first. You picked it up and we decided, after you said it was a baby and it was dead, Beth, you remember you went down the ladder and you cried out and you said it was dead, we decided that you would wrap it in that old denim jacket Hubbard kept in the barn, we decided to put it in the old well and you did it while I waited." His voice dwindled to silence.

"Only it wasn't dead," the voice behind him said.

Randy screamed and whirled around. From the shadows, near a wobbly-looking stack of hay bales, a dark figure stepped forward. Randy's terrified shriek cut through the darkness again.

"I knew better than to believe you, Randy. I didn't trust you to take the baby—*our* baby—to some family who wanted to adopt her. That's what you *told* me, right?" Donna Porter emerged from her hiding place, an altogether more fearsome sight in the light than she had been in the gloom of the eaves and hay bales. She stepped closer to Randy, her face contorted and her body rigid. "The whole setup was wrong. Why would you pick graduation night? And leaving her up on the loft. Why would you ask me to leave her up there? It was a doll. I put a doll in that ratty old receiving blanket just where you told me to leave the baby. Why should I have trusted anything you said? First you said you'd marry me, that we'd make a life, you and me and the baby. Then you said it would kill your father, he was sick and he'd have a heart attack. God, you blamed anything that ever went wrong in your life on anyone but yourself. You wanna know the bottom line, Randy? You made a mistake when you betrayed me. You'd have been better off to just admit you couldn't handle being a father. A lot of guys get that honest and live to tell about it."

Randy barely waited for her to finish. "It was an accident, Donna. We had too much to drink and Beth just kicked—"

"Shut up, Randy. When I realized you were up to something, I went to Beth for help. And to warn her away from you. She only agreed to the graduation-night ceremony to prove that I was wrong. But I wasn't. You gave her quite a party."

Randy's lips pressed together, bloodless and tight.

When she spoke again, the venom in Donna's voice had dissolved. "At least I saved my little girl from you. Her name is Linda and she's my gift. You did me a favor, the way it worked out, because I got to keep her and I'm glad. She's beautiful, Randy, dark-haired and tall, a good dancer, that's what she wants to be and she's pretty enough, she's sleeping in my car now but you'll never see her. I'll cut off your balls before I let you near her. I just needed to make sure that you knew you didn't get away with anything."

It was over. He knew the truth now, knew that I'd known about Donna since before graduation. Afraid for her baby, Donna had come to me and together we devised the subterfuge. Randy was the only one who thought a baby died. Donna and I knew it was a doll Randy had kicked onto the concrete floor.

The veins bulged on the side of his neck and his face turned red. A noise, more a growl than anything human, came from his throat. Then, to my amazement, he unclenched his fists and said, "Does Hubbard still work for old man Talley?"

Donna, taken aback, simply nodded her head.

And suddenly I realized why he asked. Randy stomped to the ladder, climbed down, and headed straight for the stack of wooden crates beside the rear door.

Where Hubbard always kept a bottle of cheap bourbon, one of his many stashes around the farms he worked.

Randy's memory served him well. Donna and I hurried down the ladder after him. He was silhouetted against the wall, his head thrown back and the bottle raised to his lips.

"I've spent ten years paying for something I didn't do," he said when he came up for air. He raised the bottle to his lips again; the gurgling sound sickened me. "No need to keep my promise now, is there? It was penance. Shit, you think I didn't feel bad? So I gave up drinking. But now there's no need." Already, his eyes were drifting out of focus and his words were beginning to slur.

I considered taking the bottle away from him, but the thought of touching him disgusted me. I had done what I'd set out to do. If this was closure, it wasn't all that satisfying. Tired and sad, I let Randy's jacket slip to the floor. Donna and I watched him take several more gulps of bourbon before we turned away from him.

We were still eight or nine feet from the door when a piping little shout from the field outside the barn cut through the silence. "Mom! Where are you?"

Donna stiffened and then backed away. "She was sleeping. She promised to stay in the car," she said, her words barely more than a whisper.

The little girl's frantic voice called out again. "I'm scared, Mom. Where *are* you?"

"I'm coming, Linda. Go back to the car, honey," Donna shouted as she disappeared into the darkness.

Trembling with the anger that had finally replaced the confusion, the regret, the guilt I'd carried for all these years, I turned to stare at Randy, a poor, pathetic figure of a drunk. "Don't you feel anything? Remorse? Shame? Gratitude that you aren't a killer?"

"Sure," he said before he lifted the bottle again. A thin stream trickled from the side of his mouth; his legs tangled as he stepped toward the door. "Lots of things. Angry that you tricked me." He giggled and lurched toward the door. "But I feel forgiveness, even though you lied to me."

Repulsed, I pivoted on my heels and fled the barn, sprinting after the two dark figures, mother and daughter, walking side by side to the blacktop. They turned north, toward the dirt road where Donna had parked her car.

My own breath roared in my ears as I ran along the footpath toward my own car. If I'd been walking, if I'd been calm, I might have heard Randy pounding down the path behind me. But I didn't; he straight-armed me from behind and I went down, unprepared, unable to break my fall. I landed heavily, choking for air, the blackness of the sky falling down on me as I fought to maintain consciousness. Time shrank, expanded, until finally I became aware of my face against the wet grass and the awkward twist of my legs under my body.

Then I heard a car start, its engine revving angrily and its wheels spitting gravel.

My lungs had filled again and I could breathe. As I pushed myself to a sitting position, I heard Donna shout a garbled, terrified warning. I got to my knees but was nearly knocked over by a wall of sound, horrible smashing and grinding noises from down the road. I straightened to a standing position and looked toward the awful sounds.

Randy's car, one headlight pointing crazily at the moon and a plume of steam pouring from its pleated front end, had slammed into a huge oak tree. Frozen in the other beam stood Donna, wrapped in agony, like an unfinished Pietà.

By the time I reached the car, Randy Darlick was sitting by the side of the road, dazed and blank-faced, cradling the still and lifeless body of ten-year-old Linda Porter in his arms. He rocked back and forth, stroking her dark hair and whispering into her broken little chest.

"You shouldn't have been on the road," he said over and over. "Oh God, your mother should have kept you off the road."

A dark thought swooped out of the night and circled around me, a wish that I had left the past, with all its lies and secrets, alone.

about the editors

Robert J. Randisi, who founded the Private Eye Writers of America, co-publishes and co-edits *Mystery Scene Magazine,* and is a co-founder of the American Crime Writers League.

Marilyn Wallace, the author of several novels including the Anthony Award–nominated *A Single Stone* and *So Shall You Reap,* is a member of Sisters in Crime and the editor of the five-volume *Sisters in Crime* anthology series.